GOD STILL
DON'T
LIKE UGLY

GOD STILL DON'T LIKE UGLY

MARY MONROE

Kensington Publishing Corp.
http://www.kensingtonbooks.com

DAFINA BOOKS are published by

Kensington Publishing Corp.
850 Third Avenue
New York, NY 10022

All Kensington Titles, Imprints, and Distributed Lines are available at special quantity discounts for bulk purchases for sales promotions, premiums, fund-raising, and educational or institutional use. Special book excerpts or customized printings can also be created to fit specific needs. For details, write or phone the office of the Kensington special sales manager: Kensington Publishing Corp., 850 Third Avenue, New York, NY 10022, attn: Special Sales Department, Phone: 1-800-221-2647.

Dafina and the Dafina logo Reg. U.S. Pat. & TM Off.

ISBN-13: 978-0-7582-0025-9
ISBN-10: 0-7582-0025-0

First hardcover printing: September 2003
First trade paperback printing: August 2004
First mass market printing: July 2008

10 9 8 7 6 5 4 3 2

Printed in the United States of America

ACKNOWLEDGMENTS

Thanks to David Akamine for the editorial feedback and emotional support. Thanks to Sheila Cunningham Sims, Maria "Felice" Sanchez, Anita "Wuzzle" Sanchez, and Heather King for being my very good friends. I love you all.

To Andrew Stuart (The Stuart Agency): you are the best literary agent in the world. Karen Thomas, I don't know what I would do without you. I couldn't ask for a better editor.

Very special thanks to the many reading groups and bookstores. Your support means so much to me. Much love to Peggy Hicks for organizing my book tour and Black Expressions Book Club for featuring my novels as main selections.

To my fellow authors: Timmothy B. McCann, Donna Hill, Mary B. Morrison, and Zane—LOL (lots of love)!

I am especially grateful to my fans for demanding this sequel to GOD DON'T LIKE UGLY. I had fun writing it.

Mary Monroe

CHAPTER 1

I used to wonder what I would look like if I had been born white. Now I know.

The white woman standing on the steps of the wrap-around porch of the shabby clapboard house could have been my twin. As far as I could tell, sandy blond hair and a narrow nose were the only things she had that I didn't have. I had to repress a gasp. I had to remind myself that this woman and I shared the same amount of blood from the same man. Black blood.

Throughout my plane ride from Richland, Ohio, to Miami, where I'd originally come from, with the help of several glasses of strong wine, I had composed and rehearsed several speeches. I had no idea what the appropriate things were to say to a father who had deserted me when I was a toddler, more than thirty years ago. What I wanted to say was not what I planned to say. It would have been too much, too soon. *Good to see you again, Daddy. By the way, because of you, I had to spend ten years of my childhood living under the same roof with my rapist. But don't worry, my playmate killed him for me and we didn't get caught.* I had promised myself that I would say something simple and painless. But now my head was spinning like a loose wheel and I felt like I was losing control of my senses. I didn't know what was going to slide out of my mouth.

Confronting my daddy was going to be painful enough. But having to deal with him and a *white* woman who looked like me at the same time was going to be another story. Especially since I'd hated my looks for so many years.

I sat in the cab parked in front of the house on Mooney Street that steamy afternoon in August, looking out the window at that ghostly woman standing on her front porch, looking at me. The makeup that had taken me half an hour to apply was now melting and slowly sliding, like thick mud, down the sides of my burning face. I had licked off most of my plum-colored lipstick during the cab ride from the airport. Warm sweat had almost saturated my new silk blouse, making it stick to my flesh like a second layer of skin.

When the impatient cabdriver cleared his throat to get my attention, I paid him, tipped him ten percent, and tumbled out of the cab, snagging the knee of my L'eggs pantyhose with the corner of my suitcase.

As soon as my feet hit the ground, I looked around with great caution, because this was Liberty City, the belly of one of Miami's roughest, predominately Black areas. I had hidden all of my cash in a cloth coin purse and pinned it to my girdle, but I still clutched my shoulder bag and looked around some more. I would have been just as cautious if I'd just landed in Beverly Hills. As far as I was concerned, the world was full of sharks; no place was safe for a female on her own. Especially one who attracted as much turmoil as I did.

It appeared to be a nice enough neighborhood, despite its reputation. The lawns were neat and the few Black people I saw seemed to be going on about their business like they didn't have a care in the world. In front of the house to my left, a man in overalls was watering his grass with a hose, while a gospel singer wailed from a radio on the ground next to his feet. The man smiled and greeted me with a casual wave. I smiled and waved back.

An elderly woman, looking bitterly sad and walking with a cane, shuffled pass me. "How you doin' this afternoon, sister?" she asked me in a raspy voice, hawking a gob of brown spit on the cracked sidewalk, missing my foot by a few inches.

"I'm fine, thank you," I replied, hopping out of the way as the old woman dropped another load of spit. "Sister," I added as an afterthought, even though the old woman didn't hear me. It was a word I had to get used to now. Especially because of the *sister* with the blond hair on the porch looking in my direction.

The glare from the blazing sun made the woman on the porch squint. Then she shaded her eyes with a thick hand that displayed rings on every finger, including her thumb. She stared at me with her mouth hanging open. She seemed just as stunned as I was by our matching features. I was glad that she was the one to break the awkward silence. "Honeychile, come on up here so I can hug you! I been waitin' a long time for this day."

For a few moments, I just stood in the same spot, looking toward the porch, blinking hard to hold back my tears. Words danced around in my head, but I still didn't know which ones to release.

A limp, plaid bathrobe that looked more like a patchwork quilt covered the woman from the neck on down to her wide, dusty bare feet. It pleased me to see that blood wasn't the only thing we shared. Judging from her size, she enjoyed food as much as I did. I couldn't tell where her waistline was, but the belt to her bathrobe had been tied into a neat knot below her massive chest. Her body looked as much like an oil drum as mine did. I had been wearing a size twenty-four for the past ten years. I couldn't lose a single pound no matter what I did. To me, diets were a rip-off and exercise was too dangerous for people in my shape. An obese woman from my church had had a heart attack and died while trying to do sit-ups. Therefore, I ate everything I wanted to. I figured that since we all had to die eventually anyway, I might as well enjoy myself along the way.

I had been stout every day of my life. My mother said I'd been such a butterball of a baby, she had to diaper me with pillowcases. I was finally comfortable with being large, but it was more important that I was now comfortable with just being myself. With me, comfort and strength were one and the same. It had enabled me to do a lot of things that I had been afraid to do for years. Like tracking down the daddy I hadn't seen since I was three years old. Unlike some of the other abandoned children I knew, I had refused to write my daddy off until I got some answers. I wanted to see him again and I wanted him to see me.

At least one more time.

CHAPTER 2

The cloudless sky looked like a blue blanket. I welcomed the cool breeze that suddenly caressed my face. From the corners of my eyes, I could see streams of hazy, black smoke floating from several different directions. It smelled like everybody on the block was barbecuing. I couldn't have picked a better day to return to Florida.

"Hurry up and come on up here on this porch right now. I been waitin' long enough." The woman stomped her foot and anxiously opened her arms. The sun made the rings on her fingers glisten as she beckoned me to join her.

"So have I," I managed, my voice cracking. My suitcase and feet felt like they weighed a ton as I dragged myself toward the house. The narrow walkway was lined with bright yellow dandelion flowers and neatly trimmed grass. I almost tripped over a discarded bicycle wheel.

I made my way up the porch steps and set my suitcase down, not taking my eyes off the woman's round, sweaty face. Now that I was closer, I could see that her eyes were blue. But they seemed cold and empty. I didn't feel good about having such a morbid thought about a woman I didn't even know. "You have beautiful eyes," I said. I swallowed hard and slid my tongue across my lips.

"And so do you," she replied with a wide smile, blinking her eyes like she was showing them off. Now those same eyes seemed full of warmth and life. Her plump cheeks were smeared with chocolate and bread crumbs. She started fanning herself with a newspaper and balancing her weight from one foot to the other. Out of nowhere, a huge, dusty-gray cat, its belly almost dragging the ground, waddled up the porch steps and started rubbing its side against the woman's leg. "Go on back home, Clyde," she hollered, gently kicking the cat away. The woman sniffed, folded her arms, and leaned her head back to look at my face some more. She had a deep, down-home drawl, but the tone of her voice was the same as mine. "Girl, I am so happy to finally meet you! You are just as pretty as Daddy said you were," she squealed, fanning my face with her newspaper, too.

Pretty was one of many words that I had never associated with myself and when other people did, it made me even more nervous and self-conscious. My moon face, three chins, small black eyes, and dark brown skin were features I had always avoided looking at. Even though I stood in front of my mirror every day applying makeup, I only focused on my features one at a time, closing my eyes when I could.

"You . . . you must be Lillimae," I stammered, as I rushed into my half-sister's arms. The bear hugs we gave one another must have made us look like two huge grizzlies to the man next door, still watering his grass. Out of the corner of my eye, I saw him staring at us, scratching the top of his head.

"Come on in this house, girl." Lillimae draped her heavy arm around my shoulder, rubbing it so hard it started throbbing.

I picked up my suitcase and followed Lillimae into a living room congested with too many chairs, two well-worn, brown vinyl couches facing one another, and a large TV with a wire coat hanger for antennae. An air conditioner whirred from a side window, forcing the leaves on a nearby rubber plant to flap.

I could smell the familiar aroma of turnip greens and other favorites that I could only describe as exotic. Smothered pork chops, cornbread, and macaroni and cheese were just part of a feast already decorating a table I couldn't see.

"Lordy, Annette, you don't know how long I've wanted to meet you! All my life I wanted a big sister to look up to." Lillimae wiped a tear from her eye and sniffed.

"And I've always wanted a sister, too," I replied dryly. "When I was little, the only reason I wanted a sibling was so I could have somebody to boss around." I laughed but I wished I hadn't. It made my throat hurt.

"Well, I bossed around my baby sister and brother when we was kids. Now I wish I could take all that back." Lillimae paused and dabbed sweat off my chin with her thumb. She patted my arm and gave me a thoughtful look. "Because ain't nobody supposed to torment the ones they love. There's enough others goin' to do that."

I blinked and nodded in agreement. The people that I had loved had been the ones who had hurt me the most. I had come to Florida, hoping to heal my heart. Daddy had helped break it in two.

I set my suitcase on the freshly waxed linoleum floor and followed Lillimae to one of the couches. When we sat down, the couch squished and squeaked and almost flattened to the floor from the strain of our combined weight. And that had to be at least five hundred pounds.

"It's so nice to finally get you down here!" Lillimae grinned, squeezing my hand. I flinched as the rings on her fingers dug into my flesh. "All that prayin' I done has finally paid off. Praise the Lord."

"Is . . . is Daddy here?" I asked, looking around the room.

Daddy's blood was all over the place. Two of the peach-colored walls in the living room were practically covered with pictures of other young faces that also resembled mine, down to the same flat, sad eyes and bloated cheeks.

Before Lillimae could respond, my daddy, also wearing a long, drab bathrobe, shuffled into the room, sliding a limp, wet towel across his face. I gasped and covered my mouth with my hand to keep from screaming. The once-handsome man who had fathered me looked like he had just stumbled out of a mummy's tomb. The healthy head of thick, black hair I remembered had been replaced with a receding halo of thin white cotton. The proud, inky-black eyes I had admired so much as a child now looked gray and tortured. Deep lines crisscrossed his face like a road map. Lips that looked like raw liver couldn't hide his snaggle-toothed grin. The few teeth he had left would have looked better on a serpent. His broad shoulders had shrunk and now drooped like the shoulders of a man who had yoked a heavy load far longer than he should have. He had never had much of a butt. But now his backside was as flat as a board, making it look like he had a very long back supported by a pair of frail, slightly bowed legs. His belly resembled a huge cummerbund.

"It took you long enough to get here," Daddy snapped, weaving toward me, his bathrobe dragging the floor. The booming voice I remembered had been replaced by a weak, scratchy growl. "I sent you your airplane fare five years ago!" His eyes watered as he stared at me like he was seeing me for the first time.

"I'm sorry, Daddy. I had a lot of things to take care of first," I explained, rising. "Muh'Dear . . . she didn't want me to come back down here."

At the mention of my mother, Daddy stopped and turned away, tossing the towel on top of a goosenecked lamp in a corner behind him.

"I figured that," he mumbled, shaking his head. His exasperation was obvious, but that didn't faze me one bit. I was just as exasperated as he was. Maybe even more so. "Ain't you around forty-somethin' now, girl?" Daddy asked, facing me with one eyebrow raised.

"Me? Oh—well, I'm thirty-five. My birthday was last week," I stammered. My words hung in midair while I groped for more. I pressed my lips together and blinked stupidly.

Daddy grunted and made a sweeping gesture with a hand so gnarled, it looked like it had never been straight. "Oh yeah, that's right. You was born durin' dog days. Well, that's old enough for you to be doin' what *you* want to do. I was beginnin' to think that I wouldn't get to see you again 'til the Rapture. Ain't that right, Lillimae?"

Lillimae chuckled. "Daddy got a notion in his head that the world's goin' to end any day now. He won't even buy nothin' on credit no more."

I was too nervous and confused to go to my daddy. I wanted to hug him and slap him at the same time. More than thirty years was a long time to be separated from somebody you loved. He had a reason to be angry with me for taking so long to come see him, but I had even more of a reason to be angry with him. *He* was the one who had run out on my mother and me at a time when we needed him the most. It was time for him to answer for what he had done.

CHAPTER 3

I was devastated that long-ago morning when Daddy deserted my mother and me, leaving us in a run-down shack with just ten dollars and some change to our names. A tornado had swept through Miami the night before, destroying most of our few possessions. That had been enough of a trauma. For many years I had blamed that storm for helping destroy my family, but Daddy had put his plan in place even before that.

His cruel departure was unexpected and thorough. I knew he wasn't coming back, because he took everything he cared about with him.

Everything but my mother and me.

I never got over losing my daddy. He had been the most honorable, gentle, dependable man I knew back then. He'd loved us with a passion and I had adored him. Like a slave, he had worked in the fields from sunup to sundown almost every day to support us and we had depended on him. He'd kept my mother and me happy by spending most of his meager wages on us. He would wear his shoes until the soles flapped, his clothes until they fell off his body, and sometimes he'd go without eating a meal so we could have seconds. But like it was a rug, he had snatched that security from under us and left us struggling around like we didn't know which way to turn. And we didn't. It was almost like being blind. I always knew that someday I would track Daddy down and make him sorry.

My mother had shed so many tears and spent so much time in the bed those first few days, I felt like the parent. I had to help her bathe, comb her hair, and cook. And all that had frightened me. It had been a heavy burden for a three-and-a-half-year-old child.

I had grieved, too, but behind my mother's back. I could not count the number of times I'd wallowed on the ground behind an old orange tree in our backyard crying until I'd made myself sick. I didn't want my mother to know that I was in just as much pain as she was.

"Don't worry. We'll be all right," I assured her. My mother must have believed me because right after I said that, she stopped crying and leaped out of that bed.

It didn't take long for us to spend that last ten dollars and change. After we ate all the food in the house, we ate berries from a nearby bush and oranges from the tree that I'd cried behind. My mother didn't believe in going to the welfare department for assistance. Other than a distant aunt we rarely saw, there were no other relatives that I knew of for us to turn to. Both of my parents had taught me that it was wrong to steal, but that didn't stop my mother and me from sneaking into other people's yards in the middle of the night to steal fruit, vegetables, and anything else edible. One night we got caught snatching a chicken out of a man's backyard. The man turned a dog loose on us that chased us all the way back home with that doomed chicken in a pillowcase squawking all the way. We got our best meals at church each Sunday and from food we stole out of the kitchens of some of the white people my mother did domestic work for.

Like an answer to a prayer, one of my mother's female friends moved to Richland, Ohio, and shortly afterward encouraged us to join her. She even sent us the money to cover our fare. In the middle of the night, my mother and I tiptoed out of our house owing back rent and loans, taking only what we could carry. Just like thieves. A segregated train took us from one pit of despair to another.

That year was 1954.

It was hard to believe that I'd made it to 1985.

As weak and sad as Daddy now looked, I would make sure that he knew just how much he had hurt us by sacrificing us for that white woman. And I would never let him forget that because I couldn't. Anger consumed me as I looked at him. The knife that had been in my back for so long only shifted its position.

I managed to postpone my wrath and wrapped my arms around my daddy. His body was as rigid as a tree trunk. He had the strong, musky smell of a man who didn't waste money on man-made fragrances. He leaned back and stared through me as if I were not there, bug-eyed and unblinking, like a dead man.

Finally, Daddy hugged me back with limp arms that trembled. He hesitated for a moment before he rested his knotty head on my shoulder. "Annette, I am so, so sorry for what I done to you and your mama. I can't change the past, but I swear to God I'll be there for you from now on." Then, my daddy cried like a baby.

And so did I.

CHAPTER 4

As much as I had hated living in Ohio those first few years, I made the best of it. Living in shacks and wearing secondhand clothes were the only things I'd ever known, but to lighten our load, my mother took in an elderly boarder. Mr. Boatwright, a homely, one-legged man with beady black eyes, a suspicious smile, and a mysterious past was a poor substitute for my daddy but he'd made my life easier. For a little while, at least. He showered me with the things I enjoyed the most, like toys and money. And even though I was already the largest first-grade student at Richland Elementary, which he complained about all the time, he helped me grow even larger by stuffing me with unnecessary snacks.

Within months after Mr. Boatwright's arrival, he revealed a side of himself that nobody but me would ever see. When we were alone, he no longer treated me like the granddaughter he never had. He treated me like a secret lover. He spent more time in my bed than he did his own. I got to know his tired, plump body as well as I knew mine. The endless wrinkles that covered him like a suit of armor, nappy gray hair, and the stump where his leg used to be all formed a grim picture that has been permanently seared into my brain.

In his scratchy voice, spraying my face with foul, yellow spit, he told me, "You ain't the prettiest gal in the world and I could do a lot better. Ain't too many men would touch a child as black, fat, and ugly as you. You done good to open up *my* nose, girl. I'm real particular." He added threats that kept me silent for years. "You ever was to tell about that little thing we do, I'll have to kill you. . . ."

Mr. Boatwright secured his threats by whupping me on a regular basis and waving a gun in my face. Not only did all that keep my mouth shut and my legs open, but my mother idolized this old man and so did everybody else I knew. I never even had a ghost of a chance.

"Brother Boatwright is more of a daddy to you than your own daddy was," my mother insisted whenever I complained about Mr. Boatwright whupping me. "Forget about Frank. You ain't never goin' to see him again nohow."

No matter how hard my mother and Mr. Boatwright tried to make me forget my own daddy, I couldn't. My life was like a jigsaw puzzle that I had been trying to put together for years. The only piece still missing was Daddy.

As much as I had wanted to see my father again, I suddenly found myself wishing I could be anywhere but back in Miami. I decided to put that and Mr. Boatwright and his threats out of my mind and focus on the real reason I had made the trip to Florida: to straighten out my tortured life.

There were just the three of us at the dinner table, but Lillimae had prepared enough food to feed twice as many people. As appealing as everything on the table looked and smelled, I couldn't eat. My stomach was in knots and my head was spinning and had been from the moment I got out of the cab that had brought me from the airport.

If Daddy and Lillimae were as uncomfortable as I was, they didn't show it. They inadvertently entertained me by loudly gobbling up mashed potatoes, macaroni and cheese, and greens like they had not eaten in days. A platter of grilled catfish, the flat, black eyes still intact, stared at me. Daddy and Lillimae stared at me, too, as if it were my responsibility to keep a conversation going. I did the best I could. I regaled them with details of my plane ride, the delay I encountered when I went to retrieve my luggage, and the cab ride from the airport. These mundane things didn't even interest me, but Daddy and Lillimae hung on to my words as if listening to me deliver their favorite psalm. When their eyes were not on me, I peered into a bowl next to the catfish that contained lumps of mysterious, root-like items in thick, brown gravy. Whatever it was, it must have been good, because Lillimae and Daddy dipped into that bowl with a vengeance.

It was hard to keep my eyes off Daddy's face. However, between him and Lillimae, his face was the easier one to tolerate. Seeing a white version of myself was a shock to my system. Lillimae's existence was a profound reminder of Daddy's betrayal. But I knew I had to work around that if I wanted to keep Daddy in my life this time. No matter how much it hurt.

"Sister-girl, you ain't barely ate a bite. Now, them greens is screamin' too loud for you not to eat 'em. But don't worry about them smashed potatoes. They are sure enough lumpy. I can feed what we don't eat to that greedy cat from next door. Clyde. That mangy old feline would eat a rock," Lillimae told me, chewing so hard her ears wiggled. An onion strip hung from her bottom lip like a ribbon. "I told Daddy not to smash them potatoes with a spatula."

"The mashed potatoes taste fine but I . . . I ate on the plane," I muttered, sliding food around on my plate with a slightly bent fork. "And, I've been trying to lose a few pounds anyway," I lied.

Daddy nodded and snapped a mighty pork chop in two with his sparse teeth. Lillimae burped and snatched another huge chunk of cornbread from a cracked bowl next to my plate. She slapped the cornbread with a gob of butter and continued stuffing her mouth. It pleased me to see somebody else appreciate food as much as I did, when I was in the mood to eat. It brought tears to my eyes to have to ignore all the good food sitting in front of me. But every time I tried to swallow something, a huge lump in my throat blocked the way, almost making me choke.

Daddy took a long swallow from a can of beer and let out a great belch. "You ain't got to lose no weight, girl." He paused and gave his chest a punch with his fist; then he belched again, covering his mouth and excusing himself. "You look fine just the way you is." Daddy grunted and punched his chest again. "Black men like women to have some meat on them bones." That sounded strange coming from him. I had only glimpsed the *white* woman one time that he had left my mother for. From what I had been able to see, there had not been a lot of meat on her bones. Daddy gave me a sharp look and asked harshly, "How come you ain't married yet? What's wrong with them brothers up there in Ohio, lettin' a fox like you run loose?" Before I could respond, he turned to Lillimae. "Girl, pass me that bowl of smashed potatoes." Daddy eagerly scooped up what was left of the potatoes, but not before Lillimae dipped her spoon in again.

"I'm engaged," I said proudly. "Jerome, my fiancé, is a high school guidance counselor." I paused and turned to Lillimae. "And he is so handsome." I felt it was necessary to let it be known that even a plain, heavyset woman like me could attract a good-looking man who loved me enough he wanted to marry me. Other than the man who had raped me for ten years, Jerome was the only man who had ever put me first in his life. That was something I couldn't even say about my daddy.

With raised eyebrows, Daddy and Lillimae looked at one another, then back to me with wide smiles on their faces.

"Well, I declare. My girl done outdone herself." Daddy beamed proudly, grinning so hard the skin on his bottom lip cracked. "You done found you a educated man, huh?" He sniffed and wiped a speck of fresh blood from the crack on his lip.

I smiled and looked away before answering. "I didn't find him, Daddy. He found me."

I spent the next fifteen minutes bragging about Jerome Cunningham and how good he was to me and for me.

CHAPTER 5

The few letters and telephone conversations I had shared with my daddy during the last five years had not revealed much about him and his new family. But when he and Lillimae started talking, while we were still eating dinner, I heard everything I had been anxious to hear. And a few things I didn't want to hear.

Even though Daddy had admitted that he was sorry he had deserted my mother and me, he made it clear to me that he was happy with his new family. My other two half-siblings, Amos and Sondra, were both in the military, stationed somewhere in Germany. Daddy had retired from a security guard position at a rough high school and now lived on a monthly pension check.

Other than an occasional dinner with a pushy grandmother he referred to as "Miss Pittman," Daddy had no love life. "I don't miss havin' no lady friend," he insisted, a faraway look in his eyes. "Women done got me in enough trouble to last me from now on."

Immediately after the elaborate meal, Daddy excused

himself from the table in the middle of a sentence. He ran to the bathroom, moaning and cussing all the way.

"He's got weak bowels," Lillimae whispered, rising from the table.

I had almost forgotten how kicked-back people were down South. It was late in the evening and Lillimae was still in her bathrobe from that morning. There was now gravy on her bare feet that had dripped off her overflowing dinner plate. She ignored the gnats hovering above her toes, but every few minutes she lifted her feet and shook them.

"Poor Daddy. He's so proud and independent, it took me a year to talk him into movin' in with me so I could look after him. And not a minute too soon, girl. Miss Pittman was just about to reel him in like a carp."

"What-all is wrong with Daddy? He doesn't look too well," I said with concern, tapping my fingers on the naked wooden table situated in the middle of the small kitchen.

"Oh, he's in pretty good health for a man his age, but he was so lonely livin' alone. And in a neighborhood that was so rough even the cops got robbed on the streets. I was just as lonely as Daddy was." Lillimae paused and leaned down to scratch the side of her foot. Then she started removing plates from the table.

"I'll help you clean up," I offered. I stood up, my legs feeling like lead pipes. I massaged my thighs, frowning at the hole on the knee of my pantyhose that I had ruined crawling out of the cab.

She waved me back to my seat. "You just sit there. You're company. It ain't every day I get to see family." She paused and continued talking with her back to me. "Uh, some folks wouldn't want nothin' to do with a man's outside woman's kids. Sharin' the same blood wouldn't mean a damn thing to them."

"Well, I don't feel that way." I sniffed and coughed to clear my throat. "Speaking of blood, where is your mother these days?" I asked, returning to my seat with a thud so hard, my tailbone ached.

I had no love for the woman who had ruined my life, but I wanted to know more about her. Muh'Dear had always advised me, *Know thine enemy, because knowledge is power.* I had to know for myself what it was about the woman who had managed to weaken my daddy and lure him away from his responsibilities.

Lillimae let out a deep sigh and pressed her thin lips together so tight it looked like they had disappeared. Then she started talking in a low, controlled voice. "Oh, she took off when I was ten. I heard that she lived in Key West for a few years. Mama's family didn't want nothin' to do with me and Sondra and Amos, so we couldn't keep up with Mama's life. I just found out three years ago that she's back in Miami with a new husband. I have two other half-sisters that I've never even seen or talked to." Lillimae blinked and smiled sadly. "That's why it was so important for me to meet you."

"Oh." The kitchen window was open and smoke from one of the houses next door streamed in, making my eyes burn and itch. I blinked and rubbed my eyes. "It's too bad you don't get to spend time with her," I managed. Nobody knew as well as I did how painful it was not to have much of a family. My mother and my Aunt Berniece had been the only relatives I had when I was growing up.

Lillimae continued talking as she started washing dishes. "Mama's baby brother Lester married a woman I went to school with. Roxanne McFinney. How a cracker like him ended up with such a nice lady is beyond me. I talk to Roxanne every now and then. We go to the same dollar-a-load washhouse. She tells me that my Uncle Lester is so racist, he won't even wear black underwear. Lester would bite Roxanne's head off if he knew she associated with a mutt like me in public. But Roxanne still sneaks by here every now and then anyway."

I didn't know where Lillimae's bathroom was, but I could hear Daddy still moaning and cussing. He flushed the toilet about every other minute.

"Poor Daddy. I been tryin' to get him to go to the doctor to get somethin' for his stomach. But you know how stubborn some of our Black men are when it comes to their health. And they act like they know everything. Daddy had a runnin' buddy who wouldn't listen to nobody when he got these growths on the back of his neck. Even when one started oozin' pus. Well, bein' so stubborn got Brother Hamilton nowhere but in a hole at the Oak Grove Cemetery over in Alabama." Lillimae paused and motioned me back to the living room.

I sat down on the dangerously weak couch. She sat down across from me on a wobbly bamboo chair.

"How long can you stay down here?" Lillimae asked, fanning her face with the tail of her bathrobe, revealing puckered fat on her thighs that reminded me of blisters. It was a struggle, but somehow she managed to cross her massive legs. I didn't even try to do that, because it was too much trouble.

I looked at my watch before answering. "Just a few days. I need to save some vacation days for my honeymoon cruise."

A broad smile appeared on Lillimae's face and she shook her head and clicked her teeth. She rubbed the side of her neck and looked at me, blinking hard. "Girl, would you believe I spent my weddin' night in the emergency ward gettin' my jaw wired up? My man beat the livin' daylights out of me for slow dancin' with his best man." She chuckled and let out a deep sigh. "My thirtieth birthday at that. Me and Freddie Lee had already been together for ten years and had two babies."

"You must have had some wedding reception. Are you still married?" I didn't laugh. There was nothing funny about a man hitting a female. I still had nightmares about the beatings that Mr. Boatwright had showered me with the few times I tried to keep him out of my bed.

Lillimae shook her head and shrugged. "That thing I married took off before the ink dried on our marriage license. Freddie Lee—that's my husband's name—was so jealous, he didn't even allow me to go to male doctors. Every time I left the house and came back, he made me take off my panties so he could sniff 'em to see if he could smell another man's juice. I broke his black ass up from that real quick, though. One time I went out and ate the biggest bowl of pinto beans and cabbage greens I could find. Then I washed it all down with some home-brewed beer. My panties was nice and ripe by the time I got home for him to sniff 'em. I didn't have to worry about none of his foolishness after that." Lillimae paused and laughed so hard, a huge tear rolled down the side of her face like a marble.

"Where is this Freddie Lee now?" I asked.

Lillimae gave me a serious look and groaned. "He's in Lauderdale, livin' with his mama. She manages one of them bait shops and he works with her." Lillimae paused and grimaced. "Freddie Lee can be such a worm hisself sometimes. No wonder he loves sellin' worms now." Lillimae sniffed and then a thoughtful look appeared on her face. "But he is a good daddy to our two precious little boys. That's why I didn't mind lettin' him have them for the summer. When I call to talk to the boys, me and Freddie Lee talk, too. We still love each other. I know we'll eventually work things out and hook back up. If not for us, for our boys. A child needs both parents to feel whole." Lillimae gave me a mournful look and quickly glanced over her shoulder in the direction where Daddy was. "I'm sure you know what I mean by that."

"I do," I said flatly.

"Besides, I can't stand bein' lonely, so I'm just about ready to put up with anything if he decides to come back. Even that panty thing he used to do. Daddy is seventy-two years old now. He won't be around to keep me company too much longer. I've been so blessed to have him with me all these years."

"I wish I could say that," I muttered grimly.

Lillimae gasped and frowned. "Excuse me?"

"Oh, I didn't mean anything by that," I said levelly, listening as Daddy flushed the toilet again.

CHAPTER 6

It was another twenty minutes before Daddy returned from the bathroom, mopping his face with a wet towel and straightening his bathrobe.

"Lord, I wish I hadn't et them peppers. Lillimae, can you run out to the drugstore and get me some more Maalox?" he grunted, a severe grimace on his face. "Carry Annette with you so she can sight-see."

I waited with Daddy in the living room while Lillimae went to put on some clothes and shoes.

Sitting next to me on the couch, Daddy placed his hand over mine and squeezed, smiling so hard his eyes watered. "Annette, I can't get over how fine you turned out. But then, good-lookin' females run in my family."

I listened with interest.

"Daddy, do you have other family? Aunt Berniece said something about you having a brother somewhere. I'd like to get in touch with your other relatives, if you don't mind." I thought that at this stage of my life, it was important for me to know as much as I could about my background. I wanted to have some answers for the questions I expected from the children I planned to have with Jerome.

Daddy sighed and shook his head and then an unbearably sad smile crossed his face. "St. Louis was my only brother. He passed last year. He would have been eighty last week. He had a bunch of kids but I don't know where none of 'em at. Both of my sisters, twins named Collette and Corinna, passed before you was born." Daddy paused and giggled. "Big-foot gals, both of 'em." He sniffed and got serious again, massaging his chest. "A car wreck is how they died. They come into this mean old world together and they left it together. Comin' home from a revival one night, a possum jumped in front of the car and they ran off the Yammagoochee Bridge over in Alabama. Both of 'em died in my arms after me and some boys from the church pulled 'em out of that car. There was a hospital less than five minutes away, but we couldn't carry them there on account of it was still segregated at the time. Right after Kennedy got in the White House and him and the rest of the decent white folks made new laws, they closed that hospital down to keep from havin' to doctor on Black folks." Daddy's lips quivered and his jaw twitched, almost as much as mine. He sniffed and continued. "Corinna left a little girl behind that her man took off somewhere right after the funeral. He was one of them Geechees so I suspect he took that child off somewhere to one of them islands where I think he came from." His jaw still twitching, Daddy paused and blinked fast and hard. But a single tear still managed to slide out of his eye. "I declare, I loved that little gal as much as I love my own." He paused again and grinned, wiping the tear off his cheek with the back of his hand. "You ever gwine to be *my girl* again?" He sniffed hard and downgraded his grin to a weak smile.

"I've always been your girl, Daddy. And I always will be." I patted Daddy's shoulder and looked away, sucking in air so hard a sharp pain rolled through my chest. "How come you didn't tell me Lillimae looked like *that*?" I asked in a whisper, leaning my head close Daddy's.

He looked at me with genuine surprise. "Look like what?" He glanced toward the back room, where Lillimae was slamming closet doors and banging dresser drawers shut.

My face was flaming as I caressed my cheek and cocked my head to the side. Talking out of the side of my mouth, I said in a controlled voice, "She can pass for white."

Daddy shrugged. "I can sure enough understand you havin' a beef with white women . . ."

I gave Daddy a thoughtful look and a smile. "My closest female friend back in Ohio is white. I don't have a problem with white women. But it was a real shock to find out that my own sister looks like one."

"Well, Lillimae ain't white. At least not by these rules the white folks done laid down. And while we on the subject, every nigger I know claim to be part Indian. Even me! Only ones ain't braggin' about havin' Indian blood is the Indians. Shoot. White blood, Indian blood, don't matter how much of it you got. If you got any Black blood at all, you Black in this white man's country. Case closed. Lillimae is a Black woman and she proud of it." Daddy paused and gave me a thoughtful look. "And I hope you proud of your color, too."

"I am, Daddy. I wouldn't want to be anything else."

I could not believe that I had only been in Florida for a few hours. It seemed more like a few days. Daylight was coming to a dramatic close. Lightning bugs and dim streetlights lit up the night as Lillimae and I made our way from the living room to her old Chrysler. She kept it parked in a narrow driveway by the side of her house. The full moon, shining like a huge silver ball, looked like it was about to drop right out of the darkening sky. It gave me an eerie feeling.

It was still just as hot as it had been when I'd arrived that afternoon. All of the doors to the neighboring houses were standing open. People in their nightclothes had gathered on their front porches. They were fanning, drinking, and listening to radios playing everything from Gospel to the Blues.

After the visit to the drugstore, Lillimae and I stopped at a vegetable stand. She wanted to pick up more turnip greens and a bag of red-skinned potatoes. The place was crawling with sweaty people pushing shopping carts, loaded with everything from watermelons to ten-pound plastic bags of raw peanuts.

There was a long line of customers at three of the four checkout aisles. Since Lillimae had only two items, she rushed to the express lane. I stumbled along behind her, chewing on a handful of grapes that I had snatched off a counter next to the greens.

The cashier, a middle-aged blonde who would have been pretty without the dark circles and heavy bags under her large blue eyes, smiled as we approached her counter. She had chatted with the white man ahead of us, telling him how sorry she was about his sick wife and telling him she was going to pray for him and his whole family. Naturally, I assumed she'd show us some level of courtesy, too.

Just as Lillimae placed her greens and the sack of potatoes on the counter, a sharp-featured white man wearing a manager's identification tag appeared out of nowhere. He stood rooted in a spot near our cashier, with his hairy, sunburned arms folded and a grim expression on his face. The cashier's face immediately went from a smile to a scowl. She roughly stuffed Lillimae's greens into the same bag with the potatoes, even though the bag was clearly too small. Then, she practically threw Lillimae's change at her, ignoring her request to have the greens put in a separate bag. Instead, the rude cashier waved us through her line and snapped her fingers at the customer behind us and yelled, "Next!"

I had to remember where I was, because I was tempted to

say something. By the grace of God, I was able to restrain myself. But I still glared at the cashier. Somehow, Lillimae managed to remain pleasant, even telling the woman, "Have a nice day."

I was further annoyed when the manager put his hands on his hips and watched us until we went out the door.

"I guess some things never change." I sighed as Lillimae and I approached her car parked on the street directly in front of the vegetable stand. "I'll never forget the way some white folks used to treat Muh'Dear and me when we lived down here." I snorted so hard I had to rub my nose. I was surprised to see specks of blood on my fingers. Lillimae didn't respond until she had tossed the bag with her vegetables onto the backseat.

"I would have gone to another stand if I had known that woman worked here," Lillimae hissed, gripping the sides of the steering wheel. The weather had cooled off considerably by now, but beads of sweat covered most of Lillimae's face. She was red with rage. "I work my fingers to the bone at that damn post office so me and Daddy can eat good. This is one of the best stands in town and one of the closest. But them motherfuckers'll never get another one of my hard-earned dollars. I don't have to put up with that shit."

"I would not have been as nice to that old peckerwood witch as you were," I snarled, looking back toward the vegetable stand.

The same cashier who had behaved so rudely was now standing outside on the sidewalk in front of the vegetable stand under a streetlight, looking at us. For a moment, her eyes locked with mine. I blinked because I couldn't believe the unbearably sad look on the woman's face now. I gasped when she offered a faint smile before we drove off. I let out a deep sigh and turned back around.

I saw no reason to share what I had just seen with Lillimae. As far as I was concerned, the woman was nobody. But what Lillimae said next made my eyes burn with tears.

"Her name is Edith," Lillimae told me, her voice cracking.

"Who?" I asked, my eyes staring at the side of Lillimae's head.

"That old peckerwood witch that just waited on us."

I gasped. "You know her?"

Lillimae nodded. "She's my mama."

CHAPTER 7

The first few hours of the first day of my visit with Daddy and Lillimae had already been difficult enough. Seeing Lillimae's mother at that vegetable stand had made it even more difficult.

Lillimae had prepared her absent sons' small bedroom next to the kitchen for me to sleep in. I took a long bath in a huge, claw-foot bathtub, noticing that the Florida sun had already started drying out my skin. By the time I crawled out of the bathtub, slathered Vaseline Intensive Care lotion over most of my body, and returned to the living room, Lillimae and Daddy had disappeared to their bedrooms. I waited until I was sure they were asleep. Then I padded into the kitchen to use the telephone on the wall next to the refrigerator to call up Muh'Dear, my mother.

Before I could dial Muh'Dear's number, that greedy cat from next door started clawing and thumping on the kitchen door. He was meowing so loud, I let him in before he could disturb Lillimae. Since she seemed so fond of him, I knew she would come out to feed him again. Once the cat rolled across the floor, straight to the refrigerator, I took out a slice of raw bacon and tossed it to him. He dragged it to a corner and started gnawing. He was already halfway done with it by the time I finished dialing Muh'Dear's number so I knew I had to talk fast.

Muh'Dear must have had the telephone in the bed with her, because she answered before the first ring ended.

"What your daddy got to say for hisself after all these years? I bet he done already told you enough lies to fill a hog trough," Muh'Dear said hotly.

Before Daddy's desertion, Muh'Dear had talked about him like he was the king of some proud African tribe. She even used to call him *Mr. Goode.* Now when she referred to him it was always by his first name only, Frank. And she now talked about him like a dog. I felt tremendously sad knowing that Muh'Dear's bitterness toward Daddy remained so strong after so many years. Despite Daddy's departure and all of the obstacles we had encountered because of it, Muh'Dear and I still had a lot to be grateful for. We both had nice homes, jobs, decent friends, and our health. I had a man and he was a good man. Muh'Dear loved Jerome as much as I did. "As much trouble as men is, we still need 'em," she had told me a few years ago.

I didn't agree with Muh'Dear's old-school belief about women *needing* men. But the one man I felt I did need in my life was my daddy. A bloodline was one thing a person couldn't change. It bothered me, knowing that part of my blood had run in so many different directions. I had a real daddy and siblings. I wanted to unite our blood while there was still time. The brief time that I had had Daddy in my life had meant a lot to me. Having him back meant even more. I knew that if I had never reunited with him, I would never feel like a whole person again.

I didn't appreciate Muh'Dear's negative attitude, but she had every right to still be angry.

"Annette, Frank brought you all the way to Florida to tell

you more lies. Once you see what a snake he is, you'll get him out of your system once and for all. I sure enough did."

"Daddy hasn't told me any lies, Muh'Dear. He was glad to see me," I replied, speaking low.

The cat had finished the slice of bacon and had returned to sniff at the refrigerator once again. This time, I tossed him a huge pork chop, hoping it would keep him occupied until I completed my conversation with Muh'Dear.

"Well, Frank'll be lyin' like a rug as soon as he tune up his lips. That no-good jackass. How he lookin' these days? I bet he look like he been whupped with a ugly stick. When you act ugly, you get ugly sooner or later."

"He looks the same way he did the last time we saw him," I lied. Without going into detail, I added, "He's still one of the best-looking Black men in town." I paused and sucked in my breath. "He still goes to that Baptist church on Greely Street that we used to go to when we lived down here. He's an usher."

"That don't mean nothin', girl. The Church is full of dev-ils," Muh' Dear snapped.

I was exasperated. I covered my mouth with my hand to keep Muh'Dear from hearing my deep sigh. "Muh'Dear, let's forget about what Daddy did to us. We can't change the past."

"I know that. But Frank Goode is goin' to rue the day he run off and left us the way he done. He goin' to be sorry."

"He's already told me he was sorry," I said dryly, my fin-gers twisting the telephone cord.

"Oh, he did? That's a surprise." Muh'Dear sucked her teeth and took her time continuing. "You called Jerome?"

"Not yet. I'll call him tomorrow."

"Well, you better. You ain't never goin' to find another man as good as him at your age. And you better hurry and marry him before he change his mind or before he take a real good look at you. Makeup is a mask you can hide behind but for so long." Muh'Dear laughed. "It was years before your stepdaddy found out what I really looked like."

"Go to sleep, Muh'Dear." I sighed. "Don't forget to go water my plants. I'll be home in a few days."

"Wait a minute, girl. I ain't finish talkin' to you yet." Muh'Dear lowered her voice to a whisper so I knew what was coming. "You seen that white woman? Your auntie told me that that she-puppy done dragged her white-trash tail on back to Miami."

"You mean Edith?" I saw no reason for me to whisper the way Muh'Dear often did when she and I talked about white folks.

"Who in the world is Edith?" she hissed, still whispering.

"The white woman Daddy was with." I didn't like saying things that hurt my mother but she made it hard for me to avoid.

"Oh, excuse me! So now you on a first-name basis with that pale-face Jezebel?"

"No, I'm not. I saw her at a vegetable stand that Lillimae took me to today. Uh . . . Lillimae is Daddy's oldest girl." I paused and added with a chuckle, "She looks just like me. She took off from her job at the post office to spend time with me. Daddy lives with her."

"*You* is Frank's oldest girl," Muh'Dear reminded with a hiss. "And how she look like you is a mystery to me, since you took after me."

"Well, I take after Daddy, too. Listen—I'm tired and I really need to get some sleep. It's been a long day. I'll call you again tomorrow."

"I still can't get over what possessed Jerome to let you go down there, by yourself, to prance around with—"

"Jerome didn't *let* me do anything, Muh'Dear. He doesn't own me and I do have a mind of my own. You should know that by now."

"Which is why you still single at thirty-five and I ain't got no grandchildren." Muh'Dear let out a heavy sigh before she started grinding her teeth. I rolled my eyes and shook my head as she continued. "Where is that Frank at now? Up in some bootlegger's house gettin' drunk and lookin' for another white woman to joog his pecker up in, I bet."

"He's in bed. He's not well, Muh'Dear. I think his barhopping days are over. And for the record, the lady friend he's got now is Black. Miss Pittman."

"Oh. Well, you try to enjoy yourself down there. Like I told you before you left, all I want is for you to be happy. And . . . and I'm glad Frank still in the Church. You can tell him I said that."

"I will, Muh'Dear." I hung up and smiled. I couldn't wait for that arrogant old cat to finish the pork chop. He dragged what was left of it across the floor as I shooed him back out the door.

CHAPTER 8

Long after Clyde the cat had disappeared from the kitchen, I stood in the doorway looking out into the night. Even with the back porch light on, I couldn't see much. Green vines crawled up the sides of the porch walls. There wasn't much of a backyard. But it had a clothesline, an old picnic table with three mismatched chairs, and what appeared to be an orange tree. In the yard of almost every one of the sorry shacks I had shared with Muh'Dear and Daddy during my childhood, we'd had an orange tree. I felt like I had come home. In a way, I had.

I was surprised to turn around and find Lillimae standing by the table in a muslin nightgown that barely covered her body.

"I hope you don't think I was eavesdroppin' on your conversation with your mama," Lillimae said, removing a pitcher from the refrigerator. She poured us both a glass of water and waved me to a chair at the table as she sat down across from me.

"That's okay. I don't really have anything to hide from you," I said, plopping down with a groan, drinking water I

didn't want. "Uh, that reminds me of something I've been
thinking about all evening." I drank some more water, wishing that it was something stronger sliding down my throat.

There was a blank look on Lillimae's face. "What's that?"

"I know you must be hurting right now about your
mother."

Lillimae sighed and clutched her glass with both hands.
"And you're probably wonderin' why I care about a woman
who don't care about me."

"She does care about you," I said firmly.

Lillimae gasped and gave me a dry look. "How would
you know that? You didn't know her. And what about the
way she behaved at the vegetable stand this evenin'?"

"I didn't want to tell you," I paused because I could
barely form my sentences. "Your mother came outside as we
were getting back into your car. She had a smile on her face,
but she looked like she wanted to cry when we drove off. I
bet if her boss hadn't been around, she would have run out to
the car and said something to you."

Lillimae started blinking hard and biting her bottom lip.
"Sure enough?"

I nodded. "I would have told you sooner or later. I guess
the sooner you know she cares, the better."

Lillimae folded her arms and glanced around the kitchen.
"Now that I know where my mama works, maybe I'll go
back over there and slip her a note, tellin' her to meet me
somewhere where we can talk. Would you go with me? I
don't think I can do it otherwise. I am not as bold as you."

I nodded. "I'm sure your mother would appreciate you
taking that step." I heard the toilet flush, so I glanced toward
the doorway. Every time Daddy was out of my sight, I got
nervous. It was like I couldn't look at his face enough. Because my beloved stepfather had recently died, I had been
afraid that Daddy would die before I could see him again. I
blinked even harder and returned my attention to Lillimae.

"That day Mama left us, she took me aside and told me that I had to be stronger than Amos and Sondra because of the way I look." A faraway look appeared on Lillimae's face. "She was right."

"You mean your color?"

"My lack of color would be more like it. I didn't know what she meant, but it didn't take me long to find out. Bein' a Black girl in a white body ain't no picnic. I'd give anything in this world to be as dark as you."

"But don't you have some advantages over the rest of us? When you go out alone, don't white people treat you like one of their own?"

She nodded. "The ones that don't know me do. But you don't know how hard it is to be around Black folks and have them make jokes about me lookin' white. You don't know what it feels like when white folks on my job find out I'm Black. I can't go around announcin' to the world that I'm Black, but when they find out, it's a whole different ball game. My first boyfriend's mama was into that Black Panther stuff. The first time she got a look at me, she told me to my face that she wasn't goin' to be 'eatin' with the enemy' or some shit like that."

I pursed my lips and shrugged. "You can't do anything about the way you look."

"And don't think I haven't tried. I used to wear Afro wigs and dark makeup. When I got tired of that, I started wearin' braids and all the things I saw the other Black girls wearin'. But that wasn't me. I can't be happy tryin' to be somethin' I'm not. Now my old man, Freddie Lee, ain't too fond of white folks. But even before me, all his other girls was high yellow. That confused me. And it confused our boys when Freddie Lee put 'em in a all-white school tellin' 'em he thought they'd do better goin' to school with white kids. My babies would come home cryin' every day because the white kids called them coons and niggers *and* spit on 'em." At this point, Lillimae reached across the table and squeezed my hand. "You are so fortunate, Annette. People know what you are when they look at you and they treat you as such. You don't give out no surprises."

"I've had my share of abuse because of the way I look, too," I said thoughtfully.

"But if you could change the way you look, knowin' what you know now, would you?"

I smiled. "I don't think so. Every person I've ever known has experienced some pain about one thing or another."

Lillimae nodded and shrugged. We remained silent for a moment, but the crickets and other night creatures sounded like they had a symphony going on outside. The small window above the kitchen sink was open by a few inches. A moth that couldn't make up its mind repeatedly flew in and out. I heard an old car rattle past the house before it backfired. The loud bang made us both jump.

Lillimae shut the window and returned to her seat with a groan. She had braided her hair and pinned it up on her head. Traces of face cream made her look even whiter under the glow of the weak lightbulb in the kitchen.

"Annette, I know you missed your daddy when you was growin' up, but it sounds like you still managed to enjoy life. Didn't your mama ever have any men friends livin' in the house with y'all before she married your stepdaddy?"

It took me a moment to respond. "Just one," I said stiffly, my eyes on the floor.

"Well, I hope he took up the slack that Daddy left behind." Lillimae sniffed. "Was that man in the Church?"

"Uh-huh." I cleared my throat and rubbed both my eyes. "But he wasn't the kind of man I wanted to replace Daddy."

"Regardless, a man was there to keep y'all company. My mother-in-law always tellin' me that a piece of a man is better than no man at all. She can't wait for me to take that half-ass son of hers back so he can stop crampin' her style. Every time I turn over in that big bed by myself, I know what she means. Bein' alone ought to be a sin. If that man was willin' to stay in the house with your mama, especially you bein' by another man, that was a double blessin'. Wasn't it?"

It took me a moment to respond. "Something like that," I said vaguely. Yawning and stretching my arms, I rose and headed out of the kitchen.

I didn't sleep much that night and when I did, Mr. Boatwright's face dominated my dreams.

It was like he was still raping me.

CHAPTER 9

I was glad Daddy got up early the next morning to go fishing. It was a ritual that he had started before I was born. I was surprised that he didn't want to spend as much time with me as possible. But in a way, I was glad to have the space I needed to sort out my feelings. As happy as I was to be in the same house with him, I was still uncomfortable.

Surprisingly, I felt particularly at ease alone with Lillimae. Her looking so much like me helped.

Lillimae and I ate a huge breakfast of grits and bacon before we retreated to the front porch glider. Still in our bathrobes, we sat fanning our faces with old magazines as we watched one noisy, beat-up old car after another crawl down the street.

The sun had already started its assault. The people in the houses on both sides of us had come out on their porches trying to cool off. The same old man I had seen watering his lawn when I'd arrived was watering that same lawn again.

I was glad that my half-sister was the type who liked to

talk. She seemed to enjoy telling me about how proud she was of Daddy and how he had raised her and her two siblings alone.

"We didn't give Daddy half the trouble a lot of kids give their folks. Oh, our baby sister Sondra was a little on the wild side durin' her teen years. She got pregnant when she was fourteen, but she couldn't stop dancin' up in the clubs long enough to carry the baby to full term. She settled down after her miscarriage long enough to finish school and join the army. Our brother Amos, he fooled around with some of them drug dealers and gangs, but he came to his senses after somebody shot at him on the street one night. I was glad when he joined the army, too."

"Do you miss not having a relationship with your mama's family?" I asked.

A weak smile crossed Lillimae's face. She sniffed and nodded.

"Somebody pointed out my mama's mama to me one day when I was eleven. She was workin' the cotton-candy stand at a carnival. I went up to her and introduced myself."

"What did she say?"

"She didn't have to say anything for me to know where I stood with her. She hawked a wad of spit as big as a walnut in my face. Me, her first granddaughter. I heard she treats the other two daughters my mama had with her white husband like queens."

Just then, a noisy, dusty blue Chevy, dented in the front, a red door on the driver's side, crawled around the corner and stopped in front of Lillimae's house. A young white woman, glancing around nervously, kept the motor running as she rolled down her window.

Lillimae gasped. "That's my uncle's wife. That's Roxanne. The one I told you about." She clutched my arm. Her knee started shaking against mine as she rose from her seat, pulling me up with her. Lillimae started waving with both hands to the woman in the car.

But the woman shook her head and yelled, "Lillimae, your mama died!" Then she rolled her window back up and drove off, leaving Lillimae and me on the porch staring in slack-jawed amazement until the car turned the corner.

Lillimae and I sat on the front porch in silence for about five minutes after the woman had delivered the news about Lillimae's mother's death. Finally, she turned to me and spoke through trembling lips that suddenly looked so dry I thought they'd crack. "What do you want to eat for dinner?" She sniffed and scratched the side of her neck, her eyes blinking hard. I noticed that when Lillimae was upset or angry, her eyes looked darker. Right now they looked as dark as mine.

"I'm not that hungry. Anything you fix is fine with me. Uh . . . I'm sorry about your mama."

Instead of speaking again, Lillimae sighed and gently rubbed my thigh. The glider squeaked like it was in pain as we wobbled up to our feet at the same time and shuffled into the living room. I followed Lillimae into the kitchen where she grabbed a dish towel off of the table and started wiping her face.

Standing next to her, reared back on my legs, I asked, "Is there anybody you can call?"

She whirled around to face me. Her eyes were now red with dark shadows already forming beneath them. "For what?"

"About your mama. Don't you want to know how she died?"

Lillimae shrugged, sucked in her breath, and shook her head. "I'll find out soon enough," she told me, narrowing her eyes.

CHAPTER 10

Lillimae and I spent the afternoon in front of the television watching game shows and *The Phil Donahue Show.* Around five, Daddy stumbled in with a bucket full of catfish. Two hours later, over a dinner of fish and more greens, Lillimae turned to Daddy and told him, "Roxanne came by today." Lillimae had dabbed on some makeup, but it didn't help. She couldn't conceal her pain.

Daddy stopped chewing and looked from Lillimae to me and back to Lillimae with his eyes bulging. "Well, now I know why you lookin' so much like hell, that I can smell the brimstone." He snorted. "What did Roxanne want?" Fresh black-and-gray stubble on Daddy's rough face reminded me of a briar patch. He dragged his fingers through his knotty hair and sniffed. "Musta been somethin' deep for her to come by here in broad daylight."

"She came by to tell me that Mama died," Lillimae muttered, her eyes on the plate of untouched food in front of her.

Daddy leaned back in his wobbly chair. Scratching the side of his face, he muttered to Lillimae, "Well, bless your soul." Then he let out a loud, deep breath. "Them fish sure was bitin' today. Them bad boys was all but jumpin' out the lake into my bucket on they own."

It was an awkward moment for us all. I forced myself to eat as much as I could. Without a word, Lillimae pushed herself away from the table and waddled back to the living room. Daddy turned to me with his eyes narrowed.

"I bet that piece of news about Lillimae's mama made your day," he hissed, his jaw twitching. His words shocked and angered me.

"Well, it didn't," I snapped, surprised that Daddy would think I'd celebrate the death of a woman I didn't know. "My mama raised me better than that," I added proudly, rising.

I didn't know what to expect the next day or the rest of my visit but I had already prepared myself to expect the worst. She didn't say it, but I assumed Lillimae wanted to be left alone. So instead of joining her in the living room, I decided to turn in for the night and try to get some sleep. I couldn't hear the television but I did hear a brief, muffled conversation between Daddy and Lillimae in the living room. Then the house got ominously quiet. It was hours before I fell asleep.

I had forgotten how hot Florida could be in the morning. Even with the plastic curtains covering the window in the bedroom that Lillimae had put me in, the sun's rays woke me up that next morning around seven o'clock. I would have cracked open the window, but through the curtains I could see the outline of a huge grasshopper on it outside, peeping into the bedroom.

I didn't know what kind of money Lillimae made working for the post office or how much money Daddy got from his retirement fund. But I knew it had to be enough between them that they could have lived in a much nicer neighborhood. And I was sure that they could afford to put better furniture in the house. Every piece in the house was probably older than I was. The mattress on the bed I was in was so weak, it was practically on the floor. Even without me on it. It was a struggle for me to pull myself out of the deep valley in the middle. Like the other floors in the house, the linoleum on the bedroom floor had been waxed to a brilliant shine. My bare feet stuck to the floor as I made my way around the bed to retrieve my bathrobe from the back of a chair in front of a closet with a blanket for a door. An ironing board that Lillimae had used the evening before to clean the fish on had been propped up in a corner by a door that had no knob. I had to open and close it with a piece of wire hanging from the hole where a knob should have been. I didn't know why I was feeling the way I was about people living in such squalor. Before Mr. Boatwright had ruined my life, Muh'Dear and I had lived in places not even this nice and I had been happy. I smiled and got dressed.

If the sun hadn't aroused me first, the aroma of the elaborate breakfast Lillimae was preparing would have. The smell of bacon was so strong it made my eyes water. I had all of my appetite back. I was comfortable enough to let myself relax. However, now Lillimae was the one with no appetite. She didn't even sit at the kitchen table with Daddy and me. Instead, she paced around the kitchen nibbling on a piece of dry toast and swatting flies with a potholder.

The subject of Lillimae's mother's death was not mentioned again until we read the newspaper that arrived the next day. It was then that we learned Lillimae's mother had been involved in a fatal car crash on her way home from work just hours after she had treated Lillimae so rudely.

"The funeral's Saturday," Lillimae informed me after a brief telephone conversation she had with somebody she did not identify. "It's the last time I'll get to see her so I have to go."

I didn't know what Daddy was thinking about that white

woman's death, because other than a few grunts, he kept his comments to himself. Then he went to his room where he remained until I called him out to eat dinner.

I had nothing against white people. My current closest female friend was a white woman. However, the last thing I wanted to do while I was in Florida was attend the funeral of the one who had stolen my daddy. There had been no love lost between that woman and me, but I already loved my half-sister. I had to go to the funeral because Lillimae needed my support.

"You don't have to go in the church with me, but I'd appreciate you sittin' in the car waitin' on me," Lillimae said, as we cleared the breakfast table after we'd eaten. I had not seen her shed a single tear. However, her eyes were red and swollen and she had barely eaten since hearing the tragic news.

"I'll go in that church with you if you want me to," I said, praying that Lillimae would decline my offer.

Lillimae shook her head so hard, the hairpin she had pinned her hair up with fell to the floor along with a plate she had just washed.

"Goodness gracious, no. I wouldn't put you through that. You wouldn't be welcome there. If they figure out who I am, *I* won't even be welcome there neither. They won't notice me if I stand in the back with a floppy hat or a veil hidin' my face, but you'd stand out like a lighthouse and they'd treat you like you stole somethin'. Wait for me in the car." Lillimae sighed before she excused herself. When she returned from her bedroom, her eyes were more red and swollen than ever.

CHAPTER 11

The obituary for Lillimae's mother that appeared in the newspaper didn't even list Lillimae and her siblings among the survivors. Just the two kids her mother had by the white man she had left Daddy for. The woman who had meant so much to Daddy at one time still must have meant something to him because on the day of the funeral he cried, too. Of course there was no mention of him in the obituary, either, but he wanted to go to the funeral, too. He sent flowers to the church under a fake name. Then he agreed to wait with me in the car parked across the street, a block from the church, while Lillimae paid her respects inside.

The church, a quaint little white clapboard building with a crooked steeple, was located in a mixed neighborhood. Seeing a few Black and Hispanic faces on the street made me feel a little more at ease.

It amazed me how many differences there were between white folks and Black folks. At our funerals there was enough loud weeping and wailing to wake the deceased. Some of the white people I saw standing around outside the church were acting like they were at a carnival admiring a sideshow. Big-bellied, red-faced men were smoking fat cigars and grinning. A washed-out woman was holding a homely, crying baby wearing nothing but a diaper. Young kids were playing tag and throwing rocks at a stray dog.

White folks didn't even dress the way we did for funerals. At least not at this funeral. The men had on natty, ill-fitting suits and shoes with heels worn down to the ground. I even saw a woman in a tight red dress cut so low I could see the nipples on her long, flat breast. A molly-faced teenage boy with a ducktail hairdo was hugging a boom box and bobbing his head. The only way you could tell that this was a funeral and not a wedding was by the long black hearse sitting in front of the church.

Lillimae had contacted her brother and sister, but neither one wanted to attend their own mother's funeral. That saddened me. I believed that in death, even the worst person deserved some degree of respect.

With Lillimae in the church, I was alone with Daddy in her car. I asked him the question that had almost burned a hole in my mind over the years. "Daddy, why did you do it?"

"Do what?" He gasped. "What you talkin' about, girl?"

"You know what I'm talking about. How did you end up with that Edith woman in the first place? I thought you were so happy with Muh'Dear."

Daddy was sprawled across the backseat of Lillimae's old car, chewing on a toothpick. Every now and then he lifted his head and glanced out the back window toward the church, shaking his head and mumbling under his breath.

"I was happy with you and your mama . . . but . . . well . . ." He paused and sucked in his breath as he brushed lint off the same black suit he told me he wore to all funerals. "Edith's daddy owned that grove I was workin' that summer. For a redneck, he was a good old boy to me, as long as I stayed in my place. Edith, she kept at me 'til she wore me down. Bringin' me cool lemonade drinks and sugar tits to munch on while I was pickin' them oranges for her daddy. She even slipped me a few dollars every now and then—which I spent up on you and your mama. It was her money that paid for them sunglasses I gave you for your birthday. One evenin' when I was in the grove by myself, she come at me, hissin' like a big snake. Wrapped herself around me like one, too. She started kissin' me up and down my neck, squeezin' on me. Next thing I knew, we was wallowin' on the ground. For the first time in my life, I felt like I was somethin' other than a ill-educated, farm-workin' nigger. And, it felt good."

A long moment of silence passed before I could reply.

"Was that all it took? You gave us up for that?"

"She gave up more than I did. Her family, her daddy's money. How many white folks you think would give up the good life they got to be with a poor-ass Black man, when she could have continued livin' like a king up in that big house her daddy owned? It got to her after a few years. Right after her nervous breakdown, she started kissin' her daddy's feet. Him and the rest of her kinfolks felt sorry enough for her they let her back in the family. Them schemin' crackers even had some rascal they dug up in Texas waitin' to marry her. A cousin of hers at that. And there I was, by myself with them three kids."

"At least you did the right thing by *them*."

"What's that supposed to mean?" Daddy snapped.

"You didn't run off and leave them behind." I kept my eyes on the front yard of the church, which was vacant by now.

"Girl, I tried to find y'all. I wanted to get back with you and your mama so bad it hurt me to my heart. Don't you think for one minute I wasn't sufferin', too." Daddy paused and sniffed. "I went through things I wouldn't wish on a dog. Like that time I carried Lillimae to the mini-mall to get her some new shoes to wear to church. She was eleven and just startin' to act a fool, as kids do when they that age.

Anyway, she threw a hissy fit 'cause I wouldn't get her no ice cream. I mauled her head with my fist. Girl, crackers came at me from every direction, thinkin' God knows what. I got beat down and cussed at so bad, I couldn't work for a week. Lillimae was a grown woman before me and her went out in public together again. Every time I thought about Edith, I wanted to kill her for the hell she had put me in."

It took me a few moments to absorb this information. Recalling the sad look I'd seen on Edith's face that day at the vegetable stand, I blinked hard. To give that woman the benefit of the doubt, I truly believed that if that store manager had not approached her, she would have shown her true feelings toward Lillimae. Now only God would know what Edith might have said and done. I was proud of the fact that I had a forgiving heart. Had I not, I would never have seen my daddy again.

"Are you going to go in the church at all?" I asked Daddy, glancing at my watch.

Daddy gasped so hard he started coughing. As soon as he cleared his throat he roared, "What's wrong with you, girl?! Them white folks would ride me out of town on a rail if I was to show my black face up in that church! I ain't *that* crazy."

"You were crazy enough to live with one and have three kids with her," I scoffed. I turned to look at Daddy. The toothpick between his lips was shaking as he stared at me with tears in his eyes.

Daddy let out a loud groan. "Girl, ain't you never gwine to let the past go? What's done is done. And don't you know everything happen for a reason? Maybe me leavin' you and your mama was the best thing ever happened to y'all. Sound like you and your mama done all right without me. I was just holdin' y'all down from a better life. What kind of life do you think you would have had if you hadn't moved to Ohio? What could I have given y'all?"

"Your love would have been enough for me, Daddy."

"Girl, you always had that. I thought about you every day of my life, wishin' I could hug you and see you grow up. I sure wish I could have been there when you got familiar with . . . uh, mens. That ain't a easy thing for a girl to go through. Lillimae and Sondra told me when they, uh, done it that first time. That's the kind of deal I had goin' with my girls. They knew from the cradle they could talk to me about anything. Even *that*. I hope you didn't jump the gun and slide off your bloomers too soon and for the wrong one."

"I didn't," I muttered. I recalled the first time I'd ever had sex in my life, with Mr. Boatwright when I was just seven years old. Just thinking about it made my crotch start aching so hard, I had to turn and sit on the side of my hipbone.

"I didn't think so. I can tell you too feisty to let some dude take advantage of you. Sugar, before you leave, let's set down and kick back and you can tell me more about your life in Ohio. Hear?"

I sighed and offered a weak smile and a nod. A great sadness suddenly consumed me. I would tell Daddy more about my life in Ohio, but I'd leave out the parts about the years of sexual abuse I had endured and my fling with prostitution.

And the part about me having a best friend who was a murderer.

CHAPTER 12

Before Lillimae returned from church, I spent a few minutes telling Daddy a glamorized, edited version of my life in Ohio. He beamed and nodded when I told him how well I'd done in school and how quick the telephone company had hired me. But when I started to brag about the nice big house and the fancy restaurant that Muh'Dear owned and how good my late stepfather had been to us, Daddy promptly changed the subject.

"I think I'll go back down to the lake and see if them bass is bitin' later on this evenin'. I like to keep the freezer well stocked." He grunted and let out a deep sigh. "Uh . . . I guess you and your mama didn't need me after all," he mumbled, looking at his hands like he was inspecting them.

I gave him an exasperated look and shook my head so hard that my ears rang. "Yes, we did, Daddy. Yes, we did need you. It was not easy for Muh'Dear and me to get to where we are now. You weren't there to see me grow up, graduate, nothing. You would have been proud of me. Do you know—"

Holding up his hand, Daddy cut me off and said in a voice

so weak I could barely hear him, "I am proud of you, child. I always was."

I was glad that Lillimae returned to the car before the conversation could get out of hand. She was fanning her face with the wide-brimmed black hat she had purchased for the funeral to match the black tweed suit she had on. Before she could get all the way back into her car, Daddy grabbed the back of her seat and asked, "Lillimae, you all right? Ain't you gwine out to the cemetery to see your mama get buried?" I was surprised at how strong he sounded now.

Lillimae mumbled something unintelligible under her breath and slapped her hat back onto her head backward. Then she said in a hoarse voice, "As far as I'm concerned, I done already done that."

Daddy groaned and slid back into the corner of the backseat, rubbing his head.

Before Lillimae started the car, she glanced back at the church. I followed her gaze and watched as four grim-faced pallbearers hauled her mother's casket out of the church and slid it into the back of a dusty hearse. As Lillimae eased her car away from the curb, a faint smile crossed her face and stayed there. We rode home in complete silence.

Daddy only stayed in the house long enough to get out of his suit and to get his fishing equipment. He took a coal-oil lamp to the lake with him so I knew that he was planning to spend as much time fishing as possible.

A few minutes after Daddy's departure, Lillimae joined me on the living room couch. She was clutching a damp handkerchief, tapping her eyes and nose. She had changed into her ratty old housecoat and had removed her shoes. I was surprised to see a serene look on her face. Despite her swollen, bloodshot eyes and smeared lipstick, she looked so much better now.

Surprisingly, I had shed a few tears myself the night before. There was something about people dying that did strange things to my emotions, even when it was somebody I didn't really care about. Especially people who died from unnatural causes. I had even cried when my best friend, Rhoda Nelson, killed old Mr. Boatwright and that sucker had raped me. Thinking about Rhoda made a huge lump form in my throat. The lump would have been even larger if I'd known then that Rhoda was in the process of returning to my life to wreak more havoc.

"Are you all right?" I asked, touching Lillimae's shoulder.

She nodded. "I am now." She didn't look at me as she continued speaking in a steely voice. "Mama didn't even look like herself. She looked like a dried-up old prune. Her skin was all pasty and pale. Her neck got broke in the car crash so her face looked lopsided. They said the car looked like a train had slammed into it. The drunk that broadsided her car walked away with nothin' but a few scratches and a few cracked bones. Him bein' Black made it even worse. Roxanne's husband was mumblin' all kinds of racist shit about goin' after that drunk. Right there in the church with Reverend Spool just a foot away! Motherfucker."

I released a deep, painful sigh. My head felt so heavy I could barely move it, but I managed to shake it. "So the people in the church did talk to you," I said, my hand still on Lillimae's shoulder.

Lillimae shook her head so hard her teeth clicked. "Nobody said nothin' to me. I didn't get close enough to none of 'em for nobody to talk to me or hug up on me like they was doin' one another. I didn't want none of that evil racism to rub off on me," Lillimae hissed. "I heard the folks in the pew in front of me talkin'. That's how I know what I know. Then that cracker preacher was goin' on and on about what a good Christian woman Mama had been and how much she had done for her family." Lillimae let out a strange laugh. "Gnat butter! I had to hold myself back from jumpin' up and tellin' them devils all just how much she done for *me*! No woman in her right mind would turn her back on her kids." Finally, Lillimae turned to face me. "Daddy done his job *and* hers because he loved his kids—"

I stared at the floor. My eyes started to burn and itch and I could feel bile rising in my throat.

"Shit." Lillimae's last comment flustered her more than it did me and she couldn't hide it. She started blinking real hard and stroking my arm. "Now you know I didn't mean nothin' by that." She rearranged herself on the couch and grabbed my wrist. "Daddy is a good man, Annette. I hope you know that now."

I nodded. "I know that. I always did." I sniffed and forced myself to keep a straight face. "Uh . . . how did you feel being there for the first time with the rest of your family?"

Lillimae turned away again. She blew her nose into her handkerchief with a honk so profound it seemed to bounce off of the wall. It took her a moment to compose herself. She started to talk with her eyes half closed and out of focus. "I couldn't have felt more distant from them if I was on another planet. The other side of my family was right there a few feet away from me, cryin' and huggin' one another. Both of my miserable sisters are pregnant and looked like they wanted to deliver right there in the church. I couldn't comfort them and they couldn't comfort me. The only thing separatin' us was blood."

"Black blood," I reminded.

CHAPTER 13

The death of Lillimae's mother had taken a toll on Lillimae. She stumbled around the house like somebody af-
flicted with polio, running into the living room wall a few
times and accidentally stepping on the tail of that old cat
from next door. For the rest of my visit there was a look of
sadness in her eyes that found its way to me. All the mascara
and Visine I used to try and brighten up my eyes didn't help.

It seemed like every time some new sad thing happened
in my life, I grieved for all the other sad things that I had already endured. The good thing was, I had enough pleasant
things going on in my life now so there was some balance.
However, I was glad that I had only one more day before my
departure. I was anxious to return to my job, my house, and
my man.

The day before I left Florida, Daddy insisted on taking me
out to dinner at what he considered a "fancy" restaurant. He
took me to Doug's Bar-be-cue, a rib joint around the corner
from his house. The deeper I traveled into Daddy's drab
neighborhood, the more sinister it looked. Unkempt, suspicious-
looking men sat on the porches of a deserted house across

the street from the rib joint, sharing bottles and whatever it was they were smoking. There was broken glass and discarded trash everywhere I looked. An old car that somebody had torched was sitting on the street and young kids were crawling in and out of it. Every house had bars on the windows, even the broken windows. Two boys that looked young enough to be my sons, their cheap plaid shirts hanging open, were kneeling on the sidewalk throwing dice in front of the restaurant. We had to walk around them.

"Keep a strong grip on your pocketbook," Daddy warned me in a loud voice. "This street is the butt-hole of Miami."

He led me into the restaurant with his arm around my shoulder and guided me to a booth in a corner next to the kitchen. There was so much smoke coming out of that kitchen, anybody who didn't know any better would have thought that the place was on fire.

A cassette player, held together with duct tape, was sitting on the counter next to the cash register. An old B.B. King song, "The Thrill Is Gone," was playing.

"I wish Lillimae had come with us. That gal love her some barbecue," Daddy told me, wrapping one of the yellow plastic bibs that the restaurant supplied around his neck after we had placed our orders. "I done told her we don't know when we'll see you again." He blinked and wiggled his nose, smiling faintly. "Long as it took me to get you to come down here and all."

"I'll just be a phone call away, Daddy," I said, drinking ice-cold water from a huge plastic glass.

Our food was delivered a few minutes later. I wasn't that hungry but I managed to eat most of the rib sandwich that I had ordered. For Doug's to be as popular as Daddy claimed it was, I was surprised to see that we were the only patrons.

Daddy sniffed and rubbed his eyes. "It's a good thing we got here early. You can't get in this place after six o'clock. You want a plate to carry with you on the plane?" Daddy asked, grinning with greasy sauce shining on his lips like lip gloss. The barbecue sauce was so spicy and hot, it made our eyes water.

"They'll feed me on the plane, Daddy," I said, sniffling and cracking a thin smile at the same time. Daddy leaned across the table and wiped my eyes with his napkin. It wasn't just the barbecue sauce that had me shedding tears. It saddened me to know that I would soon leave my daddy. All of the pain that he had caused me didn't matter anymore.

Before we finished our dinner, Daddy called every employee in the place over to our table to meet me. Four grinning men, shiny with sweat, black rubber aprons covering their big bellies, lined up in front of our booth and inspected me like I was a hog on an auction block. "This is my girl by my first wife. Ain't she fine?" Daddy patted the top of my head and beamed like a lighthouse.

It annoyed me when the elderly cook tried to flirt with me and it must have annoyed Daddy, too, because he gave the man a threatening look. "Old nigger, you lay a hand on my child and I will beat your brains out," Daddy snarled. He looked at me and winked. "I'll kill any nigger that try to take advantage of you, girl. I ain't gwine to let nobody damage you."

I wanted to tell Daddy that he was too late. After being raped by Mr. Boatwright for ten years, I was way past being just damaged. But I had survived that ordeal. Just like I had survived the ordeal of confronting my daddy. Now that I finally felt at peace, I was more than ready to go back to Ohio.

I wish now that I had refused Lillimae's offer to take me back to the airport the next morning. We had to stop twice on the way at gas stations for Daddy to use the bathroom. Each time, he made it by the skin of his teeth. Another stop and I would have missed my flight back to Ohio.

My suitcase was several pounds heavier than when I'd arrived in Miami. A hefty skycap had to use two hands to wrestle it from the trunk of Lillimae's car.

"Annette, I slid some smoked hamhocks and some smoked ham steaks into your suitcase that I fished out the freezer. Ain't no use in me lyin'—that freezer got way too much meat in it for just me and Daddy," Lillimae volunteered between sobs, offering a long hug and wetting my shoulder with fresh tears and my cheek with sloppy kisses. The well-worn beach sandals she had on kept sliding back and forth on her feet. One slipped completely off as she and I embraced. People stared at us as I leaned down to retrieve my sister's shoe and return it to her foot. In my mind, I imagined that the looky-loos assumed I was Lillimae's maid, even though I had on a sharp white blouse and new-looking slacks and she had on a faded, voluminous muumuu and a scarf carelessly looped around her damp blond hair. I was sick and tired of caring about what other people thought. I hauled off and kissed Lillimae on her cheek.

Standing next to Lillimae on the sidewalk in front of the airport wearing a shirt so freshly starched it looked like his suspenders were glued to it, Daddy blinked hard to hold back his own tears. But I had already heard him sniffling in the backseat of Lillimae's car throughout the ride to the airport. He'd blamed his discomfort on his mandatory, frequent visits to bathrooms, but I knew better. "Uh . . . I hope I see you again real soon, Annette," Daddy managed, mopping his face with a large white handkerchief. He blinked some more and cleared his throat so hard he started coughing, using the same handkerchief to swipe his mouth.

"You will, Daddy. I'll make sure of that," I said, fanning my face.

I was not going to miss that blazing Florida sun. Putting on makeup that morning had been a waste of time. Mixed with my sweat, it was now sliding down my cheeks like butter. Lillimae dabbed my wet lips with her thick finger. There was still a great heaviness in my heart, but I felt better than I'd felt in more than thirty years. I didn't know what to expect before I got back to Florida, especially since I had left Ohio with so many mixed emotions. My anger had dissipated, but I had to wonder how my recycled feelings were going to affect my mother.

After I got settled on the plane, I tried to read a few chapters from *Roots*, a book I had already read twice. But my mind kept wandering to other things. Like my own roots. My reunion with Daddy had given me a certain level of peace but there was still a lot to my own past that I had to sort out. I needed to recall as much as I could so that I could prepare myself for my uncertain future.

Flying first class was a new experience for me. I would have taken a train to Florida, but it was Daddy who had insisted on paying for my first-class accommodations. That hadn't impressed Muh'Dear at all. "Whatever that mangy dog payin' for them first-class tickets ain't puttin' a dent in all the back child support he owe!" she had snapped when I told her. In the long run I was glad to be traveling in style. There was a lot more room and other advantages that allowed me to relax. I deserved and needed the huge glass of wine a flight attendant handed to me. As soon as the buzz kicked in, my thoughts wandered back in time.

To when my real pain started.

CHAPTER 14

I never found out the real name of the woman who had helped Muh'Dear and me after we moved to Ohio. But everybody called her Scary Mary. That name fit her because she was a tall, hard-drinking, tough, wig-wearing woman that just about everybody was afraid of. Even the police.

In addition to bootlegging alcohol, Scary Mary made a good living supplying women to lonely men. She had a lot of powerful friends so the law looked the other way as she managed several prostitutes that she had wooed off the streets.

Scary Mary looked at every man as a golden-egg-laying goose. She had had several prosperous husbands. The men that didn't divorce her up and died. She often bragged about the numerous divorce settlements and life insurance benefits that she had collected.

We had lived in the same house with Scary Mary and her girls our first few months in Ohio. I was amused as I watched all the men parade in and out of that big house, leaving with empty wallets. Especially since some of those prostitutes were homely and mean. One of the regular tricks was married to a woman who had once won a beauty contest. What confused me was the fact that my own daddy had traded my beautiful mother for a less attractive woman. Since Scary Mary seemed to know so much about men and their habits, I approached her with my concerns.

Scary Mary was a woman with plain but rough looks, bronze skin, and a scar on her face that she had sustained in a barroom fight. In a voice that sounded like it belonged to a man, the old madam told me, "Annette, it ain't the beauty, it's the booty. Especially when that other booty is white. Your daddy ain't no worse than no other man. They all weak. We women got all the strength. Long as I'm alive, you and your mama ain't got nothin' to worry about." Those words appeased me to some degree and for the first time since Daddy left, I felt safe. But then I hadn't met Mr. Boatwright yet.

Richland, Ohio, was a typical small northern city. We had a town square that contained a sorry wishing well full of coins and rocks, some cheap benches, shit-dropping pigeons that drove everybody crazy, and a sturdy statue of a bronze horse with a bronze man straddling the horse's back. By the looks of the man's features, he was white. However, there was a mural on the side of the viaduct that connected the southern part of the city to the northern part that made up for that white bronze man on the horse. On the mural was the likeness of a handsome Black man in overalls and a hard hat, swinging a sledgehammer. Next to him was a heavyset, sturdy-looking Black woman with a grimace on her face, a plaid scarf knotted around her head, on her knees scrubbing a floor. That wall represented a lot to me. It was a reminder that Black people would do whatever was necessary to survive.

Richland had a few Black professionals. And on the outskirts of town were several steel mills and brickyards that kept most of the blue-collar men employed. Nearby farming communities like Marlboro and Hartville wrapped around the outskirts of Richland like a low-slung belt. A lot of the people I knew made money working on the farms.

In addition to looking after Mott, Scary Mary's adult, severely retarded daughter, I made money doing chores for the prostitutes who worked for Scary Mary. Those women were some of the nicest people I knew and some of the most peculiar. In addition to sleeping with men for money, they had other strange habits. One dipped snuff and another chewed tobacco. One even practiced voodoo and kept a goat's skull in a hatbox that she used to threaten me with when I misbehaved. Two of them didn't believe in wasting money on things like sanitary napkins and tampons when they got their periods. Instead, they plugged themselves up with old rags. My worst chore was hauling buckets of foul-smelling bloody rags and wads of chewed-up tobacco and brown spit to the trash. I worked hard for my money. Some days by the time I finished my last chore, I was just as tired as those prostitutes who had been humping men back-to-back for hours.

Some of the prostitutes had babies that I had to keep from disrupting business by guarding Scary Mary's basement, serenading them with some of the same lullabies my daddy used to sing to me. It was the closest I could get to my daddy. It made Muh'Dear furious when I brought up his name, so I rarely did.

Muh'Dear cooked, cleaned, and looked after the children of some of the well-to-do white families in Richland. She hated leaving me alone with Scary Mary and all those prostitutes but it was a real treat for me. Especially since I didn't have any friends my own age yet.

"I just worry about you so much," Muh'Dear told me when she retrieved me from Scary Mary's house one day. We had just moved into our own house a few days earlier. "Scary Mary is a good woman and a godsend to us, but her line of business ain't healthy for you to be around too much. I'm goin' to see if Reverend Snipes can't advise us." My mother was such a pretty woman. She was fairly petite with light brown skin, delicate features, and dark hair so thick and beautiful people thought it was a wig. I didn't like the sadness on her lovely face when she worried about me.

To keep my mother happy, one of the prostitutes regularly washed and straightened my hair, while another one held me down as I yipped and bucked like a nanny goat about to be slaughtered. With a Camel cigarette dangling from her thick lips, my hairdresser blew strong smoke in my face and yelled, "Annette, you better get use to fixin' yourself up. How you expect to get a man with your hair lookin' like a sheep's ass, girl?" It was a little too soon for me to be getting that kind of advice, even from a prostitute.

My mother's concern for my virtue intensified. At Reverend Snipe's insistence, she moved Mr. Boatwright in with us so he could baby-sit me while she worked as well as to help us with our bills. All the immoral things that I had witnessed in Scary Mary's house didn't come close to corrupting me as much as Mr. Boatwright did by raping me.

It was the second time in my life that a man had betrayed me.

Now that I had my peace with Daddy, I had to work on getting Mr. Boatwright's legacy out of my system.

CHAPTER 15

By the time I'd reached my teens, I was so used to Mr. Boatwright clambering into my bed, it seemed like second nature. Besides, by that time I had other things to be happy about. An old, white retired judge that Muh'Dear had worked for let us move into one of the many nice houses he owned on Reed Street, located in one of the nicest neighborhoods in town. Every well-kept yard had either a buckeye, willow, or fruit tree. There were no old, beaten-down cars littering the driveways. Just shiny Cadillacs and other impressive cars. The old judge even changed his will so that the house would go to Muh'Dear when he died.

Jerry "Pee Wee" Davis and Rhoda Nelson, kids my age, lived on the same street. Jerry's daddy was a barber and Rhoda's daddy was the only Black undertaker Richland had at the time. Pee Wee was homely and unpopular, but Rhoda was the most beautiful Black girl I had ever seen. She had more confidence than Miss America and was as fearless as a bounty hunter. Rhoda was dark like me and had long, blue-black hair that reached halfway down her back. She had green eyes, but behind them lurked something even darker than our complexions. However, I didn't see it as something evil at the time. There were too many other things obscuring my vision.

Even though Pee Wee and I became quite close, I never confided in him the way I did with Rhoda. When she was a child she had witnessed a policeman shoot and kill her eldest brother, David, so she was particularly sensitive when it came to traumatic situations. She was appalled when I told her about Mr. Boatwright. On a regular basis, she tried to make me expose him. But that old sucker's threats carried far more weight than Rhoda's anger.

"I've had it with you and that nasty old man. If you don't hurry up and do somethin' about him, I will," Rhoda told me after she had helped me abort the baby that Mr. Boatwright had impregnated me with. I ended up in the hospital. Instead of telling Muh'Dear the truth then, I let her think that some boy I refused to name had seduced me. The pain that that episode caused my mother almost destroyed me. But I loved her too much to burden her with the truth.

"Mr. Boatwright's old and always sick," I reminded Rhoda. "God'll take care of him soon. He won't live too much longer," I insisted.

I was right; Mr. Boatwright died a few months before Rhoda and I graduated from high school. But it wasn't God that took him out, it was Rhoda. One night while Muh'Dear was still at work, Rhoda slipped into Mr. Boatwright's bedroom and held a pillow on his face until he stopped breathing. It was the same year that we also lost Martin Luther King Jr. and Bobby Kennedy.

"Buttwright's in good company," Rhoda told me as I stood behind her in her pink-and-white bathroom waiting for her to finish her egg facial. It wasn't enough that Rhoda's family pampered her; she treated herself like a princess. Maintaining beauty was a full-time job for Rhoda. She spent more on beauty products than I spent on clothes.

"Yeah, he sure is," I mumbled. "It's just a shame that after all he went through when he was a little boy, he had to turn out so bad. Look where it got him."

After Mr. Boatwright's funeral, when Rhoda had helped me pack up his things for Muh'Dear to donate to the Salvation Army, she and I had come across some old, faded, dog-eared newspaper clippings from a southern newspaper. We had read about how Mr. Boatwright had been abandoned as a child and shuffled from one bad environment to another. He had also suffered abuse so severe it had cost him a leg.

Rhoda gasped and whirled around so fast to face me, her egg facial cracked before it was supposed to.

"Millions of people get abused when they are little! They don't go around rapin' people! Don't you be standin' up in here feelin' sorry for that old goat!" Rhoda roared. She sucked in her breath and lowered her voice. "Get me a towel." Rhoda's family had moved to Ohio from Alabama a few years after we'd moved from Florida. While I had worked hard to rid myself of my southern accent by imitating white girls on television so that I would seem less "country," Rhoda spoke with a definite drawl. But it sounded cute coming from her. In fact, the accent made her even more charming to me. She sighed. *"Great balls of fire."*

"You're right," I muttered, holding her in place by her shoulder while I wiped her face with a fluffy white towel that I had snatched from the back of the bathroom door.

"You are finally free," Rhoda reminded, patting her face then inspecting it in the mirror above the sink.

I declined her offer to give me a facial. I always did. I knew that there was only so much I could do to improve my face. Since I cried so often, I had started wearing a lot of makeup to hide the dark circles around my eyes and the puffiness underneath. I left Rhoda's house and went home to cry some more.

I had to agree with what she had just said about Mr. Boatwright, but I still didn't feel right about how he died and I knew then that I never would.

Right after graduation, with Mr. Boatwright's blood still fresh on her hands, Rhoda married a handsome Jamaican and moved to Florida to help him run his family's orange groves. Pee Wee joined the army a few weeks later. At first, I didn't know what to do with myself. Since Mr. Boatwright was no longer standing in my way, I decided that it was time for me to move on, too.

Rhoda called me up a lot, regaling me with details of her new life and how happy she was with her first child on the way. She ended each phone call by telling me, "Put all of that Buttwright mess out of your mind and get on with your life, girl." Knowing that I was the only person who knew about her killing Mr. Boatwright, I now felt like I was in a different type of bondage and Rhoda was calling all the shots.

Desperate to move out on my own so that Muh'Dear would never know just how miserable I was, I took advantage of my relationship with Scary Mary. For a few weeks I stole a few of her customers to raise the money I needed to leave home with. As much as I hated what I had become, a prostitute, my biggest fear was somebody finding out and telling my mother. I knew that my own mother had done "what she had to do" with a few of Scary Mary's customers during some trying times to keep us off the streets. But I didn't want her to know that I, too, had stooped that low. However, I didn't think about all that until after I had turned my first trick.

"Ooh, girl. You such a nice, juicy, young thing." The trick paused long enough to lick his lips. "I wouldn't mind seein' you again," he added with a wink. I cringed and couldn't wait to get away from the man who had just paid for my body. He was one of the most disgusting men I submitted to.

His vile body had slid on me, in me, and off of me, all within a matter of minutes. One date with the same man was all I would allow myself. Giving up my body in hellish places like cheap motels, up against brick walls in dim alleys next to garbage bins, and on the backseats of cars was bad enough. But one time I even went to one man's job with him and allowed him to fuck me from behind while I leaned over his desk. He was a short, squat man with light skin and moles all over his chin. He worked as a night watchman at a downtown office building, but he claimed to have all kinds of money in the bank from selling some property somewhere.

Afterward, while he was peeing in an empty Styrofoam coffee cup, he asked, "You would do anything for money, huh?"

"What do you mean?" I asked, rearranging my clothes. He had ripped my panties to shreds trying to remove them so fast. It didn't make any sense for me to put them back on. I slid the panties into my purse along with the fifty dollars he had just handed me.

The trick slapped his hairy hands on his hips and gave me a critical look, screwing up his face like he didn't like what he saw. "I can't get none of them other gals to come to me, I have to go to them. And they particular about what motels I carry them to. I got a heap of money in the bank and a wife that won't let me touch her with a stick. I thought I was gwine to have to beat my meat. I guess you'll have to do for tonight. You just don't care about nothin'," he remarked. Waving his hand dramatically, he looked me up and down with a fierce scowl on his plain face. "No shame, no rules, no nothin' long as you get paid. Like a Gypsy. I guess you ain't got them highfalutin standards, huh?"

"I guess not," I said sadly. I promised myself right then and there that he would be the last one. I couldn't stand to degrade myself any longer for any amount of money. It was

CHAPTER 16

I was apprehensive about leaving Muh'Dear alone after all we had been through together. Even though she had a lot of friends now, there was no special man in her life. And there hadn't been since Daddy's departure, fourteen years earlier.

Before I could finalize my plans to flee Richland, Muh'Dear got involved with a new man, a lonely old widower named Albert King. Not one of the horny old geezers that Scary Mary had tried to dump off on her, but a dignified man that everybody loved and respected. However, a big red flag went up in my mind right away, because Mr. Boatwright had been the same way at first. As pessimistic as I was, I didn't believe that lightning could strike twice in the same place.

However, I still approached Muh'Dear's new man with extreme caution. Especially since she had met Mr. King through Reverend Snipes, the same meddlesome old preacher who had cursed us with Mr. Boatwright! That alone was enough to make me keep my distance.

Mr. King was nothing like Mr. Boatwright. He wasn't some one-legged old man with nowhere to go, like Mr. Boatwright. Mr. King was the owner of the Buttercup restaurant and he had enough money to live a comfortable life. He owned his own home, so I didn't have to worry about him moving in with us. He didn't have any family left, but he had a lot of friends. He had severed a two-year relationship with another woman so he could be with my mother. I avoided being alone with Mr. King. When he came to the house while Muh'Dear was out, I hid behind the curtains and re- fused to open the door. When I couldn't avoid being alone with him, I remained distant and suspicious.

Mr. King had called the house for Muh'Dear one day and I'd been sharp with him. I had hollered at him the way I did those annoying people who called up on the telephone trying to sell something or asking nosy questions for a survey.

"Annette, you don't like me, do you?" he asked in a whiny voice. He was breathing through his mouth, groaning, hiss- ing and making low whistling noises that I knew he couldn't help. As annoyed as I was, I felt sorry for this old man.

I waited for Mr. King's breathing to return to normal. Then I sucked in my breath, hoping I didn't sound like I be- longed in a barnyard myself like he sounded. "I don't know you well enough to hate you," I told him coldly. "I'll tell Muh'Dear you called," I added with impatience. I wondered what made Muh'Dear take up with a man who had obvi- ously started falling apart. With all his wheezing and breath- ing difficulties, it seemed like he was one step away from his grave.

With a low, weak voice he said, "Well, I hope you do get to know me soon. I love your mama and I think she loves me. Me and Gussie Mae get along real good, so I'm gwine to be comin' around yonder to see your mama whether you like it or not. So you can stop all your foolishness right now!" Mr. King stunned me by being so direct.

But I didn't back down. "What you and my mother do is

none of my business," I snapped. "If my mama wants to make a fool of herself, I can't stop her."

I heard him gasp and suck on his teeth. "One thing your mama ain't, is a fool."

"Well, I'm not, either. Now if you don't mind, I'm watching *American Bandstand* right now."

He sighed and mumbled something unintelligible before he spoke again. "Look, girl. I would never do nothin' to harm you." He paused and steadied his voice. "I cut my teeth on God."

"So did Satan," I reminded.

"What you say?"

"Nothing," I muttered. I rarely sassed old people and I wasn't proud of myself for doing it now. I cleared my throat and softened my voice. "Uh . . . I'll tell Muh'Dear you called," I said sheepishly.

Mr. King let out another sigh, this one longer and deeper. "Child, I know you was real fond of Brother Boatwright. Everybody was. Even me." He paused and laughed. "Even though he departed here owin' me several hundred dollars. Bless his heart." Mr. King paused again and cleared his throat. "Anyway, your mama done told me all about the special joy he brought to your life." His last comment almost made me choke on my own tongue. "But I ain't the type to get too close to young people. It breeds contempt. Matter of fact, I don't really like to keep company with women that still got kids livin' at home. Especially gals. They can get a man in a heap of trouble."

I absorbed this information and listened with interest now. Clutching the telephone with both hands, I cleared my throat and asked, "What . . . what do you mean by that?"

"Well, the reason I broke up with Sadie Watson was because of her teenager daughters. Them some fast girls and they out to cause trouble. Both of 'em got babies and not a man in sight to help raise them kids. Naturally, they ripe to start up some devilment so they won't be the only ones miserable. That Betty Jean was always tryin' to provoke me. Sittin' on my lap, huggin' on me, beggin' me for money. That youngest one, Sarah Louise, was even worse. Kissin' me on my jaw every chance she got." He sighed again. "I'm too old to be gettin' caught up in somethin' . . . uh . . . unholy. I got too much to lose."

I suddenly felt more at ease. "Well, I'm too old to let one of my mother's men get caught up in something unholy with me," I said stiffly, scratching myself between my thighs. It had been weeks since I'd turned my last trick, but I still felt unclean, no matter how much I bathed and scrubbed myself. After each bath, I sprayed my crotch with whatever smell-goods were available. Now I had to deal with an irritating inflammation that my excessive use of the sprays had caused.

"Look, girl. I ain't got no kids of my own. I ain't a young man no more, so I doubt if I ever will have any. But I still love kids. I helped my use-to-be business partner raise all five of his young'uns. Then, after he passed, I helped send all of 'em to college. Even though they don't even call me or send me a card, unless they wantin' money, I still care about them kids. I want to see all kids succeed in life. Black kids especially. Now the Lord done blessed me. I got a few bucks in the bank and I can't take none of it with me when I lay my burdens down and go to meet my Maker. I want to enjoy life while I still can. All I want to do is make somebody happy. Right now that somebody is your mama . . . and you. If I ever say or do somethin' you don't like, you seem like the kind of gal would put me in my place. Your mama didn't raise no fool. Am I right?"

"You're right," I said contritely. My head felt heavy as I bowed it. While I was between thoughts, I noticed some faint, inch-long, slightly crooked black lines on the kitchen wall I was facing. I rubbed my fingers across the lines until I realized they were the markings that Mr. Boatwright had made with a pencil to measure my height over the years. I snatched my hand back like I'd been burned. With my heart pounding against the inside of my chest, I realized Mr. Boatwright still had some control over me.

Even from his grave.

Before I could speak again, Mr. King did and I was glad. I wasn't sure what was going to come out of my mouth anyway. Especially with additional thoughts of Mr. Boatwright, even more potent than the ones I'd had a few moments earlier, dancing around in the front of my mind.

"And you got too nice a voice to be soundin' all grumpy anyway." He laughed. "You ought to be singin' in the choir. I'll mention that to Pastor Jenkins."

I was glad to know that Mr. King and I were on the same page. I knew that I was not the only girl in Richland to have had the kind of trouble I'd had with one of Muh'Dear's men friends. Thank God Mr. King was bold enough to stand his ground.

That conversation broke the ice enough for me to accept Mr. King in my life. I regretted my behavior and wanted to retract my remarks but it was too late. However, it was not too late for me to change my attitude toward him. So I did, right then and there.

"Uh . . . I'll tell Muh'Dear you called. And . . . Mr. King, you have a nice evening."

Now that I was comfortable with Mr. King, I encouraged Muh'Dear to secure her relationship with him. It eased my mind to know that she would not be lonely when I did move away. Even though I didn't know a soul in Pennsylvania, she surprised me by encouraging me to go.

I was bowled over when she surprised me with a ten-thousand-dollar cash gift from an insurance policy that Mr. Boatwright, of all people, had left for us. Now I felt even worse about selling my body. The money I had collected from all those horny men was pocket change compared to the ten thousand dollars. I was even more anxious to get away from the scene of my crimes now. I *had* to leave Ohio. Even if I had to flee on foot.

I left on a Greyhound bus, crying and waving to Muh'Dear until the bus turned the corner.

CHAPTER 17

So much happened to me during the years I lived in Erie, Pennsylvania. It was hard for me to keep the events in order when I allowed myself to think about them. I slid in and out of meaningless relationships with meaningless men and had a fairly active social life, but I continued to have nightmares about Mr. Boatwright. Some mornings I woke up on the floor, tangled up in my bedcovers from trying to hide from Mr. Boatwright's ghost.

I joined a church and I got a job working on an assembly line in a factory, but I was not happy. I still missed Rhoda and Pee Wee. They had saved me in so many ways, so many times. In fact, it was a telephone call from Rhoda that had stopped me from throwing myself out of the window of a dingy hotel, during one of my many moments of despair.

Pee Wee was special in other ways. He had been the only boy that Mr. Boatwright had felt was sexless and harmless enough to be around me, not that any other boys had tried to get into my pants. The nights that Pee Wee had been allowed to sleep over at my house during our early teens, volunteering to sleep on our living room floor in his sleeping bag,

Mr. Boatwright had insisted that Pee Wee sleep on a pallet on my bedroom floor instead.

Unlike some of the other boys from Richland who had been snatched up by Uncle Sam and dispatched to go fight a senseless war in a place a lot of us had never even heard of before, Pee Wee returned from Vietnam intact. I was pleasantly surprised when he paid me a surprise visit one night when he came to Pennsylvania to visit relatives.

I had several reasons for climbing into my bed with Pee Wee. His appearance was one. The army had recycled him. He was no longer the skinny, loud-mouthed, sissified little boy I had grown up with. He was at least four inches taller and had packed on more than sixty pounds. His long, narrow face had filled out and he had a sexy mustache. A pair of slightly slanted black eyes that I had never paid much attention to before now sparkled like diamonds. He was gorgeous. Especially naked.

He stood over me as I lay on my bed, naked, too, feeling as big as a banana boat. But my size didn't bother him, so I didn't care what I looked like as long as he liked what he saw.

I didn't jump up and shout like I wanted to, though. I just gasped. When Pee Wee gave me an amused look, I pretended like I was reacting to the scorpion tattoo on his chest. I was already weak, so even without that bottle of wine we consumed, I couldn't help myself.

After all the unfulfilling sex I had had with Mr. Boatwright and the other men, I never expected to know any physical pleasure, other than feeding my face. But Pee Wee was a wonderful lover. He even taught me a few tricks that he had picked up from the whores he had spent time with in Vietnamese brothels that he claimed he'd been "dragged" to.

Sex was such a mystery to me. It seemed strange that something that good could also be bad if done with the wrong person. Despite old Mr. Boatwright's belief that I enjoyed his lovemaking, it had felt like hell to me. Here I was doing the same thing with Pee Wee, but it felt like heaven. Especially when I had an orgasm. It was the first one in my life and that made Pee Wee even more special to me. It was almost as sacred as sharing my virginity, a prize that Mr. Boatwright had helped himself to.

I felt like a big fool doing some of the things I did with Pee Wee that night. And I knew I probably looked like a big ox in some of the positions I let myself get coaxed into. I was like a dope fiend, devouring Pee Wee for the next few hours like he was a drug. I licked and humped like I was getting paid to do it. He laughed when I humped him with so much vigor he fell off the bed.

"Just relax, girl," he told me, jumping back on top of me, stabbing deep inside of me with his finger. We spent a whole night wallowing in each other's arms.

By the time Pee Wee rolled off me, I was practically delirious. But my rapture was temporary. He left the next morning before I even woke up. I was alone again, except for the bruises on my body and the fear of Mr. Boatwright's ghost coming back to haunt me some more.

Not long after my passionate rendezvous with Pee Wee, another man eased his way into my bed, one I thought was just as ready to get married and settle down as I was. I was half right. Levi Hardy up and married another woman while he was still involved with me. I was devastated. I felt like the woman men avoided in public, but could tolerate enough to use for their own selfish needs. I felt like a urinal, just another place for men to dangle their dicks. I didn't know what was so wrong with me that only Rhoda could see the beauty in me on an ongoing basis. That's why it had always been so easy for her to control me.

During a visit to Florida to comfort Rhoda when the younger of her two sons died, I found myself missing my father more than ever before. I didn't know it at the time, but he was in Florida, just a few miles away from Rhoda's house. If I had reunited with him then, I know now that I would have avoided some of the other pain that was waiting to consume me.

I cried until I almost lost my voice during the very next telephone conversation with Rhoda. Not over Pee Wee running out on me or that other man dumping me for another woman, but over a royal mess that Rhoda's older brother Jock had slid into.

Jock Nelson, his mind half gone after injuries he had sustained in Vietnam, had impregnated the teenage daughter of a Klansman. The girl wanted Jock to marry her and she wanted money for her and Jock to run away with. If she didn't get her way, she threatened to go to her daddy and claim that Jock had raped her.

Rhoda was on fire and predicted what she called a "bloodbath" if the girl carried out her threat. I had not witnessed that level of anger from Rhoda since I told her about Mr. Boatwright. That anger didn't last long because a few weeks later that white girl died in a freak bathtub accident and Rhoda was her old self again.

"See, God really don't like ugly," Rhoda told me in an unusually calm voice. "That white bitch got what she had comin'."

I didn't know why, but I sat looking at the telephone, long after Rhoda had hung up. I suddenly became profoundly uneasy. Something that I could not even bring myself to think about kept trying to creep into my mind, but I wouldn't let it. I knew in my heart that there was more to the story involving that white girl than Rhoda had told me. I told myself that if it was meant for me to hear the whole story, someday I would.

With the news of the white girl's death, the stunt that Pee Wee had pulled on me, and the fact that I had not gotten over Levi dumping me to marry another woman, I decided it was time to run away from my problems again.

During a brief visit to my aunt Berniece in New Jersey, I learned from her that my father was in Miami and that I had two half-sisters and a half-brother. At that point, my desire to "find" myself took on a new meaning.

When I returned to Pennsylvania I was too restless to remain there much longer. Even though Ohio had once repelled me like a snakepit, without giving it much thought, I decided it was time for me go back there to deal with the demons that had tormented me throughout my youth.

CHAPTER 18

My return to Ohio was a major event for me. In some ways I felt like I was just about to begin my life all over again. Even though, at twenty-eight, I felt like an old woman. My anger toward Mr. Boatwright was still as potent as ever. Some days I even made myself sick just by thinking about him. Being older and wiser now, I was determined to deal with my anger in a more positive way.

One thing I promised myself was, I would never let another person, male or female, abuse me and get away with it. Rhoda was too volatile and extreme when I turned to her for help. Besides, she could only do so much to support me from where she was now. The only person I had to really count on now was myself. And it was high time. I owed it to myself to increase my level of dignity if I wanted to get something out of life.

Mr. Boatwright had been the biggest personal indignation I had encountered so far. Levi Hardy marrying another woman while he was still involved with me was right behind that. I had pretty much gotten over that little stunt Pee Wee had pulled, fucking me and leaving me high and dry, but I wasn't going to forget it.

In one of his infrequent letters, Pee Wee had told me that he had attended barber's school and had opened "Pee Wee's Barbershop" in the same strip mall where the Buttercup, the restaurant my stepdaddy owned, was located. He had two chairs. His cousin Steve worked for him, cutting and styling hair. Steve's wife Helen worked in the shop also, doing manicures.

Pee Wee had a lot of customers for someone just starting out. His father, Caleb, had been one of Richland's two Black barbers. He had retired and Pee Wee acquired most of his regular customers. Even though I was still mildly mad at Pee Wee, I was glad to hear that he was doing so well.

Pee Wee and a few other people had already been in the house with Muh'Dear for a few hours when I arrived by Greyhound from Pennsylvania. They had already guzzled beer and feasted on a Thanksgiving dinner with all the trimmings.

I was glad to see that during my ten-year absence, Muh'Dear had redecorated the house with new furniture. I didn't care too much for the plaid couch and matching love seat in the living room, but the smoked-glass coffee and end tables added a nice touch. She had also painted every room the same warm shade of beige. The house looked a lot more modern than it had looked during my youth. Plush green carpets and huge live plants filled every room but the kitchen. There was a new stove and refrigerator in the kitchen. And for the first time, we had a breakfast table with chairs that matched.

With the brotherly hug and peck on the cheek I got from Pee Wee, I had a hard time believing that during his visit to Erie, we had made passionate love. I went limp in his arms, just recalling that night. For a moment, I felt like I'd left every bone in my body back in Erie. Pee Wee had to hold on to me to keep me from crumbling to the floor.

"Girl, we better get you somethin' to eat. You feel like you goin' to melt," Pee Wee noticed, clutching me by my shoulders. As hefty as I was, it was easy for him to hold me up, now that he had rebuilt his own body. Even in his thick turtleneck sweater, I could feel the bulging muscles in his arms. "Welcome home, sister. I'm so glad you came to your senses and brought your butt on back here. We got a lot of things to catch up on," Pee Wee told me eagerly. I didn't know how to interpret the wink he gave me, but I was hopeful.

The few times that Pee Wee and I had communicated, by letter and telephone, he had not mentioned the passionate night we had spent in my apartment in Erie. And that hurt. I hated myself. I wanted to hate him but I couldn't afford to lose the only close friend I had left. However, I deeply regretted the fact that I had let another man use my body. Not only with my consent, but for free.

Some grim thoughts crossed my mind and made me grimace. What if Pee Wee had not enjoyed that night with me in Erie? Had all that thrashing around and moaning he'd done in my bed been an act just to keep from hurting my feelings? Most of the men I had been with had not been that demonstrative. In fact, all one of my other former lovers had ever done was flop around on top of me, telling me in graphic terms what he was going to do to me. Then, he'd fallen asleep before doing any of it. I'd put up with that frustrating relationship for only one night. Just like Pee Wee had done with me. Had I frustrated Pee Wee? That would explain him sneaking out and not talking about that night with me. With a muffled sigh, I removed Pee Wee's arms from around me and went around the room hugging everybody else.

Rhoda, pregnant with her third child, was in town visiting her parents and to help celebrate my return to Richland. The next evening around six she swept into the house, strutting like a peacock, flaunting her yellow leather jumpsuit like plumage.

The same people who had joined Muh'Dear for Thanksgiving dinner the day before had already returned.

Rhoda dominated the gathering in the house on Reed Street that evening, showing everybody pictures of her family and home. She generated so much heat, frozen butter would have melted in her mouth. And she was as beautiful as ever, tossing that heavy mane of hair like an ox tossing its tail. Other women who looked like me would probably not have wanted to be best friends with a woman who looked like Rhoda. But it didn't bother me. I had accepted the fact that I was probably going to be a big, plain woman for the rest of my life. But I had learned to do things to enhance my appearance. I now dressed more stylishly, avoiding plaids, stripes, and large prints, and I spent a lot of money getting makeovers. Even without all that, I knew that Rhoda would have still made me feel attractive. After she had greeted everybody else that night, she complimented my appearance profusely, making me grin like a fool.

"Annette, girl, you look beautiful." Rhoda patted my hair. "Keep those braids, honey. They take ten years off your face. My husband swears he prefers a more mature look and that's the only reason I won't wear my hair braided," she squealed. Being a chatterbox was one of the things about Rhoda that always made her stand out so prominently in a crowd. All eyes were on her. "You should wear yellow sometimes. It brings out the earthy tones in dark brown skin. Look at me."

Mr. Boatwright had told me once that when I wore bright colors I looked like a fag's Easter basket. One thing I could say about Rhoda, she was sincere when it came to giving me compliments. At least I believed she was. Since she had always been the stronger one, she had nothing to gain by buttering me up with unnecessary lies. She was the only person I truly felt beautiful around.

I had no idea that this would be one of the most memorable nights of my life. After all I had been through with

Rhoda, this was the night that I would make the heart-wrenching decision to sever our relationship.

What happened was this: Before Rhoda's arrival, Scary Mary, the old madam who had lured Muh'Dear and me to Ohio from Florida, had revealed some startling information to me regarding the death of the pregnant white girl who had threatened to destroy Rhoda's family. Standing in front of me, wearing a red wig that looked like it was about to fly right off her head, Scary Mary told me how the girl had died in Rhoda's house, in Rhoda's bathroom, in Rhoda's presence. Wiping a tear from her eye, Scary Mary said, "Poor Rhoda. Seein' a po'lice shoot and kill her own brother was bad enough, but havin' that girl die right before her eyes must have been downright tryin'." I thought about how Rhoda had snuffed out Mr. Boatwright's life when he became too much of a nuisance. Right away, I *knew* that Rhoda had to be involved in that girl's death.

As soon as all of our other company left and Muh'Dear turned in for the night, I confronted Rhoda with the information that Scary Mary had shared with me, hoping she would deny any involvement.

Rhoda disappointed, but didn't surprise, me. Without hesitation, she admitted with a sigh and a strange sparkle in her eyes, "I had to do it. What else could I do?"

My mouth dropped open. I was stunned beyond belief. But the horror was just beginning. It was like a floodgate suddenly opened up and all kinds of shit spilled out.

Once Rhoda started confessing, she could not stop. Not just about Mr. Boatwright and the white girl, but *two* others! The year of our graduation, Rhoda's bothersome grandmother had mysteriously tumbled down the stairs in their house, in the middle of the night, breaking her neck in the fall. Then, the policeman who had shot and killed her older brother David died in a hit-and-run accident. I saw spots in front of my eyes because I thought I was losing what was left of my mind. I could not believe my ears. Not only had Rhoda killed Mr. Boatwright and that young white girl, but her own grandmother *and* that policeman.

It was the most difficult decision I ever had to make in my life. I knew in my heart that it was time for Rhoda Nelson O'Toole and me to part company. The burden of carrying around the knowledge of Mr. Boatwright's murder had been too much. I knew that I could not continue being friends with a woman who had admitted killing four people.

Rhoda was stunned and disappointed to say the least, but I had made my decision and I intended to stick by it. She didn't even have to warn me, because I had no intention of sharing this startling information with anyone else.

"Good-bye, Rhoda," I said, my voice cracking. She didn't respond.

When she calmly walked out of my house that night, she didn't look back, but I watched from my window until she was out of my sight.

CHAPTER 19

Rhoda had been so much a part of me, now that she was gone, I felt like I had lost an appendage. But other "handicapped" people got along okay so I knew I would, too. Somehow.

While I was trying to get a grip on myself, I spent a few weeks hanging around my stepfather's restaurant. The Buttercup was a large, family-oriented place, nicely decorated with plush maroon carpets and tables covered with starched white tablecloths. It was located in the center of town in one of our most popular strip malls.

I wasn't ready to work anywhere yet. I lived on money I had saved over the years. But I often helped out at the restaurant anyway, bussing tables and taking orders. Muh'Dear had pretty much taken over Mr. King's life. She was his head cook and she took care of his books. This relationship had empowered my mother in a way I never thought I would see. Not that Muh'Dear had ever been shy or the kind of woman to stand in some man's shadow. She didn't hesitate to speak her mind. Especially with me.

"Annette, how do you expect to get decent tips walkin'

around up in here with that long face?" Muh'Dear asked as I stumbled around like a wounded soldier, dropping trays and delivering orders to the wrong tables.

"I don't really work here. I don't expect to make any tips," I reminded.

"Well, if you goin' to do what my other waitresses do, you better get paid for it." Muh'Dear gave me a critical look. "Why you wastin' your life anyway? I ain't never seen you look this miserable." Muh'Dear paused and patted her hair which she had braided and pinned on top of her head. With the exception of a few annoying strands of gray hair and a few wrinkles on her forehead, nature had been good to Muh'Dear. She had gained a couple of dress sizes, but other than that, she was still a striking woman.

"I've never been this miserable," I replied, smacking on some French fries that a customer had left on his plate.

Balancing a tray, Muh'Dear pulled me into a corner in the steamy kitchen and felt my forehead. "What's the matter, baby?"

"Nothing," I mumbled. "Uh, the couple at table five said the food here is better than anywhere else they've eaten."

Compliments had a way of diverting Muh'Dear's attention. "Well, my job is to keep everybody happy. Now how about a smile from you? Your happiness means more to me than anybody else's."

I wore a fake smile the rest of that day. Even when the other waitresses glared at me for prancing around the dining room, keeping them from making tips and "socializing" with some of the good-looking men who ate at the restaurant on a regular basis. These hard-up men, hungry for something other than the fried chicken and waffles the restaurant was famous for, even flirted with me. They made suggestive remarks like, "Miss Buttercup, can I get a *cup* of your *butter*?" I ignored them all. Romance was the last thing on my mind. I couldn't even get a toehold on life, let alone a new lover.

And the way my life was going, I was beginning to think that I'd never feel another man's arms around me anyway.

I didn't like using my status as the boss's daughter to help pacify myself. When I got tired of receiving so many dirty looks from the real waitresses and leers from the male customers that day, I left the restaurant and drifted down the street to Pee Wee's barbershop. Why I decided to do that, I didn't know. Pee Wee had a real life and I had been reduced to the status of a peripheral acquaintance.

Even though the inside of the house Pee Wee shared with his ailing daddy looked like a train wreck, he kept his barbershop nice and neat. On one wall was a poster of John Lennon, left over from Pee Wee's Beatlemania days. There was a huge green plant in every corner. Pee Wee kept himself looking nice and neat, too. He was a casual dresser and being a barber, it behooved him to keep his hair looking nice. He kept it short with a few finger waves on the sides. He had recently grown a sexy goatee that he trimmed and washed every day. Every time I looked at Pee Wee, I thought about how lucky some woman was going to be someday when he married her. Oddly enough, marrying somebody was one thing Pee Wee never discussed, at least around me. And I never brought it up. A lot of people assumed it was because of his daddy. Old Caleb rarely left the house except to go to church. He was a fussy old man, too. I couldn't see any woman in her right mind putting up with that. And, I couldn't see Pee Wee leaving his daddy to go live with some woman.

I liked Pee Wee's daddy, but for my own selfish reasons, I was glad he was old and ailing. I figured that as long as he was around, I'd still have Pee Wee to myself, one way or another.

One of the most disturbing thoughts I had these days was knowing that sooner or later, Pee Wee would have no reason to stay single. Even I knew that there were women in Richland sitting around like spiders, waiting to drag a man like

Pee Wee in front of a preacher. I just hoped that it wouldn't be one of the gold-digging hussies I knew.

Before I reached the barbershop, one of those very wenches pranced out with a grin on her face that annoyed me so much I wanted to slap it off. I stopped and pretended I was looking in the window at the bakery next door. As soon as she disappeared around the corner, I rushed into the barbershop, slamming the door shut so hard the window rattled.

It was late in the evening and Pee Wee had put the CLOSED sign in the window. He was alone, sweeping up hair and chewing on a toothpick. I could tell that he had eaten barbecue for lunch even though I couldn't see any evidence. Even over the smell of shaving lotion, pomade, and whatever else men smeared on their faces and hair, I could still smell barbecue sauce and there were a few specks of it on his white smock.

"Was that old Grandma Foster I just saw leaving?" I asked, rolling my eyes.

"That was her granddaughter, Grace." Pee Wee laughed, flipping the toothpick into a trashcan.

"Oh. I didn't recognize her without her mustache," I muttered, standing in the door with my hand still on the knob.

"Well, I hooked Grace up with that new hair-removal crème I ordered from France. Now she don't have to worry about no upper-lip hair no more." Pee Wee took a deep breath and stuck out his chest. Which was almost twice as big and defined as it used to be. "What you got planned for the rest of the evenin', girl?" he asked, wiping his hands on his smock. He stood up straight and leaned on his broom. A few specks of sweat dotted his forehead.

"Nothing," I mumbled, speaking to him over my shoulder as I glanced out the window. Turning back to Pee Wee, I said, "Why don't you surprise me." I thought that the least Pee Wee would do was to ask to take me to a movie or ask if he could come to my house to listen to some jazz and share a bottle of wine. I was in for a much bigger and better surprise.

Pee Wee dropped his broom and slid onto one of his two swivel chairs and pulled me down onto his lap. Before I realized what he was up to, he kissed me long and hard. "Wanna take a walk around the corner?" He motioned with his head in the direction of a motel.

"What for?" I asked dumbly. "I mean . . . uh, yeah." It seemed too easy and too good to be true. I planned to get as much mileage out of it as I could. I didn't know when I'd get lucky with him again. At the rate I was going, it could take another few years.

He locked up his business and escorted me to the motel in question. As soon as we got into a room, he started nibbling on my ears, fondling my breasts and butt and telling me over and over again how glad he was that I had returned to Ohio.

"You sure haven't been acting like you were glad I came back," I snapped, enjoying his touch as we peeled off our clothes. Either he didn't hear my comment or he was too caught up in the moment to respond. Whatever the reason was, it didn't matter now. Just having a man I cared about, and who cared about me, was enough.

Even if it was just Pee Wee.

"I don't want to come here anymore," I said, before we got any more involved.

Panting, Pee Wee agreed. "I know this ain't the most romantic place in the world." He laughed. "This bed look like it's on its last leg but it'll have to do. I don't think I could last long enough to get you to your house . . ."

He didn't know the half of it. This was the same motel and the same room that Rhoda and Otis had fooled around in during high school. And as old as the bed looked, it was probably the same bed, too! Maybe it was my imagination, but I was convinced that Rhoda's smell was still in this room.

But then she was still in my blood and that scared me. With Pee Wee on top of me, I tensed up and pushed him away.

He lifted his head and looked at me with a confused expression on his face. "Look, if you don't want to do this again, I understand."

"That's not it. I . . . I'm just feeling really funny right now." I didn't want to tell him that Rhoda was the reason I was feeling so uneasy so I let him think what he wanted.

He sighed and shifted his eyes. "Hey, don't think this don't mean somethin' to me. I been wantin' to hook up with you again for a long time."

"Then why didn't you?" Now my biggest concern was about Pee Wee and me, where we had been with our relationship and where we were going.

He shrugged. "I had a good time with you that night in Erie."

"So is this going to be like that, too? Are you going to sneak off as soon as I go to sleep? If so, please leave me money for a cab."

Pee Wee wouldn't look at me as he shook his head. "What we done that night wasn't like us."

I pushed him away some more. "Well, what about now? We're still the same people. The only thing that's different is we're a little older."

A faint smile crossed his face as he looked at me and winked. "I won't leave again until you make me."

The sex was still good, but it was the distraction it provided that I enjoyed the most.

I had to get Rhoda off my mind and keep her off.

CHAPTER 20

After the tryst in the motel room, Pee Wee came to my house four nights in a row and each time we had ended up in bed. We developed a loosey-goosey relationship that we maintained in secret. I didn't know why, but I felt it best to keep it from people like Muh'Dear and Scary Mary. They meddled enough in my life. Pee Wee had always been more like a brother to me and everybody saw us as such. I cared too much about what people would think about Pee Wee and me getting together in such an intimate way.

Sometimes when I looked at Pee Wee, knowing what we did behind closed doors, I felt like we had committed incest. And if it bothered me, I knew it would bother Muh'Dear. Rhoda was the only person I had told about the night I spent with Pee Wee in my apartment in Pennsylvania. Now that she and I were no longer friends, she had no reason to blab that information to anyone I knew.

I didn't like it when Pee Wee went out with other women, especially slim, pretty women. I thought I would die when I heard about him fooling around with Glenda Mitchell. Not just because she was so thin and pretty, but because from a distance she resembled Rhoda. I was glad when I heard a week later that Glenda had run off with some musician from Cleveland.

Scorned and horny, Pee Wee crawled back to me and we resumed our slipshod affair. I accepted the fact that that was how it was going to be with us. I didn't like the role of being the woman he slept with between girlfriends, but it seemed to be the best I could do. Since I'd always felt like Mr. Boatwright's leftovers, getting somebody else's leftovers myself was all I thought I would ever get. I just didn't like what went along with it.

Once I even ironed a shirt for Pee Wee to wear out on a date with another woman, just to keep him happy. But that had happened only once and by accident. I didn't know at the time that he was dating Gladys Webster. I had called him up one night, hoping he would invite himself over and lure me to bed.

"Um, I'm gettin' ready to go to a baptism," he told me. "Listen, my iron just broke. Can I run over there and use yours?" I eagerly agreed.

Pee Wee greeted me with a quick peck on my cheek and trotted behind me to the kitchen where I had already set up the ironing board and turned on the iron.

"From now on, I'm sendin' all my dress shirts to the dry cleaners," he complained, wrestling with the iron, burning his fingers on it before it even touched his shirt. I took the iron from him and ironed the shirt myself. "I wanted to wear my turtleneck, but Gladys wants to go to that new club in Akron after we leave the church," he revealed. With a smug look on his face and a Coke that he had snatched out of my refrigerator in his hand, he leaned against the kitchen wall.

I gritted my teeth and blinked at him. Hearing that Pee

Wee was preparing to go out without another woman had a strange effect on me. I was tempted to scorch his shirt, but I didn't. I was jealous and angry with myself. However, that didn't stop me from being available when his relationship with Gladys fell apart. I was being a fool and I knew I was being a fool. But I was a happy fool.

Pee Wee had made a lot of new friends and some of them became my friends. I occasionally went shopping and to the movies with females I'd met through him. With them, Muh'Dear, Scary Mary, and an infrequent visit to Second Baptist Church, I kept myself busy. I even started working officially as a waitress at the Buttercup. That pleased Muh'Dear and my stepfather, whom I now called "Daddy King."

Unlike some of the crude women they had hired and fired, they knew they could count on me to do a good job and help the restaurant maintain its honorable reputation. Some weeks I worked overtime, simply because I had nothing better to do with myself. I watched a lot of television and I read a lot of books, but I still had a lot of time of my hands.

I knew that I could never open up with the other women I'd started socializing with like I did with Rhoda so I was a dull person to have around. Especially to the women I'd met who liked to gossip and compare their sexual escapades. I didn't want to share my most personal secrets anymore. I'd done that with Rhoda and she had ended up killing for me. It didn't bother me when my new women friends drifted away from me, one by one. It wasn't long before Pee Wee was the only close friend I had. Again.

I had a few pig-in-the-poke dates with men I met around town, but nothing ever panned out. So I was still lonely. I looked forward to my steamy encounters with Pee Wee because he was my only other option.

Muh'Dear had married Mr. King and moved in with him, so I had the house on Reed Street to myself. I was happy about that for a lot of reasons. Now I didn't have to worry about Muh'Dear's beer-drinking friends popping in three to four times a week. But Scary Mary still made her regular visits when she was in a meddling mood, which was often.

CHAPTER 21

One cold December morning, right after I got out of bed, Scary Mary snatched open my front door without knocking and entered my living room wearing black boots and a white sweat suit. She wore red wigs all the time. This particular morning she also had a scarf tied around her head and was not wearing the heavy makeup she usually wore to help hide a cruel scar on her face that she had sustained in a fight when she was young. I didn't know any other woman Scary Mary's age that got around the way she did. The woman spent most of her time tooling around town in her blue Chevy van, looking for something to stir up. A few times I had even seen her van parked in front of the houses of other people on my street that I didn't even know. She owned a huge house on the outskirts of town now, but she was rarely in it. I couldn't figure out how she managed to supervise the five prostitutes who worked for her in that house.

Like Rhoda used to do, Scary Mary barged into my house and made herself at home. Before I could even close the door, she had plopped down on my couch and crossed her spindly legs and started babbling about one thing after another. First it was her health and Florence, the foster daughter she had taken in who now lived in Toledo and rarely called or visited. Then she began talking about how she had signed her retarded daughter Mott into a group home. After that she moved on to my personal life.

"What was Pee Wee doin' sneakin' out of here the other mornin'? I seen him with my own eyes when I was on my way to that early-bird sale at J.C. Penney's," she sneered, looking at me with her eyes narrowed.

"Uh . . . he came to borrow some sugar," I lied.

"I bet he did," she chided, looking at me out of the corner of her eye.

"And to bring me my Christmas present, too," I blurted, waving toward the huge Christmas tree I had in front of my living room window. Christmas was just three days away.

Scary Mary turned her head to the side so fast her wig almost slid off. "This early in the mornin'?"

"He's got a real busy day planned and this was the only time he'd have to come by," I explained.

"Oh. Well, I didn't bring you no Christmas present. You want it, you got to come by my house to get it."

"I will," I said sheepishly. "And I'll bring yours with me, too."

"I'll be expectin' it. And I hope it's somethin' I can use!" Scary Mary grunted, shook her head, and sighed. "I don't need no more fruitcakes, no mixers, no socks, and no more perfume. I need somethin' I can *spend*."

"Yes, ma'am," I replied, my head bowed submissively. That made her smile.

"Too bad you ain't Pee Wee's type," she decided, picking lint off the legs of her pants. "I tried to hook him up with my foster girl Florence before she up and got married, but he didn't want her. If my illformed daughter Mott wasn't so limited, I'd fix him up with her. Once that medication they givin' Mott in that home tames her, I just might do that. It'd be a blessin' to keep a man like Pee Wee to ourselves. It don't matter to me which one of y'all snatch him up. Florence—if she ever divorces that nut she married, Mott . . . or even you." Scary Mary gave me a critical look. "Look like you ain't got enough sugar left in your bowl to catch any other fly." Scary Mary sniffed and smiled. "Pee Wee's gwine to make some girl a good husband. Ain't he?"

"He sure will," I mumbled.

Scary Mary could always be counted on to give me something to think about. I was glad that a busybody like her didn't know about Pee Wee and me. It was bad enough that she knew about me stealing some of her tricks before I moved to Pennsylvania. I still felt that she held a grudge against me for doing that. I didn't want to take a chance on her meddling to sabotage my relationship with Pee Wee. I knew it was in my best interest to keep this information from her. I felt the same way about other people Scary Mary knew knowing. Because Scary Mary could badger her friends so hard with her sharp tongue, sooner or later she had them revealing all kinds of secrets. Not that she was a bitter, lonely old woman; she was living the life of Riley. Once when Mr. King took Muh'Dear to the Bahamas, Scary Mary followed them and had a fling with a young island man she had met on a beach! "God ain't through with you yet, girl," Scary Mary told me with a wink.

"I hope not." I smiled.

A few mornings later, on New Year's Day, 1980, I was lying on my back in my bed with Pee Wee next to me, leaning on his arm, looking down at my face. I had already been awake for a couple of hours. There was an ashtray on my nightstand, completely filled with marijuana roaches and chewed-up wads of breath gum. Empty wine bottles decorated the floor like a gallery. Next to the wine bottles were plates overflowing with bones and bread crumbs.

"Did you ever think that you and I would end up like

this?" Pee Wee asked, belching and rubbing his head. "This close, this often, I mean."

Earlier, while Pee Wee was still passed out from the night before, I had called up my Aunt Berniece in New Jersey and asked her for my daddy's telephone number. I was excited about it and couldn't wait to call him. I had dialed my daddy's number, but I hung up when a man I assumed was Daddy answered. Just hearing his voice had lifted my spirits. I couldn't wait to dial the number again. The thought made me smile. Pee Wee assumed he'd put the smile on my face. We had just spent one of our most passionate nights together. He tickled my neck.

"Come on, girl. Talk to me." Pee Wee grabbed my hand and guided it to his crotch. He was already hard, so he didn't need any assistance from me.

"No. I never thought we'd end up this close, this often," I told him, stroking his dick anyway. "I really enjoy being with you . . . like this."

Suddenly, he let out a deep breath and roughly pushed my hand away. "Good. Then I know you won't mind me leavin' before eatin' the breakfast I know you probably planned to fix for me," he continued, sliding out of my bed. He snatched his clothes off the floor. "I gotta haul ass."

"Are you tryin' to tell me something?" I asked firmly, trying to keep the anger out of my voice.

"Yeah, I'm tryin' to tell you somethin'." He sniffed and sat down on the bed to put on his socks and shoes. "My daddy's movin' to Erie to live with his sister and I need to help get things situated. I got a real important long distance phone call to make. I'll be back this evenin'. I want to take you out to dinner before too much snow get on the ground. Dress warm."

Relieved, I sat up and reached for my robe at the foot of the bed, rubbing Pee Wee's back with my other hand. He turned to me and smiled. "I would stay longer if I could, but I really do have to make that important phone call."

I nodded. "I got a real important phone call to make myself," I said.

CHAPTER 22

As soon as I closed the front door behind Pee Wee, I dialed my daddy's phone number again. He answered on the fifth ring.

"Hello." His voice was low and weak, like an old man. He was in his seventies now so he *was* an old man. But in my mind, I still pictured him as the proud, robust young man he'd been the last time I'd seen him. I could still see him strutting down the hill toward that old shack we used to live in. When I saw my first Sidney Poitier movie, it brought tears to my eyes because he looked a lot like my daddy.

"Daddy, it's me," I said, stumbling over each word. I had to clear my throat and massage it to keep from choking. A miserably long pause followed.

"Daddy, are you still there? It's me."

"Me who?" he finally responded. Surprisingly, he sounded much stronger now.

"Daddy, it's Annette."

My daddy gasped and coughed a few times before speaking again. "Say what?"

"Daddy, I called up Aunt Berniece in New Jersey and she gave me your telephone number."

I heard him suck in his breath and mumble words that sounded like a fragmented prayer. "Hold on. Let me get myself in a chair before I fall out." I heard some shuffling around and some muffled voices on his end before he continued. "Annette? Great day in the mornin'—I thought you was dead!"

"No, I'm alive and kicking." I laughed dryly.

"Lord have mercy, girl. Where you at?" He coughed some more.

"I'm in Ohio. In a little town called Richland." I had to pause to clear my throat again. My heart was beating so fast, I had to rub my chest. "I've been thinking about you a lot, Daddy. I've been thinking about you for a long, long time. And if I had had your number I would have called a lot sooner."

"My Lord!"

"How are you, Daddy? I want to see you."

"I wanna see you, too! Where your mama at?"

"Huh? Uh . . . she lives a few blocks away from me with her new husband." Another long pause.

"Oh." Daddy sighed. "Lord, I can't believe my ears I sittin' here talkin' to *my girl*. I hope I ain't dreamin'." Daddy's persistent cough concerned me.

"You're not dreaming, Daddy. It's really me."

"Well, listen—when you comin' to see me? We just painted the kitchen and we just slaughtered a hog. I'll send you your fare!"

"I'll come as soon as I can, Daddy. Uh . . . I've really missed you a lot, Daddy."

"I thought y'all had forgot all about me." His voice had become weak and old again.

"I'll never forget about you, Daddy."

"What you been up to all these years? You got any kids?"

I laughed. "Not yet, Daddy. Get a pencil so I can give you my phone number."

"All right, baby. You hold on now. This house look like a train wreck, so it'll take me a few minutes to find a pencil. You hold on now."

During the five minutes I waited for Daddy to return to the telephone, I cried so hard my eyes burned. I was still sniffling when he returned.

"You still there, baby? What's the number and your address? I'm gwine to send you your fare as soon as I can draw the money out the bank. Hear?"

"Daddy, I can pay my own way—"

"I'm payin' for this. That's the least I can do."

"All right, Daddy." I gave him my phone number and address. "Well, I don't want to keep you too long."

"Sugar, you can keep me as long as you want to. I ain't got nowhere to go nohow."

"I have a few things to take care of, so I can't talk too long anyway."

"Uh-huh. Well, your ticket is on the way. Do you hear me?"

"Yes, Daddy."

"And listen. You tell your mama she can come with you if she want to. I'll pay her way, too. Bygones is bygones. We got plenty of room and plenty to eat. That was a mighty big hog we slaughtered. Just sittin' here thinkin' about them ribs brings tears to my eyes."

I laughed. "You take care of yourself now until I get there."

I sat staring at the telephone long after I had hung it up. As emotional as I was, I didn't cry anymore. Instead, I smiled.

I couldn't think of a better way to start the New Year.

CHAPTER 23

Now that I had talked to Daddy, I thought about him even more. He was a hard man to forget. Every time I closed my eyes, I could see his face and that made me smile. He had been so handsome and so proud back in the day. And he'd been way ahead of his time. He was the first person I'd ever heard say, "Black is beautiful." But since he hadn't stayed around long enough to make me believe that, my color had always been an obstacle to me.

I was proud of the fact that Daddy had helped integrate the South and he had the battle scars to prove it. He had endured numerous beatings from ferocious white policemen right before my eyes and bites from the dogs they had turned loose on him. But even all that had not stopped him from standing up for what he believed in.

The only snapshot I ever had of Daddy was of him drinking from a public water fountain that had a WHITES ONLY sign above it, tacked to a pecan tree. I had carried that picture around with me, transferring it from one tacky wallet to another, until it fell apart when I was fifteen. Being the man that he was, it stunned me when he left us for a white woman. But that was all in the past and I still wanted to see him again.

As hard as Daddy had worked in the fields, we hadn't had much money. We had always lived on the outskirts of Miami in shacks. Living that way hadn't bothered me because in addition to the Savior we worshipped every Sunday, we had each other. We even slept together in the same bed.

Recalling my past suddenly had me feeling as weak as a bowl of jelly. My emotions ran wild, from one extreme to the other. I was ecstatic, confused, angry, happy, and apprehensive. I had opened a Pandora's box and I didn't know how to handle it. I got light-headed when I thought about Muh'Dear and I had to ask myself, *What have I gotten myself into?*

I felt safer telling Muh'Dear over the telephone about my conversation with Daddy than I would have to her face.

"What in the world—girl, have you lost your mind?!" Muh'Dear roared. She had to stop talking long enough to catch her breath. She lowered her voice to a boom and continued, "I don't want you to have a damn thing to do with that no-good bastard after what he done to us! I . . . can't . . . believe . . . my . . . ears!" Muh'Dear sounded like she was coming through the telephone.

I rarely raised my voice to my mother and I didn't want to do that now. I managed to keep myself under control. "I don't care about all that anymore. He's my daddy and I still want to see him. And he wants to see me."

"And what about what *I* want? I don't want you to let him ruin your life."

"How is he going to ruin my life? I'm a grown woman!" I snapped, no longer able to hide my anger and frustration. "You can't tell me what to do anymore!"

Muh'Dear sucked her teeth and shot back, "Don't you sass me, girl! I ain't too old to come over there and whup your ass and you ain't too old for me to do it."

"Yes, ma'am," I mumbled contritely.

"I can't believe you doin' this to me. You choosin' him over me after all I done did for you, girl? Where was he when we was runnin' from pillar to post? Where was Frank when we had to steal food to eat a decent meal? Where was he when I had to suffer with you and that shame you got yourself into gettin' pregnant? Poor Brother Boatwright was playin' Frank's part. Where was Frank? He was God knows where, lickin' his white woman's flat ass. And now you tellin' me you want to hook back up with him?" Muh'Dear started choking on her words.

"Muh'Dear, please don't do this to me. You stop that crying. I am not choosing Daddy over you. What's wrong with me having both you and him in my life now? Other than you, he's all I have."

Muh'Dear clicked her teeth and groaned. "You got your Aunt Berniece and her husband over there in Jersey. You got everything you need."

"I don't have my daddy."

"You don't *need* no daddy now! You ain't got no daddy, girl! A real daddy would never have done to you what Frank done."

"He made a mistake and he regretted it, Muh'Dear. Aunt Berniece told me that he tried to find us after he moved back from Texas." My ears were ringing and my eyes started burning from the tears I couldn't hold back. I refused to give in and neither would Muh'Dear.

Muh'Dear gasped and said hotly, "I bet he did. After that white bitch got through with him, where else could he go? We don't need him now, nohow! We doin' fine without him."

"You have Daddy King and you have a lot of friends. I don't have anything in my life. I'm tired of being alone."

"Alone? What?! How can you say you alone? We both got Mr. King. He is your daddy now. You got Pee Wee and Rhoda. And you know you can always count on Scary Mary and her girls if you just want somebody to talk to. Your problem is, you too picky. Shame on you. Still single at your age with all these fine, single Black men in Richland." Muh'Dear's voice softened. "Sugar, how come you won't get to know some of them nice young single men at the church? Deacon Brewster's been tryin' to hook you up with his nephew Jacob for months. Jacob just bought a brand new car."

"I don't care if Jacob Brewster just bought a brand new chariot," I said through clenched teeth. "That man couldn't turn me on with a pair of pliers. I don't want him. And Pee Wee doesn't always have time to spend with me that much anyway."

"What's Rhoda's telephone number? I am goin' to call up Rhoda and tell her to come pay you a visit. She the only one can talk to you that you'll listen to."

"Not anymore, Muh'Dear." There was a long pause while I waited for Muh'Dear to respond. "Are you still there?"

"I'm still here. I had to go take a pill." Muh'Dear paused again and cleared her throat. "I am so glad Brother Boatwright ain't alive to hear all this foolishness."

"Please don't bring up that man's name," I snarled. I screwed up my face and held up my hand and swallowed so hard my eyes closed all by themselves. "I don't want to talk about Mr. Boatwright anymore." Things looked fuzzy when I opened my eyes and my butt had started itching.

"Have you been drinkin'?" Muh'Dear sucked her teeth and let out an impatient sigh.

"No."

"Smokin' that stuff? And don't lie to me. I know what that stuff smells like and I done smelled it in that house over there after you and Pee Wee done fiddled around. I bet Brother Boatwright spinnin' in his grave. Lord have mercy on your soul, girl." The more I heard Mr. Boatwright's name, the more my butt itched. I couldn't even sit still and I was too angry to even scratch myself.

"Daddy's sending me the money for a plane ticket," I said calmly.

"And where is all the money he owe me for back child support? Is he sendin' that, too?" Muh'Dear shrieked.

"I really want to see my daddy." I sighed with defeat as I rubbed my chest, which had started aching so hard I could barely breathe. "But if it hurts you that much and you don't want me to see him, I won't."

"I don't want you to have nothin' to do with that man! Aarrgh! He's a demon! He's evil! Don't you know that?"

My ears were ringing and burning now. My butt felt like it was on fire. "What do I tell him?" I felt like I was falling apart, a few pieces at a time.

"I don't care what you tell him. After what he done to us, you don't owe him nothin'."

After I hung up from my conversation with Muh'Dear, I crawled back into bed. It was still damp from Pee Wee's juices, but I stayed in the same spot for the next six hours. Crying.

CHAPTER 24

Four days after my conversation with Daddy, I received a special delivery envelope from him. In it was a money order. It contained enough to cover a round-trip plane ticket to and from Miami. First class, Daddy had instructed in a note paper-clipped to the money order.

I had not seen or talked to Muh'Dear since I had told her about my conversation with Daddy. I had taken a few days off from my job at the Buttercup, so she and Daddy King didn't expect to see me there. When I didn't return to work the following Monday, my stepfather came to the house.

"Annette, we was worried about you," he told me, removing his hat and fanning with the tail of his overcoat as soon as he entered the door. In his late seventies now, my stepfather was even older than Daddy was. Daddy King didn't have much hair left, but he still had firm features and all of his teeth. He dipped his head and peered at me over the top of the thick glasses he wore. The only thing I didn't like about him was that he was the same shade of reddish brown that Mr. Boatwright had been. Arthritis caused him to walk with a slight limp.

"I'm all right, Daddy King. I just needed to be by myself for awhile. I guess Muh'Dear told you about my daddy. You want something to drink?" I waved him to the couch.

He shook his head and removed his glasses and wiped them with the tail of his plaid flannel shirt. "She sure did and I told Gussie Mae to her face she was wrong for puttin' you on that spot. She ain't got the right to live your life."

Hearing that I had at least one ally gave me the hope I needed. "What did she say?" I asked anxiously.

"Well, I won't repeat it 'cause I know it'd only make you feel even worse. I think I will have a glass of buttermilk." He fanned his tired face with his hat.

Daddy King was a sensitive man. He tried to avoid a lot of confusion and turmoil. I knew that it had not been easy for him to come talk to me about such a tense situation. The strain showed on his face.

"Will you talk to her? She might listen to you."

"She might and she might not. She pretty well set in her ways, you know," he replied. Wheezing, he followed me to the kitchen.

I sighed. "All my life I've bent over backward trying to make her proud of me."

"And you did, child. You her pride and joy. But you gotta look at things from her point of view. She don't want to see you get hurt." Daddy King paused to drink a full glass of buttermilk in one long gulp. A white line remained above his top lip. "She ain't gwine to rar back and let nobody do nothin' that might hurt you. She real, real proud of the fact that she got you through life in one piece. Somebody was to harm you, that woman would bring down the whole world," he rasped, wiping the milk off his lip with the back of his hand.

My mind flashed on Mr. Boatwright and the dozens of times he had raped me. After what Daddy King had just said,

I tried to imagine what Muh'Dear would have done to Mr. Boatwright, had I exposed him for the monster he was.

"When I was with that Sadie, she didn't care if them gals of hers burned city hall down and run off with Godzilla, just as long as they didn't keep her from watchin' them soap operas she was so addicted to." Daddy King was a tall man, but he was so thin his clothes always hung on him, leaving almost enough room for another person. He looked like a scarecrow. "Ain't you glad to have a mama that care so much about you?"

"I am."

I walked Daddy King to the door where he paused and patted my shoulder.

"Now your mama is a good woman and that's the main thing. Even though I think she wrong for wantin' to keep you from your daddy, she got a right to feel that way. Let's give her some time to digest this thing. Wait awhile before you bring it up again. She'll break down sooner or later."

"Will you talk to her some more?"

"Every chance I get. Now how come you ain't at work today? You know how shorthanded we been. And, by the way, one of them construction workers that eat at the restaurant every day, been askin' about you. One of the Simmons boys. He eats like a stevedore so I bet him and you would get along real good." One of the few things my stepfather had in common with Muh'Dear was, he also wanted to see me settle down with a man. Any man. The Simmons man he had just mentioned had a prison record and babies by four different women.

"I'll be in tomorrow."

I walked my stepfather to his car and waited until he drove off before I waddled back inside and folded myself back onto the couch.

When I returned to work three days later, Muh'Dear

acted like the conversation she and I had had about Daddy had not occurred. She cornered me in the kitchen five minutes after my arrival, buttoning the back of the plain blue uniform I had to wear.

"Deacon Brewster just called to make a dinner reservation for him and his wife this evenin'. Lord, I hope Margaret don't wear none of that loud perfume of hers that leaves the dinin' room smellin' like Scary Mary's whorehouse on a busy weekend. He's bringin' his charmin' nephew Jacob, too. You remember him, the nephew that just got divorced from that girl he picked up over there in them Philippines. Ain't that nice?" Muh'Dear paused just long enough to take a deep breath. "Poor Jacob's depressed. I told Deacon Brewster, there's a slew of single Black girls around here that's itchin' to cheer Jacob up. He asked about you. Ain't that nice?"

"That is nice. Listen, I've been thinking about trying to go back to work for the telephone company. They had an ad for switchboard operators in the newspaper last week."

"I'm glad to hear that. You got too much goin' for you to be sweatin' away the rest of your young years bein' a waitress. Which, by the way, is years that ain't so young no more. Do somethin' with your life before it's too late. God ain't through with you yet, but you got to meet Him part of the way. Don't expect the Lord to do all the work like he been doin' so far. He outdid hisself when he blessed us with Brother Boatwright and then Mr. King. Why don't you go in the restroom and put some rouge on your jaws before the Brewsters get here."

CHAPTER 25

I waited two more days before I called Daddy back. He was happy to hear from me again, but disappointed that I hadn't called sooner.

"I wanted to call you, but I misplaced your telephone number. Hold on. Let me find a pencil so I can get it again." He returned in less than a minute. "This time I'm gwine to scribble it on my Medicaid card. I ain't about to misplace that." I gave him my telephone number again. "You get that money I sent?"

"Yeah . . . "

"When you comin'? You better hurry up if you want some of that hog we slaughtered. Them pork chops we cut up and stuck in the freezer is screamin'."

"I can't come down there right now, Daddy. Uh, Muh'Dear's not doing too well and she needs me here to take care of her." I didn't like lying, but I didn't see any other way out of this mess.

"What's wrong with her?"

"Oh, nothing serious." I lowered my voice to a whisper. "Just female problems."

"Well, I'll be here whenever you do decide to come. I ain't gwine nowhere."

"You still have my address?"

"It was on the same scrap of paper I wrote your phone number on that last time that you gave it to me. The same scrap of paper I lost. Give me your address again, too."

I received a letter from Daddy the following Friday. And another one a week later. Not a week went by without a letter from Daddy. Every time I opened my mailbox and spotted an envelope with his spidery handwriting, I got excited. Each time I heard from him, he wanted to know when I was coming to visit him.

The same day John Lennon was murdered, December 8, 1980, Daddy stopped asking when I was coming to visit him. When we did communicate, we discussed everything but that.

The telephone company had hired me back. After a while, it seemed like I had never left my job as a switchboard operator in the first place. I was determined to keep myself busy.

I even volunteered to do things that Muh'Dear used to have to beg me to do. Once a month, she and Daddy King and Scary Mary cooked food and donated it to a homeless shelter. Then they not only served it, but also after everybody had eaten, they cleaned up the mess. I had always gone out of my way to avoid spending an entire day at the shelter. Now I looked forward to it. I even started going around with Muh'Dear and Scary Mary to visit sick people from the church, cooking and cleaning for the ones who lived alone. These were things I should have been proud to do and I was. Muh'Dear and I had so much to be thankful for now. Just like Scary Mary and Daddy King had shared their good fortune with us, we shared ours with people not as fortunate. "Baby, one day God is goin' to bless you with even more. A husband, children, good friends. Just be patient," Muh'Dear told me. I didn't want to seem greedy, but even with as much as I already had, I did want the things that Muh'Dear believed God had in store for me.

Pee Wee was still making his regular trips to my bed but I continued to go out with somebody's unattached male relative just to keep Muh'Dear off my back.

I even went to a Christmas party with Deacon Brewster's nephew at one of his white co-worker's sparsely furnished tract house near the trailer camp on the outskirts of town. I hadn't been in this shabby neighborhood since we'd lived in it, before we moved to the house on Reed Street. It was a place I did not miss. Old cars and motorcycles lined the unpaved streets. Somebody had parked an old school bus on the side of one of the streets and was living in it. Dog shit littered the ground like works of art. A three-legged dog yipped at my legs as we made our way up onto a porch with two steps missing.

"Don't step in none of that dog dooky. I don't want you to embarrass me by trackin' up Mark's floor," Jacob advised me, leading me by my arm.

I felt like I was being led to a slaughter. I prayed that they would have plenty of alcohol available. That was the only way I could see myself surviving this night.

Jacob Brewster was the kind of man every Black woman wanted her daughter to hook up with. He had a good job working at one of Richland's steel mills, he drove a big, new car, he liked to spend money on his women, he was devoted to his mama, and he went to church every Sunday. But he still lived with his domineering mama and he had the face of a mule and the breath of an ox.

"Annette, since you don't want to dance with me, do you mind if I dance with Ingrid Dobbs? She been eyeballin' me all night," Jacob whispered in my ear, spraying the side of my face with his sour spit. He had been drinking heavily and could barely stand up straight. But he was so clumsy anyway, I didn't want to take a chance on him grinding his thick-soled running shoes into my feet. The fly on his wrinkled gabardine pants was open. His wiry black hair had been plastered to his head with the same foul-smelling pomade Mr. Boatwright used to wear.

"Go ahead. I don't know any of these new dances anyway." I waved him to the dance floor, looking at my watch instead of him.

As soon as Jacob weaved his way across the floor, a man I had never seen before stepped from behind the couch I was sitting on and plopped down next to me. Other than me, he was the only person on the premises dressed nicely. He had on a dark blue suit, a light blue shirt, and black shoes that shone like new money. Ironically, I had on a dark blue silk dress with light blue cuffs and collar and a pair of black pumps. Being somewhat superstitious, I took these coincidences as a sign.

A good sign.

CHAPTER 26

I never thought I would see the day that I'd be glad I'd accepted a date with Jacob Brewster. But Jacob wasn't the reason I was feeling so frisky now.

The stranger who had come over to me seemed to glow more than the lights on a lopsided Christmas tree propped up in a corner, obscuring a poster of Ronald Reagan on the wall.

"I don't know any of these new dances, either," he told me, flashing some of the whitest, straightest teeth I'd ever seen in my life. "I'm Jerome Cunningham. And you are?" He was so polite, it startled me. My eyes got wide and I held my breath as I looked around to make sure he was talking to me. He grabbed my limp hand and shook it.

"Hi, Jerome. I'm Annette," I said, coughing to clear my throat. Handsome men rarely approached me. Well, they *never* approached me. And this one was breathtaking. He was tall and even in his smart suit, I could see that he was nicely built. He had light brown skin and a helmet of curly, dark brown hair. His lips were a little too thin for my tastes but his small, slanted eyes were dazzling. I couldn't believe he was addressing me. I quickly scanned the room. Since I was the only Black woman present, I assumed he had either come with one of the attractive white women or alone.

"You want another drink?" he asked, frowning at the empty glass sitting on the coffee table in front of me.

"Oh, no. I've had enough," I said quickly, holding up my hand. The last thing I wanted to do was get drunk. Pee Wee had not visited me in a while and I was righteously horny that night. Jacob didn't appeal to me that way, but I still didn't trust myself alone with him without a clear head. He had already goosed my butt a few times, telling me he couldn't wait to get me back to my house because he had a big surprise for me. He had put a lot of emphasis on the word *big*. I had a big surprise for him, too: he wasn't getting into my house or me this particular night or any other night. I wasn't that desperate as long as I remained sober.

"Then how about something to eat? Have you tried that pasta salad?" Jerome looked me up and down, smiling with approval. His knee was dangerously close to mine. I didn't even try to imagine what was going through his mind. I placed a throw pillow on my lap because I didn't want him to see that my thighs were taking up twice as much room on the couch as his.

"As you can see, I haven't missed too many meals," I laughed. Sometimes, joking about my weight myself made it easier for me to deal with. "I'm the last one in here that needs to be eating."

"In some countries, large women are revered. They even have ceremonies in some of the villages in Africa to fatten the skinny women up before they marry them off." Jerome sniffed and looked me over some more. "Every woman in my family is stout. My grandmother was so big, she couldn't even get out of the bed the last year of her life. My daddy, may he rest in peace, loved my big-legged, big-hipped mama.

Me, I feel like he did: the more there is of the woman, the more there is to love."

I was *really* feeling frisky now. "I've already tried that pasta salad and it's nothing to write home about." I leaned toward him and whispered conspiratorially, "White folks don't know the first thing about cooking. I don't even know what that green stuff in that black bowl is."

"Turkey dressing," Jerome whispered back, wiggling his nose.

We both laughed.

"I never would have guessed that. I can't wait to get my hands on some decent food again," I said, feeling so at ease I felt I could say anything to this man.

"Well, in that case, you have to let me fix dinner for you one evening soon. My mama's folks come from Louisiana so you know we all know how to burn. Would you let me do that, Annette?"

"Okay," I said meekly.

My head started spinning when it dawned on me that this handsome man had asked me for a date. I thought I'd lose my mind when he slid his arm around my shoulder. I don't know how I did it, but somehow I managed to remain composed. I removed the pillow from my lap and smoothed my dress, resting my hand on my knee. I froze when Jerome took my hand in his and squeezed it. No man had ever done that to me before in my life. Not even Mr. Boatwright or Pee Wee. I was certain that Jerome noticed the sweat on my palm, but he was too nice to acknowledge it.

"Looks like you and I are not the only ones here who don't know the new dances, Annette." He motioned toward two women dancing together, practically knocking everybody else off the floor. "I love to watch white folks dance, don't you? They hop around the dance floor like blind rabbits."

I laughed again. I was proud of the fact that I was laughing for the first time in weeks.

"These are some nice people, though. But they are fun to watch. You haven't seen anything 'til you've seen them do the bump." We laughed again. My hand was still in Jerome's and he was squeezing it even harder. I wondered what he was up to. I knew from experience that most men would fuck a goat. If sex was what he was after, he had come to the right place. He could have slid me down on that couch and had his way with me right in front of that whole room full of people.

And I would have enjoyed it.

CHAPTER 27

"Lord have mercy! I have seen these white folks try to do the bump but *that's* what they always do, no matter whatever else they call themselves doing when they get on a dance floor." Jerome shook his head and laughed. "One night I was watching *The Dinah Shore Show* and she got loose. I thought my television set was going to fall off the stand. Now, I can do a mean bump, but I don't want to get up there and make a fool of myself doing a dance that goes back that far."

Just then, a tall, blond woman bumped into the coffee table, knocking several drinks to the floor. "See what I mean?" We laughed again. By now I had laughed so much my chest was aching. "You're Albert King's daughter, aren't you?"

"Stepdaughter. He married my mama not too long ago. My real daddy lives in Florida." I couldn't believe how comfortable I felt talking to Jerome. I cleared my throat and crossed my ankles, hoping I looked as dainty as some of the pretty white women prancing around the room. I knew that I didn't and never would, but the way Jerome was looking at me, I felt like I did. "You must be new in town. I don't think I've ever seen you before."

"Well, I was born here but when my daddy died when I was fifteen, Mama remarried and we moved to Buffalo. After my stepdaddy passed away, my mama and the rest of the family moved back down here. I came back for my brother's wedding last month and decided to stay when I heard they had an opening for a guidance counselor at Richland High. They hired me on the spot. I was pretty lonesome up there in Buffalo by myself, anyway." I almost wet my control-top panties when Jerome looked in my eyes and told me, "I'm glad I came back to Richland now. Buffalo didn't have women as fine as you up there." I slid my free hand to my side and pinched myself to make sure I was not dreaming.

"That's nice," I muttered.

Still holding my other hand, Jerome looked around the room. He groaned when he looked over at Jacob, who was glaring at us from a corner with one hand on his hip, the other hand clutching yet another drink. Jerome scratched his finely chiseled chin before returning his attention to me. "Is Jacob your man?"

I gasped and almost fell off the couch, I was so taken aback. "Good God; no!" I said quickly. "His wife from the Philippines left him and he was depressed. My mama kept at me to go out with him, so I finally did." I rolled my eyes and groaned.

"So I don't have to worry about some jealous boyfriend jumping on me if I visit you?" There was a pleading look in his eyes and that confused me. I had to wonder why such a good-looking man was trying so hard to get in good with me. Men that looked like him usually had women fighting over him. I froze when a wicked thought crossed my mind: maybe he looked at me as a meal ticket now that he knew that my mother and stepfather owned a big restaurant. Jerome had a good job and it sounded like he was from a good family. I dismissed that wicked thought and scolded myself for being so suspicious.

"No, you won't have to worry about that," I said. I don't know why Pee Wee's face entered my mind, but it did and that saddened me. "I don't have a boyfriend," I said firmly. I wasn't sure how to categorize my relationship with Pee Wee and I didn't want to give him up. But Pee Wee dated other women so I had every right to date other men.

Somebody dimmed the lights when the deejay announced that he was going to play some old Motown favorites.

"Now I *can* slow dance," Jerome told me, gently pulling me up. I didn't want to dance, until I spotted Jacob stumbling across the floor toward me with his hand held out.

"Me, too," I said quickly, letting Jerome lead me to the dance floor.

With Smokey Robinson singing "The Tracks of My Tears" in the background, I fell in love for the first time in my thirty-something years. As soon as the dance ended, Jacob came over to me while I was still on the dance floor in Jerome's arms.

"I'm ready to go! These crackers don't know how to party. Let's go over to the Red Rose," Jacob snapped, clutching my wrist. "My brother playin' in the band over there tonight. And, I heard they servin' free Cajun popcorn. I'm 'bout to starve up in here tryin' to eat this dog food Mark 'nem whupped up."

Then I did a bold thing. I turned to Jerome. "You sure you don't mind giving me a ride home?"

An amused look appeared on his face, but he seemed pleased. "I don't mind at all," he told me.

"Jacob, do you mind if I catch a ride home with Jerome?" I asked sweetly, smiling at Jacob even though he had a scowl on his face that made him look even more ridiculous. He had screwed his face up so tight, it looked like he had one eyebrow.

"What? Do I mind? Hell, yeah, I mind! I spent three dollars on gas to bring you out here!" Jacob howled, slurring his words. His eyes looked like they were about to pop out of the sockets.

I gasped when Jerome quickly reached into his pocket and fished out a wad of bills. "That should take care of your gas," he told Jacob, folding a few bills into Jacob's shirt pocket.

I didn't even look back as Jerome led me out the door, but I could hear Jacob snorting like a bull.

I didn't get to enjoy any passion with Jerome that night. In fact, he didn't even want to come in when we got to my house.

"I have to get up early to take my mama to church in the morning," he explained. "But, I will be seeing you again, *and again*, if you want me to." There was a pleading look on his face. It made him look a lot younger than the thirty-six years he claimed to be. "I like you already, Annette."

"I like you, too," I said, smiling demurely.

Jerome didn't even have to write down my telephone number. He memorized it on the spot. Then he surprised me with the longest, most passionate kiss any man had ever laid on me. I was so taken aback, I didn't even close my eyes. I was sorry I didn't. I was facing Pee Wee's house. It was too dark for me to see him in his bedroom window upstairs, but I knew he was up there watching. Pee Wee didn't smoke cigarettes, but he loved him some weed. He was smoking a joint in his darkened room and I could tell because when he sucked on it, I saw a tiny, bright-red flash.

CHAPTER 28

Even though Jerome had made a good first impression on me, the next time I saw him, a week after we'd met, he behaved more like an oaf. But that didn't bother me. I was not about to let his behavior change my opinion. I figured he was my last chance at a lasting relationship. So, like he was a football, I took him and ran.

My first date with Jerome was a date from hell. He arrived at my house smelling like beer, his hair askew, with a pair of brown slacks and a white shirt in a paper bag that I had to iron for him to wear. On our way to the movies, his Mercury ran out of gas. There was a gas station two blocks away but we walked six blocks, in the snow, to another one because it was cheaper. During the walk back to his car, he slid on some ice and spilled gas on the leg of my slacks, so I smelled like gasoline the rest of the night.

Once we got to the theater, five minutes into the movie, he complained about the French movie I had suggested.

"Why any moviemaker would choose to make a movie with subtitles is beyond me. Any movie worth being dubbed in English should have been made in English in the first place."

"Well, you didn't want to see that teenage slasher movie at the Strand," I reminded, reaching for the one small box of popcorn he had purchased. He complained that the popcorn was too dry for him, yet he held onto the box like it was full of gold nuggets.

To keep from paying for parking, Jerome had parked in an alley six blocks from the theater. He had only saved a dollar, because that's all the parking lot charged after five. During the walk from the theater to his car, he slipped on some ice and sprained his ankle.

Jerome was a vegetarian so suggesting a rib joint or a chicken shack for dinner after the movie was out of the question. He didn't want to eat at the Buttercup because his ex-girlfriend had broken up with him there.

"What about dinner at Antonosanti's?" I suggested. "They serve some dynamite steamed veggies and pasta." Antonosanti's was the most expensive restaurant in town. It was owned by the Antonosantis, a shady Italian family that owned a lot of other property in Richland.

Jerome gasped and gave me a horrified look as we walked down the street with him limping and holding on to me. "Woman, have you lost your mind? That dago restaurant is the most expensive place in town. I'd go to the A&P and spend a dollar on some macaroni and a can of green beans myself before I'd go to Antonosanti's—and I bet that's all they do. Besides, from what I've seen and heard, those people aren't even clean. Our principal, old man Martinelli, he uses the toilet and leaves without washing his hands."

We ended up in a soup kitchen where Jerome purchased our dinner with a "buy one, get one free" coupon. The French bread was free, so he filled a doggie bag to take home. When he paid with his credit card, it got declined and I ended up paying the check.

Then his car wouldn't start when we left. Too cheap to spring for a cab, he escorted me home on the bus where an unruly drunk man threw up on the seat across from us.

From that point on, our dates were usually at his apartment, above a converted funeral parlor, sitting in front of his nineteen-inch, black-and-white television drinking generic beer. I didn't know what kind of money Jerome made, but I assumed he made a decent living. But he was so tightfisted with his money that he bought his clothes from consignment shops and dollar stores. Since I could pay my own way, I didn't really have a problem with Jerome's miserly habits. I was generous enough for both of us.

Jerome was a comfort to me. He was a good listener. He held me in his arms like a baby when I told him about the hard times Muh'Dear and I had endured since moving to Ohio. He almost cried along with me when I told him about the times I had nothing to eat but lime Jell-O. "One week I ate so much of that shit, my pee came out green," I told him, glad to see him laugh at that. One thing that really touched my heart was his understanding my need to reunite with my father. "I would *never* turn my back on my children," he vowed, adding with a passionate embrace, "or you." I had been looking for a man like Jerome all my life and I was going to do whatever I had to do to keep him.

Now when Pee Wee came over, he loved making jokes about how cheap Jerome was.

"I never took you to no 'all you can eat for five dollars place' and I wouldn't never haul a woman like you around on a bus at night," Pee Wee said evenly. "You could do a whole lot better than Jerome Cunningham."

"I'm glad you think that," I shot back.

"Huh? What you mean by that?"

"Why don't you tell me? You seem to know what I need," I teased.

Now that I was seriously involved with another man, Pee

Wee and I had stopped sleeping together. But he was still the closest friend I had and I enjoyed his company. He was one of the most stable things in my life.

"If things don't work out with you and your dime-store-shoppin' Romeo, let me know," Pee Wee told me. I knew then that no matter what happened to me next, I could always fall back on Pee Wee for anything I needed. Especially sex.

Sex with Jerome was another fiasco. Not counting Mr. Boatwright, I had had enough experience by now to know the difference between good sex and bad sex. Jerome was in a league of his own. He had problems maintaining an erection and even when he did, he often had an orgasm before I even got in the bed!

"I just get so excited when I'm with you, I can't help myself," he explained, laughing and shaking his limp dick at me. Juice dripping from it formed a tiny puddle on my new sheet. He played with my titties for ten minutes, thinking that would satisfy me. It didn't, but I pretended it did. I reminded myself that sex wasn't everything. Some women got along fine without it. There was a woman at my church who was jubilant because her husband had become impotent after an automobile accident.

I overlooked my frustration and concentrated on Jerome's exotic looks. With all of his shortcomings, I was still proud to be seen with such a handsome man. My new mission was to keep Jerome Cunningham happy and that's exactly what I planned to do.

CHAPTER 29

"At least you'll have some pretty babies if y'all ever get married," Muh'Dear chirped after she met Jerome. She had grinned and beamed like a lighthouse all through the dinner she had prepared for Jerome and me. They had really hit it off. Jerome had complimented Muh'Dear's cooking excessively and that paid off for him. She had sent him home with a Crock-Pot full of collard greens, a fresh pan of cornbread, and bowls of other delicious items in a shopping bag. He wouldn't have to buy food for a week. "I'll be proud to have a man like Jerome as my son-in-law."

Muh'Dear didn't have to go into detail, but I knew what she meant. By Jerome being so light-skinned and having all that curly hair on his head, there was a good chance he'd produce kids who looked like him. In my opinion, Black folks had come a long way by the 1980's, but light skin and straight or curly hair still carried a lot of weight. I tried not to let that bother me, especially since I considered myself beyond things that shallow. Rhoda Nelson, who was as dark as I was and the most beautiful Black woman Richland had ever seen, had influenced my perceptions to the point where I would never covet light skin and straight hair again.

Yet and still, I was glad to be seen with a man who looked like Jerome. However, I would have considered him gorgeous no matter what shade he was. Despite what I thought of myself, he thought I was beautiful, too. And he was proud of me. I realized that when he took me to a barbecue at his mother's house six months after our first date. It was the Memorial Day weekend.

Ordinarily, I would have spent the day with Muh'Dear and Daddy King, like I did every other holiday. But gatherings at my mother's house always included Scary Mary, who worked at being a busybody in three shifts and Pee Wee—if he was between girlfriends. The last thing I needed was to have Scary Mary clown me about Jerome in front of Pee Wee. I had eagerly accepted Jerome's invitation to his mother's barbecue.

Almost every woman at the gathering at Jerome's mother's house was just as big as I was, if not bigger. When too many of us walked through the living room at the same time, the pictures on the wall shook and everybody thought that was funny. I did, too. It was like these women celebrated being large and I considered that a good thing. It made me feel better about myself. I held my own head just a little bit higher that day.

It didn't take long for me to realize that I was the only dark-skinned woman present and I was the only one wearing my hair in braids. I had always hated my short, brittle hair. The best thing I could do for it was to hide it. I didn't like wigs, so having my hairdresser add extensions to my hair and braid it seemed like the next best thing. Besides, braids made me look younger. And at my age, every year I could conceal counted. Looking younger made me feel like I had just that much more time left to work with.

Jerome's two older brothers, both even lighter than Jerome,

had wives who were one shade away from being white. Jerome's younger sister Nadine and his mother Marlene were both about the same shade as Jerome. It didn't take me long to start feeling uncomfortable. Jerome's sister Nadine had been in a lot of my classes at Richland High, but we'd never really associated with one another back then. However, today she was the only one of the females present who really seemed to enjoy my presence.

"I hope you have a good time, Annette. My brother is crazy about you and he couldn't wait to bring you over to meet the family," Nadine told me. She laughed and shook her head. Looking at her up close for the first time, I realized she wasn't as pretty as I thought. For one thing, one of her eyes twitched and the eyeball inadvertently rolled to the side every few seconds. That crawling eye was bad enough, but there was a purple birthmark as big as a quarter on the side of her mouth. Her lips were so thin, there was more lipstick on her teeth than there was on her lips. Her reddish-brown hair was thinner than mine. In fact, I saw several bald spots that she had tried to hide with a black headband. In her case, having light skin was a blessing. She had been popular in school because of that alone. "Some of the family members are pretty remote." Nadine sighed, rolling both eyes, but each one in a different direction.

I smiled. "That's okay. I'm pretty remote myself," I said. I liked Nadine and I planned to cultivate a friendship with her. It would be nice to have a close female friend. It was time for me to step out of the darkness of solitude that I'd been in since my Rhoda days.

I was horrified when somebody produced a camera and took a group Polaroid picture of all the women, with me in the middle. As soon as the picture finished developing, I wished that I had stayed out of it. With all those high-yellow women surrounding me, I looked like a fly in a bowl of buttermilk.

It was hotter than usual for late May that afternoon. The sun had melted a candy bar that one of Jerome's nephews had left on the picnic table in the backyard of the sprawling gray house on Pike Street.

Other than a few obligatory comments about the bright yellow sundress I had on, the other women said very little to me. I stood away from the crowd listening to the women complain about the sun and how they avoided it to keep from getting tans they didn't want.

"Well, at least the sun lightens my hair. Dark hair looks so brittle," Marlene, Jerome's mother, said, looking at my spider-like braids wrapped around my head. Marlene wore way too much makeup for a woman her age. Other than wrinkles and a few black freckles dotting her sharp nose, I didn't know what she was trying to hide. Even though her slack jaw twitched when she talked and her teeth were so big she couldn't close her mouth all the way, everybody thought she was beautiful anyway. She had a raspy voice so when she talked it sounded like she had a slight case of laryngitis. "Men love light-colored hair." She sniffed, cleared her throat, and tilted her head, patting her own bleached-blond curls. She fanned her face with her hand a lot, too. She was around Muh'Dear's age so I assumed that she was going through menopause, too. I convinced myself that it was the real reason she was so forward with me. Nevertheless, I didn't like the woman, but I would tolerate her because of Jerome. I smiled as she kept talking, looking down her nose at me out of the corner of her eye. "Annette, where are you from? The Islands? The island women look so regal and undiluted. Except those shiny-faced ones who wrap up their heads in those loud-colored scarves. Now, *they* look downright fierce."

"I was born in Florida," I said tersely.

"I never would have guessed that." Marlene lifted her eyebrows, shook her head, and gave me a hot look. "Your folks, too?"

"Yes, ma'am."

"Hmmm. I know your mama and I would have sworn that she was Creole or Cajun. Maybe even Indian." Marlene shook her head again and fanned her face so hard she groaned. "You and she look so different from one another. She must have weak genes . . ."

"She's Black as far as I know," I said firmly. "If she's mixed, she never thought it was important enough to mention. I took after my daddy. He has really strong genes, I guess."

"Oh. You're going to have some interesting-looking children." Marlene sighed, looked at Jerome, then back to me with a look of concern and pity. "Well, get up and get you some of that potato salad, child. I can see you love to eat as much as the rest of us. Tee hee."

A few minutes later, two of Jerome's male cousins arrived. To my surprise, both of them had dark-skinned girlfriends. One of the couples had a newborn baby that everybody started making a fuss over right away. The baby looked like a lemon with a face. The other couple had a dark baby—just as cute as the light one—that everybody but me ignored.

As much as I loved Jerome, I wondered if I would be able to tolerate his color-struck family. I wondered what I would do the first time one of them made a negative comment about my color. Once when I had tried to be friends with a light-skinned girl at school, she flat-out told me I could never spend the night at her house. She claimed that her mother was afraid of dark skin touching her sheets and her daddy was convinced that dark-skinned people stank up everything they touched. That same girl was known for telling lies so I didn't know whether or not to believe her. When I saw that girl one day at the shoe store with her mother, I ignored her. But Jerome's family had proven to me that they had a problem with dark skin. I knew what I was getting myself into, but having Jerome all to myself was worth it.

By the end of the afternoon, the backyard was so crowded

I couldn't keep up with Jerome. Seeing the lighter-skinned people segregated from the crowd, off to themselves, saddened me and reminded me of the old South. I couldn't wait to leave.

I used the ruse that I had to go do laundry so I'd have something clean for work the next day. Nobody protested when I excused myself. Since Jerome wanted to stay to wait for his favorite uncle to arrive, I had to go home alone.

On the bus.

CHAPTER 30

I lied to Pee Wee and told him that I'd had a wonderful time at the barbecue. He had seen me from his front room window exit the bus at the corner and had come over immediately, the soles of his well-worn house-shoes flapping. He hadn't even taken the time to button the thin shirt he had on. I had just kicked off my shoes and folded myself onto the couch when he barged in, wild-eyed and frantic.

"I'm glad you had a good time," he said with a smirk, standing in my living room with his back to the door and his hands on his hips. "I . . . I guess me and you won't be gettin' together no time soon, huh?" Pee Wee whined, patting the top of his head with his hand.

I just looked at him and blinked.

He sniffed and continued, seeming uncomfortable. "That first night I seen him slobberin' all over you on your front porch, I knew it was the end of . . . you know. That thing we do . . ."

"Oh, Pee Wee." I sighed and shook my head, unable to face Pee Wee. "That 'thing we do' was going to get old, sooner or later." I looked over at him, disappointed to see him pouting.

"I wasn't complainin'," he snapped, poking his bottom lip out like a disgruntled child, shifting his weight from one foot to the other until one of his loose house-shoes slid right off his foot.

"I do love Jerome and he loves me. Besides, I thought you and Mona Lisa McCoy had a thing going," I said, waving Pee Wee to the love seat facing me, which he ignored. With a frustrated look on his face, he shook his head, then started pacing back and forth.

"Me and Mona Lisa *had* a thing goin'," he admitted. "But, you know I always come back to you when things is slow. Shit." He returned his house-shoe to his foot and stood still, folding and unfolding his arms. Then he squatted down and rolled the cuffs on his jeans a few inches above his ankles and started shifting his weight from one foot to the other.

I rotated my neck and gasped. "That's just it. You only come to me when there is nobody else to go to. I come first with Jerome," I snapped, not sure if what I was saying was true.

Pee Wee threw his hands up in frustration and suddenly remembered an appointment he had to go to, but I knew he was lying. He didn't like where the conversation was going and neither did I. It was just as well he was leaving; I needed to be alone anyway. I had a lot of thinking to do about Jerome and where our relationship was going, now that it was serious. I hoped that Jerome was worth my sacrificing Pee Wee.

Jerome rarely mentioned Pee Wee to me, but I knew that he was not too fond of him either. Pee Wee had been Jerome's barber until Jerome found out about Pee Wee spending so much time with me. Now Jerome went to the other Black barber in Richland to get his hair cut, even though I had assured him that Pee Wee was nothing more to me than a close friend. I changed the subject whenever Pee Wee's name came up during a conversation with Jerome.

I was the only Black switchboard operator at Richland's telephone company, but that didn't bother me. It was a comfortable position and the pay was adequate. I joined the credit union and purchased my first car, a two-year-old Cougar. Unlike my old job at the Buttercup, where I had worn a conservative blue uniform and comfortable shoes, I got to dress up in nice suits, dresses, and heels as a switchboard operator.

Richland High School, where Jerome worked as a guidance counselor, was only three blocks away from the telephone company. I was able to meet Jerome for lunch several times a week. It pleased me when he came into the building to my workstation to pick me up. I wanted the women I worked with to see what a good-looking man I had. Especially after one of my female co-workers had tried to fix me up with the frog-eyed brother that delivered our office supplies.

Jerome knew every cheap restaurant in town and he had a fistful of coupons for every single one. I didn't mind, because when I ate lunch alone, it was usually at Antonosanti's, a block from my work. Once when I told Jerome that I had spent twelve dollars on lunch at Antonosanti's, it brought tears to his eyes.

The Monday after attending another gathering at Jerome's mother's house, Jerome met me for lunch in the telephone company parking lot. Sitting in his car, we shared watercress sandwiches and some of the drab potato salad left over from the barbecue. He had also brought along a Thermos full of ice water that he shared with me.

Cramps forced me to leave work early that day. There was a message on my answering machine from Daddy. All he had said was, "Call me."

I called Daddy back immediately and it was the same brief conversation we always had. He gave me an update on

his declining health and bragged about a deer he had shot
and put in his freezer. For the first time in months, he asked
when I was coming to see him.

"I'm at a new job and I can't take a vacation for a year," I
told him.

"Well, what if I come see you?" he bleated, unable to hide
his disappointment.

"Uh . . . that would be nice, Daddy. But Muh'Dear is still
mad at you, you know."

"For what?" he cried plaintively.

"Daddy, you ran out on us," I reminded.

"I ain't the first man to run out on no woman—"

"You're the first man to run out on us," I reminded. "Anyway, I think Muh'Dear's beginning to come around, though.
She doesn't cuss as much as she used to whenever your
name came up." I sniffed and held my breath.

"Well, I hope she don't take too much longer now. Ain't
none of us gettin' no younger."

A few times when I called Daddy's number, my half-sister
Lillimae answered the telephone. We didn't have much to
say to one another but like Daddy, she wanted me to come
for a visit. I didn't know how much longer I could hold them
off, but I knew that Muh'Dear was still as adamant as ever
about me not seeing my daddy.

Three more years passed by and Muh'Dear's feelings toward Daddy remained the same. My calls and letters to and
from Daddy got less frequent, but I wanted to see him more
than ever now and I planned to.

Whether Muh'Dear liked it or not.

CHAPTER 31

Jerome asked me to marry him on my thirty-fifth birthday, just when I was about ready to give up on ever landing a husband. And he did it in front of Muh'Dear and Daddy King. It was over dinner in the ornate dining room in the red brick house that Muh'Dear shared with Daddy King on Cherry Street, three blocks from the town square.

Before I could reply, Muh'Dear said jokingly, "And she better accept your proposal, if she know what's good for her." Muh'Dear waved her butter knife at me and added, "Girl, with a fancy man like Jerome, it'd be pie-in-the-sky every day."

Wearing a blue cashmere sweater that I had given him for his birthday and black slacks, Jerome dipped his head and gave me a guarded look. "Well?" he asked, one eyebrow raised.

I had just stuffed my mouth full of lemon pound cake. I had to finish chewing and swallowing first. I was lucky that I could eat whatever I wanted and not worry about gaining weight. But since I was already a size twenty-four, that wasn't saying much. I had the nerve to have on a green see-through blouse and a black skirt with a split on one side, revealing my massive thigh. Jerome insisted I wear "sexy" outfits when we went out together, even if it was just to have dinner at my mother's house. One thing I had to say about the man was, he gave me the confidence I needed to feel better about the way I looked. Just the day before, I had worn a pair of short shorts for the first time in my life when Jerome took me to a pool party. Since it was August, and the temperature was in the low nineties, I didn't have to wear a coat or a sweater to Muh'Dear's house. But a chill went through me and my heart started beating so hard I had to shift in my seat.

"I guess so," I replied, wondering why I was feeling so uncertain about marrying Jerome. I knew he loved me and I *thought* I loved him. But something was missing from our relationship and I didn't know what it was. And that scared me. The last thing I wanted to do was make another mistake, marrying the wrong man.

Jerome tilted his head and gasped, his eyes stretched wide open. "You *guess?*" With a dry laugh, he grabbed his cloth napkin and used it to snap the side of my head. Then he used that same napkin to wipe crumbs off my lips before he kissed me. "I guess I'll keep you anyway."

"Annette, it don't sound like you too happy about landin' a man like Jerome," Daddy King teased. "If I was you, I'd be so happy I'd be dancin' up and down the street naked."

My stepfather looked tired and he was really beginning to show his age. I was so sorry that I had wasted the first few months of him in our lives, treating him like shit. Now, whenever he called, I dropped whatever I was doing to go to him. The Friday before, while Muh'Dear was on a shopping expedition with Scary Mary in Cleveland, Daddy King crawled to the telephone and called me at work to tell me that he had fallen down the steps in his house and couldn't get up. I ran out of my workstation like a bat out of hell to go to him. I stayed with him until Muh'Dear returned.

I reached across the table and touched my stepfather's liver-spotted hand and squeezed it. "Oh, Daddy King, you stop that. Me naked in public would really draw a lot of attention," I laughed. I took a deep breath and said seriously, "I am happy. I really am." I leaned to my side where Jerome was seated and kissed him on the mouth. His kisses were just as lame as his lovemaking. It was like kissing a fish. As a matter of fact, when he spent the night with me, he slept on his back with his mouth open and really did look like a fish when he was asleep. When he woke up in the mornings, he had the breath to match. I didn't like what I was thinking about the man I loved. I guess it was because I'd always thought of relationships between lovers as being full of passion and excitement. I had to keep reminding myself that Jerome had a lot of other admirable qualities. And, if it had taken me thirty-five years to find Jerome, how many more years would it take for me to find a man I liked better?

"Y'all hurry up and make some pretty grandchildren for me to spoil. Hear me?" Muh'Dear sniffed and blinked back a tear that was threatening to slide out of her eye.

"We will," I told her. I had to wonder if she would love a dark-skinned grandchild as much as she would love one with light skin. I already knew how Jerome's family would treat a dark, homely baby. I scolded myself for allowing such a thought to enter my brain about Muh'Dear. I knew my own mother well enough to know that she would love a child of mine no matter what it looked like. Her love for me proved that.

Muh'Dear and Daddy King were the only Black folks living on their block. Every time Jerome and I went to visit, the neighbors peeped out of their windows when we arrived and when we left. It didn't bother me, but Jerome couldn't deal with it. This particular night as we were leaving, he gave a nosy, redheaded woman in her window the finger before we got into his car.

I was horrified. "Jerome, what in the world is the matter with you? Stop acting like you were raised in the ghetto. A lot of white folks already think that about most of us anyway."

"I can't stand these racist assholes spying on me like I'm going to steal something. Peckerwoods don't have a damn thing I would want," he snarled, glaring at another woman's face that had suddenly appeared in her window.

"Some people can't get past the color of some folks' skin," I said tiredly, looking at Jerome out of the corner of my eye. I wondered about people like Jerome's color-struck family. Was it possible that people like them were oblivious to their own color-conscious condition? They must have been, because Jerome totally missed the point of what I had just said.

"We all belong to the same race. The human race. The sooner white folks get that in their heads, the better off the world will be," Jerome snorted, snatching his car door open.

He cursed white people all the way back to my house.

Two days after the dinner at Muh'Dear's house, while I was at work, my stepfather fell down his stairs again. This time he had a heart attack, too. I was so thankful that Muh'Dear was in the house with him when it happened. She was frantic when she called me. "Your daddy needs you! He done had a heart attack and he might not make it!" she screamed into the telephone. At first, I thought she meant my real daddy.

"You talked to Daddy? My daddy is dying?" I yelled. I

thought I was going to have a heart attack myself, thinking that I had waited too long to go see my daddy and that now it might be too late.

I froze and dropped the telephone.

CHAPTER 32

After I composed myself, I picked up the telephone and glared at it like it was a hand grenade. My head was pounding, I could barely breathe and my eyes felt like they wanted to roll down the front of my face. Out of the corner of my eye, I could see a few of my co-workers staring at me. My supervisor, a busybody rail-thin woman named Mrs. Kraft, came out of nowhere and stood so close to me I could smell the bourbon she'd just drunk with her lunch.

Even before I could put the telephone back up to my ear, I could hear Muh'Dear yelling, "I'm talkin' about Mr. King, girl! The ambulance is on the way! Meet us at the hospital!" Muh'Dear started crying and praying at the same time. And so did I.

I was way too upset to drive. Mrs. Kraft offered to take me to the hospital after I told her that there was an emergency involving my stepfather. Just from that, she assumed the worst. "I hope he wasn't drinking," she said smugly. I didn't even respond to her comment. I declined her offer and asked her to call me a cab. I didn't want her to see me fall completely apart. Mrs. Kraft was the nosy kind of woman who liked to soak up all of your personal business and spread it around the office. The last thing I wanted her to know was that I couldn't control my emotions.

While I was struggling to get into my coat, Mrs. Kraft called me a cab and she called up Jerome. Then she escorted me to the telephone company exit. Holding onto my thick wrist with her bony white fingers, she looped the strap of my shoulder purse around my neck like a noose with her other hand. In a concerned tone, she told me, "Jerome'll meet you at the hospital. I pulled him out of an important staff meeting, but he said you was much more important."

"I'll call you when I can," I told Mrs. Kraft in a hoarse whisper. She stood outside on the sidewalk with me with her arm around my shoulder, trying to find out more about my personal life, until the cab arrived.

Even from his hospital bed, my beloved stepfather managed to keep his spirits up, drinking weak tea and telling weak jokes.

"If I'd known I was goin' to live this long, I would have taken better care of my body," he laughed. There was a faint rattling noise coming from him with each breath he took. It gave me a chill.

It was impossible for me not to think about my real daddy whenever I was around Daddy King. I didn't know which one I loved the most. I had often wished that it had been Daddy King who had moved in with us instead of Mr. Boatwright. Daddy King was such a wonderful man. Other than an estranged brother in Oregon, Muh'Dear and I were the only family he had left.

"Well, you'd better start takin' better care of that body now before God takes it back," Muh'Dear said firmly, adjusting the three pillows she had propped Daddy King up on.

It pleased me to see my mother so happy. Other than grandchildren, she had everything else she had ever wanted. Even a few trips to the Bahamas. In addition to the beautiful house she shared with Daddy King and the restaurant they owned, she also owned the house that I occupied on Reed Street. Old Mr. Lawson, whose mansion she had cleaned for so many years, had left the house on Reed Street to her when he died shortly after my return from Pennsylvania. She let me live in it rent-free. Jerome didn't have to tell me, but I knew that he was planning to suggest that we live in that house after we were married. There was no way the man was going to pass up a deal like that.

"Jerome, you a smart man. You don't stuff yourself with all that grease and meat like the rest of us do. Once you marry this girl, you make her start eatin' better. She don't want to end up on her back, too, like Albert here. Life is too short and gettin' shorter as we stand here," Muh'Dear said, blinking her eyes rapidly, trying to hold back her tears.

When a nurse came to bathe Daddy King, Muh'Dear, Jerome, and I went down to the hospital cafeteria to try and eat something.

"I can't believe these people have the nerve to charge four dollars for these sorry-ass sandwiches," Jerome complained about the cheese sandwich he had ordered. "Fo' dollars, y'all," he drawled in an exaggerated southern accent.

"Don't worry. It's on me," Muh'Dear said quickly, already reaching for her wallet.

"Hmmm. I guess I should go on and get a Coke and a salad, too. And a piece of that pound cake. Brother King didn't look too good so we might be here for a while," Jerome decided. When he wasn't looking, Muh'Dear looked at me and shrugged.

After Muh'Dear made a big fuss over the engagement ring that Jerome had given me, one he had retrieved from a former fiancée, we ate in silence.

Being inside the hospital gave me a bad feeling. It brought back the painful memories of the dark days I'd spent lying on the second floor recovering from my abortion. Naturally,

I was uneasy and nervous. Seeing all those doctors rushing around with the tails of their smocks flapping and their hard-soled shoes clip-clopping on the marble floors was disturbing. The conversations I overheard made it even harder for me. At a table a few feet from us were three stern-faced nurses talking about a baby that had just died. The most unsettling thing I overheard was from another table of nurses: a rape victim had just been brought in. I couldn't eat after hearing that.

"Let's go check on Daddy King," I suggested, pushing my tray off to the side.

Muh'Dear and Jerome looked at one another, then to me with puzzled expressions on their faces.

"We can't leave all this good food here," Jerome whined, taking another bite from his sandwich.

"We'll take it with us," I said sharply, rising.

Muh'Dear and I left our half-eaten sandwiches on our plates, but I wrapped Jerome's and stuffed it in my purse.

I noticed something odd right away when we returned to my stepfather's room. A small vase of fresh flowers that Muh'Dear had brought and set on the windowsill had already started wilting. They had been nice and perky when we left the room, less than an hour before.

I made it to Daddy King's bedside first. He was lying on his back with his eyes stretched wide open. I set my purse down at the foot of the bed and I felt Daddy King's pulse. Then I dropped my head. I closed his eyes with my fingers and turned to Muh'Dear and Jerome standing behind me looking as grim as pallbearers.

"He's gone," I said.

CHAPTER 33

I wished that I had not touched Daddy King before we left him in that hospital bed. No matter how many times I washed my hand, it wouldn't stop itching.

I had not seen Muh'Dear so upset since Mr. Boatwright died. "Why do all the special men in our lives leave us?" Muh'Dear wailed, staring at a framed picture on her living room mantel over her fireplace of Mr. Boatwright grinning like a clown.

I didn't have an answer for her, so I kept quiet. I didn't know at the time, but that sorry picture of Mr. Boatwright that she cherished so much would end up in that same fireplace in flames. And Muh'Dear would be the one to put it there.

The same heart attack that killed Daddy King almost killed my mother, too. I had to send for her doctor to come to the house and tranquilize her. She took to her bed and refused to eat. Just like she had done when Daddy left us. Losing a loved one was a very difficult thing for my mother. She didn't want me out of her sight. I spent the night my stepfather died with Muh'Dear.

"Baby, your mother needs all the support we can give her. Let me know if there is anything I can do," Jerome told me when he called.

That evening Jerome came to the house with Scary Mary in tow. The next day they helped me make all the funeral arrangements and Jerome even volunteered to be one of the pallbearers. He stunned me by offering to pay for all the flowers. However, he looked relieved when I told him that I had already taken care of that expense.

Scary Mary wanted to sing the same two songs at Daddy King's funeral that she had sung at Mr. Boatwright's: "Let The Work He Done Speak For Him" and "I Been In The Storm Too Long." She arranged for one of her regular tricks, an albino man, to accompany her on the piano.

The same prostitute who had washed and straightened my hair during my childhood came over to wash and press Muh'Dear's hair. Muh'Dear was too weak to get out of bed to go to the beauty salon like she usually did once a week. That same prostitute also offered to go to the funeral home to wash and press Daddy King's hair, but I refused to let her put powder on his face and rouge on his cheeks. Daddy King had been too dignified a man to go to his grave looking like he was going to a Halloween party.

Running a whorehouse and being involved in God knows what other illegal activities kept Scary Mary busy. But that woman still got around like a Gypsy and she always had time for Muh'Dear and me. Being in her late seventies had not slowed Scary Mary down one bit. There were rumors floating around town that she occasionally turned tricks herself with some of her long-time customers.

"I heard that that old battle-ax can give some damn good head." It was just like Pee Wee to try and make me laugh and he succeeded. But I was too upset about my stepfather so I didn't laugh much.

Scary Mary, with a shot glass full of Jack Daniels in her

hand, kept giving Pee Wee and me dirty looks as we stood off in a corner in Muh'Dear's living room whispering the day before the funeral.

Scary Mary paused, took a sip, and belched. "Girl, you all your mama got left now. And you better look after her," the old madam told me, as she ran the vacuum cleaner over the plush maroon carpet Muh'Dear had just purchased a week ago. Muh'Dear was upstairs in her bed in a near catatonic state.

"Yes, ma'am," I whimpered.

Daddy King had had a lot of friends. We expected a huge crowd of mourners so the house had to look its best. I was grateful to have Scary Mary around doing most of the work.

"Once you lose your mama, you ain't gwine to look at life the same no more. Mama and Daddy is the next best thing to God," Scary Mary added, shaking a finger at me.

"I still got my daddy," I said, waving a dust rag. "And I love him just as much as I love my mama."

"Then you need to make him know it! After all this time, you ain't been down there to Florida to see him!" Scary Mary hollered suddenly. Just as suddenly, her voice softened and she smiled. "Pee Wee, scat into the kitchen and get me that dust broom. Annette, go reach in the liquor cabinet and bring me that bottle again. I need me another highball." Pee Wee left the room with an exasperated look on his face and returned with the broom.

"I didn't want to upset Muh'Dear," I announced, handing Scary Mary the whiskey bottle. She snatched it and refilled her glass. It amazed me how Black folks always found a reason to turn to the bottle, myself included. I had already swallowed a few glasses of wine myself that morning. The slight buzz I had, had calmed my nerves. But I couldn't wait for the funeral to be over with.

"Girl, that ain't no excuse. If I had done everything my mama wanted me to do, I wouldn't be where I'm at today. I'd still be supervisin' that chain gang in Mississippi or helpin' the military make bombs for a livin'. Behold and praise God that I don't have to do no low-level jobs like that no more," Scary Mary said with a frown, frantically dragging the broom across the carpet, concentrating on the same spot.

Two days after Daddy King's funeral, I told Jerome that I was going to visit my daddy in Florida. He supported me one hundred percent.

"You want me to go with you, baby?" Jerome was anxious to meet his future father-in-law despite all the mean things Muh'Dear had told him about Daddy. Jerome had a lot of his things in my house that he had brought over, a few items at a time. He had on a gray cotton bathrobe and a pair of loose-fitting house-shoes that day. It was a few minutes before noon and we had just crawled out of my bed. "It might be too hard on you so soon after Brother King's passing. I will go with you."

"Not this time. I need some time alone with Daddy first," I told Jerome.

I was a little annoyed at the way Jerome kept looking at my body, even though I was covered in a floor-length bathrobe. He had already fondled me a few times that day. As a matter of fact, when we were alone, he could barely keep his hands off me. But this was one time I was not interested in sex or anybody touching me. After being in Mr. Boatwright's grip for so long, I was finally the one in control of my own body. I utilized that power every chance I got. I slapped Jerome's hand and pushed him away.

"Uh, you can go on home now. I really want to be alone right now," I said.

Jerome nodded and got into his street clothes, but he fondled me for a few minutes before he left.

Right after I sent Jerome home, I went over to Muh'Dear's house. The front door was open and I found her in her bedroom, still wearing the muslin gown she had slept in the night before. She was packing Daddy King's clothes in cardboard boxes for the Salvation Army to pick up. I blinked to hold back my tears because the scene reminded me of the day Rhoda and I had packed up Mr. Boatwright's things when he died.

"Daddy's not well and I want to see him before it's too late," I said firmly. I held my breath because I didn't know how Muh'Dear was going to react.

At first, I didn't think she heard me, because she kept her head down and continued folding Daddy King's clothes. After about a minute, she sat down on the edge of her bed and let out a deep sigh, her eyes looking at the floor. Then she looked at me with a mournful look on her face.

"I'm surprised Frank is still alive with the hog-high blood pressure he had ever since I first met him. And with all the politickin' he involved hisself with, I always thought he'd spend his last day swingin' by the neck from a sumac tree or gettin' barbecued at the stake at one of them Klan rallies." Muh'Dear paused and shook her head. Even though she had just got her hair done a few days before, she had already sweated out most of her curls. Her eyes were red and swollen and without makeup, she looked ten years older. "That Frank. He was such a strong brother," she said, speaking in a voice so soft I could barely hear her. Suddenly, her voice got loud and took on a sinister tone. "What a shame it was for him to be subdued by a white woman." Her eyes got big and her jaw twitched. She sniffed and narrowed her eyes at me and said gently, "So, you *still* want to see Frank, huh?"

I nodded. "He's *still* my daddy. I've already made a plane reservation," I said hotly, folding my arms.

"What Jerome got to say about this?" Muh'Dear blinked several times. And a faint but brief smile appeared on her face.

"He thinks I should have gone down to Florida long before now. Scary Mary feels the same way," I replied, unfolding my arms. I didn't like being in the same room that Daddy King had occupied. I could still feel his warmth and it made me uneasy because I had loved him so much.

Muh'Dear sighed tiredly and rubbed the back of her neck. "Well, leave a key to the house with me so I can water your plants." Muh'Dear shrugged and finished packing Daddy King's things. Then she gave me a big smile and a big hug. "All I want in this world is for you to be happy. Go see your daddy."

I went home to pack for my trip to Miami.

CHAPTER 34

With the exception of Lillimae's mother's funeral, I had enjoyed the few days I spent in Florida. But I was glad when I returned to Richland. Muh'Dear and Jerome were glad to have me back to themselves.

Jerome wanted to get married the week of Christmas.

"We can celebrate Christmas and our anniversary at the same time every year," he told me. He had picked me up from the airport in Akron and decided to spend the night with me. We had just finished another dull romp in bed, with him flopping around on top of me like a seal, trying to arouse me with his fingers and tongue. As usual, he had ejaculated way too soon, but I was used to that by now. "Was it good, baby?" he muttered in my ear. "Tell me it was good."

"It was good," I said dryly. I had just faked my second orgasm that night. I had not experienced the real thing since my last rendezvous with Pee Wee.

Jerome didn't have to tell me, but I already knew that our celebrating two important days of the year at the same time would save him even more money. I agreed to get married on Christmas Day of that year.

The closest friend that I had at work my age, a secretary named Jean Teresa Caruso, hosted a wedding shower for me that first week in December. Jean had recently moved into a house two doors down from me and we took turns driving each other to work. Jean was so nice and persistent, I couldn't turn down her offers to go shopping and out to dinner. She was divorced and had a six-year-old daughter named Piatra, that we called P. She was going to be my flower girl. It was going to be a small wedding with just a few friends from work and church. With Scary Mary as my maid of honor, I couldn't wait to get it over with. With great reluctance, Pee Wee had agreed to give me away. My upcoming marriage symbolized another new beginning for me as well as another ending. Because of it, my relationship with Pee Wee would never be the same again. Now we really would be like brother and sister and that was all. Even though our relationship had been pretty much that anyway since I'd met Jerome, I fiercely missed Pee Wee's lovemaking.

"You think it's fittin' to have a white girl in your weddin' with so many little colored girls around here?" Muh'Dear whispered. She still liked to whisper when she talked about white people with me. Especially over the telephone, like now. "What about one of Deacon Brewsters six granddaughters?"

"This is not about color and it is *my* wedding. Besides, I promised P. she could be my flower girl and she's really looking forward to it," I whispered back.

P. was a cute, plump little Italian girl with long, curly brown hair and big, beautiful brown eyes, but she was particularly quiet for a child her age.

She reminded me of myself when I was her age. Like I did when I was a child, P. seemed to enjoy the company of grown folks more than she did kids. I didn't mind babysitting her when Jean wanted to go out and I did it for free because I liked P.'s company. When P. came to my house we usually made cookies, watched cartoons, and I read children's stories to her. But what she enjoyed most was going to the mall or the movies.

A few days after my bridal shower, a Saturday afternoon, P. stumbled up on my front porch and started pounding on my door. Jerome had just called and wanted to come over. I agreed, only if he would take me to the movies that night to see *The Color Purple*. It was not playing at either of Richland's only two movie theaters yet, but it was playing in Canton, a twenty-minute drive from Richland. Jerome had compromised and agreed to take me to the movies only if we could go to a matinee and get in for half-price. I had opened the door expecting to see him.

"Oh, P., you can't come in today. I'm waiting for my boyfriend and we're going out," I explained, looking over P.'s bare head, hoping to see Jerome's car. P.'s coat was unbuttoned, she didn't have on her snow boots, and her cap was in her hand.

"Can't I come, too?" she asked in a trembling voice.

I shook my head. I didn't like the downside of having a close relationship with this child. I had allowed and encouraged P. to expect too much from me.

"Please, Annette," she begged, tugging at the tail of my blouse.

I laughed dryly. "I'm going out on a date with my boyfriend. I don't think he would like to have two girlfriends. Wouldn't you rather spend the day with your mama?" There were not that many children in our neighborhood close to P.'s age. And most of the ones that were, were boys. Even though P. liked to play with boys, she still preferred to spend most of her time with adults.

P. dropped her head and started shifting her weight from one foot to the other.

"I don't like it at home no more," she told me, looking up at me with tears in her eyes. "It's . . . bad."

I was already cold standing in the doorway without my

coat, but P.'s words and demeanor suddenly made me feel even colder. I chose to ignore some thoughts that had popped up in my head.

"Uh . . . we can go to the mall tomorrow," I suggested.

"I don't want to go tomorrow. I want to go today!" P. said sharply, stomping her foot, poking out her bottom lip.

Any other adult would have scolded the girl and sent her home, but I stood there for five minutes arguing with a child. I probably would have stood there longer than that if the telephone on my living room end table had not rung.

It was Jerome and he was canceling our date.

"Sister Hawthorne slipped on some ice and sprained her ankle so she can't take Mama to play bingo today," Jerome explained, talking in a low voice. I could hear his bothersome mother mumbling in the background. "Mama said if she wins, she'll owe it all to you."

"I didn't even know your mama played bingo," I said stiffly, curling the telephone cord around my finger. I heard my front door close. I turned around and P. was strolling across the floor with that same pout on her face. She stopped right in front of me, staring at my face with eyes that looked like they belonged on a puppy.

"Yeah. Mama's been playing bingo for years." In a whisper Jerome added, "You know how old folks can be. They can be just like kids when they want something. They don't stop 'til they get their way."

"Jerome, I know just what you mean." I sighed and rubbed the top of P.'s head. "Call me later on . . . if you can," I said in defeat.

Now that Jerome was not going to come over, I had a lot of free time on my hands. I took P. with me to the mall to exchange a see-through negligee that Jean had given me for a flannel bathrobe.

After P. and I spent an hour window-shopping and admiring the Christmas displays, she started whining to go to the toy store on the other side of the mall. It took me ten minutes to talk her out of that notion and that was only after I promised her that Santa Claus was going to bring her enough toys for Christmas. It was true in a way. I had already purchased and wrapped for her every one of the same toys that she wanted to go look at. She had a slight cold and looked so peaked I felt sorry for her so I compromised by taking her for pizza instead.

"That's your third slice now. Finish that and let's go," I told P. as we shared a booth in Francisco's Pizza Parlor across from Ernie's Record Store. There was loud disco music coming out of the record store and flashing colored lights from a strobe on a card table right outside the entrance. My trip to the mall usually included a visit to Ernie's, which is where I planned to go after the pizza. I needed to replace several Bob Marley tapes that Pee Wee had borrowed and not returned and I wanted to buy a few new ones as Christmas gifts for Pee Wee, Jerome, and his family. As snooty as Jerome's mother was, she had a passion for reggae music and had even told me which tapes she wanted.

"I don't want your mama mad at me for spoiling your appetite for dinner," I added, wiping sauce and root beer from P.'s chin with a napkin.

"Oh, she don't care how much I eat. She let me have some Gummy Bears this morning," P. told me, talking and chewing at the same time. "And some cherry pop."

"Well, I'm not your mama and I don't think you should be overdoing it," I said firmly, wishing my mother had curtailed my eating habits when I was a child. I couldn't count the thick biscuits and pork chops my mother had charmed me with to keep me happy. According to Muh'Dear, she had breast-fed me and had weaned me off of her milk with pork sausages before I was a year old. Thirty-five years later and I was still sucking on pork sausages, two and three at a time, every chance I got.

Even though it was the middle of winter and we had just had one of the severe snowstorms that Ohio was famous for, the mall was so warm inside I had removed my heavy wool coat and rolled up the sleeves of my thick angora sweater. When I got up to go get more napkins to wipe sweat off of my face, I casually glanced out of the window and noticed something that made me almost lose the five slices of pizza I had consumed. Prancing like a reindeer out of the record store was a petite Black woman wearing a navy blue jump-suit and high-heeled, black leather boots. She was holding a black leather coat in one hand and a shopping bag in the other. There was a proud look about her. She held her head high and her shoulders back. Her silver hoop earrings sparkled like diamonds.

My tongue felt like a big rock threatening to slide down my throat. For a moment, I knew what it was like to be para-lyzed. I couldn't move and I couldn't speak. All I could do was stare and blink my eyes.

I was looking at Rhoda, the woman who had killed the man who had raped me throughout my childhood.

CHAPTER 35

W hen I was able to move again, I grabbed a wad of napkins and almost knocked three other patrons down trying to get back to my booth so fast. I sat down so hard, a sharp pain rolled through my stomach.

"I'm almost finished," P. told me, coughing and gobbling up another slice of the pizza, spilling soda on the table.

"Take . . . take your time," I said nervously, using the napkins I had just picked up to wipe off the table instead of the sweat sliding down the sides of my face. I beckoned for the waiter and ordered another pizza and a half-carafe of white wine.

"What's wrong, Annette?" P. asked, giving me a puzzled look. "Did you want that last slice of pizza?"

"Uh . . . no. You go on and eat it. I'll eat some of the next one. I . . . I just thought about something that made me nervous," I replied, looking toward the door.

"You look so funny now," P. stated, looking at me with her eyes blinking rapidly. "You sick?"

"I'm fine. Just be still!" I snapped.

The waiter delivered another pizza and the wine. I ignored the pizza, but I poured myself a glass of wine so fast, I spilled most of it on the table. I couldn't get some in me fast enough. I didn't stop drinking until it was all gone. P. gobbled up as much of the second pizza as she could by herself, eating so fast she almost gagged.

"You can slow down. I don't want any more pizza," I told her, belching so hard my chest felt like it was going to explode.

Chewing frantically, a frown appeared on P.'s face and she pushed the pizza away.

"I don't feel so good now," she complained, rubbing her stomach.

I didn't feel so good myself and I felt even worse knowing that I had allowed P. to overindulge herself.

"We'll sit here for a little while," I offered. "Then we'll both feel better."

Now that I was tipsy from drinking the whole container of wine by myself, I was afraid to drive. I was also afraid to go back out into the mall. The last thing I wanted to do was face Rhoda Nelson again. Especially this close to Christmas and my wedding.

There was a back door out of the pizza parlor. It was for the use of employees only and there was a big sign above the door that said just that. But I wasn't going to let it stop us from leaving that way. I slid into my coat, snatched up my package from the lingerie store, and turned to P. "Quick— follow me and run like hell!" A stunned teenage employee walking toward us just looked and shook his head as P. and I rushed toward the back door, flung it open, and fled. P. seemed to be enjoying our unplanned escapade and ran along with me, giggling until we reached my car.

"How come you didn't want to pay?" P. asked, trying to catch her breath as she fastened her seat belt.

"What?" I hollered, tossing my package into the back-seat.

P. sniffed, rubbed her nose, and looked over at me as I secured my seat belt around my heaving chest. My heart was beating so hard, I thought I was going to have a heart attack.

"You didn't pay for the pizza and stuff," P. said with a devilish look on her face.

"Oh, shoot!" I smacked the steering wheel and gritted my teeth. "Well, we'll just have to pay double the next time we go there for pizza," I offered, speaking more to myself than to the confused child on the seat next to me. I didn't know when I'd go back to that mall again. But knowing that I might run into Rhoda there, I knew it wouldn't be anytime soon.

I knew I couldn't drive until the buzz had worked its way through my head. So P. and I tumbled out of my car and walked across the parking lot and spent the next two hours in a hardware store across the street from the mall.

"Now, we can't leave until I find something to give to my boyfriend for Christmas," I told P., praying more for Rhoda not to come into this store than I was for the employees at the pizza parlor not to track me down.

Jean wasn't home when I attempted to drop P. off, so I took her home with me and I was glad that I did. She kept me so busy wrapping Christmas presents that I didn't have time to think much about Rhoda.

About an hour later, Jean called and told me to send P. home.

"I don't want to go home. I want to spend the night with you," P. insisted, almost in tears.

"No, you have to go home now," I said sternly. "It's Christmastime and you should be spending more time with your own family."

With a profound scowl, P. put on her coat with so much reluctance that she put it on inside out.

As I was walking P. to her house, I advised her not to tell her mother that I'd allowed her to eat so much at the mall pizza parlor and that we had left without paying for our orders.

"You can keep all of that a secret, can't you?" I asked, leading the girl down the street by her hand.

P. was taking too long to respond.

"P., did you hear me?"

"I heard you," she replied weakly. "I can keep a secret."

I stood outside on the sidewalk in front of Jean's house until P. made it inside, dragging her feet and looking back at me with a hopeless look on her face. It had started to snow again so my vision was obscured. For a moment, I just stood there blinking at the big, green-shingled house that Jean occupied. Jean and P. had painted pictures of elves and fairies on the wall of their front porch. The place reminded me of a big, sad dollhouse. A light came on upstairs and P.'s face appeared in a window. She stayed there until I left.

Alone in my house again, I was still so occupied with other things—cleaning up the mess in the kitchen, watching television, and hand washing a few pairs of my panties—that I didn't think much about Rhoda. But when I went to bed, Rhoda was all I could think about. It had been close to around this same time of the year when I'd last seen or talked to her.

I had thought about her often over the years. Naturally, I did it more around this time of the year. I knew that her family had moved away, and as far as I knew, she never came to Richland to visit anybody so I couldn't come up with a reason for her to be back in Richland now. Hours later, I was still tossing and turning, almost falling out of my bed thinking about Rhoda. I kept telling myself that I had mistaken some other woman for her. There were a couple of other petite, young Black women in town who resembled Rhoda from a distance . . .

When I got up the next morning, I had convinced myself that I had not seen Rhoda.

But I was wrong.

CHAPTER 36

Two days after my visit to the mall, Jerome and I went to the Red Rose nightclub to hear a jazz band from Cleveland that somebody had told him about. Jeffrey Rose, the nightclub owner's nephew, sang with the band and the club was anxious to give the boy some exposure. I should have known that there were other reasons for Jerome to want to go out and spend money when he didn't have to. I found that out before we even left my house.

"I won a raffle down at the office. Buy one drink, get one free. And all the free buffalo wings you can eat," Jerome confessed with a grin so extreme it almost divided his face. "If we eat enough, you won't even have to cook dinner tonight."

Another snowstorm had hit Richland earlier that day. Snow was still coming down like curtains. Most people had the good sense to stay home that night. Even though Jerome had snow tires on his car, the car skidded so much on the icy streets that I was a nervous wreck by the time we got to the Red Rose. And I didn't try to hide it.

"I'd feel better if we had walked over here," I complained,

gripping Jerome's arm as we stumbled, slipped, and slid across the parking lot.

"Not in all this shit," he snapped, snow covering his bare head like a white cap.

I had a scarf on my head and a muffler around my neck. But snowflakes the size of quarters all but covered my face. My cheeks and eyes burned from the cold wind that was howling at us like a wolf. Being so fair-skinned, Jerome's normally yellow-toned face now looked bright orange. His nose was almost blue.

"Old Mr. Boatwright used to walk over here from our house in the snow, at night, two and three times a week. And he didn't have but one leg," I said with my teeth clicking and my hands feeling numb even though I had on thick gloves. I was more disgusted with myself than I was with Jerome. I couldn't believe that I had let him woo me out into this miserable weather just because he had won a raffle to get some free drinks.

"Well, I am not old Mr. Boatwright," Jerome growled, snatching open the heavy metal door leading into the tiny bar with its postage-stamp-size tables. "And that's probably why he's residing at the cemetery now." Jerome's teeth were clicking just as hard as mine.

We were the only two patrons in the dimly lit Red Rose for the first hour after the band started playing. And it was a wretched band at that. The sax player was trying to play and smoke at the same time, the guy on the keyboard played off-key, and Mr. Rose's poor young nephew couldn't carry a tune in a bucket. I felt sorry and amused at the same time.

Jerome was in heaven. So far he had only had to buy one drink. One of the band members covered our next two rounds. And the waitress couldn't bring more buffalo wings to our table fast enough for Jerome.

The Red Rose was popular for a lot of reasons. The owner was so generous he allowed his regular customers to run up long tabs before he collected, if he collected at all. I knew this because Mr. Boatwright had died owing the club a fortune that Muh'Dear had settled herself, calling it her last act of "Christian duty" in Mr. Boatwright's honor. The club offered food to go and I often stopped by myself to pick up fried chicken dinners for Jerome and me. It was a cozy little place and after I got more relaxed, I was almost glad that I had come. That feeling didn't last long.

I was facing the door but I didn't see her come in. It was like she had come out of nowhere.

Rhoda!

This time I *knew* it was her. Standing alone on the dance floor in front of the bandstand, she had on a long, dark skirt, boots, and the same leather coat that she had had with her at the mall. Her long hair was in a ponytail. While I sat there in slack-jawed amazement, the band started playing a tune I'd never heard before, called "Crack The Whip." Rhoda started gyrating like a stripper and my mouth dropped open so wide, my chin ached. Every member in the band egged her on as she removed a leather belt from her waist and started waving it in the air, cracking it like a whip. In all the years that I had hung around with her, I had never seen Rhoda get so loose in public—or anywhere else, for that matter.

"Now there's a sister that's feeling the holiday spirit. You need to loosen up more," Jerome told me, beckoning for the waitress, snapping his fingers and bobbing his head to the music. He was enjoying every minute of Rhoda's outrageous performance. I could feel sweat oozing out all over my body. I snatched a napkin off of the table and started to wipe and fan my face.

I had managed to shut my mouth but I was still horrified.

"I'm as loose as I'm going to get," I declared, my heart beating against my chest so hard I thought the buttons on my cotton blouse were going to pop off. I moved to a chair on the opposite side of the table so I could face the wall—not to keep from looking at Rhoda, but to keep her from looking at me.

The band finally stopped playing but they hooted, hollered, clapped, and whistled like they had no shame whatsoever. I turned to see Rhoda walking away from the dance floor, clutching a huge bag filled with fried chicken so potent it teased my nostrils all the way across the room. I watched her until she glided toward the door and disappeared.

A couple of minutes after Rhoda's departure, a few more patrons entered and the band stopped sending us drinks. Now, Jerome was just as ready to leave as I was.

By the time we left the club there was so much snow coming down we could barely see two feet in front of us. Jerome led me to his car with his arm around my shoulder, cussing all the way. I didn't even bother to remind him that it had been his idea for us to come out into this raging blizzard in the first place.

Jerome drove me back to my house and left without coming in for his usual "nightcap," which included a few minutes in my bed. But that was only after I feigned cramps and a headache.

Once I got inside, I couldn't sit still long enough to enjoy anything on television. Seeing Rhoda a second time in the same week was a heavy load to carry and I needed to talk to somebody about it. But my options were limited. I couldn't call Pee Wee for obvious reasons. I couldn't talk to Muh'Dear about Rhoda and every time I called up Scary Mary, all she really wanted to talk about was herself. I called up Jean. Not to talk about Rhoda, because Jean didn't know the history of this subject, but I figured that a neutral conversation with an uninvolved party would be the next best thing.

"Annette, is it my imagination or is there something bothering you?" Jean asked. I could hear P. singing along with the television in the background.

"What do you mean?" I managed.

"You've asked me if I was going to apply for that supervisor's position four times in the last ten minutes. And each time I told you I wasn't. You nervous about the wedding?"

"Yeah. That's it. I am nervous about my wedding," I said quickly.

"Well, don't be." Jean sighed. "I just wish I was in your shoes."

I spent the next hour talking to Jean about our jobs at the telephone company, her desire to marry her boyfriend, and other mundane things that I would forget as soon as I got off the telephone.

I went about my business the next few days. I had enough going on in my life that I was soon able to put Rhoda on a back burner.

One of the reasons I tolerated Richland was because it was a small town. It was a lot more intimate than Miami and even Erie, Pennsylvania, the town I'd tried to hide out in a few years ago. But even if Richland had been twice its size, it would still not be big enough for Rhoda and me to occupy at the same time. Not after the way our friendship had ended.

No matter how I tried to ignore it, I knew that if Rhoda was back in town to stay, I would have to deal with her, face-to-face, sooner or later.

I just didn't know when or how.

CHAPTER 37

My upcoming marriage to Jerome, and Muh'Dear and Scary Mary's constant meddling, were not enough to keep my mind off of Rhoda. I was always looking for other things to occupy myself with. I volunteered to work overtime when nobody else would and I took long drives down the highway, ignoring the bad weather. I also spent as much time as I could with Jean. There was usually a lot going on with her and it was always a temporary relief.

However, there was one thing going on in Jean's world that disturbed me, to say the least. It had to do with P. and Jean's boyfriend.

During my frequent visits to Jean's house, I started noticing things about P. that alarmed me. Whenever Jean's live-in lover, Vincent "Vinnie" Gambiano, got too close to P., she became even quieter. It was no wonder. Vinnie's appearance was unsettling, even to me. He was not some evil-eyed gargoyle with fangs. Basically, he was not bad-looking at all. He had a pleasant, square-shaped face with full, bow-shaped lips that he loved to part so that he could show off his sparkling white teeth. But Vinnie wore a long, greasy ponytail, and had a scarred nose that had been broken more than once. He had cold, black eyes with eyebrows so thick it looked like two black caterpillars had crawled up his face. He didn't have much fashion sense because every time I saw him he had on something dark and outdated. He even wore dark, ratty turtleneck sweaters when he accompanied Jean and P. to the church that they belonged to.

Vinnie and I went way back. He had been in most of my classes all through high school. He had been one of the smartest, neatest boys in the whole school. A lot of kids had teased him about coming to school in a suit with his black hair slicked back with something oily every day, but none of that seemed to bother Vinnie. His grandmother had raised him and it was her that he had always aspired to please.

When the old woman died during our junior year, Vinnie went to live with his Uncle Luigi, a shoe-store manager who drove an old hearse that he'd plucked from a used-car lot for half the asking price. Almost immediately, Vinnie took a strange turn. He stopped wearing suits, grew his hair long, and dropped out of school in our senior year. He started hanging out with some rough people, doing everything he could to look just as tough. Like beating up other kids, smoking, and drinking alcohol in public. He even started speaking like them, using foul words and bad grammar. I'd see him barreling through town, driving his uncle's hearse like it was a Batmobile.

According to the rumors, Vinnie had fathered three babies by three different girls. Among Vinnie's shady new friends was a bull of a man named Big Pete, who owned a newsstand that sold only the sleaziest of the men's magazines. Big Pete, a beefy-faced Greek immigrant, was also a small-time loan shark. He would send Vinnie out to visit people who had fallen behind on their loans. Vinnie's job was to chastise these unfortunate deadbeat individuals. It must have been true because I'd heard it from Scary Mary and she knew everybody's business. And I did see a lot of people associated with Big Pete hopping around on crutches and wearing casts on their arms.

Even though he was always cordial to me, Vinnie even made *me* nervous when I visited Jean. But there was something more than that where P. was concerned. She would barely face him when he talked to her. A few times when he thought nobody was looking, I saw him wink at that little girl. A chill shot through my body like a bullet when Jean told me that Vinnie had given up the job he used as a front, driving a cab, to stay home and take care of P. while she worked during the day.

I was scared to death for P. because I knew all too well what was going on behind Jean's back. At least I thought I did. I had lived through that experience myself with Mr. Boatwright for ten agonizing years.

With all of the things going on in my own life, and Rhoda streaking through my mind like the tail of a comet, I still spent a great deal of my time worrying about P. It was especially difficult for me because I knew that whatever was going on between that child and Vinnie, I was in no position to do anything about it.

Even though Jean was madly in love with Vinnie, other men constantly asked her out. It was no wonder. She had violet eyes like Liz Taylor and a cute nose that turned up at the tip. She had thick, jet-black hair that she wore in a short style with bangs. But she was self-conscious about being overweight and hairy. She rarely wore skirts and it was just as well, because she had hairy legs that she refused to shave. But since that didn't seem to bother Vinnie, she thought he was the best thing that had ever happened to her. She bent over backward to keep him happy. As hard as it was for me to believe, Vinnie did the same for her. He sent roses to her at work and he took her out to dinner at least twice a week.

Working for the telephone company didn't pay Jean, or me, the kind of money we needed to live in the nice houses we lived in on Reed Street. I would have had to move to a much cheaper place if Muh'Dear hadn't owned the house I occupied. Vinnie paid Jean's rent and helped with her other bills. And when Jean's mother passed away, Vinnie cut a trip to Brooklyn short so he could come home and be with Jean. I had to admit to myself that the man did have some redeeming qualities. But so had Mr. Boatwright.

I was happy when Jean told me that she had decided to put P. in a nursery school. A Black friend of hers had recently opened a licensed child-care center in her home.

"Vinnie was against it but I went for it anyway. My friend has a little girl herself around P.'s age. Maybe being around other kids more will help P. get over her shyness," Jean told me, fumbling with a huge tuna sandwich in the telephone company lunchroom. "Besides, it's inconvenient for Vinnie to pick P. up from school every day, and then baby-sit her until I get home from work."

I gave Jean a thoughtful look. "A little girl should not be alone around men too much anyway. Something bad might happen to her." I don't know why I said what I did, but it had been on my mind so much lately, I wasn't surprised when the words slid out.

Jean gasped and dropped her sandwich on our lunchroom table. A raw onion ring slid out.

"Vinnie's the only father P.'s ever known. He'd jump in front of a bullet to save her, so I know he wouldn't let anything happen to her," Jean said breathlessly, toying with the onion ring she had dropped.

"I meant . . . well . . . things happen to little girls all the time."

Jean blinked and gave me a look that made me wonder if she even knew what I was talking about. "Well, I know

Vinnie would never do anything to hurt P. Even . . . even though . . ." Jean stopped and started fumbling with her sandwich again.

"Even though *what*, Jean? Has P. ever told you anything about Vinnie that you should be concerned about?" An ominous feeling came over me.

"Oh, you know how impossible kids her age can be!" Jean waved her thick hand dramatically. She was obviously flustered as she continued in a low voice to keep co-workers at the end of the same table from hearing. "P. got a little pissed-off at Vinnie one time because he tickled her under her arms while I was at the nail shop. She was crying when I got home."

I looked at Jean with my eyes narrowed. "Is that all she ever told you?" I had not touched the steak sandwich in front of me.

Jean bit a great big plug out of her sandwich and started talking and chewing at the same time. "Oh, she told me that he kissed her one time. But it was her fourth birthday."

"Did you see him do it?" By now I had lost my appetite completely. I wrapped my sandwich and slid it off to the side.

Jean stared at the wall and her voice got even lower. "I was at work that day."

"So, Vinnie kissed P. when he was alone with her?" I asked through clenched teeth. "In your house?" My stomach turned. Nobody knew better than I how agonizing it was to kiss a man you didn't want to kiss. Especially to a frightened child. Mr. Boatwright's sloppy kisses used to make me puke.

Jean nodded. "On the lips," she whispered, blinking nervously.

"And what did you do? Did you talk to Vinnie about it and tell him not to be doing something like that?"

"I didn't do anything," Jean admitted, refusing to face me. "I can't afford to lose him."

That did it! That was all I needed to hear. It was way too late for somebody to help me, but not too late for me to help another victim. I knew it was none of my business, but I felt it was my responsibility to do *something* to help P.

And I was going to.

CHAPTER 38

The same day I had the conversation with Jean about Vinnie kissing P., Jean went home right after lunch, claiming she was sick. The next day I heard that she had decided to take a few days off to take care of a "personal problem" that had suddenly come up. Concerned, I called her house twice that morning and left messages with Vinnie. He must not have given them to her because by the late afternoon, she had not called me back.

On my way home from work that day, I stopped at a pay phone near city hall and dialed the number I had looked up for the county social services. An operator with a nasal voice answered.

"What department, please?"

"Excuse me, ma'am. I'd like to talk to someone about a, uh, possible child-abuse situation," I whispered, glancing over my shoulder.

"Would you speak up, please?" the woman said in a crisp and impersonal voice.

Being a telephone operator myself, I knew how annoying

it was to have an individual on the other end of the line who was not speaking clearly. It was such a thorn in my side, I often hung up on people when they called and mumbled something I could not understand. The last thing I wanted was for this woman to hang up on me. I didn't know if I'd have enough nerve to call back. I cleared my throat and hollered as loud and clear as I could without attracting attention, "I have reason to believe that a child in my neighborhood is being sexually abused."

The woman asked my name and address, but I refused to reveal that information. She transferred me to another number. This time a man answered.

"Sir, I need to talk to someone about a child-abuse situation."

He cleared his throat and said quickly, "I'll transfer you to Child Protective Services." The telephone went dead. I called right back and the woman with the nasal voice answered again. I ordered her to transfer me to Child Protective Services. The woman who answered sounded Black and that put me more at ease.

"Ma'am, I don't want to give my name or address, but there is this little girl who lives in my neighborhood. Uh . . . her mother has a live-in boyfriend, with a shady reputation, and I believe he is molesting the little girl."

"Have you witnessed any inappropriate behavior between this man and this child?" She had a crisp voice that had enough authority in it to make me feel like I'd reached the right person.

"Uh . . . yes and no."

The woman let out a deep, tired sigh. "Well, have you or have you not?" This woman's impatience and indifference startled me. I thought that if anybody would be eagerly interested in hearing about a child being abused, it would be the people in her position. If they were not, then who? And society wondered why children were reluctant to expose their abusers. My head felt so heavy I was afraid it was going to roll right off my shoulders.

"I've noticed him looking at the child in a lewd way, see. Every time the child is around him, she gets really nervous and quiet. I don't think that's normal. And, the little girl's own mother told me that this man kissed the little girl on the lips."

The woman let out another tired sigh. "What you've just described does not constitute child abuse."

Now I was impatient. "Look, lady, I—I went through the same shit when I was a child! I know all the signs! Now somebody has got to do something to help this little girl before it's too late! Isn't that what you people do? This same man makes his living breaking people's legs and arms and God knows what else. He's a beast!" I couldn't remember the last time I had felt so emotional. I started itching all over.

"Would you please give me the names of the parties involved and the address?"

I gave the woman the information she requested and was about to hang up.

"And you are a friend of the child's mother?"

"Huh? No, I didn't say that. I don't want to get involved—"

"You *are* involved—"

"Just send somebody out to that address to investigate, *sister.*" I hung up before the woman could say anything else, proud of myself for making it this far.

CHAPTER 39

After the clumsy telephone call I had just made to the Child Protective Services, I was too wound-up to go home, so I went to the Buttercup. Muh'Dear was bustling around in the kitchen, barking orders at the dishwasher and one of the busboys.

"Muh'Dear, if you knew something somebody was doing, and it was something real bad, would you turn them in?" I asked in a low voice, glancing around.

"It depends on what it was that the somebody was doin'." Muh'Dear started dicing celery. "I hate when them folks from the projects come in here. No matter what they order, they complain. Would you believe one of 'em sent back a rare steak because it wasn't rare enough? If they want raw meat they should be eatin' at a white restaurant. I don't know why niggers start trippin' once they get their hands on enough money to eat out. I wish they'd stick to eatin' at rib joints and chicken shacks. But then, I know a lot of them folks don't know no better. Bless their savage souls. Me and you used to be the same way." Muh'Dear paused and wiped her hands on the tail of her apron. She offered me a broad smile. "I'm so glad me and you got class now."

"Muh'Dear, what if somebody was doin' somethin' nasty to a child? Like kissing and feeling on their private parts. Maybe even . . . uh . . . raping them. Would you turn them in?"

"I wouldn't have to. I'd beat the dog-shit out of 'em myself." Muh'Dear grabbed a carrot and started dicing it, too. "I ain't never had to worry about nothin' like that, praise the Lord." Muh'Dear patted the top of my head and stuck a carrot stick into my mouth.

I smiled weakly and left.

The next few days I made several bogus trips to the store, just so I could drive past Jean's house to see if I noticed anything different. I didn't.

Jean returned to work two days later, looking like a fish-wife. Her face was bloated and red, her hair looked dirty, and her clothes looked like she had slept in them.

"I've decided to take P. out of the wedding," she said, hardly looking at me. I was standing next to her desk as she moved stacks of files from one drawer to another.

"Oh, no. P. was really looking forward to being in my wedding. Did she change her mind? I know she's shy, but—"

"Annette, that's not it. Listen, I don't want you to take this the wrong way, because I don't want you to think of Vinnie as a racist."

I gasped and rotated my neck. "Vinnie doesn't want P. in my wedding because I'm Black?"

"Something like that. Now, you know Vinnie has Black friends, but he was raised by an old woman that never looked at things like race from a modern point of view. Vinnie believes that P. being in your wedding would be sending out the wrong kind of message. He doesn't like to look like a jerk to his friends."

I gagged and started gasping for air. When I composed myself, I asked, "How in the world is P. being in my wedding going to make Vinnie Gambiano look like a jerk? Which, by the way, he already is. None of Vinnie's friends are coming to my wedding. How would they know about P. being my flower girl?" I wailed.

Jean's eyes got big and she cocked her head to the side. She rotated her neck even more skillfully than I did. "Well, this is a small town and people do talk, honey. Vinnie and Pee Wee know some of the same people. You know, from hanging out at the Red Rose bar and all?" Jean sighed and set the last stack of files on top of her desk and gave me a mournful look. "I hope it's not too late for you to get another little girl."

"Jean, did something else happen in your house?" I asked quietly. I could see our supervisor peeping at us from around the copy machine across from Jean's desk. I lowered my voice and leaned closer to Jean. "Did it, Jean?"

"Annette, I don't know what you mean." Jean bowed her head and narrowed her eyes. "Just what are you thinking, Annette? Who have you been talking to?"

I shrugged. "I haven't been talking to anybody about Vinnie except you and little P. But this seems kind of sudden. Why did Vinnie wait all this time to pull P. out of my wedding? And why are you letting him decide that? He's not her father."

"He pays the cost to be the boss. You know how good he is to P. and me. I don't want to move out of my house and if I upset Vinnie, that's exactly what I'd have to do." A wan smile crossed Jean's face and she shrugged. "You know how unpredictable men are. Hey—how about lunch at Antonosanti's? I feel like pizza today. My treat."

I let out a deep, noisy breath and slapped my hands on my hips. "Well, are you and P. at least still *coming* to my wedding? Tell Vinnie he doesn't have to come if he doesn't want to. I won't miss him and that'll mean a lot more wine for us to drink."

Jean slapped her forehead with the palm of her hand. "How could I forget to tell you! Vinnie's got to go visit his uncle that moved to Toledo on that same day and he wants me to help him drive. You remember his Uncle Luigi who used to drive around in that cute little hearse? But guess what? After you and Jerome come back from your honeymoon cruise, let's drive up to Cleveland for a nice lunch. Wouldn't that be nice?"

"It would be nice, Jean." I sighed in defeat and went back to my workstation.

Vinnie picked Jean up from work that day. He rolled into the telephone company parking lot with snow chains on the wheels of Jean's Thunderbird. A knitted cap covered his head. The cap had long flaps on the sides that covered his ears, making him look like a hound dog.

P., looking like a little bear in her brown snowsuit, with her smudged little face pressed against the window in the backseat, looked at me and waved. Even with that surly Vinnie glaring at me, I escorted Jean over to her car.

"Hi, Vinnie," I said dryly, forcing myself to smile. I wanted to straighten out his crooked nose with my bare hands.

"What's goin' on?" he grumbled, his eyes shifting nervously. I could see grease on the neck of his natty sweater. "You better lay off them greens, that cornbread, and them fried chicken parts, lady. You about to bust right out of that pretty green dress," he added, looking me up and down with a frown. He followed that with a low, throaty laugh.

I ignored Vinnie's rude remark about my weight and motioned for P. to roll down her window. The wind was whistling in my ears, like it was taunting me, too.

"Annette, I can't be your flower girl," she pouted, blinking. I could see that she had already been crying, but she screwed up her face and started crying again. "Uncle Vinnie . . . says . . . says . . . I've been bad." P. paused, sniffled, and glanced at Vinnie. Jean was still standing outside the car next to me with her eyes staring at the ground.

"Well, I am sorry you all won't be at my wedding, P., honey," I said, giving Vinnie the evil eye he deserved.

"Yeah, I'm sorry, too," Vinnie snapped, gunning the motor. Like a trained puppy, Jean trotted around the car and climbed in. She kissed Vinnie on the cheek before she even closed her door.

As long as I live, I will never forget the sad expression on P.'s little face that dreary day. Even though we looked nothing alike, it was like I was looking at myself when I looked at her.

I didn't know if an investigator had paid Jean a visit or not and I knew Jean would never tell me. I just had to wait and see what happened next.

CHAPTER 40

In a surprise move, Jerome decided that he didn't want to get married in church. He wanted to get married in his mother's house. Muh'Dear told me she didn't care if I got married in an outhouse as long as I was happy. And since all of Jerome's siblings had been married in Marlene's house, it seemed like the right thing to do so I went along with it. That way, he argued, we could save money for the Mexican cruise we planned to go on for our honeymoon. Even though Muh'Dear was paying for half.

"We could use that money for some new furniture," Jerome insisted. "I don't want us to start our life together with all that tired old junk we both have now."

I agreed with Jerome that we needed new furniture, but I refused to go along with him about picking up wicker items from a flea market where he often shopped. When Muh'Dear offered to buy us new furniture, Jerome decided we had to have crushed velvet couches and a matching love seat. Like a docile lamb, I went along with that, too.

Since Muh'Dear owned the house on Reed Street, I lived

rent-free. I had agreed to keep up the property taxes and the maintenance. And that was well within my budget. After paying rent on the apartment I'd had in Pennsylvania for ten years, this was a dream come true for me. I was so happy that things were finally going so well for me, that I often let it cloud my judgment. Jerome was taking advantage of me left and right, but I couldn't see it then. He usually presented his schemes to me while I was in his arms.

After a tiresome five minutes of sex, I had also agreed with Jerome that he would move in with me after we were married. Shortly after Muh'Dear married Daddy King and moved in with him, I had moved into Muh'Dear's old bedroom. I had recently moved back into mine. For some reason, I felt more comfortable there, after all. I refused to move from it again to the one that Mr. Boatwright had occupied, like Jerome suggested. I had already said no twice but that didn't stop Jerome. It annoyed me when he badgered me about something, but he never gave up without a fight.

"That other bedroom has a better feel to it and a better view," he insisted as he squeezed my breasts and tangled his legs around mine. Sadly, he was not arousing me, but he thought he was. "I'll be a lot more passionate in a bedroom I'm happy in," he added.

I was learning something new about Jerome all the time. Even though he showered me with attention, he was also his own biggest fan. He loved getting his way and I usually let him have it. But I wasn't the girl I used to be. Standing up for myself was a new characteristic that I fully enjoyed. I had stopped growing physically, but my personality continued to expand in positive ways. My biggest regret was that I had not developed this new attitude sooner.

Irritated, I slapped Jerome's hand and kicked his legs away. "You can just stop right now about that bedroom. If you want to sleep in that room, you go right ahead. I am not moving from the one I've been sleeping in all these years," I told him. I had tried to compromise by suggesting that we move into the bedroom that Muh'Dear had slept in. "Muh'Dear's old bedroom is nice, too. It even has a chifforobe built into the wall."

"I don't like that room. It has no view at all and it's too small," he exclaimed, kicking the bedcovers to the floor.

Sometimes Jerome made me feel like a plantation mammy. I had to scold him, advise him, and nurture him like one. When he behaved like a spoiled child, that's the way I treated him.

"Jerome, like I said, if you want to sleep in that other bedroom that bad, you can sleep in it alone," I said firmly. I got my way, but I knew that the subject would come up again later.

I didn't care how much he begged and whined about us moving into Mr. Boatwright's old room. I would never sleep there. It would have been like sleeping in a cemetery and I told him so.

"Exactly what happened in that room?" he asked, his eyes dancing with curiosity.

"Mr. Boatwright, the old man who used to live with us, he died in it," I mumbled. My words sounded distant and hollow. Even after so many years, Mr. Boatwright was still a difficult subject for me.

"Oh. I didn't know that. Your mama told me how close you were to that old brother. My daddy died at home, too. I couldn't go in his bedroom for a year. We'll stay in your room, baby. But we definitely need a new bed. We've just about fucked the hell out of the one you got now."

Even though Pee Wee and I had not been lovers for years, on one hand, it saddened me when I heard from Scary Mary that he was seriously involved with a woman he had met at the Red Rose bar. On the other hand, it pleased me when Pee

Wee confessed that he was not comfortable knowing that Jerome was going to be living right next door to him. I had assured Pee Wee that he would still be welcome to visit me every day if he chose to. However, I planned to tell him that he would have to stop entering my house without knocking and making himself at home by stretching out on my couch like he was now.

The last thing I wanted to do was hurt Pee Wee's feelings. Next to Jerome and Daddy, Pee Wee was the most important man in my life and I didn't ever want to lose his friendship. That's why I didn't bring up the fact that I'd seen Rhoda. If Jerome had not been in my life, I could have talked to Pee Wee right after my first sighting of her in the mall. But over the years, she was the one subject I'd purposely avoided talking to Pee Wee about. There was too much I wanted to say about her to Pee Wee. But, I couldn't. At least not yet. With my wedding, wondering how my relationship with Daddy and Lillimae was going to develop, and my concerns about P., I already had enough to keep my mind working overtime.

"Old boy know about us?" Pee Wee asked, looking at me out of the corner of his eye. "And . . . uh . . . do Jerome know about that . . . uh . . . thing we used to do?" Pee Wee made an obscene gesture with his fingers.

"No!" I snapped. "Nobody but you and I know about *that thing we used to do*. Let's keep it that way," I said, walking around, picking up the empty beer cans that Pee Wee had scattered about the living room. Jerome liked a clean house and I did, too. But living alone for so long, I had a habit of neglecting my housecleaning duties.

Pee Wee frowned and shook his head in disgust when I lifted one of Jerome's jockstraps off the floor and stuffed it inside my bra.

"Annette, I know it ain't my business, but I think you could have done a lot better," Pee Wee said suddenly.

"Better than what?"

Pee Wee waved his hand dramatically, frowning even more. "Better than Jerome," he snapped in a high-pitched voice.

"Didn't you tell me that already?"

"Well, I'm tellin' you again. How you goin' to feel at all them family visits with that color-struck crew? How you goin' to feel if you have dark-skinned babies?"

"I am beyond that color thing and I thought you were, too," I hissed and gritted my teeth. "What would Black people talk about if we were all the same shade? That subject is so tired and old and I am sick of people bringing it up. Especially you."

"Yeah, but—"

"But nothing, Pee Wee." I threw up my hands in exasperation. "Look, you just don't like Jerome or anything about him. Including his whole family."

Pee Wee shook his head and gave me a thoughtful look. "Now don't be comin' at me like that. You got it all wrong. His sister Nadine's cool. I was supposed to take her to our prom, but she got the measles. I was—" Pee Wee stopped talking abruptly and looked away.

I gasped. "What? You never told me that. So you only took me to the prom because Nadine Cunningham couldn't go? I ought to slap the shit out of you," I yelled, shaking an empty beer can at him. I sat down on the couch and stared at him with contempt.

Pee Wee guffawed and held up his hand. "Don't be clownin' me, girl." He paused and got serious. "I was scared to ask you. You and that high-and-mighty Rhoda thought I was a fag. Oh, I know about all them times y'all hid from me. I couldn't even get you to go to the movies with me— why would I think you'd go to the prom with a 'fag-ass punk,' as I overheard you and Rhoda's brother Jock refer to

me one afternoon. I just happened to be listening outside
Rhoda's bedroom door that day."

"You know Jock was crazy and mean, even before he got
injured in Vietnam. I was just gossiping along with him so
he wouldn't get mad at me." I lowered my head and bit my
lip to keep from laughing. "Well, why did you invite me to
the prom?"

"Because you was the girl I wanted to take. Besides, Nadine had asked me to go with her, I didn't ask her. It took me
a whole day to get up enough nerve to ask you. And even
then I had to smoke a joint."

I looked over at Pee Wee and blinked stupidly. "I know
you don't like Jerome. But, can't you be happy for me?
Life is too short and I've spent enough of mine being miserable."

A sad look crossed Pee Wee's face—a face that I noticed
was getting better-looking each day. . . .

"Did I ever make you miserable?" he asked.

"No, but you know what I mean. I want you to be happy
for me," I wailed.

"I am. I just don't want to see you end up regrettin'
nothin'."

"I'm thirty-five, Pee Wee. And, look at me. I am no Diana
Ross. How many more chances will I get to marry?"

"Well, do you see Marvin Gaye, may he rest in peace, sittin' up in here with you? Women ain't standin' in line waitin'
on me. Don't I deserve a chance?"

I gasped. "A chance for what?"

"I want somebody to cook and clean for me and keep me
warm at night when I crawl into the bed. Shit." Pee Wee
looked at me with an anxious look on his face. I had to say
the most appropriate and noncommittal thing possible for
his benefit, as well as mine.

I sighed. "Get a maid and some woolen pajamas."

Pee Wee rolled his eyes, let out a groan, and offered me an easy smile that he promptly replaced with a moderate scowl. "I always thought that one day . . . you know. Oh, hell, girl. How come you ain't marryin' *me?*"

I laughed and waved my finger at Pee Wee. "Be serious. And stop spilling beer on my clean carpet!"

"Why won't you marry me?" he whined. "I ain't good enough for you?" A puppy-dog expression appeared on his face. "I know I'm a little on the dark side and my hair looks like Nap City, but I ain't no bad dude to look at. And you know I can afford to support you in style. A woman like you deserves the best and I should be the one to give it to you. Not what's-his-butt. Shit."

I stared at Pee Wee with my mouth hanging open, giving him one of the most exasperated looks I could come up with. I didn't appreciate him joking with me about something as serious as marriage. But the days of us being alone in my house were numbered so I decided to humor him. "And just why in the world would you want to marry me *now?* I've known you most of my life."

Pee Wee shrugged and chuckled. "Looks like I'm goin' to be stuck with you the rest of my life anyway. I ain't movin' from my house, you ain't movin'. We'll probably be livin' next door to one another from now on anyway." Pee Wee paused and clapped his hands together, then started rubbing his palms together. "Just think of all the money we'd save if I moved in with you or if you moved in with me."

"Now you sound like Jerome." I laughed.

"I ain't Jerome."

"Look, let's pop open another beer before Jerome gets here."

"Thanks, but no thanks. I think I'll go over to the pool-room for a while." Pee Wee rose and stretched. I walked him to the door, my arm around his waist. I was disappointed when he pulled away from me. "You know I was just jokin' about us gettin' married, don't you?"

"I know you were," I said. "You always could make me laugh, even when I didn't want to."

CHAPTER 41

I looked around my living room to make sure that I had not overlooked any empty beer cans or other trash. This was going to be an important night for Jerome and me so I wanted everything to be perfect, or as close to it as possible. He was coming by later to pick me up for a dinner at his mother's house, where I would be presented to some of his other relatives.

I promptly forgot about the clumsy conversation I had just had with Pee Wee. I laughed when I thought of him marrying me. It was a bizarre joke. But after thinking about it some more, it didn't seem so funny.

And the thought of having to clean up behind Pee Wee made me howl. In all the years I'd known him, I'd only been inside his house a dozen times. Even before his daddy moved away back to Pennsylvania, every room in Pee Wee's house looked like a crime scene.

There was so much junk piled up in his three bedrooms, he couldn't even shut the doors. His kitchen sink was usually full of dirty dishes. The last time I'd visited him, I had to sit on the floor because there had been no room on any of his seats. If Pee Wee and I ever did get married, which was highly unlikely, I would have my work cut out for me every day.

But the same was true of Jerome, in a way.

I didn't think about it a lot, but I knew that Jerome's stinginess was going to cause problems in our future. He got tears in his eyes one night when I told him I wanted to enroll all the children we planned to have in private schools. Whenever Jerome didn't want to argue with me, he lured me to bed where I ended up purring like a kitten. After a few perfunctory thrusts, he stood up in my bed naked and told me, "I'd rather teach my kids at home before paying somebody to teach them."

I was truly going to miss the great sex I had shared with Pee Wee. I was sorry that we had not gotten together "one last time" before my wedding. But it was too late now. Looking on the bright side, there was always a chance that Jerome's bedroom techniques would improve over the next forty or fifty years, if we lived that long and remained faithful to one another. It was a depressing thought, but it was all I had to go on.

Jerome got stuck in traffic going to and coming from the airport in Akron to pick up his Uncle Willie from Columbus. He called me from a pay phone on his way back.

In one long breath, he told me, "Baby, put on your best dress. That yellow one, because it makes you look like a sunflower. I want you to look your best for Uncle Willie. He can't wait to meet you. The way I've been bragging about you, he said you got a lot to live up to. Mama's running around in the kitchen right now, cooking up a storm. My sister Nadine's making a pound cake. Aunt Minnie's driving over all the way from Sandusky in her brand-new Ford. She just got a face-lift so tell her how good she looks. We'll pick you up and by the time we get to Mama's house, dinner will be ready. I love you, baby."

"I love you, too, Jerome."

Jerome had a key to my house so he let himself in while I was still getting dressed. He raced upstairs and into my room. He stopped dead in his tracks and let out a long, low wolf whistle as he rubbed his palms together.

"Girl, I am scared of you." He tilted his head, folded his arms, and smacked his lips. "Every time I look at you, I tell myself I'm the luckiest man alive."

I grinned demurely as Jerome rushed over to zip up my dress. I had to pry his arms from around my waist so I could get my shoes out of the closet.

"Hurry up, baby. Uncle Willie's in the car and we need to stop by the liquor store to pick up some champagne. Uncle Willie is springing for the best." Jerome whistled and rubbed his hands together again. "Girl, I can't wait to get you back here to myself. I won't eat much at Mama's house because I'm going to *feed* on you later on tonight."

"You stop that," I snapped, slapping Jerome's hand as he massaged my butt.

I let out a deep breath as I wiggled my feet into the black pumps I had fished out of the closet. "I don't like these frequent gatherings, Jerome. I'm nervous enough around your family as it is."

Jerome waved his hands above his head. "You don't have anything to be nervous about around my folks. Now come on. Uncle Willie's been complaining about his butt getting numb from sitting so long, all the way from the airport. I know what he needs. He needs him a juicy-butt woman to get his blood circulating. He almost got whiplash trying to look at this big-legged sister standing in front of the Red Rose. I tease him all the time about him fucking my aunt to death. She died while he was on top of her. What a sight that was. It took three of us to lift that big sister out of that bed."

I gave Jerome a serious look. "Do all of the men in your family prefer big-boned women?"

"I already told you we did. Uncle Willie, with his hot-natured self, loves him some big women! I'm going to have to keep my eye on him around you. I have to warn you, Uncle Willie is quite a ladies' man. Even though there is enough of you for both of us, you are all mine. Now let me warn you about my uncle. Uh, he didn't finish high school, so he's not that sophisticated. He talks rough sometimes and he acts even rougher. But he's a proud man and he deserves the highest respect."

"You don't have to worry about me. I can handle your uncle," I said, patting my hair. To look less ethnic, I had removed my braids. I had to agree with Jerome that I looked better with my hair in a French twist and bangs. Even though this particular "do" made me look my age.

Jerome kissed me on my neck and gave me another squeeze around my waist. "Girl, you just wait 'til I get you back to this house to myself. I'm going to have you scream-ing like somebody scalded you."

I groaned and made a mental note to come up with a mys-terious, fictitious, *untreatable* pelvic condition so I wouldn't have to have sex with Jerome too often in the future. I al-ready had him thinking that my periods lasted twice as long as they really did. Like Mr. Boatwright, Jerome was a man who couldn't stand to get too cozy with a bloody woman.

"Let's go, baby," I said, running out the door behind him.

I saw Pee Wee peeping out of his living window with a disgusted look on his face as I sashayed out to Jerome's car with my coat in one hand and a sweet potato pie in the other. Jerome was carrying my purse.

The huge, red-faced man sitting in the front passen-ger's seat of Jerome's car looked at me and did a double take. His eyes got big as saucers as his face froze with his mouth hanging open like a trapdoor. I stopped dead in my tracks, almost choking on my own tongue.

With my mind a whirl of confusion and fear, I thought

back to a night seventeen years ago. Not having the insight back then to know that my actions might someday come back to haunt me, I had sold my body to every man willing to pay. Jerome's Uncle Willie had been one of those men. The last one. He was the same night watchman who had used me and treated me so rudely afterward. It was like I got tunnel vision all of a sudden for just a few seconds. All I could see was that man sitting there glaring at me. My legs almost buckled. I shook my head and blinked my eyes a few times.

I wanted to run. I wanted to hide. I wanted to drop dead on the spot from shame. I wanted Pee Wee to get out of his window and come out and rescue me.

"What's wrong, baby? You look like you just saw Caesar's ghost." Jerome opened the back door of his car and pulled my arm, guiding me like I was a blind person. But I remained in the same spot, shaking like a sumac leaf. My feet felt as heavy as cement blocks.

"I don't feel well," I mumbled. There was a lump in my throat and a knot in my stomach. I couldn't tell which one felt worse. "Maybe I should stay home." I couldn't take my eyes off the man in the car and he couldn't take his eyes off me. I stumbled back a few steps.

"Stop acting crazy. Don't you want to make a good impression on Uncle Willie? He's paying for the other half of that cruise you're so determined for us to go on," Jerome said impatiently. His fingers dug into my flesh as he pulled me toward the car again.

I don't know how I did it, but somehow I managed to get into the car, folding myself onto the backseat like a sack of sand. Jerome briefly introduced me to his uncle and was gracious enough to keep the conversation going all the way to his mother's house. I said less than five words as Jerome bragged about what a beautiful, decent, hard-working, clean, generous, and sexy woman I was.

"Uncle Willie, ain't this woman something else? I can't

wait for you to get to know her as well as I do," Jerome said, talking so fast he had to cough to catch his breath.

Mr. Willie turned around and gave me a sharp look, shaking his head as he spoke. "I can't wait," he growled, his lips snapping brutally over each word. "She sure enough is somethin' else." He glared at me some more, shook his head, and turned back around.

CHAPTER 42

As usual, most of Jerome's female relatives ignored me. Even though I was practically a member of the family now. However, his sister Nadine was her usual cordial self to me. She always attempted to pull me into a conversation no matter what the subject was.

"Annette, I can certainly tell you're a woman in love. Your face is just glowing," Nadine told me in her nasal voice.

I had not secured another close Black female friend after Rhoda. I hoped that one day soon, Nadine would fill that position. Nadine and I had already spent several Saturday afternoons shopping in Cleveland, getting our nails and hair done and going to lunch together. I looked forward to the day I could introduce her to my newly found sister, Lillimae.

Nadine and Lillimae made me realize how wonderful it was to have females to bond with. But it saddened me to know that I could never replace Rhoda. As much as I loved Lillimae and Nadine, I could never feel as free with them the way I had felt with Rhoda. But like Mr. Boatwright, Rhoda was part of my past and I had accepted that.

"I *am* in love," I muttered, watching as Mr. Willie glared at me and shook his head. The scowl on his face was so severe, it looked like he was in pain. I didn't need a psychic to tell me that he was going to be trouble.

Jerome's mother, Marlene, wearing a pink chiffon dress, had already set the table and was prancing around on four-inch heels ordering everybody around the dining room like a drill sergeant. "Annette, didn't I tell you to sit between Jerome and Willie? You and Nadine act like a couple of schoolgirls." Marlene reminded me of Muh'Dear because cooking and cracking the whip were her strongest points. Waving a napkin, she continued, "Jerome, you don't have to sit so close to Annette. You're stuck with her for the rest of your life, so give yourself some space tonight. You'll have plenty of time to snuggle up to her." As much as Jerome and I loved the bright yellow dress I had on, Marlene looked me up and down and frowned. "Annette, I guess you want to get as much mileage as you can out of that frock." She turned sharply away from me and snapped her fingers. Then she opened her mouth to bark again. First, she sneezed and turned back to me. "I was hoping you wouldn't splash on none of that Giorgio, Annette. Cheap perfume is bad for my sinuses. And what did you do—swim in it? My goodness!" She waved the white napkin at me and started talking with her other hand covering her nose. "Annette, you better sit at the end of the table after all." Marlene waved me to another chair. "No, wait. That's still too close to me." Instead of allowing me to sit at the table with the rest of the adults, Marlene seated me at a card table that they had dragged into the dining room for Jerome's two young nephews and niece. I was pleased when Jerome got up from the table and sat with the kids and me.

I was even more pleased when Nadine took the seat next to Jerome. "I'm wearing Giorgio, too," Nadine said with a wink.

As uppity as Jerome's mother was, she was a fairly decent cook. She had roasted a duck and stir-fried all the vegetables. With a smirk she yelled across the room, "Annette, you might recognize these dinner rolls. I picked them up from your mama's restaurant. I hope you're half as good a cook as she is. I want my boy to be well taken care of."

"Mama, you don't have a thing to worry about. Being with Annette is just like being with you," Jerome said, not noticing the snickers from his siblings. Nadine shook her head and tapped my foot with hers under the table. "Uncle Willie told me when I was a little bitty boy that a smart man always marries a woman like his mama."

"Mrs. Cunningham, Jerome is just playing with you. I could never be the woman you are," I said distantly. Knowing that my goose was probably already cooked, thanks to Mr. Willie, I was not too particular about what I said now. I had nothing else to lose, so I kept talking. "I just hope that I make Jerome as happy as you have, anyway."

Marlene glared at me with her mouth hanging open. Like Nadine, Jerome's mother was not as pretty up close as she was from a distance. Marlene's small, beady black eyes were too close together, her nose was crooked, and one of her cheekbones was higher than the other, making her face lopsided. I wondered if a woman who looked like Marlene would have thought so highly of herself if she'd been born with skin as dark as mine.

Jerome's Aunt Minnie from Sandusky cleared her throat. "Annette, the key to keeping your man happy is to always look good for him. No matter what you have to do. It's such a shame my husband Clarence had to up and die on me so soon." Miss Minnie lifted her chin and patted her cheek. I didn't comment on her recent face-lift because she still had a few wrinkles and folds.

As hard as I tried not to look at Mr. Willie, every time I

turned my head in his direction, his eyes were on me. There was no mistaking his contempt.

"So, now what do you do for a livin', Annette?" Even though Mr. Willie said it nicely, there was still a fierce scowl on his face as he addressed me. These were the first words he had spoken to me since the ride from my house.

"She's a switchboard operator," Jerome said proudly.

"And she was the smartest girl in my algebra class," Nadine added.

"Mmm-huh," Willie nodded. "When I was your age they only gave jobs like operators to those squeaky-voiced white girls. Black girls had to do some of everything to make a buck."

"That's for sure. My mama cleaned houses and cooked for most of her life. When I was little, I remember a job she had spreading manure on some politician's farm. I used to help her," I said evenly. I didn't particularly care for duck, but I managed to take a few bites.

"Spreading manure? Yegods." Marlene clucked and shook her head. "I'd do anything to get out of doing something that ghoulish." She sighed and looked around the room from Jerome to her other two sons. "Boys, just being a woman in this world is a mighty cross to bear. Some of us have to do some of the most unspeakable things so we can take care of our loved ones. I've been telling Nadine that all her life." Marlene turned to me with a rare smile and said, "Well, be thankful you had a mama willing to do whatever she had to do. Just look where she's at now."

"She owns the Buttercup restaurant now," I announced proudly.

"I know. I used to go by there a few times before I moved away from Richland. I didn't know Gussie Mae was your mama," Mr. Willie grunted, waving a tall flute of wine in front of his pink-and-brown lips.

"Oh, Miss Gussie's a sweet woman. Goes to church every

Sunday," Clifford, Nadine's sharp-featured husband, said. He occupied the seat next to Marlene. "She cooks and serves free food to the homeless on a regular basis."

I smiled proudly. I didn't want to brag about the fact that my mother had also started giving cash donations to the homeless, too. I didn't care what anybody thought or said about me now, I was proud of the person I had become. I was so bold as to now believe that the people in my life should consider themselves lucky to know me. I just hoped that Jerome was one of those people.

Marlene patted Clifford's shoulder and grunted. "It's a crying shame Annette's mother associates with wenches like that Scary Mary," Marlene said with disgust, shaking her head and waving her fork high in the air. "That woman gives the rest of us a bad name. If Annette's mother and Annette could shovel shit to survive, Scary Mary could have, too! A Black woman running one of those . . . those . . . *houses*. Shame, shame, shame. I didn't even know snake pits like that still existed in America. That whole business is so . . . so third world."

I was surprised when one of Jerome's brothers defended Scary Mary. "Scary Mary's cool. It's because of her generous donations that they can keep that youth center open. Lord knows, Black kids need all the help they can get to keep them out of trouble."

"Scary Mary also helps my mama cook and feed the homeless," I said, holding my hand up defensively. "Even if the woman is a madam, she's got a good heart and she doesn't judge people."

Jerome beamed proudly; his mother just looked at me and blinked. Mr. Willie glared at me and shook his head. Everybody else in the room smiled at me, even the children.

Then the conversation suddenly shifted to family matters that didn't concern me, so I excused myself to go to the bathroom. I made it just in time to throw up in the toilet. When I opened the door to leave, Jerome's ferocious uncle was standing there, blocking the doorway.

The contempt in his eyes could not be measured.

CHAPTER 43

"Ex . . . excuse me," I mumbled, attempting to walk around Jerome's angry uncle. I even offered him a smile.

The huge man stepped to the side, preventing me from moving. His face was close to mine and his foul breath made me cough. "Get thee behind me, Bride of Satan," Mr. Willie commanded.

"Uh . . . I . . . uh . . . I . . ." I couldn't believe the gibberish coming out of my mouth. I felt more like a spectator than the recipient of his wrath.

Mr. Willie rolled up the sleeves on his shirt, like he was preparing to punch somebody out. In a way he was. And I was his target. Wiry, reddish-brown hair covered his thick arms as he folded them.

"So. We meet again," Mr. Willie said gruffly as he reared back on his stump-like legs and started to rock back and forth on his feet.

I attempted to walk around him again but he was determined to keep me from moving. He wobbled to the side and blocked my path.

"Where do you think you gwine?" he sneered, stabbing my chest with his thick finger.

"I'm going back to Jerome," I said, trying to sound firm, my arms hanging limply down my sides.

"You ain't gwine noplace, Whore of Babylon."

"But . . ."

"But nothin'!" He paused and let out a loud belch, shaking his head as he looked me up and down. "Jerome always was the family fool, but I never expected him to settle for a sloppy, leftover whore like you." Mr. Willie sucked in his breath and stuck out his barrel of a chest. He looked just as disgusting as he did that night he paid me to use my body. Deep lines formed a wide "V" on his forehead. Gray hairs stuck out of his flaring nostrils.

"Jerome doesn't know anything about . . . what I did before I met him," I hissed, glancing around, a pleading look on my face.

"I didn't think he did. Well, if you think I'm gwine to let that boy get involved in somethin' he'll regret, you way wrong. Just look at you—with your nappy-headed self."

I wrung my hands nervously. "This is none of your business, Uncle Willie."

Mr. Willie was clearly horrified by the way I had just addressed him. He gasped and moved back a step. Then he stopped and stared at me with his mouth standing wide open. For a moment I thought he was going to laugh because there was such an odd expression on his face. But then he screwed up his face into a frown so extreme it looked like he had on a mask.

"Gal, don't you never fix your lips to call me 'Uncle' ever again. I will never be no uncle to the likes of you, with your nasty self. For your information, Jerome is my blood. My blood is my business." He snorted. "My nephew deserves a decent woman. A *sanctified* woman who's been splashed by the blood of Jesus—not the cum of a hundred and one heathens! Not some two-ton whore willing to sell her rank pussy for a few dollars. And, by the way, you was one of the cheapest pieces of tail I ever come across. Fifty dollars! Them other gals charged twice as much and they was worth it and more. You wasn't!" Mr. Willie interrupted his assault on me just long enough to catch his breath, then said harshly, "And for the record, you wasn't even worth the fifty dollars! Shame on you! A two-dollar food stamp was about all you was worth. Look at you. You got the nerve to come up in this house in that loud yellow dress, lookin' like a big, black cow peepin' over a bale of hay."

"Oh yeah? With all the squealing and sweating you did that night I was with you, you must have had a good time with this big, black cow! You didn't care what I looked like then," I reminded, trying to keep my voice low.

"I could have had a good time with a bar of soap on a rope!"

"Then why didn't you do that in the first place?"

"I wish I had." Mr. Willie growled and wiggled his nose, not taking his eyes off my face.

I felt like the lowest form of life known to man. But I also felt that this man was no better than I was! Women wouldn't go around selling their bodies in the first place if it wasn't for horny men like him.

"I wish I could take back what I did, because I didn't have to do it. I was young and I was foolish," I mumbled, hardly recognizing my own voice.

"Foolish? You got that right. Well, you ain't good enough for Jerome. I suggest you get your big, black ass the hell up out of this family's life! My mama would do a jackknife in her grave if I let that boy marry a sloppy Jezebel like you."

"You're not going to tell Jerome, are you? Let me tell him in my own way, in my own time. Please."

"You . . . just . . . watch . . . me . . . now!" Mr. Willie rubbed his neck and blinked. "I know you don't think I'm gwine to let him marry you first. Do you think I'm that stupid?"

"What . . . what do you want me to do?" I whimpered.

"Devil, you do whatever the rest of them strumpets do. Find you a man that don't come from a respectable family like mine. I don't give a bejoojoo what you do. I know what you ain't gwine to do, and that's to marry into this family. Especially with your homely self. I seen better-lookin' faces in a pigsty." An amused expression appeared on Mr. Willie's face as he continued attacking me. "You'd give birth to young'uns with hooves and scales, I bet."

Just then, Jerome entered the hallway in front of the bathroom and strutted right over to me, draping his arm around my shoulder.

"Mama's about to serve the drinks," Jerome said, a puzzled look on his face as he looked from his uncle to me. "Baby, you really do look sick. I'll take you home in a few minutes if you want me to. Just stay long enough to have a drink. You are going to be part of this family and I want you to get used to everybody." Jerome wiped a layer of sweat off my cheek with the back of his hand, then felt my forehead. "Hmmm. Feels like you have a fever, too."

I nodded.

"It was nice talking to you, Unc . . . uh, *Mr.* Willie," I mumbled, my words tasting like something contaminated.

"I bet it was," he said with a smirk, both of his fleshy cheeks twitching. "And I didn't get to say everything I wanted to say, but I'm sure I will, *if* I see you again." There was no mistake about the threatening tone in his voice.

I was so light-headed, I could barely feel my feet as I followed Jerome back to the living room. I had perspired so much that the top part of my bright yellow dress was soaking wet. My stomach was in cramps and my eyes felt like balls of fire.

"Baby, I am so proud of you tonight. I'm so sorry you don't feel too well," Jerome said lovingly as we entered the living room where everyone was.

"I'll be fine," I managed, pressing my lips together to keep them from quivering. Mr. Willie was standing in a corner glaring at me with his arms folded. He flinched, shook his head, and took a drink when Jerome kissed me.

I felt like I had slid into the deepest bowels of hell and been sucked up into the jaws of the Beast.

CHAPTER 44

I needed a drink more than anybody else in the living room at Jerome's mother's house. But even a straight shot of vodka didn't dull the pain. Nobody even noticed when Jerome and I slipped away from the crowd and went to his car.

"I know you don't feel well, baby, but I wish you would have said good-bye to everybody before leaving," Jerome whined, helping me into his car. "And don't be shy around Uncle Willie. Don't call him 'Mr.' when you see him tomorrow; call him 'Uncle Willie' like the rest of us did tonight. He'll like that."

"Jerome, I'm really sick and I need to get home right away." The alcohol that I had been able to get down churned violently in my stomach. The inside of my mouth tasted like bile.

"Well, take care of yourself. I'd like for us to take Uncle Willie to the Buttercup tomorrow night for dinner. Your mother makes the best sweet potato pies in town."

I nodded and placed my head against the window, praying that Jerome would drive fast. I wanted to be alone as soon as possible. I stayed pressed against that window all the way back to my house.

"I'll call you later tonight. I would stay with you now, but my uncle is the head of the family and I need to spend some time with him." Jerome lowered his voice and continued. "I just hope Uncle Willie's not expecting me to hook him up with some female company like he did the last time he came to visit. Since my aunt died, he's been hornier than ever. Scary Mary's girls just love him to death."

I nodded and started to open the car door. I paused and looked at Jerome. "Jerome, you love me for who I am, right?"

He gave me a puzzled look before he grinned. "Yeah. But you know that already."

"If you found out that I was not the woman you thought I was, would it matter?" I delivered the words with extreme caution. At the same time, I wondered if it would make a difference if the worst-case scenario did come to pass.

"Remember how Flip Wilson used to say, 'what you see is what you get'?"

"What? Jerome, what in the world are you talking about?"

"Well, I like what I see and even what I can't see in you. I am not perfect and I don't expect you to be. I can't imagine you having a secret so deep and dark—don't tell me something strange, like you used to be a man." Jerome laughed. "I don't think I could deal with that!" He leaned over and kissed my cheek and laughed again. "We got some baby-making to do and you'd have to be a *real* woman to be able to do that."

I laughed dryly. "Don't worry. I'm all woman and I always have been."

Jerome kissed me at my front door and waited until I got inside before he left.

Before I could cross the living room floor, my phone rang. It was Muh'Dear.

"Listen. I been thinkin'. It won't make no sense for your daddy and your sister . . . uh, *half*-sister, to stay in no motel when they come up for the wedding. Frank can sleep in Brother Boatwright's old room. That Lillimae can sleep in my old room."

"That's nice, Muh'Dear. I know Daddy'll be glad to hear that," I said distantly.

"Are you all right? You sound a little strange."

"I'm fine, Muh'Dear."

"It's just the weddin' jitters. I had 'em both times I got married. That Frank. He was so frisky the day we got married, I had to hide from him to keep him from makin' a fool of hisself in front of the preacher. Oh, I never thought I'd live long enough to see you get married. And to such a fine young man!" Muh'Dear chuckled. "And Brother Boatwright was so afraid that all the decent young Black men would be dead or married to somebody else by the time you got grown. If only he could see how you turned out."

"Muh'Dear, I am really tired. Can we talk tomorrow?"

"All right, baby. You get some sleep."

I flung my overcoat on the back of the love seat facing my couch and dragged myself into the kitchen to rinse out my mouth.

Sleep was the last thing on my mind. All I could think about was Mr. Willie and his vicious threats. I recalled that ugly night I had let him have his way with me during my terrible teens. Before he had leaned me over his desk to enter me from behind, he had pushed me down on my knees and held my face against his vile, naked crotch. It had taken me three days to get the taste of his slimy dick out of my mouth. Now it looked like he was going to screw me again.

I had no idea how I was going to deal with my dilemma. But it was a comfort to know that Jerome didn't care about the things he didn't know about me. Or so he said. I made myself a strong drink. For a while, I felt fine. I was even feeling good enough to be enjoying a late-night edition of *Soul Train* on Channel 7. But my equilibrium was short-lived.

About an hour later, just as I was about to dial Jerome's number, my living room door swung open. I was in my nightgown, sitting on my living room couch, clutching the telephone. It was Jerome storming into my house. His face looked like the mask of the red devil. His cheeks were twitching, his lips were quivering, and his eyes looked like they were about to explode. Black veins had popped out on his forehead.

"Get your husky ass off that telephone!" Jerome roared. He kicked the door shut and stood facing me with his hands on his hips.

"Jerome, listen, baby," I began, holding up both hands. "Let me talk to you."

"You nasty-ass, low-down, funky, piece-of-shit, cock-sucking tramp!" Jerome was boiling with rage. In the blink of an eye, his face turned purple.

"Let me explain—" My voice was as weak as a kitten's.

Jerome started strutting in my direction, his hands still on his hips.

"How in the hell can you explain yourself?! Uncle Willie explained it for you, you bitch! Do you know what a fool I felt like, in front of my family, listening to that unholy shit you did?!" Jerome shot across the floor and jumped on top of me, pinning me down on the couch with his knee against my chest.

The back of my head hit the arm of my couch so hard I blacked out for a split second. "You heifer! Gimme back my ring!" Jerome grabbed my hand and forced the engagement ring that he had given me off my finger, almost breaking my wrist. "I can't believe it! I can't believe you'd let me get this far with your musty, black, cocksucking self! What if I had found out all this *after* I married your big ass? You bitch!"

As soon as he rolled off me, I stood up, facing him. "All

right. You've said what you had to say and you got your ring back, so leave." My voice was much stronger now. "And while we are at it, I have a few choice names for you, mother-fucker. You get your high-yellow, dickless, no-fucking, CHEAP ass the hell up out of my house!"

All the blood drained from Jerome's face. Now he looked almost as pale as a ghost. "Oh, I'm going, all right. But first I'm going to whup your whoring ass—" Jerome poised his fist and brought it down across the side of my face. I stumbled back a few steps, with him moving with me, ready to hit me again. I had never experienced so much rage before in my life and most of it was coming from me.

I balled my own hand and when I hit Jerome back, right across his lips, he hit the floor so hard, the lamp on my end table crashed to the floor.

"You let me tell you something, motherfucker. If you ever hit *me* again, I will kill you. Now get the hell out of my house!" I had removed my shoes but that didn't stop me from kicking Jerome in his side while he was still stretched out on the floor.

He grabbed the seat of my couch and pulled himself up. Blood was squirting from his lips. He slid his hand across his mouth, and then looked at his blood in disbelief.

"Bitch! You—you hit me," he choked. Tears and blood were sliding down his chin onto his neck. Strings of snot dangled from both sides of his nose. His wild eyes wouldn't stop blinking, as he shook his head from side to side.

"And I'm going to hit you again if you don't get the hell up out of my damn house. Nobody, but nobody, hits me and gets away with it," I yelled so hard my cheeks ached.

Even with this ruckus going on, my mind flashed on Mr. Boatwright. I had him to thank for all the anger I had internalized for so many years. It dawned on me that for the rest of my life, the wrath I should have bestowed on Mr. Boatwright, I would aim at anybody else who abused me. I knew it wasn't fair, but in my situation, worrying about what was fair to somebody else was not my problem. I had too much to make up to myself.

"You are going to burn up in hell, you lying wench," Jerome shrieked.

"Well, you are going to burn up *before* you get to hell, if you don't get out of my house." I spun that man around by his shoulder and pushed him toward the door. Then I helped him out with a swift kick in his ass with my heavy, bare foot. When I saw the blood he'd left on my clean carpet, I wanted to run out of that door and whup him some more.

Instead, I stood in the window and watched Jerome limp all the way back to his car. He didn't even turn on his lights as he shot off down Reed Street like a cannonball.

CHAPTER 45

Life had been so cruel to me. So many things beyond my control had caused me to make some truly stupid choices and I had paid dearly for my stupidity. Each time I had a setback, I thought about how happy I had been when Rhoda was in my life. I didn't know how I was going to get over my breakup with Jerome without the understanding female support I so desperately needed.

At this point, I looked at my half-sister Lillimae as a wild card. She seemed to be enough like me that I could eventually trust her with my deepest, darkest secrets. Her devotion to Daddy was an indication that she was a compassionate person. But I needed to get to know her better. And I planned to cultivate a closer relationship with her by calling her and writing her more frequently. Having met her and reuniting with Daddy had done wonders for my morale. But even so, I was moving forward with them slowly and carefully.

I rarely went to church anymore and I had not even prayed much lately. I knew I had to get over Jerome as soon as possible. However, I was too weak at that time to even turn to God. Instead, an hour after Jerome's departure, I started pacing my living room floor, so angry with myself, I kicked the foot of the couch. But that only added to my discomfort.

With my big toe throbbing, I got on the phone to start calling people to tell them that the wedding was off. I planned to offer a brief and vague explanation that Jerome and I had decided to see other people. I started with the most difficult person I knew.

"Was it another woman?" Scary Mary asked as soon as I got the words out. "Was Jerome the jealous type? I bet he was."

"Yes, ma'am." It was a good thing I was sitting down now because I was so weak and wobbly, I felt like I needed a cane.

"Was he generous?"

"No, ma'am. He was a cheapskate, too."

"Holy moly! Then you done the right thing. My second husband was jealous and cheap, too. He tried to choke me one day because he got it in his head that I was creepin' around with a preacher from Jacksonville. Well, him chokin' me was the biggest mistake he made in his life. You don't clown a Black woman when she got a hot skillet in her hands. Mine happened to have some corn in it that I was frying. I let him have that corn, right upside his head. He been bald-headed ever since." Scary Mary would have rattled on for hours if I had not cut the conversation short. "Before you get off the telephone, I got one more thing to say: I'll pray for you, child."

I waited a few moments before I dialed Muh'Dear's number. I was surprised that she reacted so calmly. "I was suspicious of that Cunningham family anyway. That mama of Jerome's was jealous about Judge Lawson leaving us that house. Don't you worry, baby. You'll get through this. I had a bad feeling about this night when Jerome's mama came by to pick up them rolls. As old as that lazy heifer is, she ought to know how to cook her own rolls by now."

It was well past midnight by the time I called up Pee Wee.

"Jerome and I broke up tonight. I know it's late, but I don't need to be alone right now. Can you come over?" I held my breath and waited.

Without hesitation, Pee Wee said, "I'm on my way."

Even after I had neglected him for years to be with Jerome, Pee Wee hopped out of his bed and rushed over to my house, with an overcoat over his pajamas. Just like a trained puppy.

"What he do to you?" Pee Wee asked as soon as he got in my door. He rushed over to my coffee table and poured wine into two glasses that I had already brought from the kitchen. "You want me to kick his ass? You want me to slash the tires on his car and put some sugar in his tank? Oh, I'll fix him up real good."

I shook my head and held up my hand. "Before we go any further, I need to tell you some things about me that you don't know," I said evenly.

"So, what's up?" Pee Wee handed me a glass of wine and sat down on the couch while I stood in the middle of the floor, pacing like a tiger.

"I am no angel," I began, gulping a huge dose of wine.

For a moment, he just stared at me with a blank expression on his face. Then he covered his mouth with his hand. He threw back his head and guffawed so hard, he started choking. When he straightened up, he had tears in his eyes. His lips were quivering like he was gearing up to laugh some more. "I could have told you that. And guess what? I ain't no angel myself. What's your point?" He pressed his lips together and laughed under his breath, taking quick sips of wine.

"You stop that!" I slapped the side of my thigh and that

made Pee Wee get serious. He sniffed and blinked, looking at me like he was looking at me for the first time. "Pee Wee, what I'm about to say is hard enough. Now you just sit there and listen for a minute," I ordered, drinking some more.

Pee Wee drank from his glass as I talked. He was so anxious he couldn't sit still. He kept crossing and uncrossing his legs and caressing his goatee.

I cleared my throat. But my mouth was still dry and my throat hurt so, it was painful for me to talk. "When Rhoda got married and moved away and when you went to the army, I turned a few tricks with some of Scary Mary's customers. I needed to scrape up enough money to leave home with." I tilted my head. Out of the corner of my eye I stared at Pee Wee in a fever of anticipation. I didn't know what I expected him to say or do, but I was surprised by his mild response.

"Go on." Pee Wee nodded and waved his glass at me.

"That's it. I was a prostitute."

"Well, ain't you a dark horse." Pee Wee gave me an amused look and shook his head, saluting me with his wine-glass. "You just full of surprises, girl."

I held up my hand and said quickly, "It was just for a minute, but Jerome found out about it and he broke up with me. His Uncle Willie from Columbus was my last trick. He blabbed."

"Is that all? Girl, I thought you was goin' to tell me you did somethin' *real* crazy." Pee Wee paused and grinned as I continued.

"Jerome got real violent with me," I said flatly, sighing heavily.

Pee Wee froze and an evil look crossed his face. "Did he hurt you?"

I shook my head. "No. But I beat the dog-shit out of him." We both laughed. "Pee Wee, do you still want to be my friend?"

"Yeah. Why wouldn't I?" my dear friend said gently, giving me an affectionate look.

I didn't know what I had done to deserve a friend like Pee Wee.

"What about me . . . doing what I did with those men?" I asked in a meek voice.

Pee Wee let out a deep sigh and shrugged. "So what? What about it? I mean, what do you want me to say?"

"You can say whatever you want to say. How does what I did make you feel toward me now? Do you realize what I just told you? Do you know what it means?"

Pee Wee sniffed and rubbed his thigh. He finished the wine in his glass and poured some more, shaking his head as he spoke. "I guess I done run up one hell of a tab."

"What do you mean?" I turned my head to the side and gazed at him from the corner of my burning eye.

Pee Wee snapped his fingers. "I mean what I just said. As many times as we hooked up, I must owe you everything I got but my citizenship."

"Is that all you have to say about . . . this thing I just told you?"

Pee Wee shook his head. "Just one more thing. I hope them other tricks gave you some big money, 'cause you got some damn good pussy."

"You nasty thing, you!" As hard as I tried not to, I laughed anyway.

Pee Wee slapped his knee and clicked his teeth. "Aw shit, girl. I got too much invested in your black ass to be runnin' out on you over some shit like that. I ain't Jerome." Pee Wee shook his head and exhaled before he looked at me again, giving me a thoughtful look. "What happens when Jerome cools off?"

"Nothing." For emphasis, I shook my head vigorously and narrowed my eyes. "I never want to see him again as long as I live."

"Well, that's the best news I done heard all year." Pee Wee rose and held out his hand to me and nodded toward the steps leading to my bedroom. "Come on, girl. Let's go upstairs. We got a lot of catchin' up to do."

I sighed. "What the hell," I said, rising.

I locked my front door and propped a chair up against it—in case Jerome decided to come back. I smiled at Pee Wee, feeling warmer and more comfortable than I had felt in a long time.

Then I took his hand and led him upstairs to my bedroom.

CHAPTER 46

In a town as small as Richland, it was hard to avoid Jerome and other members of his family. A few days after our violent breakup, I ran into one of his brothers at the mall. He turned as red as a tomato and looked at me like I had leprosy.

A week later I ran into Jerome's mother at Miss Rachel's, the upscale hair salon that catered to Black women. Marlene ignored me completely as I sat there getting my hair rebraided, while she got her hair dyed in the seat right next to mine.

Even Jerome's sister Nadine shunned me when I saw her shopping for groceries at Kroger's the following Saturday afternoon. She left the market before I did and when I went out to my car, she was leaning on her car, looking at me and shaking her head.

When I did see Jerome, it was at the movies. I was with Pee Wee, Jerome was with a stout, dark-skinned woman I'd never seen before. He gave me one of the meanest looks anybody ever gave me.

Ironically, Jerome's Uncle Willie was not the only one of my former customers I saw. On two separate occasions I ran into other men that I had slept with for money. Either they didn't recognize me or they didn't remember me because they ignored me. But it didn't bother me one bit. I really had nothing else to lose now.

I cheered myself up by spending as much time as I could with Pee Wee. When he developed a cold and didn't want to leave his house, I went over there. Before we could find a spot with enough room for us to fuck, I had to clean up his living room. He had a couch that let out into a bed, so that was good enough, once I removed all the fast-food containers and dirty clothes.

"And don't think I'm going to let you kiss me. I don't want to catch your cold," I told Pee Wee, glaring at him stretched out on his couch-bed in a sleeping bag, waiting to clamber back on top of me.

"You just better hurry up and get out your clothes before my dick go back to sleep," he told me in a weak voice. Even sick with a cold, Pee Wee gave me more pleasure than Jerome ever did. I was just as weak as he was by the time we finished. I limped home, feeling like a different woman. And I was. I felt like I had just come back from the dead.

I stuffed all of the clothes, cassette tapes, and other things in my house that belonged to Jerome into old grocery bags. A few days later, when Pee Wee was feeling better, he drove me to Jerome's apartment. He waited in his car when I went to knock on Jerome's door.

"What the hell do you want?" Jerome roared, standing in his doorway in a pair of boxer shorts. "If you thinking about crawling back to me—"

"Don't flatter yourself, nigger. It'd be a cold day in hell before I crawl for you or any other man," I snarled.

Jerome gasped and stared at me with a look on his face so harsh my flesh crawled.

"Look, woman—"

"No, *you* look." I pointed to Pee Wee's car. "I got the shit you left in my house out here. If you want it, you better bring your sorry yellow ass out here to get it."

Jerome gasped and stretched his eyes open as wide as he could. "Woman, who in the hell do you think you are to be bringing that black-ass nigger over here?" Jerome shouted, shaking his finger in my face.

"Do you want your shit or not? And you better hurry up because I got more important things to do with my time—with that black-ass nigger I brought over here with me," I said, folding my arms.

Jerome gave me a hot look and then he slammed the door in my face. I returned to Pee Wee's car and told him to drive to the city dump. Whistling and puffing on a joint, Pee Wee helped me toss Jerome's belongings onto a mountain of other debris.

Back in the car, Pee Wee leaned over and kissed me. "You feel better now?" he asked, caressing my chin.

I took a deep breath and let it out before I replied. "Better than I've felt in years," I said. "Take me home so I can call up my daddy."

Daddy was disappointed about not being able to visit Ohio and see me get married. But he wanted to see me anyway.

"I might go see Daddy again for a few days," I told Muh'Dear the next day.

"I see." Muh'Dear sniffed and cleared her throat. "Why don't you make your daddy come up here? It ain't fair for you to go down there every time." Muh'Dear's suggestion stunned me. Her change of heart startled Daddy so hard, he had to take a pill when I called to tell him.

"You sure your mama ain't layin' in wait for me, ready to bounce a fryin' pan off my head?" He laughed as he chewed on an aspirin.

"No, Daddy. I think she's ready to see you again anyway."
I laughed, too.

I was glad that I had something to keep me from thinking
about Jerome. Daddy's upcoming visit was like an elixir for
my morale.

CHAPTER 47

A lot of people assume that women my size love to go grocery shopping. I was one big woman who would rather get a whupping than shop for groceries. That's why I ate out as much as I did. I spent a great deal of my paycheck on expensive restaurants—McDonald's, Burger King, and every place in between.

My meals at the Buttercup were free, but I had to limit my visits there to two or three times a week because of Muh'Dear. It didn't matter to her if I'd come in with Pee Wee and Jean in tow; Muh'Dear still took me aside to badger me with a siege of perfunctory questions and comments. "Did you find a new boyfriend yet? I don't want you to be alone at your age. You keepin' that house clean? Cleanliness is next to godliness. You payin' your bills on time? You don't want to mess up your credit."

Shopping for groceries brought back too many painful memories. Throughout my youth, when Mr. Boatwright was still alive, he used to drag me all over town to gather up the foods he enjoyed cooking. During those days, we'd purchased most of our food at a discount market called The Food Bucket, where the quality of the food was low and the service was even lower. We had to stand in long lines behind people taking their good old time to locate food stamps and checks they couldn't cash at any other place. The clerks were rude and the other patrons were even ruder. They jumped ahead of other people already in a checkout line; they knocked over displays, and shoplifted in plain view. Mr. Hood, a bowlegged, elderly security guard, had been at The Food Bucket ever since I could remember. I had never seen Mr. Hood do anything but hold customers hostage, boring them to exasperation with long-winded updates of his health.

Now that I shopped alone and paid for my purchases with my own money, I bought my groceries at Kroger's or the A&P, which were both considered upscale compared to The Food Bucket.

I still hated shopping for groceries, even at the nice stores. This particular Saturday evening was no different. I only grabbed what I needed and rushed back to my car and headed for home.

I didn't like cold weather but I had to admit that I liked the way Ohio looked in the wintertime. A fresh blanket of fluffy snow covered the ground and houses and the city snow trucks had come out earlier and cleared the streets. I took my time driving home, admiring how the trees looked with their branches heavy with thick wands of snow and ice. Almost every yard had a snowman and that brought back some painful memories. Mr. Boatwright used to play with me in the snow when I was a child. Before he had started abusing me, he used to help me build snowmen. After he started putting his hands on me, the snowmen became snow*women*, complete with scarves and aprons. "I just love me some females," he told me with a look in his eyes that told me what was coming next: a trip to bed. I was glad that none of the snow people I saw now in the yards along my way were feminine.

The backseat of my car was covered with assorted fresh meat and several bunches of greens. This was part of the food I planned to cook for Daddy and Lillimae. They were due in later that night from Miami.

It was the first week in January. I was glad that Christmas had come and gone. It had been a dark day for me. Instead of marrying Jerome on Christmas Day like I had planned, I had spent the day with Muh'Dear and Pee Wee. Later that night, I had talked on the telephone with Lillimae and Daddy for over an hour, anticipating their first visit to Ohio.

Driving home from Kroger's, I stopped my car so abruptly at the stop sign across from Jean's house, my head lurched forward. My neck muscles got so tight I was afraid they'd snap. There was a thin film of snow on my windshield so I had to turn the wipers on to make sure I was seeing what I thought I was seeing. At first I thought I was seeing some kind of an illusion. I blinked hard and rubbed my eyes. Unfortunately, my eyes were not playing tricks on me. Standing in Jean's front yard, along with her brooding boyfriend Vinnie and her young daughter P., was an older white man I didn't see in public that often anymore, Carmine Antonosanti. He owned Antonosanti's, the most expensive restaurant in town. I had first met him when I was thirteen, the same year I met Rhoda Nelson. Mr. Antonosanti had been so close to Rhoda's family that she called him Uncle Carmine. Rhoda was the one who had introduced me to him at her house one day after school.

According to Rhoda, this old Italian man and her daddy had served in the army together. Rhoda's daddy had saved Mr. Antonosanti's life on a battlefield somewhere in Germany and because of that, Mr. Antonosanti had become one of Rhoda's family's most important friends. Standing between Jean and Mr. Antonosanti—a walking cane in each of his gnarled hands—was Rhoda Nelson. Even though Rhoda had married Otis O'Toole, I still thought of her by her maiden name. I kept thinking her name over and over in my mind as I blinked my eyes so hard they started to ache.

Seeing Rhoda at the mall and the Red Rose nightclub had traumatized me enough. Seeing her this close to my own house with my friend Jean was excruciating. I could no longer ignore the fact that Rhoda was back in Richland, Ohio, and I had to find out why and what she was up to. But the most important thing about her return was how it would involve me.

Rhoda was living proof that Mother Nature had her favorites. My former friend was as breathtakingly beautiful as ever. At thirty-five, she still had the face of a cover girl. Her long black hair hung down her back like a silk scarf. After having three children, she was still a size four, a size I couldn't even fathom. As hard as it was to believe, there actually were women who looked like Barbie dolls and Rhoda was one of them.

I had not talked to Rhoda since the week of Thanksgiving in 1978, the night she had confessed to me that in addition to murdering Mr. Boatwright, she had murdered three other people. That was the night I had told her I could no longer be friends with her. Not long after that night, the rest of Rhoda's family moved away. Their empty house, which included the mortuary her father had owned and Rhoda's life-size dollhouse, had all mysteriously burned to the ground.

I had often wondered about what had happened to Rhoda's handsome father and her beautiful mother. I had even asked Scary Mary, but even she didn't know. After a while, I stopped asking. Seeing Rhoda now was like seeing a ghost and, in a way, it was.

Standing next to Rhoda was a little Black girl around P.'s age. This little girl, who was the image of Rhoda, had to be Rhoda's daughter, the child she had been carrying in her belly the last time I saw her. I didn't torture myself by looking at Rhoda's daughter for more than a moment. I had seen enough. The child was just as dazzling as her mother.

The small crowd was very animated—talking, laughing, and waving their arms. But P., sullen and mute, was standing a few feet away from the boisterous group, sucking her thumb. She was the only one who noticed me sitting in my car staring with my hand shading my eyes. A faint smile crossed P.'s face and she waved at me. Knowing P. as well as I did, I was certain that she missed coming to my house as much as I missed her coming.

I slid down in my seat as far as I could as my car shot across the street like a guided missile.

CHAPTER 48

After I parked in front of my house, I had to sit still for about five minutes with my window rolled down. I needed to feel the cool air on my face so I could focus on what I was doing. Breathing with my mouth open, I felt as clumsy as a seal trying to undo my seat belt and maneuver myself out of my car. My big legs felt as heavy as tree trunks as I lifted them. I finally tumbled out, my shoes sliding, even though there was no ice on the ground. I looked across the street at the empty spot where the Nelsons' house had stood before a mysterious fire consumed it a few years earlier. Then I looked down the street toward Jean's house. The crowd was still there. Since I'd had the conversation with Jean about Vinnie taking P. out of my wedding, Jean and I didn't get together as often outside of work. And even then, we talked about everything but Vinnie and P.

I watched P. tug on the tail of Rhoda's coat, then point in my direction. I cringed when Rhoda looked in my direction for a brief moment, giving me the same blank stare she would have given a stranger. Without acknowledging me, Rhoda returned her attention to Vinnie Gambiano, who was standing so close to her, skinning and grinning, you would have thought that they were lovers.

I dumped my packages on my porch and sprinted across my yard to Pee Wee's house. I knocked for several minutes before he came to the door.

"What's up?" he drawled, a toothpick dangling from his lip, a damp towel draped around his shoulders. I looked over his shoulder and I could see that his living room was once again a huge mess. Hand weights and a barbell were on the floor next to a pizza container and a beer can. A dirty T-shirt was on top of a lamp, the sleeves dangling like snakes. I was more than willing to clean house for Pee Wee again, if that's what I had to do to get him alone.

"Can we talk?" I asked breathlessly. Now that Jerome was out of my life, I felt that I could once again use Pee Wee as the sounding board I desperately needed now.

Pee Wee glanced over his shoulder first. "I'm just gettin' out the shower. Can this wait?"

"Do you have somebody in there with you?" I asked impatiently, trying to look past him again.

"Ain't nobody here but me," he said, opening the door wider as he made a sweeping gesture with his hand.

I snorted so hard, the insides of my nostrils burned. "Did you know that Rhoda was back in town?" I asked gruffly. My manner startled Pee Wee. He widened his eyes and gave me a confused look. "Man, don't look at me like I'm crazy," I yelled, stomping my foot. "Just answer the question."

"Yeah." He shrugged, removing the toothpick from between his lips. "I knew Rhoda was back in town. Why?"

My mouth dropped open. "How come you didn't tell me?"

He shrugged again. "I thought you knew. She been back a few months."

"She's back here to stay?" I managed, blinking and rubbing my nose.

Pee Wee nodded. "Uh-huh. She live over on Noble Street

now, next to the bowlin' alley. That Jamaican she married sure knows how to treat her. I heard the dude filled up that house with brand-new furniture and done already contracted to have a pool dug in the backyard as soon as the weather breaks." Pee Wee whistled and shook his head. "One thing I can say about Rhoda: what she wants, she gets. That sister always was out of my league." Pee Wee lifted his head and gave me a suspicious look, his eyes half-closed. "What's up with you and her anyway? Every time I brought up her name you changed the subject."

"That's what I need to talk to you about. Will you call me or come over as soon as you can?" I asked, looking over Pee Wee's shoulder once again. Soft jazz was playing from the cassette player he kept on a stand in his living room. He had burned something in his kitchen. I could still smell the smoke.

He nodded. "Yeah. I can do that." He glanced toward my house and scratched the side of his neck. "I thought your daddy and your sister was comin' up from Florida today."

"They won't get here until around eleven tonight."

"Can't we talk tomorrow? I was thinkin' about slidin' over to the poolroom for a while. And after that, I'm goin' over to my cousin's house to watch the game so it'll be real late when I get back home."

"I need to talk to you before you do all that. This can't wait that long," I said impatiently. I never asked much of Pee Wee and when I did, he always came through.

"I'll be over in a little while," he told me, a puzzled look on his face. "This better be worth it," he said sharply. He sniffed and gave me a threatening look.

"It is," I assured him with a firm nod.

CHAPTER 49

I had suffered the consequences of my actions more times than I could count. Now that I was approaching middle age (already there, according to some folks), I was more concerned about doing what I thought was right, no matter what price I had to pay.

The telephone call that I had made to the Child Protective Services alerting them to P.'s situation had taken a lot of nerve on my part. I had done it because I knew that it was the right thing to do. However, I didn't have enough nerve left to follow up on that call. Besides, I had other things on my agenda that I had to address now. Like Daddy and Lillimae coming to visit—and now, Rhoda's reappearance.

Keeping my mind occupied helped keep me from thinking about my violent breakup with Jerome. The return of Rhoda and what I was going to do about it would certainly cancel out any more thoughts about Jerome. At least for the time being.

Even though it had been years and I had made a promise to Rhoda, I could no longer keep silent about the crimes she had confessed to me. Seeing her today, grinning with her

Italian friends and looking so beautiful, had a strange effect on me. I think I would have felt better about seeing her if she'd lost some of her beauty and if she had seemed more restrained. I wondered if Rhoda ever thought about what she'd done to those people and if she ever felt remorse. That morbid secret suddenly felt like it wanted to explode right out of my head on its own. I *had* to finally release it in a more dignified manner.

"Did Rhoda ever tell you why she and I stopped being friends?" I asked as soon as Pee Wee entered my living room a few minutes after I'd left his house.

Knowing he loved jazz as much as I did, I had popped an old Nina Simone tape into my cassette player. I had tossed my overcoat on the back of the couch and slid off my shoes. The soft carpet felt good against my feet, but I had started itching all over since I'd seen Rhoda. I stood facing Pee Wee, scratching my arms and neck as I talked.

Pee Wee shook his head and gave me an indifferent look. "Not really. She gave me the same weak-ass story you gave me. Somethin' about y'all growin' apart." Pee Wee rooted through my tape collection on the floor. "You ain't got no Bob Marley?" he asked, squatting on the floor.

"They are all at your house," I reminded, sinking down hard onto the couch with my arms folded. "Pee Wee, I trust you. You are the only person I can tell something this serious."

Pee Wee looked up from the tapes and slid his tongue across his bottom lip. "Oh, this must be river deep, judging from the look on your face. Should I have a drink first or should I sit down?"

"You better do both," I whimpered, wringing my hands.

I sucked in my breath and closed my eyes for a few moments. When I opened my eyes, Pee Wee was staring at me with a horrified look on his face.

"Girl, what in the hell is the matter with you? I hope you

ain't about to have no screamin' fit, or no nervous breakdown or nothin' else that I can't handle up in here," Pee Wee
said with alarm.

"I'm fine. Just go get the drinks," I said, breathing through
my mouth as I waved Pee Wee from the room.

He literally ran into my kitchen and returned with a six-
pack of beer. He popped open one for himself and one for
me, placing the other four on the floor next to his feet as he
plopped down on the love seat facing my couch. I was pacing the floor, looking toward the door.

"Pee Wee, Rhoda killed Mr. Boatwright," I blurted out. I
stood stock-still and held my breath, clutching the can in my
hand before I took a swallow.

Pee Wee shrieked like a loon and started choking on his
beer. I had to run across the floor to slap him on the back.

Between coughs and wide-eyed expressions, he said,
"Oh, come on, girl. Don't be playin' with me. Why you
comin' out with some crazy shit like that?"

"I swear to God. And he wasn't the only one—"

Pee Wee held up his hand, frowning ferociously. "Hold on
now. Let's take this slow. You tellin' me that itty-bitty Rhoda
killed old man Boatwright *and* somebody else? Well, tell me
why you think she killed Boatwright first, and then tell
me about the rest." He paused to let my words sink in. Then
he gave me a thoughtful look before taking another sip of his
beer.

"Uh. She didn't like him. I know he had everybody believing that he was all holy and saved and stuff, but he wasn't."

"Exactly what did the old brother do that made Rhoda kill
him?" Pee Wee asked, wiping his wet lips with the back of
his hand.

"Uh . . . he was mean to her so she smothered him while
he was sleeping."

Pee Wee laughed, shook his head, and slapped his knee.

"Don't laugh. I'm telling the truth. I've been carrying this around too long. When I saw her today, I knew I had to get this off of my chest. It's time I did the right thing by telling."

"Well, the right thing would be goin' to the cops and tellin' them."

"I can't do that—"

"You think you doin' the right thing by tellin' *me*? What do you expect me to do?"

"I just want you to listen. I wanted somebody else to share this with." The room got so quiet you could hear a pin drop. I could no longer hear Nina Simone.

"So who else did Rhoda kill?" Pee Wee asked seriously, leaning his head forward, toying with the tip of his goatee.

"Her grandmother," I said flatly. I couldn't believe that I was finally revealing Rhoda's unspeakable crimes to another person. I was frightened and relieved at the same time.

Pee Wee just stared at me with his mouth hanging open. His hand froze in midair. "Now *that* I can understand. I can't tell you how many times I wanted to off that old battle-ax myself." He let out a groan and started scratching the side of his neck.

I sighed and started pacing the floor again. "I'm not through. You need to hear it all."

CHAPTER 50

Before I could continue my lurid confession, Pee Wee leaped from his seat and took the stairs three at a time to get upstairs to the bathroom. He returned to his seat within minutes and snatched up his beer and took a long swallow.

"You mean the sister killed somebody else?" he asked with his eyes stretched open so wide, I was afraid that his eyeballs would pop out and roll across the floor.

"Uh-huh." I nodded, sitting down hard on my couch. "She sure did." I took several deep breaths, not taking my eyes off of Pee Wee's face. His mouth was hanging open. He slid his tongue back and forth across his bottom lip.

Pee Wee blinked a few times, returned his eyes to their normal size, and rubbed his neck. "Girl, this is some of the most off-the-wall shit you ever told me."

"And I hope you're believing me because every word of it is true."

Not taking his eyes off of me, Pee Wee drained his beer can and popped open another one with his teeth. He tilted his head and motioned with his hand for me to continue.

"Remember that cop that shot Rhoda's brother, David?

Well, she killed him, too. And when she was still living in Florida, she killed a white girl named April that her brother Jock got pregnant. April was threatening to tell her racist daddy all kinds of shit. She said that if Jock left her, she was going to say Rhoda's husband was the one that got her pregnant."

Once again, Pee Wee stared at me in slackjawed amazement. "Why you tellin' me all this crazy shit, girl? Is this got anything to do with you and Jerome bustin' up?"

"Forget about Jerome!" I snarled, rising from the couch, waving my arms. "None of this has anything to do with Jerome Cunningham."

Pee Wee shook his head and rubbed his eyes. He leaned back in his chair and screwed up his face like a coin purse. The look on his face was so extreme, I thought he was in pain and I guess he was. He started rubbing his chest and moaning. "Girl, you a mess. I—you serious, ain't you?"

"I swear to God. You know me well enough to know I wouldn't be making all this up."

"Let me ask you somethin'. Did you witness Rhoda do any of this shit?"

"Huh? No, I didn't. But she told me out of her own mouth!"

"Damn! And I thought your little confession about that prostitutin' thing was a pip."

A wave of sadness crossed my face and it seemed like the room got darker, but it was only my mood. "You don't believe me, do you?" I waved my hand in exasperation. "Why would I be lying to you about something like this?"

Pee Wee exhaled and let out a deep breath. "Hell if I know." He paused and leaned his body so far to the side, I thought he was going to roll right out of his seat. "Why did you wait so long to tell me this outrageous shit?"

"Rhoda made me promise not to tell anybody. I didn't because I was afraid that if she got caught, I'd be in trouble my-self for not telling. You know how strange the law is." My hands were trembling.

"In the first place, if Rhoda wanted to make sure she never got caught, why she tell you all this shit? And another thing, how could she have killed four people and got away with it? The woman ain't no bigger than a snap bean." Pee Wee groaned and started tapping his knee with the bottom of his beer can. "One of my hands would make two of hers. Yours would, too, for that matter."

"She smothered Mr. Boatwright with his own pillow while he was sleeping. Everybody thought he just died in his sleep that night. She pushed her grandmother down the steps and the old lady broke her neck. And remember how Rhoda was always running into things with that old car her daddy bought for her and her brother Jock? Well, when she ran down that cop, everybody thought it was just a hit-and-run. With that white girl in Florida, Rhoda threw a radio in the bathtub while the girl was taking a bath and electrocuted her. I swear she did."

"But you ain't seen none of this shit."

"No. But why would Rhoda confess to it all if it wasn't true?"

"Sound like to me Rhoda girl got a serious problem, but it ain't murder. If that sister told you some funky shit like that, she got her a mental problem. Ain't you never heard of pathological liars?"

"Of course I have, but why would Rhoda make up lies like that?"

"Because if she is a pathological liar, tellin' lies is what she supposed to do. At least that's the way her mind see it. And the bigger the lies, the better. My cousin Claude in Erie is a kleptomaniac. He'd steal your mind if he could. Stealin' and lyin' ain't so bad if the person doin' it don't know no bet-ter. They ain't no worse than alcoholics."

I sank back onto the couch, folding my arms. I didn't know why I was trembling. One thing I knew about Pee Wee was that I could trust him.

"Pee Wee, I knew Rhoda better than anybody. And it all made sense to me. She had a reason to kill all four of those people."

"The old lady, the cop, and the white girl, I could see her havin' the ass with them. But old man Boatwright was like a granddaddy to all of us. What could a harmless old man like Boatwright have done to Rhoda to make her kill him?"

"Didn't I just tell you he wasn't what he seemed to be?"

"Like how? The old dude could barely get around on that one leg of his. Hell. He was even more harmless than Rhoda. His head was always up in the Bible and shit."

"You don't believe me, do you?" I pouted. "I've wasted my time and yours by sharing this with you."

"Oh, I believe you, all right. I believe Rhoda told you some crazy shit and you believed her. But I don't believe what Rhoda told you. What I do believe is what I just said— the girl was a pathological liar and still could be. Is all that shit she told you the real reason you cut her loose?"

I didn't realize I was still trembling until I looked at my hands. The can of beer in my hand was shaking so hard, beer spilled out. Suds covered my hand like a glove.

I shook my head. "I was scared. I thought that if Rhoda got caught, I'd go down with her."

"Well, if what she told you is true, and she gets caught, you goin' down with her anyway." Pee Wee ran into the kitchen and returned with a paper towel, mopping sweat off his face.

"Pee Wee, you have to promise me you won't tell anybody what I just told you."

Laughing, he sat back down, dropping the paper towel to the floor. "Oh, you ain't got to worry about that. What you need to be worried about is why Rhoda told you that pack of lies in the first place. Did you ever sit her down and try to figure her out?" Pee Wee shook his head and gave me a pitying look. "I always thought that out of the three of us, you was the one with the most common sense." He laughed again and drank some more. He stopped laughing when he saw how hard I was staring at him. He let out a gasp that resembled a croak. "You really believed that woman. Didn't you?"

I nodded. "Why would a smart girl like Rhoda tell lies like that? She wasn't crazy. You know her daddy would have taken her to the best shrink money could buy if he thought she had a problem."

"And how do you know she wasn't cracked? If you'd have seen a cop shoot your brother dead like she done, you'd be havin' some serious problems, too, I bet." Pee Wee took a quiet, quick sip from his beer can, and then let out a loud belch. He slapped his chest before letting out another belch, frowning, and shaking his head. "Now, Rhoda was my girl way before I met you. She wasn't like the other girls I knew. She seemed too perfect. Even when we was kids, I knew she was carryin' around some heavy shit from seein' her brother get killed. Why her folks didn't take her to a shrink, I don't know. But I never said nothin' to her about how strange she was. She was always cool with me."

"She gave me the coldest look today when I saw her," I said, staring at the wall behind Pee Wee.

"I would have, too. You was the only girlfriend she had and you was good for her. She used to tell me all the time how she didn't know how she'd make it without you to talk to."

"Rhoda told you that?"

Pee Wee nodded. "All the time. You was a lifeline to her. Then you up and dropped her like a bad habit without tryin' to get to the root of her problem? Hell, no wonder she gave you the evil eye today."

I gasped and felt a tug at the bottom of my heart. Then I

felt a twinge of sadness and regret. I had to wonder what Rhoda would say if she knew I had just blabbed on her. I also wondered what she would do to me. Fear gripped me so hard, my neck suddenly felt like a noose had been placed around it. I had to loosen the top buttons on my blouse so I could breathe. "Pee Wee, promise me you won't tell Rhoda what I told you. Or anybody else."

"Oh, you ain't got to worry about me spreadin' them bare-butt lies. I ain't that crazy. If the girl really was bold enough to put somebody's lights out, I wouldn't want to be on her shit list. Now you promise me somethin', Annette."

"What?"

"Promise me that if you and Rhoda do get back together, you try to talk her into gettin' some therapy." Pee Wee drained his beer can and started moving toward the door, shaking his head and laughing and humming that ominous theme music from *The Twilight Zone*.

CHAPTER 51

It saddened me to know that Pee Wee had taken the news I'd shared with him so lightly. But I was glad that I'd finally told him. As off-the-wall as it was, his reaction had given me something else to consider. His theory about Rhoda's behavior made as much sense as anything else. It was possible that Rhoda was not the ghoul I thought she was. I had to ask myself: What if Rhoda had lied to me about smothering Mr. Boatwright and killing those other three people? What if she had a medical problem that interfered with her telling the truth? Hadn't I read about people telling lies to get attention? Good God! I had a hard time concentrating on the drive to the airport to pick up Daddy and Lillimae.

Richland didn't have an airport. The closest one was in Akron, about thirty-five miles away. Pee Wee had offered to ride along with me, but I had declined his offer. His reaction to what I'd told him about Rhoda also had me wondering how it was going to affect my relationship with him. Pee Wee was the most levelheaded person I knew. The last thing I wanted to lose him over was him thinking that I was crazy or worse. Even so, I was anxious for him to meet the rest of my family. I had invited him to join us for the Sunday dinner I planned to prepare.

Muh'Dear had already made it clear that she had no desire to come to the house to see Daddy. That saddened me. "Frank Goode will never get another chance to hurt my feelin's," she had assured me. However, just her agreeing to let Daddy and Lillimae stay with me in the house on Reed Street told me I was making progress. I was comforted even more when she told me, "I hope Frank don't get in my face and clown me when I do decide to see him. I'll bounce somethin' hard off his head so quick he'll be listenin' through his nose." Her laugh that had followed the comment gave me even more hope that one day my parents would be friends again.

Scary Mary invited herself to the Sunday dinner I planned to host, but I would have invited her anyway. Jean couldn't join us. However, she did agree to come over to meet Daddy and Lillimae later that night. That is, if she could get away from Vinnie long enough. Vinnie liked to keep a short leash on Jean these days. Work was the only place she was allowed to go to without his permission or without him nipping at her heels. After Vinnie had pulled P. out of my wedding, I had lost what little respect I had for him. I shouldn't have, but I talked about him like a dog to Jean every chance I got. I knew she didn't appreciate it and she made that clear.

"Annette, if you don't like Vinnie, that's your business, but I do love him. You trashing him is not going to change that. You really need to get over what Jerome did to you and get a life," Jean told me.

The last thing I wanted anybody to think was that I was still reacting over my breakup with Jerome. I still loved Jerome and I wanted him to be happy, even if it was without me. But Jerome had nothing to do with the way I behaved regarding Vinnie Gambiano or anybody else.

I still didn't know if the Child Protective Services investigators had approached Vinnie and Jean to follow up on that anonymous telephone call I had made about P. But something had happened in Jean's house. Now the curtains stayed closed all day, every day. And I rarely saw P. outside in her front yard playing like I used to. Jean had stopped calling and visiting my house two or three times a week and I had stopped calling and going to visit her. It was a shame that another man had brought some more unhappiness into my life.

Things would never be the same again for Jean or me.

CHAPTER 52

I had assigned Daddy to Muh'Dear's old room. I insisted that Lillimae sleep in my room. I planned to sleep downstairs on the living room couch during their visit.

Even though I had clean sheets, I had bought new ones for the beds. The last thing I wanted was for my daddy and my sister to wallow on sheets that I had fucked Jerome and Pee Wee on.

Daddy gasped as I helped him unpack the rest of his things the following Saturday evening. "With all this frilly she-stuff in here, I'm liable to forget my true nature up in here." He laughed, waving his hand around the room, frowning at the yellow curtains and white bedspread. "Girl, why you gwine to sleep on a couch when you got that other big, empty bedroom across that hall yonder?" He nodded toward the door with a puzzled look on his face. Mr. Boatwright's old room represented a lot of unresolved pain for me. I only went into that room when I had to. Like, to store old clothes and other things I wasn't ready to part with. The last time I had entered the room, two years ago, I discovered spider webs in every corner. I left them there and had not been in the room since.

"Uh, somebody died in that room," I explained, sitting down on the new four-poster I had installed to replace the one Muh'Dear had slept in for more than twenty years. The mattress and springs were so firm they didn't even creak under my hefty behind. It was the bed that I had hoped to share with Jerome and conceive my children. When Pee Wee paid me a visit, we sometimes ended up wallowing around in it, just to add some variety to our clumsy routine. I had put new sheets on it, too. Pee Wee and I did other things to keep our relationship from getting boring. After a few too many beers and maybe a strong joint, we rolled around on a pallet on the living room floor. I was thinking about my romps with Pee Wee so there was a smile on my face when I cleared my throat and said, "Death makes me nervous, Daddy."

Standing in the middle of the floor, Daddy looked at me with a confused expression on his face. "Oh? Well, do say." He shook his head and dragged his fingers through his wiry hair. "Now, I don't blame you for that. My dead grandpa's haint floated above my bed one night when I was a young'un and scared me so bad I busted the bedroom door down tryin' to get out that room so fast. Who was it that died in that room, anyway?"

"Uh, that boarder we had living with us for a few years. An elderly, sickly old man. He died in his sleep." I paused and caressed my chin, my eyes looking around the room. "I hope you and Lillimae are hungry. I've been cooking all evening." I rose from the bed with a grin.

"Elderly and sick, huh? I bet it was a stroke."

"Something like that," I said quietly.

"I know that old brother had to be good to y'all. Your mama don't take no mess off nobody."

"He was, Daddy. And you're right about Muh'Dear. She wouldn't take mess off any man."

Daddy sighed sadly and shook his head. "Not even me. When I come home from servin' for Uncle Sam overseas, I had a little, uh, social ailment I caught from one of them French gals over yonder. Your mama batted my head with a plank."

I gasped. "I never knew you were in the service."

"Oh, there's a whole lot you don't know about me, girl. We'll get reacquainted, don't worry. I ain't never turnin' my back on you no more."

I cleared my throat and looked away. "I know you won't, Daddy," I said, my eyes getting misty. "Now, hurry up. Come get acquainted with a couple of my friends. There will be plenty of time for us to talk later."

After an extended visit to the bathroom, Daddy joined Lillimae, Scary Mary, Pee Wee, and me at the dinner table. Steam was still rising from the huge bowl of collard greens I had dumped from a CrockPot. I had fried two whole chickens and made a huge pan of cornbread from scratch. Okra and corn were swimming around in a bowl of tomato sauce. I had bought a gallon of vanilla ice cream to go with the peach cobbler that Scary Mary said was "screaming loud and clear" from a plate next to the cornbread.

As soon as Scary Mary got me alone in the kitchen after the elaborate dinner, she started whispering. "How come you didn't tell me your sister was walkin' around lookin' like a white woman? And how come y'all didn't tell me Frank Goode was such a good-lookin' man? No wonder that white woman snatched him from your mama and ran. He'd have opened up my nose, too." Scary Mary's wrinkled old eyes sparkled like I had never seen before. Other than for money, I had never seen her show any interest in men. Even though she had been married several times.

"Thanks for helping me do the dishes." I deliberately avoided responding to Scary Mary's shallow questions and comments. I had something more important on my mind. Muh'Dear's conspicuous absence had made me more than a little uneasy. Since she had softened enough to allow Daddy and Lillimae to stay at our house, I thought that by the time they arrived, Muh'Dear would agree to join us for dinner. I was wrong. I was pleased that so far, Daddy and Lillimae had refrained from asking about Muh'Dear in front of two busybodies like Scary Mary and Pee Wee.

I was glad when the telephone in the kitchen rang. Hoping it was Muh'Dear, I didn't take the time to dry my hands. I sprinted across the kitchen floor and grabbed the phone, dropping it twice from my wet hand before I could even say hello. It was Jean. I waved Scary Mary back to the living room where Pee Wee, Daddy, and Lillimae were.

"Annette, I don't think I can make it over there this evening. We got a little problem on our hands," Jean told me. She could not hide the terror in her voice.

I gripped the telephone with both hands. "What's the matter?" I didn't want to ask, but I had a feeling her little problem had something to do with Vinnie. I had seen him earlier in the day, lurking around the side of Jean's house, looking on the ground under a window like he had lost something.

"P.'s gone," Jean announced in a shaky voice.

"Gone where?"

"I don't know!" Jean cried. "Somebody took her."

"Jean, the only person who would want to take P. is her daddy. Why don't you call him?"

"Tony? He's the last person who'd take P. Didn't I tell you he hasn't been to see her in three years?"

"Why don't you call him anyway? You and I both know how unpredictable men are."

"I . . . I tried to reach him. His wife told me he's been locked up in county jail for the past two weeks for beating up his landlord."

"Where else do you think P. could be?" I asked, getting more nervous and frightened by the second.

I heard Jean sniff a few times before she answered. "We

don't know. She was outside jumping rope and making a snowman most of the day. I got so busy in the house I didn't realize how much time had passed before I went to check on her. She wasn't in the yard and none of the kids around here have seen her."

"Well, you know how kids are. I think I heard that ice cream truck a little while ago. She probably followed it like I used to."

"It's wintertime, Annette. That truck doesn't come around this time of the year," Jean snapped. "I'm sorry. I didn't mean to yell at you. It's just that . . . that P.'s been gone since early this morning," Jean choked. "She never misses her lunch. And her granddaddy picks her up every Saturday afternoon to take her shopping. She would never miss that."

"Oh. Maybe she wandered off and got lost. Maybe she's afraid to come home because she thinks she's going to get a whupping." P. was one of the most obedient children I knew. Disobeying her mother was way out of character for her. "She's got to be lost."

"That's what Vinnie and my daddy said." Jean paused and sucked in her breath. "P.'s been lost before, but she's always found her way home."

"Where's Vinnie?" I asked evenly.

"Huh? Oh, he's here. He's blown out a fuse in his brain trying to figure out where P. is. We are about to go out again and look for her some more."

I became so uneasy I could barely talk. Without knowing all the facts, but with what I did know, I immediately felt that Vinnie knew more than he was saying. "Well, if you want me to help—"

"Oh no, you don't. You stay right home with your daddy and your sister. I'll come over as soon as we locate P. Vinnie said after we find my baby, he'd come to your house with me, if you don't mind."

"Uh, you can tell Vinnie that he can come, too," I said.

"Now you go on and find your child, Jean." I hung up the telephone and had a brief cry. The main cause of my grief was obviously P.'s disappearance, but also the fact that the missing child could have been me at an earlier time.

There was no way I could not get involved. A missing child was everybody's business.

"Uh, that was a friend of mine from down the street. Her little girl is missing and I need to go see what I can do to help out," I announced, immediately after returning to the living room. Daddy and Lillimae were tired from their long plane ride. They didn't protest when I suggested that they turn in for the night.

Pee Wee and Scary Mary insisted on accompanying me to Jean's house. Another neighbor, a pretty brunette, greeted us, standing in Jean's doorway with her arms folded like she was on guard duty. "Jean and Vinnie are out looking for P.," she told us.

"Do you know where they went? We'd like to help search," I said in the gentlest voice I could manage.

The woman coughed and looked up and down the street before responding. "I don't know why, but Jean insisted on going out to the city dump with a flashlight. She borrowed my son's old collie to see if he could sniff the way."

"What? Why would P. be way across town by herself, at the city dump? I know Jean doesn't think somebody . . ." What I was thinking was so horrific, I couldn't even finish my sentence.

I could not imagine somebody taking P. to a nasty dumping ground and leaving her there among trash that included the bags of Jerome's things that I had discarded. Only if—I couldn't even bring myself to think the worse.

"The police said somebody found one of P.'s snow boots out there," the woman stammered, wiping a tear from the corner of her eye.

Unbearably grim thoughts crossed my mind, but I refused

to pay attention to them. I shook my head so hard I saw spots.

Pee Wee started cursing.

Scary Mary waved her hands high above her head and prayed in a loud voice, "Lord, please be with P."

"Oh no," I muttered, stumbling back a few steps. If Pee Wee hadn't caught me in his arms, I would have fallen off Jean's porch.

I didn't like the thoughts that wouldn't leave my head no matter how hard I shook it. My stomach started churning. I covered my mouth with my hand, hoping I wouldn't throw up the dinner I had spent so much time preparing and eating. I tried not to think about Jean out there in the dark, in a dump site, with a flashlight and a dog.

Looking for her child.

CHAPTER 53

I had arranged to take the following Monday and Tuesday off so that I could spend more time with Daddy and Lillimae. That Monday evening I offered to take them to dinner at Laslo's. I wanted to keep myself busy so I wouldn't have to think about P., wondering where she was and what had happened to her.

Laslo's was the nicest place in town for steaks, but everybody who worked there and most of the people who dined there were white. I thought that eating in a place like Laslo's would be a nice experience for Daddy and Lillimae.

Big mistake.

Right away Daddy and Lillimae started to complain about one thing after another: our table was too close to the kitchen, white customers were giving us dirty looks, it took too long for us to get waited on. There was nothing that they didn't complain about.

"And them smashed potatoes tasted like wallpaper paste. How can anybody enjoy something like that?" Daddy laughed.

"And the toilet is enough to scare anybody into constipation," Lillimae complained, glaring at a sirloin steak the size of a small saucer.

Daddy snorted and shook his head. "Tell me about it. I wasn't half done doin' my business on that toilet before it started flushin' by itself!"

I sighed and shook my head. "Stop that," I scolded. "I thought you two would like to eat out at a really nice place for a change. This place is a world away from the greasy rib joints you usually go to. This is how the other half lives."

Daddy and Lillimae looked at one another, then at me. "Baby, we ain't the other half; we the ones in the middle," Daddy told me, looking up toward the ceiling with a frown. "Now what in the world kind of music is they playin' up in here?"

"It's 'Strangers In the Night' and that's Frank Sinatra singing it," I told Daddy as he rolled his eyes. "You can't expect a place like this to be playing something by B.B. King."

Daddy and Lillimae looked at each other and shrugged, then they looked at me.

"Is this the kind of music white folks listen to when they eat out?" Daddy asked, laughing some more.

I sighed and nodded.

Living in a cosmopolitan city like Miami for so many years hadn't refined Daddy and Lillimae at all. As much as I loved my daddy and my sister, I loved them just as they were. Their lack of sophistication was endearing. I watched in amusement as they struggled through the rest of our meal.

On top of everything else, our waitress was rude. Lillimae was the only one that the scowling redhead was courteous to. She smiled at Lillimae and addressed her first each time she came to our table. A lot of the Black people I knew didn't go to Laslo's that often because they felt that some of the servers were racist. I had not eaten at Laslo's that often and until today I had never had a problem.

The last straw was when the waitress refilled Lillimae's water glass and ignored Daddy and me. Lillimae beckoned the waitress back to our table.

"My daddy and my sister would like a little more water, too," Lillimae said loud enough for the people three tables away to hear. With a stunned look on her face, the woman poured more water onto the table than she did in our glasses.

Finally, she left the check on the table in front of Lilli-mae.

"Well, that heifer sure won't get a tip," I grumbled, lifting the check, poring over it to make sure she didn't overcharge us.

"Don't you leave that cow nothin'," Daddy hollered, loud enough for the woman to hear. "Somebody need to tell that wench that we in the middle of the 1980's—not the 1950's! And this ain't the South."

My face was burning. Not with embarrassment, but with anger.

Lillimae shook her head and waved her hand at me, a devilish smile sitting on her face. "If you don't leave nothin', she'll think you forgot. I'll take care of the tip," she announced, rooting through her purse. She fished out two pennies and dropped them on the table, making sure the waitress saw her. "That's how you tip for bad service. Come on, y'all." Lillimae glared at the waitress and all the other looky-loos as we waltzed out.

There was not much to see in Richland, so "sight-seeing" was not an option. However, I did suggest that we take an extended drive throughout the city so I could point out our few landmarks. By the time we returned to my house, Daddy was snoozing in the backseat of my car like a big cat and Lilli-mae was anxious to get to my bathroom so she could use a toilet that didn't interrupt her while she was sitting on it.

A few beers seemed to restore their equilibrium. Sitting

next to me on my living room couch, Daddy stared at the side of my head and let out a deep sigh. "I am so glad to see you again, sugar. You don't know how glad I am."

I blinked hard to hold back a tear that was threatening to reveal itself. "Uh, maybe by summer we can plan a family reunion," I said weakly.

Daddy and Lillimae looked at one another, their faces expressionless. Turning to me, Lillimae said, "I thought we'd already done that when you came to Florida."

I shook my head. "I mean all of us. Amos and Sondra, too."

"We'll all get together someday soon," Lillimae told me. "If you don't mind, I'll give 'em both your address and telephone number so y'all can talk some."

"I'd like that," I said gently. "I'd like for us all to get together soon. I want all of my family together." A stiff look on Daddy's face told me he needed some clarification. "Not Muh'Dear, Daddy. Just us for now."

Lillimae gave me an address and some telephone numbers so I could contact my other half-siblings at the military base in Germany where they were stationed. But for some reason I knew in the back of my mind that I would not make the first move. I had to handle things a little at a time. I had to deal with Muh'Dear and Daddy's reunion first.

I wanted to see some more closure in my family before it was too late. One thing I felt I didn't have was a lot of time. Muh'Dear and Daddy were not getting any younger. As far as I knew, they were both in fairly good health and I realized they could both probably outlive me because I was not getting any younger, either. But time was still not on my side.

While Daddy was snoozing again on the living room couch, Lillimae and I attempted to watch television. I had moved from the couch to the floor and curled up on a throw rug with my head on one of the throw pillows from the couch. Lillimae had stuffed herself into one of my wing-armed chairs across from me.

I don't even remember what was on television because we spent that time talking. She did most of it. She shared with me her concerns about her rocky marriage, her love for her sons, her disgust with her weight, and the fact that the other children her mother had given birth to lived right in Miami and she couldn't spend time with them.

"And I am so sorry about your weddin' bein' called off. Maybe that Jerome wasn't the man for you, after all. You don't have to tell me if you don't want to, but I have a feelin' he was a scoundrel in the makin'. So many men are," Lillimae told me with a smile. "But I know in my heart there is another one out there more suitable for you."

"I am sure there is," I said sadly, wondering what Pee Wee was up to.

To make our conversation more interesting, I told Lillimae all about Scary Mary and her sordid activities.

"I figured that old sister had a hidden agenda that first time I met her. The way she didn't look me straight in the eye when she talked and all," Lillimae laughed. "Well, anyway, that Scary Mary woman still sounds like a good friend to you and your mama." Lillimae sighed and turned her head to the side, staring off into space. "Bosses, co-workers, they come and go. Next to family, friends is the most important individuals in a person's life. I hope that in time, you and I will be both to one another." Lillimae paused and ran her tongue across her lips. There was a faraway look in her eyes as she continued. "I got a few girlfriends. Sisters from the church, co-workers, neighbors. But I don't feel that close to any of them. I don't really feel as comfortable talkin' to them as I do with you. I feel like I can share anything with you. I hope you feel the same way about me."

"I do," I said. And I meant it.

I wanted to open up my entire life to my sister and I knew that one day I would. I knew that I had to tell her about Mr. Boatwright and what he had done to me. I knew that I had to tell her about Rhoda and what she had done for me. And when I did, I would leave no stone unturned. I had not seen Rhoda since I'd seen her standing in Jean's front yard. And with everything going on with P., I couldn't pump Jean for information about Rhoda yet.

The only person in my life I wouldn't give Lillimae too much information about was Pee Wee. I didn't want her to know how weak I was when it came to him and how weak he was when it came to me. As mysterious as my relationship was with that man, there was something sacred about it and I wanted to keep it that way.

Like Lillimae, he was another wild card in my life.

CHAPTER 54

That Sunday when I got up after a restless night filled with nightmares, Pee Wee called to say that P. was still missing. Now, I also planned to use my time off to help look for P. I didn't have to do that, though. Around noon, Pee Wee called my house again.

"I . . . I guess you done heard about poor little P." His voice was low and labored, which was rare for Pee Wee. I had not seen or heard him cry since his sissified, teenage years. He had cried like a baby and fainted when President Kennedy got assassinated. He was crying now so I knew what he had to tell me was bad.

I braced myself. "Did they find her?"

Pee Wee composed himself and let out a deep sigh before continuing. "So you don't know."

"Know what?" I was getting impatient. "Did they find the child or not?!"

"Turn on Channel Two news." Pee Wee let out another sigh, then he hung up.

Richland, Ohio was not a crime-free city. We had our share of barroom brawls, domestic disturbances, and burglaries, but murder was something that didn't happen in our city that often. The year before, we had had only one murder. An ex-con had returned to exact revenge on the person who had sent him to prison. That crime didn't garner that much attention. But what we had to deal with now was the worst thing that had ever happened in the history of our city.

The television reporter could barely get the story out without stopping to clear her throat. In a raspy voice, she revealed that before dawn, a homeless woman had discovered P.'s body on the ground behind a Dumpster in an alley just six blocks away from Jean's house. P. had been dead for several hours. In addition to being strangled with her own knee sock, she had been raped and beaten. I was on the floor sitting with my knees held against my chest when Lillimae entered the living room from upstairs just a few minutes later.

"Annette, what's the matter?"

"Somebody killed a little girl from down the street," I said hoarsely. "Somebody killed that child and threw her away like she was a piece of garbage."

"What little girl?" Daddy asked, weaving his way down into the living room. "Who was her peoples? This the little missin' girl y'all was talkin' about last night?"

I nodded. "My friend Jean's daughter."

Lillimae stumbled to the couch, clutching her chest. "Lord have mercy! Do they know who did it?" As soon as Lillimae hit the couch, she started fanning her face with her hand. Living in Florida, she didn't own much heavy clothing. She had not been prepared for our winter weather. She had one of my sweaters on over a muumuu that she had slid into.

"No," I said, turning off the television, forcing myself to keep my opinions to myself. It was too soon for me to say what I was thinking. But as soon as I had heard the news, I believed in my heart that Vinnie Gambiano had had something to do with that child's murder.

I immediately called Jean's house. When Vinnie answered, I hung up the telephone so fast and hard it fell out of its cradle.

I grabbed my coat and started down the street with Lillimae and Daddy running along with me. When we saw all the police cars in front of Jean's house, we decided to delay our visit. With long faces, we returned to my living room, where Lillimae sank to the floor, with Daddy struggling to pull her up.

"I feel for that child's mother. I don't know what I would do if somethin' happened to one of my boys," Lillimae sobbed.

"Children is the most precious gift the Lord gives us," Daddy said. Looking in my direction he added, "I know that now."

In the meantime, I stumbled to my kitchen and spent a few minutes on my wall telephone talking to Muh'Dear. P.'s murder and other heinous crimes dominated the conversation for the first five minutes.

"I don't know what this world is comin' to. Why men rape is beyond me. I just read about some demon out there in California that they say had raped three teenager girls. Some shyster of a lawyer got him off and then that same demon up and raped another woman," Muh'Dear hollered.

"I guess he got off for that one, too." I sighed.

Muh'Dear cleared her throat and sucked her teeth. "Yes and no," she said gruffly. "That last woman he raped was burnin' up with that new disease they can't cure. AIDS. Now he got it. See, there. When somebody act ugly, God treat 'em ugly, 'cause He done showed us he don't like ugly." Muh'Dear paused and sniffed hard. "Too bad P. didn't have a deadly disease." Muh'Dear sighed. I was glad when she changed the subject. "Uh, your daddy ask about me?" Her voice cracked, but I didn't know if it was because of P. or Daddy.

"You know he did, Muh'Dear. He knows you don't want to see him, but Daddy still wants to see you," I told her. Daddy had entered the kitchen and was now standing right next to me, listening. He frowned at the mention of his name. Muh'Dear quickly diverted the conversation back to P.

"Ain't nothin' but a devil would do that to a child. I hope when they catch him, they slice his nuts off before they send his ass to hell."

"I feel the same way, Muh'Dear," I said stiffly. As far as I was concerned, whatever punishment they gave the perpetrator, it wouldn't be harsh enough.

Daddy folded me in his arms as soon as I hung up the telephone and started leading me back to the living room. "God sure was good to me. He didn't let no harm come to you all them years I wasn't there to protect you," he said.

I smiled and nodded.

I finally made it to Jean's house that evening around six. The police were gone, but the house was full of other neighbors, friends, and relatives. Vinnie, gadding about with no shirt on, was in tears the whole time. Poor Jean was inconsolable. A doctor had sedated her and sent her to bed. I didn't get to see her at all.

About an hour after my arrival, old Mr. Antonosanti showed up, accompanied by his male nurse and three ferocious, stout Italian men. According to Scary Mary, Mr. Antonosanti had been sick for years and was dying from a rare liver ailment. The three stout men and Mr. Antonosanti were all dressed in black. Stomping across the floor in their heavy black shoes, huddling together, they reminded me of a herd of bulls.

"I won't die until the monster that killed my little Piatra is dead," Mr. Antonosanti vowed in a weak voice.

Harming a child was the one sin even I could not forgive. I wanted to see the person responsible suffer.

Jean had never explained her relationship to the Antonosanti family to me. But I learned from a woman who identified herself as one of Jean's cousins that Jean's mother and Mr. Antonosanti were first cousins. Knowing the connections and the money the Antonosanti's had, I knew that the police would make P.'s case their highest priority.

However, Richland was a small city with not many resources. The cops in our little Mickey Mouse police department spent most of their time writing out speeding tickets, chastising drunkards, locating missing pets, and kicking back. I didn't expect them to solve this hellish case quickly, if at all. And even if they did, I couldn't see them administering a punishment that fit the crime.

That was why—as much as I hated violence and people taking the law into their own hands—I hoped that the Antonosantis got to P.'s killer first.

CHAPTER 55

I could not imagine the pain Jean was experiencing, but I was feeling like hell myself after hearing the news about P. I could hardly eat or sleep. Being an outsider and feeling the way I did was one thing. But to a parent, losing a child to murder had to be unbearable.

During some of my loneliest days, I fantasized about having a child of my own someday, whether I had a husband or not. I had even considered adopting at least two. While I was in my senior year in high school, my social studies class went on a field trip to our county orphanage. Ironically, it was located across the highway from our county asylum. I had learned from the orphanage director why some of the kids had ended up in the orphanage. The reasons varied. Some of the kids had severe physical and mental handicaps; some were incorrigible and it had been too much of a hardship for their families to keep them. But the saddest ones to me were the ones nobody wanted because of the way they looked. One cone-headed boy in his late teens was transferred from the orphanage to the asylum, the same day of our field trip.

I knew right then and there that if I ever did adopt children, I'd take the ones nobody else wanted. I didn't care how severely handicapped or incorrigible they were. After learning the history of some of our local orphans, my own painful childhood seemed like a picnic. Mr. Boatwright was still in my life at the time of my field trip. I had come home to him that day, grateful that he was the only evil in my life.

But then there were also days when I was glad I was childless. Just the thought of someone brutalizing a child of mine made me temporarily blind with rage. It was a horror I knew I would never get over. The truth hurt and the truth was: no one could protect a child. Not the parents, not even God.

According to the newspaper report, P.'s face had been battered beyond recognition and her arm had been broken in two places. Jean's daddy had made the painful trip to the morgue to identify P.'s body. I had been told that the old man had fainted immediately afterward.

Jean was not doing well at all. Two more days went by before I was able to talk to her. By then, she was practically out of her mind, staring at me through glazed eyes. It had only been four days since the murder, but Jean had already lost weight from not eating. Her face was already gaunt enough that I could see her cheekbones for the first time since we'd become friends. Those pretty violet eyes of hers that I admired so much were bloodshot and almost swollen shut.

Vinnie sat next to Jean on the plush blue couch in her living room with his arm around her shoulder, gripping her like he was afraid she'd break loose. But then every time Vinnie attempted to rise, Jean pulled him back down and guided his arm back around her shoulder.

I didn't know what-all P. had told Jean about Vinnie's actions toward her when Jean was not around. However, since Jean had told me herself about P.'s claim that Vinnie had kissed her on her mouth, that alone should have been enough to put Jean on her highest alert. Instead, here Jean was now, weeping like a widow and clinging to Vinnie like a vine, knowing how much P. had hated and feared him.

Jean's behavior toward Vinnie disturbed me. I had heard of cases where the mothers of abused children, *who knew about the abuse*, chose to stay with the abuser! I had attended junior high school with a girl whose mother had kicked her out of the house for "tempting" the mother's husband and getting pregnant by him. And if that wasn't bad enough, the girl's two older brothers had been fucking the hell out of her, too. What really got my goat was the fact that when the girl finally exposed her father and her brothers, a well-known businessman and two star athletes, everybody got mad at her and said that the girl herself had taken advantage of her father and brothers. Ruining her family must have been a greater crime than the abuse she had suffered, because that girl committed suicide. It was no wonder so many kids kept secrets of that nature to themselves.

I had convinced myself that the only people who understood the shame of females like me, were females like me. I was only sorry that I had not been able to reach out more to P. However, I had tried to help by making that anonymous telephone call to the Child Protective Services. But even that had not been enough to save that child.

"I think I saw P. running down the street, trying to get home," Jean told me, talking as she licked tears and snot from her bottom lip. Her eyes were so red and swollen, she looked like she had been severely beaten. She had on the same soiled, stiff duster she had on the last time I saw her. "P.'s so slow-witted and clumsy. Runs into walls, sometimes gets lost a block away from home. She lost her way again and hasn't made it home yet." Turning to Vinnie, Jean added, "Honey, don't worry. P.'ll be home soon."

"No, she won't, darlin'," Vinnie sobbed, his eyes darting from side to side each time I looked in his face. The oil, or whatever it was that he wore on his hair, had dripped onto the shoulders and neck of his shirt and the sides of his face. He looked like he was melting right before my eyes. Just like that witch in *The Wizard of Oz*. He cleared his throat and slid his hand across the top of his head, then dabbed at the sides of his face with his sleeve.

Vinnie was nervous, but that was nothing new. He often fidgeted when he was around me. I wasn't that much larger than Jean, so I knew it was not my size that intimidated him. I had always treated Vinnie cordially to his face, so I had to assume that he didn't like me because of comments Jean had told him I'd made about him.

I didn't care if Jean had told him that every time she and I were alone, I bad-mouthed him for treating Jean like a piece of property and for putting his hands, and his mouth, on her child. I was glad he knew that I had his number. I liked seeing him squirm and, in an odd way, I hoped that I would be around when he met his downfall. It all had to do with what I had experienced with Mr. Boatwright. I didn't know whether to call it revenge or justice, as long as Vinnie got what he had coming. Even if he wasn't the one responsible for P.'s murder, he had done enough to P. to warrant some degree of punishment.

I didn't know what Jean and the other people I knew were thinking, but I had a strong opinion about this hellish crime: this was no ordinary rape and murder; this was a crime of passion. I was certain that P. had known her killer and that she had done or said something to push him over the edge. But what could a five-year-old child do to anger someone to the point of murder?

Through narrowed eyes, I glared at Vinnie Gambiano's brooding face and I saw Mr. Boatwright. And I recalled the numerous threats Mr. Boatwright had made to me. *If you ever tell anybody about us, I'm gwine to kill you.*

I could have been wrong about Vinnie being P.'s killer. But knowing that some other child-killing monster could be on the loose in my neighborhood didn't make me feel any better. I knew in my heart that it was a macabre thought, but I still hoped that it was Vinnie.

"What are the police saying?" I asked, directing my attention to Vinnie.

"Uh, nothin' much. They are continuin' their investigation," he replied, clearing his throat and scratching the side of his hard face. His beady black eyes, baggy and cloaked with dark circles, turned as flinty as steel. His greasy ponytail, more than a foot long now, swung every time he moved his head.

"I know they'll catch the monster who killed P. And it won't be long," I said bitterly. "I don't care how careful that bastard thought he was, somebody is going to find something he overlooked."

Vinnie shifted in his seat as sweat slid down the sides of his face. "Uh, I think Jean should get some rest now, if you don't mind," Vinnie said with bite in his voice. He caressed Jean's face until she stopped moaning. He then rose from the couch and ushered me toward the door, eyeing me sharply. "You better get on home yourself before it gets any later. It ain't safe for a woman to be roamin' the streets by herself at night." He added with a smirk, "Even you. Them rapists don't care who they grab."

"Tell me about it," I hissed.

"Anytime," he sneered, looking at me like he wanted to rearrange my face.

Vinnie didn't blink as I stared into his cold eyes. It was hard to believe that this was the same individual who had sat in front of me in so many of my classes throughout my years at Richland High. I couldn't count the times he had made me laugh with his classroom antics, tossing spitballs and making barnyard noises out the side of his mouth. He had been one of the few kids in school who had not picked on me. He had had a soul back in those days, but it had left his body a long time ago.

"Thank you for your concern, Vinnie, but I think I can take care of myself." I let out a heavy breath.

"Oh, I don't doubt that," he said, looking me up and down with contempt, shaking his head. He slammed the door so hard and fast behind me, he caught the tail of my coat in it.

CHAPTER 56

My feet felt as heavy as concrete on the icy sidewalk as I dragged myself back to my own house after leaving Jean's. Normally, I would have been slipping and sliding and even falling a few times. But I was too angry to lose my balance. And I was glad I left when I did because being in the same room with that smug Vinnie had been excruciating. There was so much I wanted to say to him and about him, but for Jean's sake, I had to keep my feelings to myself. At least for the time being.

It seemed like the whole neighborhood was in mourning. Even though it was fairly early in the evening, houses were already dark and few people were on the street. Since P.'s murder, I had not seen a single child playing alone outside on my street or any other street in Richland. What I did see were parents walking with their children, even to the corner store, holding on to them for dear life. I knew that our little city would never be the same again. I had read in the newspaper that a lot of people had gone out and bought guns and attack dogs. The family in the house across the street from Jean's had put their house up for sale.

"It's a cryin' shame that your visit to us in Florida got messed up with a funeral and now here one done ruined ours," Daddy lamented as we all dressed to go pay our last respects that Saturday morning. Lillimae stood in front of Daddy, adjusting the stiff necktie he had fished out of his suitcase. "And for a white girl."

Lillimae and I both gasped and glared at Daddy. "Daddy, a little girl is a little girl. And in case you forgot, the *white* woman in Florida who died used to be your wife," I said evenly. I turned to Lillimae for confirmation.

She spoke with her eyes staring at the floor. "And that same woman just happened to be my mama." Lillimae looked in my eyes and blinked; I looked away.

P.'s murder touched a lot of people. Mayor Doyle appeared on Channel 2, pleading with the perpetrator to turn himself in. Mr. Carmine Antonosanti had put up a $20,000 reward. He stood right up on television and vowed, "I will say it again—I will not die until the monster that killed Piatra is punished!" As old, weak, and close to the grave as that old man was, everybody knew he still had a lot of power. Somebody was going to pay for P.'s murder, one way or the other. I was glad to know that so many people cared about P.

I couldn't help but wonder if people would have reacted the same way if what happened to P. had happened to me when I was a child.

For the first time that I knew of, whole families of Black people flocked to the funeral of a white person. One good thing that came out of P.'s funeral was the fact that Muh'Dear attended. It put her in the same room with Daddy in more than thirty years. I was glad that room happened to be in a church. I was confident that there was little chance of Muh'Dear saying something offensive to Daddy there. She had already demonized him, but it seemed like she never ran out of nasty things to say whenever his name came up in a conversation. I saw Muh'Dear sneaking glances at Daddy several times, with a look in her eyes that I could not interpret. Each time, a faint smile appeared on her face.

Muh'Dear had parked her Oldsmobile in a no-parking zone. The car had been towed while we were all in the church. Muh'Dear couldn't ride with Scary Mary in her van because the five prostitutes who worked for Scary Mary had taken up all the room. Pee Wee had come with Daddy, Lillimae, and me in my car. Muh'Dear had no choice but to ride with us to Jean's house after we all left St. Mary's, the Catholic Church Jean's entire family had attended for years.

"Annette, did you see Rhoda and her husband and little girl? They sure are a good-lookin' little family," Muh'Dear said, sitting in the front seat of my car fanning her face with a folded handkerchief. I was glad that Pee Wee was driving my car. I didn't think it was safe for me to drive and keep an eye on Muh'Dear and Daddy at the same time. Muh'Dear glanced back at me and said dryly, "I heard that Rhoda's husband treats her like a queen."

Even though it was cold enough to have the heater on in the car, Muh'Dear was sweating like a coal miner. Like me, she sweated when she was nervous, angry, or emotionally challenged. I could not imagine what she was feeling or thinking about being in the same car with Daddy and one of the children he'd had with the white woman he'd left us for.

So far, at least as far as I knew, Muh'Dear had not said one word to Daddy or Lillimae since they had arrived in Richland. And I was not surprised, but I was hopeful. Daddy and Lillimae were sitting like mutes in the backseat with me, with Daddy in the middle. It was such a tight fit with the three of us that I had to press my thighs together so close that the friction was almost unbearable. Within minutes I could already feel the skin between my thighs chafing. Even through my thick pantyhose. One sideways glance at the grimace on Lillimae's face told me that her massive thighs were in just as much pain as mine.

Daddy's bony hand, resting on my knee, looked like a piece of wood. He had on the same natty suit he had worn the day of Lillimae's mother's funeral. I could tell it was the same suit because the top button on his jacket was navy blue and all the other buttons were black.

Every few seconds Lillimae sobbed and moaned under her breath, the same way she did during the ride home from her own mother's funeral a few months earlier. Except for a few moans and groans, Daddy remained silent all the way to Jean's house.

"Muh'Dear, Rhoda is a lucky woman. She's always been lucky," I muttered thoughtfully, folding and unfolding my sweaty hands, rubbing the side of my thigh, trying to reduce my discomfort.

Rhoda had occupied a pew with her husband and her daughter across the room, offering me a brief smile as she wept on her husband's shoulder. I had no choice but to smile back.

It was a mob scene at Jean's house by the time we arrived. In addition to family and friends from our neighborhood and a few co-workers, the crowd included a flock of old Italian women dressed from head to toe in black, shroud-like outfits. A couple of the women even had veils partially covering their faces. One toothless old crone in a wheelchair, a thick black shawl draped around her shoulders, was Jean's great grandmother from Naples, Italy. This old woman cried the whole time I was in Jean's house, babbling every few minutes in Italian.

We had all delivered food to Jean's house before the funeral.

"Other than pizza and spaghetti, what else do Italians eat?" Scary Mary had asked me that morning before the funeral.

"They are people, just like us. I'm sure they will appreciate anything we bring," I told her.

Scary Mary played it safe. She had brought a few berry pies. I played it safe, too. I brought lasagna. Muh'Dear, so proud of her culinary talents, brought a huge bowl of collard greens, a pan of cornbread, and several sweet potato pies and an assortment of other goodies, saying, "Italians ain't goin' to be the only folks in Jean's house. Black folks will want some *real* food up in there to sink their teeth into. Besides, almost every Italian in town eats at the Buttercup at least once a week. Them folks got the good sense to know good food when they eat it. Shoot."

It didn't matter what we brought. Hardly anybody was eating much, anyway. However, almost everybody was walking around like zombies, slurping wine. Even me. I needed it to help calm my nerves. I didn't feel comfortable in the same house with Vinnie *and* Rhoda, the two most diabolical living people I knew.

Rhoda and Vinnie didn't need wine, they needed the Exorcist.

CHAPTER 57

It was hard for me to remain civil in Jean's house, but acting was something I was good at. Nobody could tell how disturbed I really was.

It was obvious that Vinnie was trying to avoid me. Every time I got near him, he moved to another part of the room. When he was not hovering over the table that contained the bottles of wine, he was grazing like a Clydesdale horse at the dinner table, sampling some of everything. Even with his back to me, I could tell when he was smacking and chewing on something by the way his ears wiggled.

This was the first time I had seen Vinnie in a suit since high school. And I was glad he had cut his hair. He actually looked like the Vinnie I had known in school. But no matter what he did to his outside appearance, I felt that he should have been trying to improve what he had inside. Vinnie was paying more attention to Scary Mary's prostitutes than he was to Jean. And I was not the only one who noticed that. More than once I saw Jean's uncle, old Mr. Antonosanti, take Vinnie by the arm and lead him to Jean.

About an hour into this tense visit, I turned around and

there was Rhoda staring at me from a dim corner with her daughter standing next to her. Rhoda stepped toward me, her heels click-clacking on Jean's hardwood floor, looking like a ray of sunshine penetrating a dungeon. Her daughter walked along beside her.

I stumbled and splashed wine on the lap of the loose-fitting navy blue dress I had chosen to wear. The black suit Rhoda had on made her look even slimmer. I didn't remember her chest being so flat, though. As a matter of fact, she had always been so proud of her bosom; she had showed it off in tight, low-cut blouses most of the time. I assumed that her three pregnancies had taken a toll on her body, like most of the mothers I knew.

This was the first time I had ever seen Rhoda in a hat. It was a derby, or something close to it. It was also black and sat perched at an angle on the side of her head. Muh'Dear, Scary Mary, and most of the other Black women present had on hats so garish I wouldn't wear them for Halloween. I had been avoiding hats, because that was one thing I had always associated with older women. Seeing one on Rhoda reminded me that that's exactly what we both were now: *older women.*

"Hello, Annette. I'm glad you were able to make it," Rhoda said, her eyes red from crying. She dabbed at her eyes with a white handkerchief that she had in her neatly manicured hand. "It's good to see you again." She sniffed and offered a nervous smile. "I didn't know you and Jean knew each other."

"Uh, yeah, we both work for the telephone company," I croaked, looking for some gray hair and wrinkles on Rhoda. I didn't see any. The wine I had wasted made my dress stick to me. But that didn't bother me half as much as Rhoda's sudden appearance. "It's good to see you, too, Rhoda. You're looking as young as ever."

The child with Rhoda was standing as rigid and stoic as a

soldier. Her eyes were the only things moving on her when she blinked. Unlike the other children in the room, with their smudged faces and disheveled clothing, this child was impeccably neat. Her long, blue-black hair looked like it had been put on her head strand by strand. Her complexion, the same shade of dark brown as Rhoda's and mine, was as clear as glass. The girl had the same small, upturned nose as Rhoda and the same sparkling green eyes. It was like Rhoda had literally duplicated herself. At the time, I didn't know if that was good or bad.

With my face covered excessively in makeup and my huge body hidden inside my sharp, loose-fitting dress, I reminded myself what some of the kids I'd attended school with had told me so emphatically: a baboon in makeup and a dress is still a baboon. It bothered me that after so many years and all the fuss that Jerome had made over me, my feelings of inferiority were still disturbingly strong. Even though I was now standing before the same person who had first encouraged what little self-esteem I did have. A pain that started in my head shot all the way down to my feet. I immediately started shifting my weight from one foot to the other. The bottom of my right foot was itching. The only reason I didn't bend down and remove my shoe to scratch was because I didn't want to act like a baboon, too. It was bad enough looking like one.

"This is my beautiful daughter, Jade." Rhoda nudged the girl with her elbow and snatched the girl's thumb out of her mouth. "Jade, this is Annette. When I was a girl, Annette was my best friend."

Jade sniffed, rubbed her nose, and gave me an indifferent look. "I don't care," she mumbled, returning her thumb to her mouth. Rhoda frowned and gently thumped the side of Jade's head with her fingers, causing Jade to flinch and smile at me. "It's nice to meet you, Annette. Mommy told me all about you."

Rhoda's husband Otis was standing across the room talking to Pee Wee and Vinnie. Tall and undeniably trim, Otis was aging gracefully. A few faint lines on his forehead and a few strands of gray hair at his temples gave him a distinguished look. Bushy black eyebrows framed his slanted black eyes; his teeth looked unnaturally white next to his deep-chocolate skin. When we were still teenagers, Pee Wee looked like a dog-faced scarecrow next to Otis. Now, Pee Wee was just as handsome as Otis. Otis smiled and waved to me. I smiled and waved back. Pee Wee looked in my direction, one hand in his pants pocket, his other hand holding a glass of wine. There was a surprised look on his face. I could only imagine what was going through his mind seeing me talking to Rhoda after all of that stuff I'd told him about her killing folks. My eyes locked with Pee Wee's. When I realized he wasn't going to be the one to look away first, I did. I returned my full attention to Rhoda.

"Where's your son Julian?" I asked Rhoda.

"He's away at school," Rhoda replied, smiling proudly. "The same military school in Huntsville, Alabama, that my daddy attended and he's first in his class, too. Some people say my boy reminds them of John Kennedy, Jr." Rhoda beamed. Then she sniffed and pushed Jade's hair back from her face. "Children are such a blessin'. So, Annette, are you married or what?"

"No. I came close but things didn't work out. I'm still looking for my Mr. Right. I'm not sure if I ever want to have kids, though. I enjoy being footloose and independent," I said stupidly. Other than my clandestine romps with Pee Wee and my new relationship with Daddy and Lillimae, my dead-end-ass job was the most exciting thing I had going.

Rhoda could have seen through me with her eyes closed. She gave me a knowing look. "Bein' married and havin' children hasn't interfered with my independence one bit. You won't believe how havin' a family will enrich your life. Look what it's done for me." Rhoda leaned down and covered Jade's cheek with hungry little kisses. "And my husband, oh girl, the man just gets better and better each day." She leaned close to my ear and whispered, "If you know what I mean." Rhoda winked and then said loudly, "I am so blessed." Finally, she let out her breath and smiled broadly.

I couldn't tell if Rhoda was as uncomfortable as I was but I was surprised when she motioned me toward the couch, pulling Jade by the hand with her. Even on such a sad occasion, almost every man present was looking at Rhoda, admiring her beauty.

Before I could join Rhoda on Jean's couch, I had to weave my way through the crowd to the bathroom to empty my bladder. When I returned to the living room, I had to refill my wineglass. It was going to take a strong buzz and a lot of nerve and luck to get me through the rest of this evening and my unexpected reunion with Rhoda.

The day seemed to be getting darker and darker.

CHAPTER 58

"So. Are you back in Richland to stay or what, Rhoda?" I said. I sank down as gracefully as I could on the couch next to her.

Rhoda's daughter stood off to the side, giving me guarded looks with her arms folded on the arm of the couch.

Rhoda nodded and cleared her throat. "Oh, I'd had enough of Florida with all those big-ass grasshoppers gettin' tangled up in my hair and that blazin' sun wreakin' havoc on my skin. And I hope I never see another lizard again as long as I live." Rhoda paused and brushed off Jade's dress with her hand. "I talked Otis into movin' back up here. He's the foreman down at the steel mill on Patterson Street, you know." I listened while Rhoda brought me up to date. She ran a licensed childcare center out of her house and P. had been one of her charges. She had met Jean through the Antonosanti family and that's how they had become friends. P. had been Jade's closest little friend. Rhoda's father, the undertaker, had retired. He and her mother had moved to New Orleans to be closer to Rhoda's ailing maternal grandmother. The other relatives, her white uncle Johnnie and his sister Lola, who had lived with Rhoda's family in the house across from mine, had both returned to Alabama. An electrical problem had caused the fire that had burned the Nelsons' house to the ground.

"I am so grateful that the good Lord had removed us all out of that house before the fire," Rhoda said, a wan smile on her face. "If He hadn't, I probably wouldn't be standin' here talkin' to you right now. I feel so blessed." Rhoda patted my arm.

I nodded. "I do, too." I paused and cleared my throat. "Where is your brother Jock?"

Rhoda's older brother Jock had sustained some serious injuries in Vietnam. He had spent some time in a veteran's hospital afterward. Battle fatigue, a mental condition common among men who had been injured on the battlefields, had changed Jock forever. Except for sex, Jock could no longer function as a normal man. The trouble he encountered once he had been released from the veteran's hospital had included him impregnating the white girl in Florida that Rhoda had claimed she killed, more than five years ago.

"Oh, he's in New Orleans, too. One of the reasons Daddy retired was so he could devote more of his attention to Jock." Rhoda paused to take a sip from her wineglass and to adjust her hat. "I had a little chat with your mama a few minutes ago. She sure does look good, considerin' the rough life she's had. She told me about your stepfather's passin'. I'm so sorry."

"Thank you, Rhoda. Daddy King was a wonderful man and I'll never forget him and all he did for Muh'Dear and me. He left the Buttercup and his house to Muh'Dear."

"So I heard. Well, your mama deserved all that and more. She damn well earned it." Rhoda screwed up her face and continued, "Even after *scruuuubin' floors* and all the rest of the shit she did, she still looks like a queen. I'm glad to hear that she's finally livin' like one now. Women like her are livin' proof that you can't keep a good woman down. Especially a good Black woman. You and I were so fortunate to have strong family foundations. We'll never have to worry about life beatin' us down. Will we?"

I shook my head, but I kept what I was really thinking to myself. The way I saw it, life had beaten me down a long time ago. "I sure hope not." I smiled. I gasped when Rhoda surprised me with a hug. "I am so glad to see you again," I said, my voice trembling, sweat rolling down the back of my neck. I really was glad to see her. When I tried to embrace her back, she stiffened and pulled away.

In a raspy voice, Rhoda told me, "I've missed you, girl." She slid away a few inches and sniffed, fresh tears on her face. "I prayed we'd at least see one another one more time. You were the first and only real girlfriend I ever had. I am so happy to see you again!" she squealed, pinching my arm.

I never thought I would see the day that Rhoda would be so humble in my presence. It pleased me.

"I've been thinking about you a lot, Rhoda," I said, holding back my tears.

"I . . . I was nervous about approachin' you at first. I didn't know how you would react," Rhoda admitted in a low voice.

I sighed. "You don't have to be nervous on my account. I'm the same Annette you grew up with."

"I hope you are," Rhoda said firmly. "I really hope you are the same Annette I used to know."

It seemed so eerie, but appropriate, that a funeral had brought us back together. It was ironic that somebody's death had driven a wedge between Rhoda and me. Now another death was responsible for our reunion.

I had missed not having Rhoda in my life. Other than Pee Wee, she was the only other person I could tell my deepest, darkest secrets. It gave me great pleasure to announce to her, "My daddy's here and so is one of my half-sisters." I looked around the room trying to locate Daddy and Lillimae. They were both standing across the room in front of Scary Mary, along with several other guests as Scary Mary held court. Her mouth was moving fast and she was waving her hands like she was directing a symphony.

"Uh, that's him with the plate in his hand. That heavyset woman next to him, that's my sister, Lillimae." I pointed Daddy and Lillimae out to Rhoda.

Rhoda shaded her eyes and looked from Daddy to Lillimae, then back to me, pursing her lips and widening her eyes. "I was wonderin' who they were."

"Uh, my sister inherited her mother's coloring," I said.

"She sure did." Rhoda laughed but covered her mouth and stopped when she saw the serious look on my face.

"But she'll tell anybody in a hot minute that she's Black," I said proudly.

"I can see that your daddy was a good-lookin' man in his day," Rhoda remarked, giving my daddy critical looks. "And your sister, she looks a lot like you," Rhoda exclaimed, turning to me.

"You'll like them," I said firmly, smiling shyly. "They're good people."

Nodding, Rhoda sniffed and rubbed her nose. "You want us to rescue them from Scary Mary? Your daddy looks like he's in some serious pain."

"No, that's all right. He looks like that most of the time," I replied, holding up my hand. "They seem to be enjoying whatever it is Scary Mary's babbling about this time," I snarled, then laughed so hard my chest ached.

Rhoda let out a disgusted sigh. "Scary Mary hasn't changed and never will. Still upstagin' everybody else. Let them enjoy her latest dog and pony show. I can meet them later."

"We're having dinner later on tonight at my house. Muh'Dear won't be there, but my daddy, my sister, Pee Wee, and I am sure Scary Mary and her girls will be there, too. You, Otis, and Jade are welcome to join us if you'd like. I still live in the same house on Reed Street."

"I'd like that very much, Annette." Rhoda gave me a warm look and excused herself.

As soon as Rhoda walked away, Muh'Dear strutted over to me and started whispering, "You didn't tell me that that girl of Frank's was white. And Lillimae is such a dainty name. I had a sweet cousin named Lillimae."

"Lillimae looks white, Muh'Dear. But she's as Black as we are." I leaned closer to Muh'Dear and said gently, "Do you think she looks like me?" I was surprised that nobody but Rhoda had mentioned this already.

Muh'Dear sighed, gave me a thoughtful look, and nodded. "I guess she do. But you way prettier. And she ain't missed too many meals, neither. That girl got hips as wide as the Mississippi." Muh'Dear laughed and slapped my shoulder. "And what's up with all them rings on her fingers? She tell you?"

I nodded. "When she was a little girl she had a crush on Ringo Starr."

"Who?"

"One of the Beatles. He wore a lot of rings so Lillimae started wearing a lot of rings."

Muh'Dear gave me a puzzled look and shrugged. "Whatever. I guess that wasn't as bad as Pee Wee runnin' up and down the streets wearin' that Beatle wig when he was a young boy. I'm glad you didn't do nothin' silly when you was a child. We can thank Brother Boatwright for that, may he rest in peace 'til we get there. He kept you under control."

"He sure did," I snapped, almost biting my lip. Muh'Dear didn't notice the sarcasm in my voice. Just thinking about that old rapist made my blood sizzle and my flesh crawl.

"Anyway, I just had a lovely chat with Lillimae and she's such a nice girl. Loves her some collard greens now. Since hardly nobody else is eatin' much, she only ate one helpin'. Poor thing. I'm goin' to cook her a whole pot of greens to eat by herself before she goes back to Florida. She's so much like you, praise the Lord. I'm surprised Frank done such a good job raisin' her by hisself. Where is the rest of his half-breeds?"

"Amos and Sondra are in the army, stationed in Germany," I said flatly. My head was still reeling from my encounter with Rhoda.

Muh'Dear gave me a dry look and shrugged her shoulders. "I noticed Frank still like my cookin'. The food I brought is the only thing I seen him eat so far. I told him and that white girl of his to come by the restaurant for dinner before they leave." Muh'Dear sniffed and raked her fingers through her hair. She cackled. "And I don't know why Frank was so surprised to see me still lookin' as good as I do. It ain't no secret about Black women agin' better than white women. I'm glad he see that now. Of course, your half-white half-sister Lillimae havin' Black blood, she won't wither up as quick as a real white woman. I bet that hag over there by the window in that wheelchair is younger than me." Muh'Dear nodded toward Jean's great grandmother, still weeping and babbling. "I'm goin' to go up to Frank and make sure he tastes them hush puppies I brought. When we was together that man ate hush puppies like they was peanuts, poppin' them in his mouth a handful at a time."

My chest tightened and I gave Muh'Dear a sharp look. "You haven't said anything about the way Daddy looks."

Muh'Dear gasped and raised her eyebrows, an amused look on her face. "I was tryin' not to!" she snapped, blinking rapidly before she shook her head and let out a deep sigh. Her voice rose sharply. "He look older than Methuselah and uglier than Uncle Remus, Mr. Bojangles, King Kong, and the Tar Baby put together." Muh'Dear paused long enough to catch her breath. "And he got more lines on his face than a corduroy jacket." She slid a strand of gray hair off her face.

I was tempted to remind her that she had just as many lines on her face as Daddy had on his.

I shrugged and ran my tongue across my bottom lip before I spoke again. "I guess you just answered my next question."

Still looking amused, Muh'Dear asked, "And what question was that?"

"I was just wondering if . . . if Daddy still excited you. I remember how affectionate you and him used to be when I was a little girl. . . ."

Muh'Dear cussed under her breath and gave me the most disgusted look that she could come up with. She narrowed her eyes into slits and spoke through clenched teeth. "I'd rather kiss a cobra on the lips. That sucker couldn't turn me on with a monkey wrench." She started to laugh so I didn't know how serious she really was.

I was exasperated and I didn't try to hide it. Since Muh'Dear was having so much fun tormenting me, I wanted her to know how I felt. I gritted my teeth and rolled my eyes at her. "You didn't say anything mean to Daddy, did you? I hope you didn't. Not with a priest up in here." I held my breath and waited.

With a twinkle in her eyes, Muh'Dear told me, "Girl, I know how to behave." Then she let out her breath and pursed her lips, a thoughtful look on her face. "But I still ain't forgot what he done to us."

I looked at my feet. "Daddy's not that well. I'm glad he's got Lillimae. She takes real good care of him," I offered.

Muh'Dear giggled; I frowned.

She stopped giggling and cleared her throat. "And I hope I live long enough to be as big a burden to you," she said. A serious look suddenly appeared on her face. "I didn't mean that the way it sounded. I know you'll always be there for me, too." She squinted her eyes so hard that her pupils crossed as she waited for me to respond.

"Why wouldn't I be?" I mouthed. I exhaled when Muh'Dear rubbed my back and gave me a quick smile before she pranced across the floor to a spot next to Daddy and tapped him on the shoulder. There was a look on his face that I could not describe. He didn't look surprised or annoyed, but I couldn't tell if he was glad to be facing Muh'Dear or scared.

With all of the gloom in Jean's house, a warm feeling came over me as I watched my parents greet one another with a hug. I smiled for the first time since walking in Jean's door that day.

It was just a shame that it took funerals to bring out the best in some people.

CHAPTER 59

Rhoda didn't make it to my house after the gathering at Jean's. But Muh'Dear, Pee Wee, and Scary Mary and her entourage did. I didn't know what Muh'Dear and Daddy had talked about at Jean's house. But they must have had a pleasant conversation because she sat right next to him on my living room couch.

My parents were not acting loud and ugly, they were not scowling, and they were not rolling their eyes at each other. However, they did look uncomfortable and they were the only ones in the room who had not removed their coats. Muh'Dear's hands were cupped in her lap and her legs were crossed at the ankles and her face was as stiff as a mask. Daddy's arms were folded and his eyes looked as unfocused as a newborn baby's. I moved closer so I could hear what was going on. At about the same time, Pee Wee plopped down on the arm of the couch next to Muh'Dear and whispered something in her ear and a broad grin appeared on her face. Whatever it was Pee Wee said to her, it must have been interesting enough for her to share with Daddy because she leaned over and whispered in his ear and he grinned, too.

I had always been able to count on Pee Wee to lighten my load. Tonight was no different. He steered Muh'Dear and Daddy into conversations so neutral (sports, his barbershop, politics) that there was no way they could step on one another's toes. My fear that they would lock horns had almost dissipated.

"White folks sure don't grieve the way we do. Did y'all see how that Vinnie and the rest of them wops was drinkin'?" Scary Mary said, speaking in a low voice even though no white people were present.

"Them dagoes don't like to be called wops," Muh'Dear insisted with a nod, looking at Daddy like she needed a confirmation from him. Daddy looked like he could have been knocked over with a feather. His face remained expressionless as he blinked and nodded.

"Anyway, I didn't see none of them dagoes shed a single tear." Scary Mary continued, "Us, when we have a funeral, we boo-hoo for a straight week."

"Everybody else was drinkin' just as much as those Italian people. And that frail old woman in the wheelchair cried nonstop the whole time we were there," I reminded.

Scary Mary, pacing the floor like a panther, gave me an exasperated look and threw up her hands. Her floor-length, robe-like black dress swished with every step she took.

"That Vinnie ain't got no nature," Fanny Mae, Scary Mary's most outspoken prostitute, growled. Even though she was in her late forties and had eyes like a frog, she was Scary Mary's most popular employee. On any given day, horny men lined up to fuck her.

Over the years, Scary Mary had employed dozens of women. Fanny Mae had been with her the longest. Like Scary Mary, Fanny Mae was a hard-looking, coarse woman from a rough little town in the Deep South where the women ate poke salad every day and carried switchblades in their bras, even to church. I thought I would scream when Fanny Mae's weapon fell out of her bra during P.'s funeral. I was thankful that I was the only one who noticed it.

"And how Jean could put up with his Mickey Mouse dick in the bedroom is beyond me," Carlene, Scary Mary's youngest and newest prostitute, added. Looking more like a girl from some Asian country than a Black girl born in Pontiac, Michigan, Carlene was still learning the ropes. She had once implied that by being young and pretty, she was a cut above the more seasoned women in Scary Mary's stable. But Scary Mary had brought her back down to earth by telling her, "Gal, I don't care how young and pretty you think you are. To them tricks, you just another piece of tail. And you better believe that the cat you got between your thighs smell just as fishy as the rest of ours. When it comes to turnin' tricks, it ain't the beauty, it's the booty." Carlene was lucky that Scary Mary had rescued her from a brutal pimp in Cleveland. Carlene continued, "Even after Vinnie got with Jean, he never stopped comin' to the house. She want somethin' else to cry about, somebody ought to tell her that."

I couldn't figure out what it was about Scary Mary and her women, but I enjoyed their company. In addition to Pee Wee, they were the support system that kept me going. I was glad they had all come home with us. This was one night that I needed as many distractions as possible.

Poor Daddy. He didn't know what to do with himself. I hoped that I was the only one who had noticed him sneaking glances at Fanny Mae's and Carlene's big legs in their short little dresses. I could also see that Daddy was clearly embarrassed, but he laughed along with the rest of us at the prostitutes' comments.

Once while Muh'Dear was laughing, I saw her place her hand on Daddy's knee. Then the atmosphere shifted to a more serious mood.

"I'm sendin' my baby girl up to Toledo to stay with my

mama 'til they catch the maniac that killed P.," Fanny Mae said.

"And I pray they catch that devil soon," Scary Mary growled, slamming the top of my coffee table with her fist. "I pray he dies in the most unspeakable way possible."

CHAPTER 60

A lot of people in Richland didn't approve of Scary Mary and her role in the sex industry. When she had tried to buy a motel to expand her shenanigans on a very conservative street, the people in that neighborhood made a fuss that caused such an uproar that people as far away as Cincinnati were talking about it. Our city newspaper ran a quote from an unidentified man who not only lived in the neighborhood that Scary Mary wanted to corrupt but who was also one of Scary Mary's regular tricks. "Sure I get a lot of good sex from Scary Mary's girls. But that doesn't mean I want them operating in my backyard where my kids can see them!"

I don't know what else went on, especially behind the scenes, but Scary Mary promptly abandoned that idea. She quietly continued to run her operation out of the big house she lived in across town three blocks from the church we all attended.

Even though I had spent some of my earlier years living in the same house of shame with Scary Mary and the prostitutes she had working for her then, I never felt truly comfortable being in that environment. But that didn't stop me from visiting Scary Mary's house from time to time. I knew that she was not the one-dimensional she-devil some people made her out to be. Sure she was immoral, greedy, manipulative, and opportunistic, but she was also generous, sensitive, patient, wise, and spiritually stronger than any other woman I knew. Her advanced years had not diminished her strength. In fact, to me it seemed like the older she got, the stronger she got. That's why I went to Scary Mary's house after everybody had left my house. Daddy had already turned in for the night and I had left Lillimae sitting in front of the television.

Usually, when I did visit Scary Mary's house, I rarely went beyond her kitchen. Even on the days when her house was closed for business, which was usually during holidays, a day after a raid, or a funeral. I didn't like to roam around too much in Scary Mary's garishly furnished house because I didn't like listening to all of the moaning, groaning, and noises from bedsprings creaking coming from the three bedrooms upstairs.

Scary Mary occupied the only bedroom downstairs near her kitchen—she had beds and a jukebox in her basement that she put to use on really busy days and nights. When she had what she called "civilian" overnight guests, meaning people not involved in her sordid business activities or her prostitutes' children, she assigned them to her basement.

Business was slow at Scary Mary's place the night I went there after P.'s funeral. Not because of a lack of tricks but because three of the women who worked for Scary Mary were spending time with family members and doing other things a lot of people don't think prostitutes do. Ida Mae, one of the absent women, was working for free with some church group to help collect clothes for underprivileged kids. Another prostitute named Ethel, a singer that never got the break she needed, was entertaining terminally ill patients in a cancer ward at a nearby clinic. Lucille had taken her kids to Disneyland. The house seemed like such a lonely, quiet place with just Scary Mary, Carlene, and Fanny Mae present.

Carlene, clutching a large glass of red wine and wearing a flowered bathrobe, pulled out a seat for me at Scary Mary's kitchen table. Fanny Mae, wrapped up in a pair of white flannel pajamas that made her look like a pear-shaped mummy from the shoulders down, set a cup of steaming hot coffee on the table in front of me.

Scary Mary, perched on a stool by her sink, was coating her legs with Vaseline. Why she was wearing a see-through negligee was a mystery to me. Her long, flat breasts flapped when she moved and it was not a pretty sight. Large, pink sponge rollers were dangling off her red wig.

"So, Annette, you run off and leave your daddy and your off-white sister in the house alone?" Fanny Mae asked, picking her teeth with a straw from the broom she had just used to sweep the kitchen floor. Her hair was also rolled with pink sponge rollers. She was going through menopause and was always having hot flashes.

I sighed. "They won't miss me. My daddy's asleep and my sister was watching *I Love Lucy* reruns. She encouraged me to get out of the house. I know I won't sleep much tonight."

"Well, a whole lot of folks won't be sleepin' much tonight or no other night 'til they catch whoever killed that little white girl," Fanny Mae said, fanning her face with a pot holder.

"And I'm one of 'em," Scary Mary croaked. "I won't stop prayin' for that to happen until it do. I heard from one of my contacts at city hall that the po'lice done made P.'s case their number one priority. Praise the Lord." Scary Mary waved her hands high above her head, the same way she did in church when she got happy.

"Hmph! Do say. I wonder if the po'lice would be investigatin' this hard if it was a Black child involved," Fanny Mae scoffed, clearing her throat and toying with a loose thread hanging from the cuff of her pajama-top sleeve.

"Let's hope we don't have to find out," Carlene said in a strong, loud voice. "Not that I don't care about white kids," she added in a noticeably softer tone. Carlene's hair was in braids and her face was covered in a pasty-looking white facial mask. It made her look so much younger than her twenty years.

"Annette, I know you feelin' this whole thing way down deep. That child was crazy about you," Scary Mary said gently, now sliding Vaseline on her face and neck.

"And I'll be feeling it for a long time," I admitted. So far I had ignored the coffee cup in front of me. But I did want something to drink. Without asking, I lifted the glass of wine out of Carlene's hand and took a long swallow. After diffusing a belch, I let out a long, deep sigh.

I stayed at Scary Mary's house until almost eleven that night. When I got back to my house, Lillimae was still up. Still sitting in the same spot in front of the television that I had left her in, she was soaking her feet in a hot pan of water.

For the first time I noticed how rough her feet looked. She had calluses as big as walnuts. I knew it was because of her walking around outside, stepping on rocks and other debris in her bare feet so much when she was relaxing at her house.

"If you used Vaseline you wouldn't have to do that," I advised, frowning at the dead skin floating on top of the water in the pan. I stood in front of her, stretching and yawning as I removed my coat.

Lillimae shook her head. "My skin's too far gone for that. It wouldn't even absorb no Vaseline. The soles of my feet are so tough, last month I stepped on a nail and I didn't even bleed."

"And everybody thinks that white skin is so fragile." I sighed and crossed over to the television to turn on the eleven o'clock news.

Before I knew what was going on, Lillimae gasped. "Listen to that," she hollered, waving her arms. "Move out the way!"

I stumbled backward and moved off to the side of the television and listened to a special news report. I could not believe my ears. The police had a man in custody for P.'s murder!

And it wasn't Vinnie.

CHAPTER 61

It was too good to be true. The man who had raped and murdered P. was off the street.

"He looks like somebody's old grandfather!" Lillimae roared, wringing her hands, standing with her feet still in the pan of water. "Who would have guessed that a man his age could still get a hard-on!"

"You'd be surprised," I said nastily. "Some of those slimy old devils never run out of juice." Of all the men I had ever known intimately, including Pee Wee, old Mr. Boatwright was the one who could get a hard-on the quickest and keep it the longest.

The elderly white man on the television screen was attractive in a subtle kind of way. He had a head full of neatly coiffed gray hair, large eyes with pencil-thin eyebrows, and a nice set of teeth. He had the nerve to be smiling as the police escorted him, in handcuffs, into our police department. Dressed in a dark suit and tie, the suspect looked more like a banker than a sex-crazed child rapist and killer.

According to the news report, a twelve-year-old girl had been abducted on her way home from a neighborhood convenience store in Canton, twenty miles south of Richland. Some time during the night, she had escaped from her abductor and had been found wandering naked down a dark, rural road. She had been raped, beaten, and left for dead in an area near a cow pasture. Well, the girl lived and she was able to identify a neighbor as the perpetrator. Her clothing, her blood, and other evidence had been found in his car. The police had picked up the man at the home of one of his six adult sons. One of his sons lived in Richland in a house one block from the house that P. had lived in. As soon as the police questioned the man about P., he confessed.

I turned off the television and let out a deep sigh of relief.

"Thank you, Jesus," Lillimae mouthed. The news had excited her. She mopped sweat from her face and then fanned herself with the tail of her housecoat. Then she lifted her feet out of the pan of water and blotted them with a towel. We toasted with fresh cans of beer before we turned in for the night.

I went to work the next day feeling better than I had felt in weeks. Even though thoughts of Jerome and Rhoda were still haunting me, I now had a different issue to address. I had misjudged Vinnie and I had to humble myself and restore what was left of my relationship with him and Jean.

Jean had not returned to work yet and I had no idea when or if she ever would. Rather than call her house, I decided I would just drop by on my way home from work that day.

I called home to let Lillimae and Daddy know I was going to be late getting home because I wanted to go by to see how Jean and Vinnie were doing after hearing the news about P.'s killer being in custody. But before I could tell Lillimae what I planned to do, she cut me off.

"They are not goin' to charge the man that was on the news last night for killing that P."

"What do you mean? That little girl identified him and

they found her clothes and blood and stuff in his house!" I screamed. "He's got to be the one!"

"For that little girl, yeah. But not for P."

My tongue started to ache but I ignored the pain and continued in a weak voice. "Lillimae, the news said that the man confessed. His son lives right around the corner from Jean's house."

I heard Lillimae suck in her breath and sniff. "They just said on the news that the man has mental problems and was in the county nuthouse up until two days ago."

"But he said he killed P. Maybe he slipped out of the asylum that day. Maybe . . ."

"Annette, the man did confess to kidnappin' P. But he also confessed to kidnappin' every other missin' child but the Lindbergh baby." Lillimae sniffed again and cussed under her breath. "Now what did you call to tell me?"

"Nothing," I mumbled. "I was just calling to see how you and Daddy were getting along."

I hung up the telephone and spent the rest of my lunch hour sitting in my car in the telephone company parking lot with the worst headache I ever had before in my life.

CHAPTER 62

W hen I got home that evening, Daddy was already in the bed asleep and Lillimae was in the kitchen organizing dinner.

"Is Daddy all right? He sure sleeps a lot," I said with concern.

"That's because he likes to sleep. He slept through the last hurricane we had," Lillimae informed me.

Just as I opened my mouth to speak again, the telephone rang. It was Pee Wee calling me from Muh'Dear's house.

"Your mama told me to call your house and see how everybody was doin'," he said. I could hear Muh'Dear mumbling in the background. One thing that had always pleased me was the fact that Pee Wee and Muh'Dear got along so well. Even during the times when Pee Wee and I were not sleeping together, he'd kept up his relationship with my mother. Especially after Daddy King died.

Muh'Dear had always wooed Pee Wee with lavish meals and juicy gossip. Two or three times a month he dropped by Muh'Dear's to see if she needed anything done around the

house. She had become so fussy that she was almost impossible to please. She had called three different plumbers to
come to the house to take care of a leaky faucet in her bathtub and she was still complaining about it leaking. Now Pee
Wee was over there with his toolbox. Even when something
in Muh'Dear's house wasn't falling apart, Pee Wee went over
there to check on things anyway.

"We are all doing fine," I said tiredly. "Daddy's resting,
Lillimae's fixing dinner, and I'm just . . . I'm just here."
There were times when I couldn't stop myself from sound-
ing like a sick old woman. Like now.

"You don't sound too good at all," Pee Wee remarked. He
didn't sound too good himself.

"I'm not," I admitted.

"Well, since you still got company, I won't ask if you
want me to come over to . . . uh . . . keep you company. But
I'll be home in a little while. You want to come over to my
place? And you won't have to worry about steppin' in no
mess or helpin' me wash my dishes. I had a lady from the
church come to the house to do some light cleanin'. She got
my floors lookin' so spiffy we could eat off of 'em."

"I don't think so. I don't feel like socializing tonight. Tell
Muh'Dear I'll call her tomorrow."

I still wanted to see how Jean was doing. And as much as
I hated to admit it to myself, my original suspicions about
Vinnie's involvement in P.'s murder had returned.

Two days later I invited Muh'Dear to the house to have
dinner with Daddy, Lillimae, and me.

"They'll be going back to Florida in a couple of days and
I don't know when we'll see them again. And I know you
don't plan to visit Miami anytime soon," I said.

"I don't think so," Muh'Dear replied tiredly. "I got to take
Frank in small doses now."

I didn't put any pressure on Muh'Dear but I told her that

if she changed her mind about having dinner with us, she was welcome to join us. Scary Mary and Carlene came over to dinner, even though I had not invited them.

"How come Carlene's not working tonight?" I asked Scary Mary in a low voice as she and Carlene followed me to the kitchen.

One thing I could say about Scary Mary was that she was still an astute businesswoman. But she now treated the prostitutes who worked for her more like a stern nanny than a madam. Scary Mary's only child, a severely retarded woman in her forties named Mott, was in some kind of a group home in Toledo. The only other family that Scary Mary had, that I knew of, was Florence, her blind, thirty-six-year-old foster daughter. Florence had tried to be my friend during our teens, but I had shunned her for Rhoda. Now Florence lived in Toledo, too, with her husband and two kids. Scary Mary didn't get to see her much because Florence's straitlaced husband didn't approve of Scary Mary's lifestyle. Since Carlene was the youngest of the prostitutes, Scary Mary used her to fill the familial void in her life.

Leaning against me as I opened my refrigerator to get her a beer, her tongue almost touching my ear, the old madam told me with a mysterious chuckle, "Carlene's back went out the other night. She got this real frisky trick that can't make up his mind what he want to do once he get in the bed." Scary Mary sniffed and winked her eye twice as she snatched the bottle of beer out of my hand and flipped off the top with a pancake flapper. "These men. They out of control. Oooh, dicks is tricky these days. In my day a man wasn't so complicated in the bedroom. If he was a real good lover, he didn't even make no noise when he did his business. He'd pile up on top of you, slide it in, slide it out, and climb off and go to sleep like he supposed to. Because of a tricky dick, I gave Carlene a few days off." I had heard this story before.

"Again," I muttered, grabbing a beer for myself.

"Uh-huh. Again." Scary Mary nodded. "But I ain't no fool. The girl is just plain lazy." She sighed and shook her head, smiling like she had a secret. "She so young and I'm so old, but I'm crazy about this child," Scary Mary said, massaging Carlene's back. "I see myself in her when I was her age."

I glanced out of the window over my sink, thinking about how I'd felt the same way about P.

Shaking her head and backing away, Carlene retorted, "My back is out! And I ain't lazy!" Carlene had on a rumpled trench coat. She slid her hands into her pockets and shifted her body into a position so extreme I thought she was going to fall across my kitchen table. She fished a stick of Juicy Fruit chewing gum out of her pocket and stuffed it into her mouth.

"Gal, you won't get far in this business 'til you start suckin' dick," Scary Mary hollered, snapping her fingers in Carlene's angry face.

"Nuh-uh . . . nuh-uh," Carlene replied, shaking her head and cracking her gum. "I ain't puttin' no nasty, stinky pecker in my mouth. Ain't no tellin' what kinds of health problems I'd end up with."

Scary Mary slapped her hand onto her hip and got so close up in Carlene's face, their noses touched. "All them chitlins, Big Macs, and fried chicken you eat is doin' a lot more damage to your health than you slurpin' on a few peckers, honey child."

Carlene dropped her head and started sniffling. Scary Mary snatched a handkerchief out of her bra and wiped tears off of Carlene's face and we returned to my living room.

God answered a lot of people's prayer the following Saturday night. Right after I returned from taking Daddy and Lillimae to the airport, Pee Wee rushed over to my house, frantic and out of breath, with his latest eyewitness report. He had just come from Jean's house. He told me that

Carmine Antonosanti had confronted Vinnie with some information that P. had shared with Rhoda's daughter Jade during P.'s last sleepover at Rhoda's house.

Rhoda and her husband had brought Jade to Jean's house to tell her story. In a child's words, Jade told how P. had revealed to her that "Mr. Vinnie made P. do the nasty with him almost every day."

Instead of denying the allegation, Vinnie Gambiano had cooked his goose by confessing that he had killed P. "by accident." Jean and Rhoda had attacked Vinnie with lamps and chairs. They had literally beaten him out of his clothes. Vinnie fled from Jean's house wearing nothing but his underwear and one shoe.

Not less than an hour later, the police found Vinnie on the ground behind Antonosanti's restaurant with a bullet in the back of his head. Old Mr. Carmine Antonosanti, one step away from the grave himself, had already admitted executing Vinnie and turned himself in to the police.

I was surprised when Rhoda showed up at my house with Muh'Dear and Scary Mary later that same night. Rhoda's face was bruised and her hair was askew from the mayhem she had participated in. But there was a triumphant grin on her face. It would be one of the most memorable nights of my life.

"Vinnie was lucky I wasn't there to help them gals whup his ass," Scary Mary said angrily, shaking her gnarled, liver-spotted fist.

"*Lucky* is one thing Vinnie ain't," Muh' Dear added. "But I blame Jean for this mess. She should have done somethin' the first time her baby told her Vinnie touched her," Muh'Dear said, handing Scary Mary a can of beer from the big bag she had brought along with her. "With all the grown women 'round this town screamin' for somebody to pester them, ain't no grown man got to go around rapin' no child!"

"From what I heard, Jean didn't believe that child 'til it

was too late nohow!" Scary Mary said hotly. Her jaws moved so fast and hard that her false teeth started to click and slip. "That child didn't have to die!"

"Kids do tell lies against folks they don't like! It ain't no secret P. didn't like Vinnie!" Muh'Dear offered, sitting down so hard on one of my chairs it squeaked.

It seemed like I was the only calm person in the room. "The man did threaten to hurt P. if she ever told," I said evenly.

Standing in the middle of my living room floor with her arms folded and a menacing look on her face, Rhoda cleared her throat and nodded at me. "And most kids usually don't lie about things like that."

"Well, I'd have believed my daughter if she had told me some nasty motherfucker was messin' with her." Muh'Dear sniffed. "All my girl would have needed to do was tell me and I'd have dealt with whoever that devil was and asked questions later."

Rhoda nodded more vigorously in my direction. I read her lips as she silently mouthed to me, "Tell . . . now."

I nodded back at her and cleared my throat. Then I said as calmly as I could, "Mr. Boatwright and Vinnie were two of a kind."

A wall-to-wall smile appeared on Rhoda's face.

All eyes were on me. I didn't know where to start.

CHAPTER 63

Muh'Dear gasped and almost slid out of her chair. "You say Brother Boatwright was just like Vinnie? What's that supposed to mean, Annette?"

Muh'Dear tilted her head and gave me a dry look, lifting both her eyebrows. Then she started blinking real hard and shaking her head.

I waited until Muh'Dear composed herself. Then I sucked in my breath and stole another glance at Rhoda before I responded. "Every chance he got, Mr. Boatwright had his way with me." My voice was ringing in my ears. "Sometimes two and three times in the same day."

The room got so quiet I could hear the clock ticking on the wall above my television set. Scary Mary's mouth dropped open and she leaned forward. Muh'Dear's eyes got as big as saucers. Pee Wee stood up and put his hands on his hips.

"Why in the world would you say somethin' like that?" Muh'Dear yelled, glaring at me. "Why would you bad-mouth a man like Brother Boatwright? With him dead and buried and unable to speak for hisself. What's wrong with you, girl?!"

"Because it's true," Rhoda announced evenly, her right jaw twitching. "That old-ass man was a lyin', child-rapin' son of a bitch."

With a loud gasp, Muh'Dear turned to Rhoda. "Both of y'all done lost your minds. Don't neither one of you drink nary one of them beers. This ain't one bit funny. What in the world is y'all tryin' to say?"

I surprised myself by remaining calm. "Muh'Dear, Mr. Boatwright started messing with me when I was seven. He didn't stop until, until . . . well, he stopped because he died." At this point, I glanced at Pee Wee. His eyes were on Rhoda. I had never seen Rhoda look as smug as she did now. Scary Mary was so still she looked like an old statue. Her mouth was hanging open so wide now, I could see the top of her dentures.

"Tell them about the baby," Rhoda insisted, making a sweeping gesture with her hand. Bracelets on her wrist clicked like coins.

"That time I got pregnant, Mr. Boatwright was the one responsible," I confessed.

Muh'Dear was beside herself. Her eyes blinked rapidly, her lips quivered. "Girl, why in the world didn't you tell somebody?" Muh'Dear screamed. She rose from her chair so fast, the chair fell over. She looked at me like I had just sprouted horns. "Don't you think you done got too old for me to whup your behind! Lyin' is one of the deadliest sins. If all what you sayin' is even half true, how come you didn't tell me, girl?"

"I was too scared. He threatened me and told me he would do all kinds of stuff if I told. He even said he would kill you if I ran away from home. You and everybody else were so in love with that old man, I didn't think I'd have a chance. I knew that Rhoda was the only person I could turn to and I knew that Rhoda would stand by me. She saw right through Mr. Boatwright and all of his lies." I turned to Scary Mary. "And your foster daughter Florence, she saw through Mr. Boatwright, too, and she was as blind as a bat."

"You and Rhoda told me everything else! Why didn't y'all tell me this shit, too? I would have believed you," Pee Wee said, his voice cracking. "I thought you told me everything."

"Not everything," I mumbled, unable to look in Pee Wee's eyes as he glared at me.

"That no-good, low-down bastard. Annette, I would have believed you if you had come to me. I knew you wasn't the kind of kid to tell lies that bold and ugly. If Boatwright wasn't already dead, I'd kill him with my own hands," Scary Mary shrieked. It was the first time I ever saw tears on her face. "Lord, you can't trust half the men on this planet. My own granddaddy put his hands on me when I was a child. He threatened to feed me to his hogs, but I told my mama anyway." Scary Mary paused and wiped her face with the sleeve of her blouse. "She didn't believe me and that's the very reason I left home when I was thirteen. Even after they caught my granddaddy messin' with one of my cousins, they still didn't believe *me*." Scary Mary paused long enough to catch her breath. "There I was, a young girl on my own durin' the Depression. I rode them train rails in boxcars with them hoboes and other displaced peoples, doin' whatever I had to do to survive them mean streets. All because some man couldn't keep his dick out of me. And that's the very reason I ended up doin' what I do now. I make 'em pay for it with cold, hard cash, every goddamn time. Me, I went one better—I started makin' 'em pay me for *other* women's pussy, too. After my granddaddy, I never let another man take advantage of me."

The room remained silent for a few moments after Scary Mary's outburst.

Rhoda broke the silence by clearing her throat first. Then she started talking in a low, controlled voice through clenched teeth. "Everybody that knew me as a child, knew better than to lay a hand on my body. And if somebody ever touches my baby girl . . . well, let's just say he'll regret it 'til the day he dies—which wouldn't be too long after that." Rhoda sniffed and turned to Pee Wee. "Brother-man, I hope you don't feel dumped on, bein' the only man up in here. All of y'all are not bad and we all know that. It's just *some* men we're talkin' about. And a precious few at that."

Pee Wee blinked and looked around the room, resting his eyes on me. "I hope y'all don't think I'm like that. I would never touch nobody's child! Matter of fact, girls ain't the only ones get messed with." He paused and there was a collective sigh in the room as we all looked at Pee Wee. He cleared his throat before continuing in a labored voice. "When I was five, livin' in Pennsylvania, before my mama passed, one of her female friends used to baby-sit me. As soon as she got me alone, she would make me put my head between her legs and . . . lick her. That nasty bitch! One time her crotch had such a unholy stench, I almost threw up in her lap. Oh, but she wasn't goin' to be outdone by no little-bitty boy like me. She made me suck on her long-ass, flat-ass titties. I bit the nipple off one of 'em, spit it out on the floor, and I ran out in the street screamin'. She fell out on the floor screamin' herself, with blood squirtin' from a hole in her tittie. Somebody went and got my mama and my daddy and they took turns whuppin' that heifer's ass, bleedin' tittie and all. I think that episode is what killed my mama. She never got over puttin' me in that predicament. That's the reason Daddy packed me up and we moved out here to Ohio."

Muh'Dear dropped her head and shook it for a moment

before she looked at me. "Annette, baby, I don't care what Brother Boatwright said he would do to you, I would have protected you. The police would have found that son of bitch in pieces by the time they picked him up. I should have known that that hound from hell was too good to be true. There he was with his one-legged, black ass, layin' up in my house, on top of my baby—I hope he's sizzlin' in hell right now!" Muh'Dear started moving about the room, picking up empty beer cans and straightening furniture. "I would have killed that son of a bitch if I'd known."

"And I would have helped you kill him," Scary Mary added, waving her fist in the air.

Scary Mary got so upset she had to leave. Pee Wee left shortly afterward.

Muh'Dear patted her chest and folded her arms. "Other than Brother Boatwright, was there any other man that took advantage of you when you was comin' up?" Muh'Dear asked, looking from me to Rhoda.

"No, ma'am," I managed.

"What about Albert?"

"Daddy King was a decent man, Muh'Dear. And he was a good husband to you. He wasn't that kind of man."

"What about your daddy? He had plenty opportunities to pester you when you and him was alone out there in them woods fishin' in them lakes when we lived in Florida."

I gasped. "Muh'Dear, Daddy was not that kind of man. He would never do something like that."

"Rhoda, I am so sorry you had to hear all this," Muh'Dear said, turning to Rhoda again.

"And my daddy was a decent man, too," Rhoda said. "But as decent and peaceful as he was, he would have taken care of old Buttwright with his own hands if Annette had let me tell him." Turning to me, Rhoda said gently, "I never told you, but one time my daddy said he'd noticed Buttwright lookin' at you the wrong way. He asked me if you'd ever said anything about that old goat touchin' you." Rhoda let out her breath and gave me a sad look. "I told him no."

Muh'Dear finally came over to me on the couch and hugged me. "You doin' okay, baby?" she asked, almost choking on her words.

"I'm fine now. I was lucky I had a friend like Rhoda to go to. Talking to her about Mr. Boatwright is what got me through it."

"I am sorry for not seein' that dead-ass motherfucker for the monster he was. I don't know how I'm goin' to make this up to you. I didn't do my job 'cause I failed you and I ain't never goin' to forget that. I don't know how I'm goin' to live with that now."

"You didn't fail me. I failed myself by waiting until now to tell you. But Muh'Dear, you can't do anything about it now. Mr. Boatwright had to answer to God. We all will someday."

Out of the corner of my eye I saw Rhoda drop her head and reach for her coat.

CHAPTER 64

Now that the horror of what I had experienced at Mr. Boatwright's hands was out in the open, I felt like I had just been released from a prison.

I felt free.

My startling confession changed Muh'Dear in ways I was glad to see. One of the first things she did was to destroy that wretched picture of Mr. Boatwright that she'd kept on the mantel above her fireplace for so many years. After she ripped it to pieces, she tossed it into that same fireplace. She bent over backward to make sure I was happy and safe. She had new locks installed on all of the doors in my house. She offered to buy me a gun, which I graciously declined. She offered me money I didn't need, she came by more often, and she started treating Daddy the way I had been praying for. She called him to check on his health and she even invited him to visit her in Ohio *and stay with her in her house.* That was a major move and it helped the healing of my emotional wounds.

"Frank don't like the weather up here so he ain't too crazy

about comin' back no time soon. But I just might take a notion and go down there to visit him and that gal Lillimae
sometime soon," Muh'Dear told me, walking through my
house, checking all the locks.

In one of her letters, Lillimae told me that Muh'Dear had
told her and Daddy what I had revealed about Mr. Boatwright. I was not surprised when Lillimae told me about an
incident involving her and one of Daddy's fishing buddies.
The man had fondled Lillimae and threatened to take her to
the Everglades and feed her to some creature if she told. Lillimae had told anyway and Daddy had beaten the man to a
pulp.

Old Mr. Carmine Antonosanti died before he could be
brought to trial for killing Vinnie and Jean was finally able to
smile once again. But she was never the same. I was not surprised when she quit her job at the phone company and
packed up and moved to Brooklyn to live with her older
brother and his family.

By the end of February, Rhoda and I were once again in-
separable. I knew that it had a lot to do with my confession.
I was so glad to have her back in my life. I enjoyed visiting
her at her lavishly decorated house on Patterson Street. Just
like the house she had grown up in across the street from me,
plush white furniture decorated almost every room. And the
smell of roses permeated the air. Her husband Otis tooled
around town in a pickup truck, but Rhoda had a Ford station
wagon that she used to haul around the four young children
she took care of five days a week. A couple of childless old
maids from her church helped her operate her child-care
center, so Rhoda could always get away to spend time doing
other things. Every Monday, Rhoda came to my job to pick
me up for lunch.

One Saturday afternoon, during a spaghetti and Chianti
lunch in her neat little kitchen, Rhoda laughed until she

cried when I told her about my disastrous relationship with Jerome. It didn't even faze her when I told her why Jerome had dumped me.

"So what if you sold a little pussy. Sooner or later every woman uses her body to get over, one way or another. How else can we keep our men in line?" Rhoda laughed.

Then Rhoda shared some of her pain with me. I hated it, but I had to admit that even I supported the "misery loves company" belief. I was glad to hear that Rhoda's life had not been all peaches and cream.

"One of the reasons we left Florida was to get away from my husband's mistress," she told me, her eyes sparkling with mischief. "A heifer almost young enough to be his daughter." A fierce scowl suddenly appeared on her face as she stared at the wall behind me. I got nervous when her eye started twitching. And I got downright scared when she balled her fist and slammed it on the table, making a napkin sail to the floor. I knew better than anybody did how much wrath she could inflict.

I picked up the napkin and slid my chair back a few inches from the table. "Uh, Otis had an affair and you're still with him? What happened to the woman?"

The last thing I wanted to hear was Rhoda telling me that she had killed somebody else. But I couldn't imagine Rhoda knowing about her husband having an affair and her not taking some *fatal* action. Maybe with middle age approaching, she had mellowed, I decided. I took a huge swallow of wine and braced myself. Then I asked, "Is that, uh, other woman . . . still around?"

CHAPTER 65

Rhoda's face softened and she leaned across the table and mumbled just loud enough for me to hear, "Well, after what I did to my husband with that friend of his, I kind of expected that kind of payback." She sighed and straightened up, rotating her neck as if it was in pain. Rhoda sighed again and rubbed her neck before continuing. "Uh, you remember that thing I did with you-know-who?" As far as I knew, I was the only person who knew that Rhoda's deceased son, David, had been fathered by Otis's best friend.

I nodded. "I'd almost forgotten about that," I lied. I cleared my throat and steered the conversation back to Otis's mistress. "Did you confront the other woman?" I stabbed at the plate of spaghetti that Rhoda had set on the table in front of me, spearing three meatballs at the same time.

"Oh, you goddamn right I did. I know you don't think I'd let some bitch clown me. Shit." Rhoda paused and held up her hand. "But I didn't hurt her, if that's what you're wonderin'. At least, not physically."

I breathed a sigh of relief. "Was she pretty?" I asked, talking with my mouth full.

We had picked up the spaghetti from Antonosanti's, where Rhoda went almost every day to pay her respects to the late Carmine's grieving family. She had started this ritual right after the old man's funeral. Her loyalty to her friends never ceased to amaze me. I guess that's why I was so glad to be back in her fold. She was the kind of person you wanted on your side.

"Was that cow pretty?" Rhoda dismissed the thought with a wave of her hand. "Only in a pig's eyes. Once I got a gander at that face, I felt sorry for her. The girl was a real piece of work. It was no wonder that Otis was the only man she'd ever been with. Or so she claimed."

"How could you feel sorry for the woman who wrecked your marriage?"

Rhoda's eyes got wide and she rotated her neck. "She didn't wreck my marriage! I felt sorry for her. And if you had seen her you would have felt sorry for her, too. She looked so much like James Brown, we all called her J.B." Rhoda laughed. "Who wouldn't feel sorry for a woman who looked like the Godfather of Soul? She even wore the same old tired Lord Jesus hairdo that James still wears to this today. She claimed she didn't know Otis was married. She packed up and went back to Mississippi that same night. As a matter of fact, I stood in her bedroom with a stick in my hand while she packed her shit. I wasn't goin' to use it, but I thought it would help her pack and it did. Oooooh, that Otis. He cried like a baby when I went home to cook his goose. By the time I was through with his black ass, he was as humble as the Pope. I used his affair as leverage to make him move us back up here. After that thing with, uh, that white girl that tried to ruin my brother, I knew I had to get out of Florida."

I chose to ignore Rhoda's comment about the white girl. I chuckled and stuffed more spaghetti into my mouth, sliding it into my jaw as I talked. "Otis is lucky you didn't divorce him."

"Now you of all people know that I am no fool. Divorcin' Otis never even entered my mind. I love bein' married. Where else would I find a man as good as Otis at my age and with two kids?"

"Good men don't cheat on their wives," I wailed, flooding my mouth with more wine.

"Girl, you got a lot to learn." Rhoda drained her glass and snatched the bottle of wine in front of her and refilled her glass before she continued. She was tipsy and had started slurring her words. "My man works his fingers to the bone, gives me the whole paycheck, and does everything I tell him to do, see. And he serves up some good dick, anytime I want it. I got a fool and I know I got a fool. I got a good thing. Dynamite couldn't separate me from him." Rhoda laughed, but there was a seriously sad look on her face. I didn't know why, but my instincts were telling me that she was leaving something out. "Don't pay me any mind. My man is not a fool—he really loves me and I love him. Eat those meatballs, girl."

Just then Jade, wearing a red dotted Swiss dress and shiny, black leather T-strap shoes, marched into the kitchen and started skipping in circles in front of Rhoda. "Mama, what's a fool?" Jade asked.

"Uh, sweetie, did you clean up your room? Did you put all your toys away?"

"No, ma'am," Jade pouted, still skipping in circles.

"Run and go clean up your room so your Auntie Annette won't think you're a little piggy."

Jade gave me a smile and skipped away.

I tilted my head and smiled at Rhoda, stuffing more food into my mouth. "Well, I'm glad you came back to Ohio. I really missed you. Oh, uh, that last time we talked right after I moved back from Pennsylvania, that stuff you told me—"

"About Buttwright?"

I nodded and slid my seat closer to the table, leaning my

head toward Rhoda's. In a low voice I said, "And your grand-mother and the cop and the white girl."

"What about it?" Rhoda now sounded as sober as a judge. Even though she had swallowed more wine.

"Was it all true?"

"Would it make a difference?" Rhoda asked, not blinking as she stared into my eyes.

I looked at the floor and shrugged. "Not really. Not now. It's in the past and we've moved on."

"Then let's leave it in the past. We don't ever have to bring any of that up again."

"Then we won't," I said, reaching for more wine.

CHAPTER 66

Rhoda knew I was pregnant even before I did. On five different occasions when I was with her, I had to run to a toilet to throw up. Once during a drive from the mall, she had to stop her car so I could throw up on the side of the freeway.

"When are you goin' to tell Pee Wee?"

My mouth dropped open. "How do you know it's his?"

"I'm not blind. Besides, I've always known that you and that brother were still foolin' around."

Telling Pee Wee I was pregnant with his baby was not something I planned to do anytime soon, if at all. He was involved with another woman and there was some talk that their relationship was serious. However, I continued to let him crawl into my bed because he was the only man who was paying any real attention to me these days.

I went out with a few other men here and there, but sleeping with them and developing a relationship was something that did not happen. No matter how hard I tried. It was Pee Wee I was with when Jerome came by my house that night, a week after my lunch at Rhoda's house.

Wearing nothing but my bathrobe, I opened my front door and went out on my porch. The night air was cool, but I was sweating like a bull. Pee Wee and I had just rolled out of my bed.

"Negro, what are you doing here?" I asked Jerome, letting my robe fall open on purpose. I wanted him to see what he had given up. Now that I had accepted the way my body looked, and the fact that men other than Mr. Boatwright found it attractive, I reveled in the attention. My breasts, as big as globes compared to women like Rhoda, were still high and firm.

"Uh, look, baby, I've been thinking about you a lot. I've had a lot of time to think things over and I still think we have a chance to make a go of things," Jerome told me, his eyes staring hard at my nakedness.

"I don't think so," I told him, letting my robe fall open even more.

"Look," he continued, holding up both hands. "What you did in the past was your business. What I care about is the woman you are now. You were a good woman to me and for me. I . . . I realize that now. I mean, we had a good thing going. We had fun, we got along real good, and we were good for one another. "

"But what I did in the past with those men would always be in the back of your mind and someday it would make a difference. Again. What do you think would happen if the rest of your family found out I slept with men for money?"

"Uh, they already know. Uncle Willie left no stone unturned. He told it all. But I don't care what they think. And anyway, that's *my* problem."

"It would be too big of a problem. If we got back together and had kids, it would be their problem, too."

Jerome shifted his weight to one side and let out a tired sigh. "I still love you, Annette. I wouldn't be here if I didn't.

I mean, I'm lonely for you, girl. I want to be with you for the rest of my life. Look, if it would make you feel any better, I got a thing or two in my past that I would like to forget. There was a drug thing when I was up in Buffalo and there was a thing with an underage girl. That's on my record and will be there 'til the day I die. It about killed my family, but they got over it. If they could get over that, they can get over anything. And—and Uncle Willie is no angel, either. Right now as we speak, he's trying to get out of going to jail for income tax evasion." Jerome was frantic and I was enjoying it. "See, I just got a big bonus at work. We can go on a cruise before and after we get married. I'll pay for everything. Come on, girl. *I need you.*"

The pleading look on Jerome's face brought tears to my eyes. I never thought I'd see the day that a man would beg *me* to come back to him. I was flattered, but it still was not enough for me to change my mind. The damage had already been done to my spirit and it couldn't be repaired.

I shook my head so hard, my braided hair batted my face. "It would never work, Jerome." Caught off guard, I didn't come across sounding as indifferent and cold as I should have. Part of the reason was, I still had strong feelings for Jerome, but I didn't want him to know that. I stood up straight and narrowed my eyes, making him flinch. "I'm not the woman for you," I added with a snap.

Jerome stumbled and cleared his throat. Now there was a desperate look in his eyes. "Don't you believe in the power of love?"

"Of course I do, but apparently you didn't when it counted. I loved you at one time and you knew it. And even the power of love can only do so much." I let out a deep breath and announced proudly, "Besides, I'm involved with somebody else." I was glad Pee Wee came to the door, wrapped in nothing but a towel, to confirm my claim.

"Hey, brother, what's goin' on? Ain't this a woman and a half?" Pee Wee said smugly, sliding his arm like a snake around my waist.

Jerome's eyes shifted to Pee Wee's arm, and then he just glared at Pee Wee. After doing that, Jerome turned around and left, walking with his head lowered. His shoulders sagged like an old man's.

"So. Brother Cunningham tryin' to get next to you again?" Pee Wee draped his other arm around my shoulder and guided me to my couch, where he pulled me down on his lap. I could feel his knees straining to support my massive weight, but since it didn't bother him, it didn't bother me.

"He can't try hard enough," I sighed, struggling to keep from sliding to the floor.

I felt bad about having to reject Jerome. He did seem sincere. But I felt even worse about knowing that I was carrying Pee Wee's baby and not knowing when and if I would ever tell him.

CHAPTER 67

Despite the fact that I had aborted my first child, with Rhoda's help, I had decided to keep the baby growing inside me. I had made enough mistakes. With life being as short as it was, it was time for me to stop interfering with God's plans for me. Not willing to risk His wrath, and a disturbing dream I had the night before, had helped me make up my mind.

In the dream, I entered my living room from the kitchen after treating myself to a late-night snack. Pee Wee had just left, but I could still see him peeping in my living room window, like there was something he just had to see. The room was dark, but a stream of light coming from an unknown source helped guide me across the room. In the middle of the floor were two open coffins. I got close enough to see that Mr. Boatwright was in the first one. Huge black spiders and maggots crawled across his face. His lips appeared to be frozen into a cruel sneer. His hair was a matted cap of cobwebs. In the second coffin was a young woman who appeared to be about the same age that the child I had aborted would have been, had she been born. I blinked and the young woman sat up, as alive as I was. And she was beautiful. Her dark brown skin was as smooth as velvet. Thick, bow-shaped lips parted, displaying a dazzling smile. There were no creatures crawling on her face and there were no cobwebs on her head. I asked her who she was.

"I would have been your daughter if you and Rhoda had not killed me before I could be born," was her response.

"I had to," I replied. *"I didn't know what else to do!"*

"Well, where I went to after you and Rhoda killed me, there were a lot of other kids already there. A lot of us never got the chance to be born so we didn't have names. What would you have named me?"

"I don't know. What names do you like?"

"I like Charlotte. That's the same name of the old woman that was already in the place that I went to when you killed me. She keeps me company."

"Then you can call yourself Charlotte."

The young woman closed her eyes and resumed her death pose in the coffin. I closed both the coffins as Pee Wee watched from the window that he was still peeping through.

I woke up shivering and crying. I knew then what I had to do. I had to keep my baby this time. Besides, at thirty-six, and no husband of my own in sight, I truly believed that it would be my last time to be a mother.

I had a lot to offer a child now and when Muh'Dear passed on, the Buttercup and the house she lived in would be mine, too. I looked forward to the experience of raising a child. With all the knowledge I had gained, and based on my own experiences, I was certain I'd be the best mother any child could have.

With renewed strength, I leaped out of bed and prepared myself for work. I called Muh'Dear during my morning break and told her that I was coming to the Buttercup for lunch and for her to have a plate of chicken wings and waffles ready for me.

"When was you goin' to tell me about that baby you carryin'?" Muh'Dear asked, pulling me into the kitchen as soon as I entered the restaurant.

"Rhoda told you?" I mouthed, looking around the hot kitchen.

The cook who assisted Muh'Dear and several other workers scurried about, almost knocking Muh'Dear and me into the wall. Muh'Dear cleared her throat, gave a stern look to her employees, and pulled me into a corner.

"If you lookin' around for them chicken and waffles, don't worry. You'll get 'em. But first you goin' to talk to me about that baby."

"Rhoda told you?" I repeated. I had to remove the scarf I had tied around my throat that morning. As good as it looked with my new green sweater, it had begun to feel like a noose.

"Rhoda ain't had to tell me nothin'. I ain't blind." Muh'Dear let out a deep sigh and dropped her head. "Well, I ain't *that* blind." She gave me a sharp look before she caressed my face. "Now that I know about Brother Boatwright's wicked ways, you done opened my eyes to a lot of things. I don't miss nothin' no more when it comes to you. You are my only child and I love the ground you walk on, girl. I was with you and for you long before you took up with Rhoda and I'll be with you long after she gone. Friends come and go, but I'm the only mama you'll ever have. Why did you tell Rhoda about the baby before you told me? It was bad enough you told her about all that other mess first."

"I didn't tell Rhoda I was pregnant. She's not blind, either."

While I was standing there, Muh'Dear picked up the telephone on the wall by the door and started dialing.

"Frank, did you know that this gal up here walkin' around pregnant? Uh-huh. I didn't think so. No, Frank, I ain't noticed nothin' 'til recently. The girl's been big as a bread truck all her life—why would I notice her puttin' on a few more pounds?" Muh'Dear paused and nodded, holding the telephone away from her face. "All right, then. Tell Lillimae I said hi. 'Bye, Frank." She hung up and turned to me. "I declare, your daddy is tickled to death. This'll be his first grandchild, too."

I gave my mother an exasperated look. "My half-sister Lillimae already has two little boys."

Muh'Dear shot me a hot look, stomped her foot, and placed a hand on her hip. "Well, this will be Frank's first *all-black* grandbaby," she said firmly. Then her voice softened. "Frank and Lillimae said they comin' up here later this year."

I sighed. "I wanted to be the one to tell Daddy and Lillimae about my baby, Muh'Dear."

"Well, do say." Muh'Dear paused and took a long, deep breath, staring at me through narrowed eyes. "It seem like you have a problem tellin' everybody but Rhoda stuff 'til it's too late. I know Pee Wee'll be a good daddy to that child. He was raised right. Hand me that bowl off the counter."

I gasped. "You told Pee Wee?" I snatched a bowl off a counter and handed it to Muh'Dear. "How in the world did you know that . . . uh . . . Pee Wee and I—"

"Everybody in town know you and Pee Wee more than just friends," Muh'Dear said smugly. She laughed, rolled her eyes, and patted my shoulder.

I was baffled. "That Pee Wee was a blabbermouth when I met him, he's a blabbermouth now!" I hissed.

"Pee Wee ain't told nobody nothin'. But y'all wasn't foolin' nobody in this town but yourselves. And I don't know why you havin' such a hissy fit. Pee Wee is a fine young man. You outdone yourself. You caught a real prize. He's a much bigger fish than that Jerome."

"We didn't think you would like us being together. I mean, Pee Wee was always more like a family member."

Muh'Dear nodded and shook her finger in my face. "He still is and I hope he always will be."

I gasped. "You told Pee Wee about the baby?"

Muh'Dear clicked her teeth and shook her head. "I ain't told that boy nothin'. But like I said, I ain't blind no more."

"Well, I hope you don't tell him. That's my responsibility." I paused and looked around the kitchen again. Some of Muh'Dear's employees had some mighty big ears. Pee Wee hearing about my pregnancy from one of those busybodies was one thing I would not allow to happen. "Uh, we'll talk more about this when you get home. Call me. Where are my chicken wings and waffles?" I had my food wrapped to go.

There was a message from Rhoda waiting for me when I got back to work. I called her immediately.

"Otis just told me that Pee Wee and that Mitchell woman broke up," Rhoda said breathlessly. "She went back to her husband and they are plannin' to move to Cincinnati." Rhoda sighed. "Poor Pee Wee was such a fool for that woman. I bet if she ever leaves her husband again, she could have Pee Wee back in a split second if she wanted him . . . and if he's still available."

"So?"

"So you need to hook him back up before he latch onto somebody else. How would you feel if the Mitchell woman changes her mind tomorrow and decides she wants to stay with Pee Wee after all? Let me tell you somethin', sister-girl, the older you get, the shorter that line of men waitin' on you gets."

"Men never lined up for me in the first place so I don't have anything to worry about," I said dryly. The men that I had turned tricks with had been the closest I ever got to having men standing in line to get to me.

"You know what I mean." I could hear Rhoda blowing her nose on her end. "Sorry. This cold is really gettin' on my nerves. My honey wouldn't even sleep in the bed with me last night. Lyin' there by myself, I thought about you and I wondered how you could sleep alone day after day, week after week, year after year. I mean, Pee Wee is as buffed and fine and raw—finally—as my husband is. So I know he can work that body—".

"Please let me worry about my own sex life. Besides, there are other single men besides Pee Wee."

Rhoda was quiet for an uncomfortably long time. "Jerome bowls on the same night as Otis and me. Uh, he and I talked for a few times and he knows you're my best friend. He was at the bowlin' alley last night and he asked how you were doin'." Rhoda paused and gasped. "Is he the one you hope to snuggle up with again?"

"I'd rather donate my body to science," I said emphatically. "Rhoda, I don't have to encourage Pee Wee to be with me. If and when he's ready to come back to me, he'll do so on his own."

I was right. Like he was following a script, Pee Wee returned to my bed and me the very next day.

To this day, I don't know why I didn't tell Pee Wee that I was pregnant with his baby then. I guess it was because we had always had such an odd relationship. He seemed to enjoy seeing other women when he felt like it. The last thing I wanted was for him to feel that I had trapped him with a baby.

As crazy as it sounded, even to me, I decided that I would just keep sleeping with Pee Wee for as long as I could. If and when he ever decided to see *only* me, I'd tell him about the baby.

Maybe.

CHAPTER 68

Being obese hides a lot of things, including pregnancy, on large women like me. Even when I was naked and flopping around with Pee Wee in my bed, he couldn't tell I was pregnant. He knew how sensitive I was about my weight. Even if he did notice that my belly was rounder than normal, he didn't mention it.

It was the same with other people I knew. I felt confident that other than Muh'Dear and Rhoda, nobody else knew I was pregnant. Like the folks who worked at the Buttercup, the people I saw at church (when I went), and Scary Mary. Carlene, Scary Mary's most useless prostitute, bragged about having a supernatural ability that allowed her to know when somebody she knew was pregnant.

"Every time I dream about fish, I find out somebody is pregnant." Carlene had made this claim so many times in my presence that I had no doubt in my mind that if she thought I was pregnant, she would bring it up. There were three other women that we all knew were pregnant. Carlene discussed them at great length every chance she got. She talked about the fact that one of the pregnant women was involved with three different men and didn't know which one was the father of her child. Another one of the three women was in her late forties, morbidly obese, and alcoholic. "With all that against her, she'll give birth to a Cyclops for sure," Carlene predicted. "The fish I dreamed about this time didn't have but one eye." The third woman, who was neither promiscuous nor experiencing a midlife snafu, was discussed just as much as the other two, though not as often but just as harshly. "She's so quiet and sneaky about her baby, she must be hidin' somethin'," Carlene reported. I was convinced that my secret was safe. Except from Rhoda.

Rhoda was the first to notice when I started showing. "Since you're already big, you probably won't get stretch marks," she told me.

"Well, thanks a lot," I said.

She chuckled. "Now, you know I didn't mean anything by that. There's nothin' wrong with you bein' a big woman. I would never make fun of you. You know me better than that, anyway. Besides, nobody's body is perfect," Rhoda said with a faraway look on her face.

I had been ashamed of my body most of my life, but I didn't think that Rhoda was ashamed of hers. She certainly had no reason to be. That's why I was surprised when we went shopping she never let me join her in dressing rooms when she tried on clothes. This particular day, she decided to bring home a new blouse without trying it on in the boutique at the mall where she had purchased it.

While I was in Rhoda's kitchen, making milkshakes with Jade, Rhoda went into her bedroom to try on the new blouse. She was taking longer than she should have, so I went to find out why. I had been to Rhoda's house several times since our reunion. I was still not used to seeing such a showcase. The off-white carpets on every floor were so plush and thick, it felt like walking on air. *White* carpets. People talked about Rhoda having white carpets on her floor like it was the height of arrogance. The thing that baffled them the most was trying to figure out how she kept white carpets clean. What they didn't know was that as soon as you entered Rhoda's front door, you were required to remove your shoes. A huge chandelier bathed her living room with golden light at night, and every piece of furniture in her living room was some shade of white.

Above a fireplace in Rhoda's sitting room was a huge oil painting of her, her husband, and both of her children. On the mantel and on the walls were additional pictures of her family. Oddly, there were no pictures of Rhoda's deceased son and her deceased brother. But I knew that Rhoda carried snapshots of them both in her wallet, the same way I had carried around a snapshot of my daddy for so many years.

I paused briefly in Rhoda's den, the room she used for her child-care purposes. This floor had linoleum and cheaper furniture, as well as the usual childproof items. We hadn't discussed it yet, but I knew that when my child came, I would leave him or her with Rhoda once I returned to work.

Rhoda's bedroom door was closed. As soon as I started to open it, she screamed, "Don't come in here!" But it was too late. "I don't want you to see me like this," she sobbed as I entered the room.

"Rhoda, you know it's—" I stopped in the middle of my sentence. I was horrified by what I saw, but I managed to remain calm. Rhoda was naked from the waist up. Gone were the two healthy, firm breasts she had always been so proud of. All she had now were two cruel scars. "Why didn't you tell me?" Taking quick, tiny steps, I marched across the floor and stopped in front of Rhoda. I stared at her disfigurement in slack-jawed amazement. "I had no idea!" I shrieked.

With her head hanging low, she wrapped her arms around

her chest. "It happened right after I had Jade," Rhoda said in a distant, almost unrecognizable voice.

"What the hell happened?" I asked, my arms waving, my eyes on her flat chest.

Rhoda took a deep breath before she started. "One mornin' while I was takin' a shower, I felt a lump in my left breast. I didn't think it was anything serious so I ignored it. I checked the lump every day for a few weeks, hopin' it would go away. One day I looked in my medical book and I read about calcium deposits and things like that. I told myself that's all it was. I didn't feel my breast again for six months, but by then it was too late." At this point, Rhoda lowered her voice to a whisper. "Not only was that same lump still there, there . . . there was another one in my other breast."

"Can . . . cancer?" I could hardly get the word out. With all the women I had known, I had never known one with breast cancer. Accidents were one thing. They could have been avoided. So could crimes. But an assault from nature had to be the ultimate crisis.

Rhoda nodded. "Otis made me go to the doctor. But like I said, it was too late. They had to remove both . . . both of . . . my breasts."

I hugged my enigmatic friend. "I am so sorry, Rhoda. I had no idea. Well, did they get all of the, uh, cancer?" The evil word burned my lips like a flame. I had always felt sorry for people who had lost a body part. The fact that Mr. Boatwright had come to us with only one leg had played a huge role in my devotion to him. The pity that I had felt for him had made it that much easier for him to lead me to his bed, like a lamb being led to slaughter.

Rhoda nodded again. "I think so. I haven't felt anything since."

"Can't you get implants or something?"

Her shoulders sagged as she shrugged and groaned. "I

tried that. As soon as I healed from the surgery, I had implants inserted. They were fine for about a year. One mornin' I woke up . . . and one had ruptured during the night. Once all the saline solution had dripped into my system, my body had a really negative reaction and I almost died." Rhoda looked at me with the most unbearably sad eyes I had ever seen. The whites of her eyes looked yellow and cloudy and were streaked with blood. Their sparkling, light-green color that I had admired for so many years had darkened by at least two shades. These were things I had not noticed until now. "From that I went to those removable things. After they kept slidin' in and out of my bra when I least expected it, I gave up on them, too."

I had to sit down on Rhoda's bed, massaging my own bosom. "Well, I am sure Otis still loves you, anyway."

Rhoda joined me on the bed, clutching the new blouse against her chest. Her knee touched mine. "Now you know why I can't leave him. What man would want me now?"

"But Otis loves you—"

Giving me a sharp look, Rhoda hollered, "What do *you* know about love? You with your *two* titties—"

"There's a lot more to me than titties! And there's a lot more to you than that, too. Looking good is not all there is to life, Rhoda. Because whether you like it or not, it doesn't last. And there's nothing you or anybody else can do about it. The best plastic surgeon in the world can only do so much to make somebody look better." I laughed. "If I thought otherwise, I'd have spent every one of my paychecks on everything from my face on down to my flat feet."

Rhoda didn't laugh. Instead, she gave me a thoughtful look and shrugged. "I never had to worry about the way I looked until . . ."

"Well, I've looked the same way all my life, but I made the best of it. Sure, I was surprised when men found me attractive. I was surprised when you told me I was beautiful. All I ever tried to do was be the best person I could be and people cared about me for that."

Rhoda smiled and squeezed my hand. "I've always cared about you, Annette. I've said it before and I'll say it again— you are the best friend I've ever had."

"You could be a lot worse off, girl. You are a wonderful mother, a good wife. You have more than a lot of other women will ever have."

"Except two healthy titties."

"You stop that!" I hollered, waving my finger in Rhoda's face. "Be thankful for all the years you did have a nice body. How would you feel if you had to live in this wigwam of blubber for all these years the way I had to? Huh? If I could, I'd slice off these two big balloons on my chest and let you drag them around for a while."

Rhoda laughed and gave me a mournful look. "Annette, I never wanted you to find out about this. I wanted to keep this a secret for the rest of my life."

"Girl, with all the gruesome secrets we already share, what's one more?" I stood up. "Go on and put on that new blouse so we can drink those milkshakes." I grabbed Rhoda by her arm and pulled her up from the bed.

"I don't ever want to discuss this again," she said firmly, sliding her arms into the sleeves of the new blouse.

"We won't," I said.

And we never did.

CHAPTER 69

A month after that tense conversation with Rhoda in her bedroom, I was invited to Florida again. My other half-siblings, Amos and Sondra, were in Florida for Amos's wedding to a German woman named Helga that he had brought home with him.

It was a bad time for me to be traveling, but I agreed to go anyway regardless of how bad I felt. Some days my morning sickness lasted until noon. My food cravings were so extreme, one night when I *had* to have some Mexican food, I got out of bed and drove around for two hours trying to find a restaurant that was still open. I had to settle for a bag of Doritos that I purchased at a gas station.

By now I was anxious to meet my other siblings so I was not going to let my pregnancy interfere with my plans. And, my half-brother had insisted on me being there to see him get married.

"Amos said to tell you that this will be a once-in-a-lifetime thing for him. If this marriage don't work out, he'll never do it again. So you'd better get yourself down here if you want to see your brother get married, girl," Lillimae advised me when she called. I was stunned beyond belief when the same invitation to Florida was extended to Muh'Dear and even more stunned when she accepted.

"I done waited too long to be a grandma. I ain't about to let you get on a plane and go off to a savage jungle like Florida by yourself, Annette," Muh'Dear told me on our way to the airport.

"I can take care of myself. Don't you know that by now? I don't need you watching every move I make, Muh'Dear."

Muh'Dear shook her head sadly. "If I had been doin' just that when that evil, slimy snake Boatwright slithered into our lives, you wouldn't have suffered nary a day of your life at his hands." Muh'Dear blinked hard, but it was too late for her to hold back her tears.

"But you didn't and now you can't. Let's put that mess behind us, too." I grabbed Muh'Dear's wrist and squeezed. "I'm a strong woman. Just like you. I got through that mess with Mr. Boatwright intact. I'm going to get through this pregnancy the same way."

I was so overwhelmed when I met Amos and Sondra, my brother and my sister, that I couldn't stop hugging them for the first five minutes. Out of the corner of my eye, I saw Muh'Dear looking at the emotional meeting in Lillimae's living room with a blank expression on her face. Knowing that these were the children that my father had had by the white woman he had left her for, had to be painful for Muh'Dear. But she handled it well. She even hugged them both a little herself.

I had seen pictures of my other siblings, but they didn't look the same in person. Amos looked like Daddy did when he was a young man and he was almost as dark. Like Lillimae, Sondra also looked like me but she was a lot darker than Lillimae.

Right after I'd first met Lillimae, we'd bonded immediately. Things didn't move that fast with Sondra and Amos. Even though they both seemed happy to meet me, they were somewhat reserved and aloof where I was concerned. When I tried to converse with Amos, he often gave quick, one-word responses and he didn't ask me a whole lot of questions about myself like I had hoped and expected. "Amos is shy," Lillimae explained when she got me alone. "He don't even like to talk to me that much. But him and Sondra both still tryin' to get used to the idea of havin' another sister."

Now, Sondra liked to talk, but when she did it usually wasn't with me. I overlooked all of that and I accepted her and Amos unconditionally. I was interested in everything either one of them had to say whether it was directed at me or not.

Muh'Dear was not impressed with the house Daddy lived in and couldn't believe anybody would want to get married in it. Right after the brief ceremony in the living room, she took me aside and started whispering, "This place reminds me of some of them hovels we used to live in before Frank acted a fool and took off with these half-breed kids' mama."

"Muh'Dear, please be nice. We came down here to have a good time," I whispered back.

Daddy was nearby and the way he screwed up his face, for a moment I thought that he'd overheard Muh'Dear's rude remark. But he sucked on his teeth and shook his finger at Sondra. "Gal, what did you just say?" he asked gruffly.

Sondra repeated a comment that she had just made. "I said, if I ever take a notion to move back to Florida, I'm thinkin' about passin'."

Everybody in the room looked at Sondra. I could hear a

few snickers. I wasn't the only one present to gasp. Daddy said what I was thinking.

"Sondra, gal, with all that nappy-ass hair on your head, your *brown* skin, and your big ass, if you even think you can pass for white, you ain't foolin' nobody but yourself!" Daddy had had too much to drink. "Look at your sister Annette. She black as hell and she happy. Ain't you, baby?" He smiled, giving me an insightful look.

Muh'Dear cleared her throat and draped her arm around my shoulder.

"I am happy," I admitted. And I was.

Lillimae and her husband Freddie Lee had reconciled. He had moved back into Lillimae's house. I didn't know why I was so surprised that he was so good-looking. Especially when I had almost married a man just as handsome myself. As a matter of fact, Freddie Lee resembled Jerome. He had the same light skin and curly hair, but he had a dimple in his left cheek that made him look even cuter. Lillimae's two pre-teen sons, Wally and Ernest, seemed bored and took off running out the back door as soon as they had stuffed their mouths with wedding cake.

What was touching about the ceremony was, after the preacher had pronounced Amos and Helga man and wife, they also jumped over a broom, like the slaves used to do when they were married. Of course, Muh'Dear had to whisper in my ear about that. "I done seen everything now. A half-white man and his all-white woman, doin' one of the blackest things in the world." Muh'Dear covered her mouth when I gave her an exasperated look.

I borrowed Lillimae's car after the reception so I could be alone for a little while. I didn't want Muh'Dear, or anybody else, to know where I was going. I drove straight to Hanley, the rural Miami district where I had been born.

I couldn't see the road for the tears in my eyes as I eased

the car down the hill to see the shack we'd been living in when Daddy left. It was gone. A tree, leaning so far to the left it looked like it was about to break in two, now occupied the spot where our old house had stood.

Waist-high weeds covered the backyard where I used to play. There was nothing left to indicate that I had ever been to this place before. A squirrel was peeping from behind a tree and ran when I tried to lure him out in the open. I had had a squirrel for a pet when I was a child, but this one wanted nothing to do with me. After a few more minutes, I returned to the car and sped back up the hill. Looking in the rearview mirror, I saw a blanket of dust rising up so high, it completely blocked my view. That dust was symbolic. It blocked out a past that I needed to forget. But I couldn't. My past had shaped my future and was the reason I had risen so high myself.

Too emotional to return to Lillimae's house right away, I headed in the opposite direction. Before long I found myself in another rural part of Miami. Atwater was where Rhoda had lived with her husband and children. I parked the car on the road and looked to the clearing where Rhoda's former house still stood. An elderly white man was on the front porch in a rocking chair. I didn't want to see any more than this, particularly the inside of the house or the back porch. The back porch was where I'd watched Rhoda nurse her child, even after he was dead.

Inside of this house was the bathroom where Rhoda had electrocuted the white girl who had threatened her family. I don't know why I had to see the two places that had played such major roles in my life, but I'm glad I did. Even though sadness overwhelmed me, I felt calmer than I'd felt in years.

My bittersweet visit to Miami ended with a hog butchering and us having a picnic in Lillimae's backyard the day after my brother's wedding. Daddy seemed happy just to have all of his children *and* Muh'Dear together with him for the first time.

It was the best year of my life.

CHAPTER 70

Daddy was as excited about my pregnancy as Muh'Dear was. He and Lillimae hopped on a plane during the middle of my last month, planning to be present for the birth.

I was surprised and pleased when Sondra and Amos started calling me once a week from Germany. Apparently it was a lot easier for them to talk to me from a distance than it was to my face. I learned during lengthy telephone conversations with them that Amos and his German wife were planning to buy a house in Munich and that Sondra had met the man of her dreams. She airmailed me her wedding pictures. I was shocked to see that her groom was a pitch-black, flat-faced lawyer from Uganda. "Ain't no tellin' what our kids are goin' to look like," she confessed. It pleased me to hear that she had put her obsession about living as a white woman behind her.

The last week of my pregnancy was the hardest. I was as clumsy as an ox. Lillimae took care of the house as well as she took care of Daddy and me. I never felt so loved in my life.

With Daddy snoozing noisily on my living room couch and me piled on the love seat facing him one evening, Lillimae waddled around the room in a flowered muumuu, dusting and straightening up furniture.

"Annette, I am so pleased everything worked out the way it did. If I hadn't met you, I probably wouldn't have gotten back with Freddie Lee. And poor Daddy." She paused and looked over at Daddy with his head back and his mouth stretched open. "He's so happy. Everything is complete now." Lillimae sighed, fanned her face with a dust rag, and looked at me.

"It sure is," I mumbled, crossing my swollen ankles.

I still felt that something important was not where it was supposed to be in my life even though that something lived right next door to me. As close as Pee Wee and I were, there was something keeping a wedge between us. Me.

My daughter was born one night in the middle of that December. My labor had started earlier in the afternoon, right in the middle of Jade's birthday party in the dining room at Antonosanti's.

"It's a sign. Us havin' daughters on the same day," Rhoda decided. She had come to the hospital later than evening. Muh'Dear, Daddy and Lillimae, and Scary Mary all grinning like they'd won a jackpot, were in the room with me when Rhoda arrived. It was truly one of the happiest moments of my life. The people I loved most in the world were all with me at the same time. Pee Wee was the only one missing. I knew that if he had known that I was in the hospital having a baby, wild horses couldn't have kept him away. As long as I had known Pee Wee and as close as we were, I wasn't sure where I stood with him. I didn't know what this new development in my life was going to mean to my friendship with Pee Wee.

Because of my age and weight, delivering a baby was not

easy for me. After my daughter had decided it was time for her to make her debut, she also decided to change her position in my body, turning herself almost upside down. I had to be cut open. My doctor insisted that I spend another few days in the hospital.

The day after I'd given birth, I opened my eyes to see Lillimae standing over my hospital bed, smoothing my hair back off my face with a damp facecloth. "Don't you worry about havin' a scar on your belly, Annette. The doctor had to cut me open for both my babies." Lillimae stood up straight, patted her belly, and sighed. "My husband says my scar is the biggest 'smile' he ever seen on me. I hope you'll look at your scar the same way and I hope you don't wait too long to share this blessed event with that baby's daddy."

Two days after I delivered my daughter, Pee Wee walked quietly into my room with a huge potted plant. I was propped up in bed, trying to season a baked potato. Daddy, Muh'Dear, Lillimae, Scary Mary, and all five of her prostitutes had just left and I was so exhausted I couldn't even see straight. It took me a moment to realize that it was Pee Wee I was looking at. *The Price Is Right* was on the television facing my bed. Pee Wee turned the television off and gave me a stern look.

"Girl, why didn't you tell me you was pregnant?" he asked in a hoarse voice, setting the plant on the windowsill. Then he slid his hand into his jacket pocket and pulled out a get-well card and dropped it on the nightstand. "I call your house lookin' for you and your daddy tells me you at the hospital *havin' a baby*."

"I've been meaning to . . ." I set the tray with what was left of my lunch on the table next to the bed. "Uh . . . all this medication got me all doped up . . . I thought I called you yesterday to tell you."

Pee Wee walked up close to the bed and for a moment he

just stared at me as my face burned. In the clumsiest move I ever saw him make, he leaned over the bed and kissed me on my forehead with homosexual indifference. It was hard to believe that this was the same man who spent almost as much time in my bed as I did. The father of my child.

"To tell me what?"

"About the baby," I whimpered.

He nodded and pursed his lips. "Did you just find out you was pregnant yesterday?"

I didn't answer. I just blinked.

"I called you yesterday, girl. Like I said, your daddy picks up the telephone and tells me you at the hospital havin' a baby."

With a look on his face I could not interpret, Pee Wee moved until his back hit the wall. With a deep sigh, he turned and moved to the side so that he was now in front of the window.

"So do this mean you and Jerome goin' to try and make a go of it after all?" he asked, talking with his back me.

"Uh . . . I don't think so." I was stunned. Pee Wee thought that Jerome had fathered my baby! Rhoda, Lillimae, and Muh'Dear were the only ones who knew the truth and I had not decided on what I was going to tell everybody else. But I knew I couldn't pass my daughter off on Jerome. Once the news got to him, he would have denied it anyway, so I'd be right back where I started. Pee Wee had been the only man I'd slept with since Jerome. It sounded like he didn't think that, though. If he had asked, I would have told him right then and there that he was my baby's father.

"Pee Wee, you should leave now. They'll be bringing the baby in for me to feed in a few minutes." My breasts felt like bricks as I struggled to rearrange my bloated body. I looked like I was still pregnant.

Pee Wee sighed as he moved toward me. "I can't wait to see your little girl," he said dryly, patting my shoulder. "Uncle Pee Wee is goin' to spoil her rotten."

"I already know that," I said sadly.

"And I know she is goin' to be a heart-breaker. Just like her mama." He bit his bottom lip and blinked. "I can't wait to see what she looks like," he said on his way out.

I was grateful that Charlotte looked just like me. I believed that I could keep the identity of her father a secret for the rest of my life, if I had to.

Muh'Dear was the proudest new grandmother in town. "And I just love the name Charlotte. That was my mama's name, you know. She didn't live long enough to enjoy a grandchild," Muh'Dear told me.

Recalling that mysterious dream I'd had made me feel even better. I now knew that both my children were in good hands, the dead one and the one I held in my arms.

Two days after I returned to my house, Lillimae had to leave Ohio to go back to work and look after her own children. But Daddy decided to stay on in Ohio indefinitely. Muh'Dear had insisted that he stay with her in the house that she had shared with Daddy King—sleeping in a separate room, though. It was a blessing to see them on friendly terms. It was one of the many things I had prayed for.

Rhoda spent a lot of her free time at my house, fussing over Charlotte.

"We've been tryin' for another child before Otis and I get too old," she told me. "Otis has always wanted another boy to replace David. He took our son's death harder than I did and still hasn't got over it."

"You think about your little boy a lot, don't you?"

"I think about a lot of things, but my children are the most important things in my life. I would die for them. Poor Jade hasn't been the same since P. died. She doesn't want to sleep over with any of her other little friends and I don't want her to. Just thinkin' about my daughter bein' in Jean's house with that Vinnie just makes my blood boil."

"Well, at least that's one more child molester nobody won't ever have to worry about again," I said thoughtfully, holding my own child closer to me so tight she squirmed and moaned.

"That's for sure. Vinnie'll get along just fine down in that inferno with old Buttwright," Rhoda hissed.

I had often wondered what child molesters thought of one another. Whatever it was, it didn't matter anymore. They would all end up in the same fiery hell and that's all that mattered.

"Nobody's sorry that old Mr. Antonosanti killed him." I sighed. It was the look on Rhoda's face that sent my mind into a whirl of confusion. I had to wonder just what really happened to Vinnie. It had appeared to be an open-and-shut case. They'd found Vinnie dead and Mr. Antonosanti had promptly confessed to killing him. It all seemed too neat and convenient. If Rhoda was involved, I didn't want to know. But if her confessions about her killing Mr. Boatwright, her grandmother, that cop, and that white girl were true, and if Rhoda thought for one minute that Vinnie had also touched her daughter, it all made sense.

"Annette, why are you suddenly lookin' so serious?" Rhoda asked, hugging her chest. She had on a baggy sweater. Even if she'd still had breasts, that sweater would have concealed them. It occurred to me that most of the tops Rhoda wore since her return to Ohio were baggy. I had wondered why. I wouldn't have to wonder about that anymore.

"Uh . . . I was just thinking about how happy having Charlotte has made me. I guess it's not fair for me to keep all this happiness to myself. I have to tell Pee Wee that Charlotte is his daughter," I said. With a laugh I added, "He worked hard for her."

"I've been tellin' you that all along. Haven't I?"

I put all the other thoughts I had just had out of my mind. None of it seemed to matter anymore now.

CHAPTER 71

A s soon as Rhoda left my house, I called up Pee Wee. He had been to the house several times since I'd come from the hospital. Like a typical man, he had purchased a lot of things that Charlotte couldn't appreciate for years. In addition to rattles, bibs, and pacifiers, he had spent a fortune on huge dolls that could walk and talk, a tea set, roller skates, and a play station. Like everybody else, he agreed that Charlotte looked a lot like me. So far, nobody but me had noticed that she had Pee Wee's eyes.

"I need you to get over here right now," I said sternly.

I heard him take a deep breath before he responded. "Uh-oh. Uh, shit. Ain't no tellin' what you goin' to confess this time. I think I should have me a few drinks before I come over there. Girl, you be comin' up with some deep shit."

"I don't want you drunk when I tell you . . . what I have to tell you."

"Please don't tell me you got a fatal disease—"

"Charlotte is your daughter."

There was a moment of silence that seemed to go on forever.

I heard Pee Wee suck in his breath and cough to clear his throat, choking on air. "What did you say?" he wheezed.

"You heard me."

Pee Wee laughed. "I—you, why in the world do you keep so many things a secret? Do you like fuckin' with my blood pressure? How do I know you ain't just clownin' me?"

"I know you didn't believe that stuff I told you about Rhoda killing all those people. And I don't know if you believed all that stuff I told you and everybody else about Mr. Boatwright. If you don't want to believe me this time, well, there's nothing more for me to say to you tonight. What I told you about Rhoda killing those people, what I said about Mr. Boatwright raping me, and what I am telling you now about Charlotte, is all true."

"What about Jerome?"

"What about Jerome?" I hissed.

"Every time he slid out of your house, I seen him. And I know y'all wasn't in your bedroom playin' cards."

"I broke up with Jerome more than a year ago. I don't know about your mama, but mine didn't carry me in her belly but nine months. Why don't you do the math?"

I heard Pee Wee mumbling under his breath, then I heard a loud gasp. "Holy shit."

"I'm getting off this phone now. If you decide this is too much for you, that's fine. I can raise my child alone. And we sure don't need your money, so you don't even have to worry about me putting the Man on you."

"Let me get in some clothes and come over there," he said evenly.

"I don't like your tone of voice and if you come over here and clown me, you . . . you are going to get what Jerome got."

"Now you gettin' all mad and I ain't even there yet. I'm comin' over there so you can tell me this to my face."

Pee Wee didn't come over right away like I expected him to. It was an hour before he pounded on my door. In his hand was the biggest bouquet of roses I had ever seen.

"Ain't you never seen a proud new father before?" he asked.

Pee Wee looked in my eyes the way no man had ever done before. I could feel his love for me. I broke down and cried like a baby.

It was all clear to me now. After all I'd been through with other men, the best one for me had been right up under my nose all along.

I wasn't prepared for what Pee Wee did a few minutes later. He spirited Charlotte and me to Muh'Dear's house.

Over dinner in front of my daddy, my mother, Rhoda, and the ever-present Scary Mary, with Charlotte on his lap, Pee Wee turned to me with a broad smile and tears in his eyes. "Girl, if we don't hurry up and get married, we goin' to have to find a church that's wheelchair accessible. I found another gray hair on my head this mornin'," he said petulantly.

"Whenever you're ready," I said, grinning from ear to ear. I meant every word I said. Because I was ready now myself.

It was so ironic that both Jerome and Pee Wee had proposed to me over dinner with Muh'Dear as a witness. It had to mean something.

"And if you run off and leave this girl, I'm goin' to hunt you down myself," Muh'Dear said sternly. "Some men have to go through hell before they figure out how good they already had it." Muh'Dear looked at Daddy.

Daddy's eyes got wide and he said quickly, "I ain't gwine nowhere. I'm stayin' rightcheer . . . where I belong."

Scary Mary gasped so hard she started coughing. Her

mouth dropped open and she looked around the table. "Frank ain't got no choice. How far do y'all think a old fossil like him would get? And who would want this black-ass nigger now anyway?" Scary Mary snarled. She finished clearing her throat by taking a long drink from a glass of Jack Daniels. Turning to Daddy, she added, "Frank, this is your last chance. You ain't got nothin' no other woman, Black or white, would want no more so you may as well stay on with Gussie Mae for good this time. And don't think you gwine to get your name added to none of Gussie Mae's property. Gussie Mae ain't nobody's fool so if you leave her again, you ain't takin' nothin' with you but what you brought." Daddy bowed his head as Scary Mary turned to Muh'Dear, who was sitting there with her mouth open now. Even after all of these years, Scary Mary's behavior still stunned some of us. "See how easy it was for me to straighten things out, y'all? You just got to be firm with men like you do with young'uns. Whup the shit out of 'em if you have to, to make 'em behave. Shit."

"Me and Gussie Mae can take care of our own business," Daddy mumbled, his head still bowed contritely, his eyes staring at the floor.

"And you, Pee Wee, you surprised me," Scary Mary said seriously. "You sure done come a long way from that little sissified bag of bones runnin' around the neighborhood wearin' that Beatle wig." Scary Mary bit off a huge piece of fried chicken and turned to me with a severe scowl on her face, chewing hard as she spoke. "Girl, if I was sixty years younger, you'd have to fight me over Pee Wee. You let him get away, I'm gwine to whup your ass anyway."

Everybody laughed.

"And I'll help," Rhoda said seriously. Then she grinned and gave me a proud look. "Annette, you've come a long way, girl."

"We done all come a long way." Pee Wee covered my hand with his. "Ain't we, Annette? I didn't think we'd get this far."

"I didn't, either," I replied.

CHAPTER 72

Rhoda had come to Muh'Dear's house with Scary Mary. Prancing behind them had been Carlene with a healthy grin on her face. She'd had to take a few days off from work because of another physical setback caused by a tricky dick. Again. This time it was a sore pussy caused by a man with a severely curved penis. What Carlene did with her life was her business, but it saddened me to see what she had settled for. But she seemed happy. Even though she was *just* a prostitute. I was in no position to judge her so when she and Scary Mary regaled me with this latest comic confession, all I did was laugh.

Rhoda's parents had left New Orleans that morning with their church group to go to Kenya. Going on an African safari had always been a lifelong dream of theirs. It was the first time that so many miles separated Rhoda from her parents and it saddened her. She had been unusually quiet for most of the evening.

When Scary Mary invited herself and Carlene to spend the night with Muh'Dear, Rhoda decided to get a ride home with Pee Wee and me.

"I don't feel too well," Rhoda announced in a mumble that I could barely hear.

"We'll take you straight home," I said.

Rhoda had never been much of a drinker. A few beers or a couple of glasses of wine usually made her either slaphappy or lethargic. The odd thing was, she had only consumed half a glass of wine with her dinner, yet she was staggering across the floor and slurring her words. In fact, she had been doing that even before drinking the wine. I assumed she had enjoyed a few drinks before her arrival or she was missing her parents, especially since they would be unreachable until they returned from their ten-day safari. Rhoda had told me that from the time she got married and moved away from her parents, she called her mother twice a week. I couldn't imagine not being able to talk to Muh'Dear for more than a few days.

"Boy, you drive careful out there with all that snow and ice," Daddy told Pee Wee, giving him a hard look. "I don't want nothin' to happen to my girl and her baby."

Pee Wee had to hold Rhoda up to keep her from falling as we made our way to the new Chevy he had purchased a few days earlier. Even though it was dark, and not a single other person was on the street, the neighbors on both sides of Muh'Dear's house peeped out of their windows. I was used to that by now. And unlike Jerome, who used to give fingers to those nosy neighbors when he and I visited Muh'Dear, Pee Wee ignored them.

Before Pee Wee could start the car, Rhoda stretched out on the backseat, belly-up.

"That little sister ain't goin' to be makin' too much noise," Pee Wee laughed, glancing at Rhoda through his rearview mirror.

"This little sister won't, either," I said, hugging Charlotte, who had been sleeping like a log for the past two hours. I sniffed, staring at my daughter's plump, beautiful dark face.

She looked like an angel dressed in yellow from head to toe. Even the blanket that Rhoda had given her was yellow.

"So, you really want to do this thing? Get married and shit," Pee Wee said, pulling out onto Cherry Street, narrowly missing a slow-moving station wagon crawling backward out of the driveway next door.

"What the hell. Why not?" I grinned. "Seems like I'm going to be stuck with you for the rest of my life anyway. Let's do it before you change your mind. I don't want a lot of fanfare or anything. Let's go down to the courthouse this coming Saturday."

Pee Wee nodded. "That's cool. My old man is too sick to be comin' over here from Pennsylvania for a weddin' anyway. And I ain't for traipsin' down no church aisle with a use-to-be prostitute like you no-how. . . ." Pee Wee glanced at me with a serious look and sniffed. "But I ain't no Jerome Cunningham. I'm takin' your black ass as is," he teased. "By the way, you got any more secrets you wanna share?"

"No, I don't. And keep your eyes on the road." I sighed and gave Pee Wee a pensive look. "It just seems so strange. Us getting married."

"What's so strange about it?"

"For one thing, I never thought I'd marry somebody like you, Pee Wee."

He gasped and glanced at me again. "What's that 'spose to mean?"

"It's just that, well, you're the boy next door."

"Well, you the girl next door. So what? What's your point?"

"Just shut up and drive before one of us says something we'll regret," I snapped with a grin.

"One more thing."

I gave Pee Wee a sharp look. "What? Please don't tell me you got some deep, dark secrets you want to share." I was alarmed and I couldn't hide it.

"Naw, it ain't nothin' like that. You know everything there is to know about me." Pee Wee paused and sucked in his breath. His window was rolled down a few inches. The cool night air felt good on my face, but I covered Charlotte's protectively when she sneezed in her sleep. "I do love you, girl. I always did. Even when you and Rhoda was callin' me a fag behind my back when we was growin' up. I used to fantasize about you . . . when . . . when I jacked off."

I gasped, then giggled. "I love you, too, you nasty thing, you." We were silent the rest of the way to Rhoda's house.

Rhoda was still passed out on the backseat when we stopped in her driveway. As soon as Pee Wee turned off the motor, her porch light came on and Otis rushed out in a housecoat, grinning and waving.

Pee Wee leaped out of the car and shook Otis's hand. "Hey, brother. Rhoda needs some help. She had too good a time."

Otis groaned and lifted his hands high above his head and clapped them. "De woman is such a hard-headed one. How many times do I tell her not to drink too much? But do de woman listen to me? No. Every time she dig a hole, she dig it deep. Oh—*Americans*!"

Otis snatched open the back door of Pee Wee's car and dragged Rhoda out like she was a sack of flour. He cradled her in his arms, struggling on the icy sidewalk to keep from falling.

I cracked open my window. "Otis, you tell Rhoda I'll talk to her when I drop Charlotte off on my way to work tomorrow," I yelled before we drove off.

Pee Wee made a U-turn and headed back across town to my house. As we walked in my front door, my living room telephone rang. I handed Charlotte to Pee Wee and sprinted across the floor to answer it, cursing at whoever it was calling my house so late at night. It was Daddy.

"Annette, that foreigner that Rhoda married just called. Ain't he one of them Geechees?"

"The man's Jamaican, Daddy. What did Otis say? We just left his house," I said.

"He said he tried to call you at home and got your answerin' machine. He called here to see if y'all had come back over here." Daddy sounded so tired. "At least that's what I think he said. I thought he was babblin' gibberish. You know I ain't good with them accents."

I saw that my answering machine was blinking. "I just got in. What did he want?"

"Well, with that foreign accent of his I couldn't hardly tell for sure. Somethin' about Rhoda."

"I'll call him right now."

"He said to tell y'all to come out to the hospital. At least I think that's what he said. I swear to God, that man harder on my ears than Donald Duck. How Rhoda and y'all can understand a word he say is beyond me."

"Hospital? What—" I paused and turned to Pee Wee standing right next to me. "It's Daddy. Otis wants us to come to the hospital." Pee Wee blinked and looked at the telephone. "Daddy, did Otis say anything else?" I asked, grabbing Pee Wee's hand. He placed Charlotte on the couch and rushed back to stand next to me with his ear cocked against the telephone.

"Yeah. With that accent he got, I ain't sure. But it sure sounded like he said Rhoda done had a stroke."

CHAPTER 73

Otis met Pee Wee and me in the waiting room at Richland City Hospital. He ran toward us with his arms stretched open and a desperate look on his face. His lips were moving but no words were coming out. I grabbed his shoulders and shook him.

"What happened?" I shouted, ignoring the indifferent stares that we received from nurses swishing around us. "I have to see her and I have to see her now!" I roared. One huge nurse standing a few feet away from us folded her arms and shot me a hot look. Every nurse on duty that night had a big bosom and a stern face. I didn't care how big and stern they looked; I was ready to challenge every single one if I had to. For once in my life I was glad that I was big, too. And I could look just as stern as anybody else.

"She's bad. She is really bad," Otis choked. "De doctor say she had a stroke. A *stroke*!" Otis paused and rubbed his head, his eyes rolling back and forth like marbles. "Her mum and daddy can't be reached so I call for you to come."

I could barely talk but somehow the words popped out of my mouth. "A stroke? No way!" Everything around me went black. Suddenly, for a moment, all I could see in that darkness was Otis's terrified face. I took a step back. "Rhoda's thirty-six years old. What's she doing having a stroke? Old people have strokes," I yelled, looking around the room, frowning at the cold-looking vinyl couches lined up along the walls. "Are you sure? We thought she was just drunk."

"Is she goin' to be all right?" Pee Wee asked, draping his arm around my shoulders. We had dropped Charlotte off with Muh'Dear.

Otis shrugged. "I don't know. Let us pray she will. I need her. I'm fin to go crazy." Otis massaged the back of his head and then shook it so hard, he had to close his eyes. I held his hand until he composed himself. "I'm fin to lose everything."

"That's not true," I insisted. "Everything is going to be all right."

One of the mean-looking nurses tried to block my way, telling me only family could see Rhoda. I was more than family, as far as I was concerned. With one hand, I shoved that heifer to the side like she was as light as a feather and I galloped toward the elevator along with Otis. Pee Wee was close behind. Nobody was going to stop me from seeing Rhoda. I wish somebody had.

I was horrified. It was the most haunting sight I'd ever seen before in my life. Rhoda's face was so contorted, her mouth was on the side. It was open in a frozen yawn and she was drooling. She was conscious, but she could not move a single part of her body, except her eyes. When she saw me hovering over her, she blinked. And then a large tear rolled down the side of her face. Dried spit and snot covered her lips and chin. This was the first time I'd seen Rhoda without makeup since we were teenagers.

"Rhoda, honey, it's going to be all right. You're going to be just fine. I promise." I had a lot of nerve making her another promise. I turned to Otis. "Where's Jade?"

"With de nice white lady next door to my house," he managed, not taking his eyes off of his wife. "De nice lady next door, she say Rhoda told to her this morning she was feeling mighty funny."

"I should have paid more attention to her at Muh'Dear's house," I muttered, recalling how Rhoda had slurred her words and stumbled around, even before drinking that wine. "I don't know what I'll do if she doesn't make it," I said, looking at Pee Wee.

"She in God's hands now. The rest is up to Him," Pee Wee said, embracing me from behind.

I turned sharply to Pee Wee and said, "We're getting rid of that car." He pulled away from me and stared at me with his mouth hanging open.

"I just bought that car," he wailed, hands on his hips, his brow furrowed.

"Like I said, we're getting rid of that car. Even if I have to burn it up with my own hands." I meant every word I said. Even if Rhoda lived, I knew that I would never ride in Pee Wee's new car again. I already felt the same way about that car as I did about the bedroom that Mr. Boatwright had committed his crimes against me and died in. I thought of it as a tomb.

I left Charlotte with Muh'Dear that night. I didn't sleep that night and I didn't go to work the next morning. I was disappointed with Pee Wee at first for not taking the day off to stay with me. But in the long run, I was glad he didn't. Being alone gave me the opportunity to focus on Rhoda's condition, which had changed considerably by the time Pee Wee left his barbershop and came to my house around noon, still wearing his smock.

"The guy at the dealership is an old army buddy of mine," Pee Wee began, clearly disappointed about having to get rid of his new car. "He let me bring the car back and trade it for another one. Same make and model, but in navy blue. And it cost us a few dollars." He paused and smiled vaguely. "And you can forget about a honeymoon cruise on *The Love Boat*."

I waved my hand impatiently. "Otis called and said Rhoda's able to talk now," I told Pee Wee. "I have to get out to that hospital immediately."

"Where's Charlotte?" Pee Wee asked, looking around the living room.

"Don't worry about her. She's with my daddy." I didn't even give Pee Wee the chance to take off his coat. I ushered him back out the door, stepping on the backs of his heels. "Why don't you go get the baby in your car. I'll call you from the hospital." I didn't even stop to look at the brand-new car, its sticker still in the window, parked in Pee Wee's driveway. I just jumped into my car.

Rhoda was sitting up in bed when I arrived at the hospital. Otis and Jade had just left. I was glad I could be alone with her. She smiled as I rushed to the bed and grabbed her limp hand.

"Rhoda, you're going to be fine." It was more of a question than a statement. Her mouth was still not where it was supposed to be. For somebody as vain as Rhoda, I knew that that had to be the ultimate nightmare.

"I . . . I . . . don't think I'm goin' to let a little stroke get me down," she managed. Her mouth remained open after she finished speaking with her enlarged tongue hanging out, resting on her quivering lip.

"I know that. You are too tough and ornery to let that happen." I held my breath when she started coughing. Her left eye crawled back in her head. I stood up, still holding her hand. "You want me to get the doctor?" Then, the same rattling noise that I had heard coming from Daddy King before he died came from Rhoda! I could not believe what was happening. I refused to believe that my best friend was dying right before my eyes. "Rhoda, I'm going to go get the doctor."

She shook her head, refocused her eye, and clutched my arm. "I'm fine."

I waited and watched in silence for a few moments. "I'm so sorry. I am so sorry I didn't pay more attention to you last night. I knew something was wrong." I blinked hard to hold back my tears. The last thing I wanted to do was fall apart in front of Rhoda.

"Girl, stop overreactin'," she snapped in a weak voice. "The doctor said it was just a mild stroke."

I breathed a sigh of relief. "Then everything's going to be all right?"

"If you mean my fucked-up mouth, yeah." I was glad to see Rhoda wiggle her lips and laugh. "And I'm not goin' anywhere anytime soon, so don't worry about what to wear to my funeral."

"I never—"

"And you never will. Now go on back home so I can get some rest."

Rhoda closed her eyes and I left.

CHAPTER 74

That following Saturday morning, just as we had agreed, Pee Wee and I went down to the courthouse and got married. I wore a navy blue suit and a yellow silk blouse and I'd gone to Miss Rachel's beauty salon and had my hair done the evening before.

Pee Wee advised me not to wear any makeup. "I love you just the way you are," he told me. "You always been beautiful to me."

I didn't bother to tell him how good he looked in his black suit and white shirt. He had gotten so much more handsome over the years, it wasn't necessary to tell him. The city hall judge who married us made a comment about us being such a nice-looking couple. It was then that *all* of the doubts were removed from my mind: I *was* beautiful. The only flaw in my ecstasy was Rhoda's latest trauma. I knew in my heart that I would be there for her, no matter what. If Muh'Dear could forgive Daddy and allow him back into his life, I could forgive Rhoda for every evil thing she'd done. She was paying for her crimes, and in the worst way.

Pee Wee moved in with me that same day. Other than that,

it was just another day. We went to visit Rhoda but she remained asleep the whole time. I was stunned but pleased
when we went to Muh'Dear's house to pick up Charlotte and
discovered that Daddy had slept in the same room with
Muh'Dear. He was still in bed when I walked into Muh'Dear's
bedroom.

"It ain't what you think. I just needed him to keep my
back warm," Muh'Dear told me with a nervous grin.

"And I'm sure he did." I hugged my mother and then I
woke up my daddy so I could hug him, too.

I called up Lillimae when I got home and we chatted for
over two hours.

"Annette, I love you and I am so happy for you," Lillimae
told me. "You finally got everything you wanted. Your mama
and daddy are back together. You got a good man, a beautiful
baby. What more could you ask for?"

"I am blessed," I told my sister. I had received letters from
both of my other siblings the same day. Yes, I was truly
blessed. Even though I had lost my stepfather, P. and Jean,
and possibly Rhoda, I still had a lot to be thankful for.

The next day Otis told me that a tour guide had tracked
down Rhoda's parents and delivered the message that he had
wired about Rhoda's condition.

It was another week before the doctor released Rhoda. I
was already at Rhoda's house, nursing a huge glass of wine,
when Otis brought her home. I was glad that he and Jade left
me alone with Rhoda.

"My parents are arrivin' from Kenya tonight. I really
need my mother," Rhoda told me in a hoarse voice, lying on
her back in her bed, propped up with three pillows. Even
though she was able to talk, her mouth was still slightly
twisted and from the grimace on her face, it looked like it
was painful for her to talk. If that wasn't enough of an indignation, she would have to drag her left foot when she walked
for the rest of her life. I couldn't imagine Rhoda having to

give up all of her fancy high heels, prancing around like one of the Rockettes, skipping rope, roller skating with Jade, and dancing in front of the band at the Red Rose bar. The glamorous life that she had enjoyed for so many years was over. Her future as a hopeless cripple was far worse than her spending time in jail. Rhoda cleared her throat and spoke again with her lips quivering. "My Aunt Lola's comin' up from Alabama to stay with us for a while, too. She's goin' to help out until . . . until—" Rhoda was too weak to continue.

"Scary Mary said she could take care of Jade and I can cook and clean for you until your family arrives," I offered, smoothing the covers on Rhoda's bed.

Rhoda shook her head. Her hair, dry and tangled, dangled about her face like natty dreadlocks. "You've done enough for me." It was a struggle for her to speak but she continued. "Besides, you should be with Pee Wee and Charlotte."

"I think you need me more than they do right now," I said firmly.

She sniffed and cracked a thin smile. "When's the weddin'?"

"Last Saturday."

"What?" Rhoda wailed weakly, her eyes bulging.

I shook my head. "We just went to city hall. I didn't want to be waltzing down a church aisle with a bunch of people gawking at me anyway. I'm too old for that." I laughed. "We'll have a reception at my house when you get better. Pee Wee moved his things into my house and he's going to rent his house to his cousin Steve and his family."

"I wish you had waited. I wanted to be there for you," Rhoda whined, sighing sadly.

"You were," I said gently as I sat down on the foot of the bed, crossing my legs. I cleared my throat and steered the conversation back to Rhoda's condition. "Did the doctor say why this happened?"

"What do you mean?"

"People our age don't have strokes."

"Well, I did."

"But you were so healthy. Was it something in your diet? Was it something you did or didn't do? I don't understand how—"

A pensive look appeared on Rhoda's face. She scratched her chin, frowning because it was covered in dried spit. "It was somethin' I did."

"But what in the world—"

In a steely voice she announced, "I did some things I shouldn't have done. And you know what I'm talkin' about."

I gave her a puzzled look and shrugged.

"Bad karma." Rhoda sighed and scraped her bottom lip with her teeth. I noticed that her left eye now looked larger than her right eye.

"What's that supposed to mean?" I knew damn well what she meant. I just didn't want to be the one to bring it up. Especially at a time like this.

"The things I told you I did . . ."

I let out a groan as a sharp pain shot through my chest. "Do you think it was that shit you told me about killing four people that overloaded your mind and caused that stroke?"

"It could be. I've thought about it all a lot since I told you. Every day. And by the way, it's five people, not four."

I gasped so hard, I almost choked on my tongue. "What?"

"You know damn well old Uncle Carmine Antonosanti didn't shoot Vinnie, girl. I was there."

I nodded. "I thought so." I looked in Rhoda's unblinking eyes. "I'm not judging you this time. That's between you and God."

Rhoda nodded and sighed. Her tongue slid out of her mouth and licked her bottom lip, making a slurping noise. "So God's takin' me . . . a piece at a time. First my baby boy . . . then my," she paused and patted her chest and added in a cracked voice, "now . . . this."

"You stop talking all that foolishness," I scolded, shaking my finger in her face.

Rhoda gave me a thoughtful look. "Annette, you said I was a good wife, a good mother, and I've tried to be a good friend."

"And all of that's true!" The words seemed to burst out of my mouth.

"But I guess all of that didn't matter. God *still* don't like ugly." Rhoda's eyes shifted and she added, "And I have a feelin' that God ain't through yet."

"And He never will be," I muttered. "But I'm still going to be your friend, Rhoda."

At this point Rhoda sighed, nodded, and gave me a weary look before she wiped a huge tear from the corner of her eye. "I'm goin' to be okay," she rasped.

Before I could respond, Otis and Jade entered the room. Otis advised me to let Rhoda get some rest.

"You will come back tomorrow?" Otis asked. "You part of the family," he added, making a sweeping gesture with his hand. I nodded and grabbed his hand and squeezed it.

Rhoda had already closed her eyes and curled herself up like a ball. I pulled the covers up to her neck and kissed her on the cheek. I was amazed that after all of the hundreds of egg facials I'd watched her give herself during our youth, her skin now felt like sandpaper.

"We'll both be okay now," I whispered in Rhoda's ear, leaving so she could be with her husband and daughter.

I suddenly felt so warm all over that I had to fan my face. I let out a deep breath and I smiled.

And then I went home to be with my husband and my daughter.

CHAPTER 1

"**I**f you don't get yourself out of this vehicle and into that motel room and screw that man, I'll go up in there and do it myself!"

I never expected my best friend to encourage me to have an affair. I always thought that she'd be the main person who would try and talk me out of it. Especially since she and my husband had been like brother and sister for most of their lives. But that was exactly what she was trying to do now. I knew this sister like I knew the back of my hand, so I knew she was not going to stop until I had stepped out of my panties, stretched out on my back, and opened my legs for a man who was not my husband. One of the reasons was that my girl was having an affair herself. I knew that if I got involved in one, she wouldn't feel so guilty.

I was still strapped in by my seat belt, and I was in no hurry to unfasten it. "I don't know if I'm ready to cheat on my husband," I admitted. Despite the words of protest that tumbled out of my mouth and my reluctance, I was not going to reject Rhoda's orders. I just didn't want her to know how eager I really was to jump into bed with another man. I liked to mess with her from time to time, just enough to provoke her. It kept our crazy relationship exciting. "I really don't know if I can do this," I mumbled for the third time in the last two minutes. I sounded so weak and unconvincing that even I didn't believe what I was saying. "So stop trying to rush me!"

"Rush *you?* Woman, we've been sittin' here for ten minutes—tick-tock, tick-tock. And you rushed *me* to drive *your* horny black ass over here." Rhoda gave me a disgusted look before she unfastened my seat belt like I was a stubborn two-year-old.

"I know that. I just need to think," I whimpered.

"You need to think about what?" she demanded, slapping the side of the steering wheel with the palm of her hand.

"I need to think about what I'm doing and why," I replied, wringing my sweaty hands.

Now that the moment had arrived, I was sitting here acting like a frightened virgin, and it made no damn sense. This had been in the works for weeks. And me—with my weak self—I was just as eager to fuck the man who was awaiting my arrival in the motel room as he was to fuck me. He had made his intentions known the moment he stuck his fingers inside my panties in a restaurant booth the first time I spent time with him in public. I'd wanted to throw him down on that restaurant table and fuck his brains out then. And that was exactly what I planned to do as soon as I got up enough nerve to take my ass into that motel room.

"Honey, I can tell you why you're doin' this. You need it. Your fuckin', uh, *fuck* quota is bankrupt." Rhoda laughed.

"That's not funny, and I wish you'd stop making jokes about my personal life," I snapped.

"I'm sorry, girlfriend," she said, stroking my hair. "All I want is for you to be happy. I'm gettin' sick of your long, frustrated face, and of the jealous looks I always get from you when I get mine. It's time for you to get yours, and I am not goin' to let up until you do. Do you hear me?"

"I sure do hear you, Miss Pimp," I said, my voice dripping with sarcasm.

"Excuse me?"

"Rhoda, if I didn't know any better, I'd swear you were getting paid for this. And for the record, I am not jealous of you. You can get that notion out of that head of yours right now. You don't have a damn thing I'd want."

"Except a man who knows and wants to take care of my needs. Now you move it. Go on now." Rhoda clapped her hands together twice like a drill sergeant, bumped her knee against mine, and motioned with her head toward the door on my side. "You go into that room so you can get laid like you're supposed to be. Shoo!" This time she tapped the side of my leg with the toe of her black leather boot.

I still didn't move. I couldn't stop myself from glancing toward the motel entrance from the motel's parking lot, where we had parked. And I couldn't stop myself from hoping that the "good loving" that the man in the motel room had promised me was going to be worth my while. Rhoda was right. My fuck quota was bankrupt. I had not had any good loving in a while. As a matter of fact, I hadn't had any loving period in a while now. I was so hot and horny, I was about ready to explode like a firecracker.

The Do Drop Inn was the kind of motel that people snuck in and out of, in disguise if they were smart. It was a cheap one-story place in an industrial area off the freeway, with a sign that advertised rates by the hour, cable TV, XXX-rated movies, a heated pool, and vibrating beds.

Last month, during Memorial Day weekend, when a sister from my church was checking into this notorious love nest with her white lover, her husband was checking out with his lover at the same time. All hell broke loose that night. The husband, an avowed racist, seemed more pissed off about his wife having a white lover than he was about her having an affair. Not only did the cops have to be called, but an ambulance, too. The two sisters ended up in the hospital; the husband went to jail. And the only reason that the white man escaped injury was because he had fled the scene before the husband could get his hands on him. It was the kind of scandal that the people in Richland, Ohio, sunk their teeth into. Especially when it involved somebody in the church.

As a member of the Second Baptist Church—even though I attended services only about once a month now—I knew that if I got caught entering or leaving a motel with a man other than the one I was married to, my goose would be cooked alive. My dull husband would die. Not because I'd kill him in self-defense, but because he'd be so shocked and disappointed, he'd probably drop dead. And knowing my mother, she'd probably come after me with a switch. Given all these facts, why the hell was I doing this? If I had an answer to that question, it was hiding somewhere behind my brain.

I shaded my eyes and scanned the parking lot, sliding down into the passenger seat of my girl Rhoda's SUV each time I thought I saw somebody we knew. "Is that Claudette who owns the beauty shop coming out of the liquor store across the street?" I said, with a gasp.

"Shit! Where?" Rhoda asked, jerking her head around like a puppet. We slid down into our seats at the same time and stayed there for about a minute. Rhoda eased up first, peeping out the side of her window like a burglar. "No, that's not her. Claudette never looked that hopeless from behind. Whoever that sister is, her ass is draggin' on the ground like a tail."

I exhaled and sat back up in my seat. "I just wish Louis had picked some other motel. One with a little more class and one where we didn't have to worry about running into somebody we know," I complained, speaking more to myself than to Rhoda.

"What's wrong with you? This is the only one of the few motels in this hick town that employs people we don't know.

You go to the Moose Motel out on State Street, and I assure you that Sister Nettie Jones, who works her mouth more than she works that vacuum cleaner when she cleans the rooms, will blab so fast, everybody we know will know about your visit before you even check out." Rhoda let out an exasperated breath, rubbed her nose, and shook her head. I looked away from her. "Lord knows, this is one straight-up, low-level place, though. I wouldn't bring a dog that I didn't like here. If Louis was a real man, he'd take you to his place."

My breath caught in my throat as I whirled around to face Rhoda again.

She leaned to the side and gave me a puzzled look. "What's wrong now?"

"I'd rather get a whupping than get loose in Louis's apartment," I declared.

"Well, other than it bein' located in a low-rent neighborhood, two doors from the soup kitchen, what's wrong with Louis's apartment? Why don't you do him there?"

"I can't do that. I'm not the kind of woman who hangs out in a strange man's apartment," I answered. When I realized how ridiculous that statement was, we both laughed, but only for a few seconds. I cleared my throat and got serious. "Please don't mention Louis's apartment to me again after today unless you have to. I want to keep this thing casual."

"Well! All I can say is, this man better have somethin' good between his legs," Rhoda retorted through clenched teeth. "If he doesn't, I'll help you slice it off with a dull knife and feed it to a goat I don't like. But I still feel that he ought to be ashamed of himself for plannin' a romantic evenin' in a dead zone like this," Rhoda said, looking around the area.

I didn't like the look on her face, and she didn't have to say what was on her mind, because I already knew. On one hand, she approved of me committing adultery, but she had a problem with me doing it with a broke-ass man like Louis

Baines. But since she'd introduced me to him and did business with his struggling catering service herself, she usually didn't harp on his financial status that much.

"You know that he is putting most of his money into his business. You are the main one who keeps talking about how you want to see a black business succeed in this town," I said in Louis's defense. "I don't expect him to take me to the Hilton . . . yet."

"I know, I know," Rhoda replied gently, giving me a smile and an apologetic look. "I just wish that he could afford to take you to one of those nice hotels near the airport, like *my* gentleman friend does for me. Did I ever tell you about that?"

"You've told me everything there is to know about you and your lover, Rhoda," I said, my eyes rolling around in my head like marbles. "Year after year after year . . ."

"Oh. Well, a real nice hotel makes it seem, uh, less illicit, I guess. I like to be with my sweetie in my house only when I have no choice. Believe it or not, I still have some respect for my husband. It's the least I can do. He's a beast, and his dick gets about as hard as a slice of raw bacon these days. But as long as he keeps his nose out of my business and hangs on to that six-figure-amount-a-year job, the only thing I'd leave him for is to go to heaven. Shit." Rhoda sniffed loudly and tapped my shoulder. "Well, what's it goin' to be?" She glanced at the clock on the dashboard. "I've got other things to do, you know."

I couldn't figure out why, but for some reason, I had to stall a little more. Even though I *knew* that I was going to go through with my first indiscretion since I got married ten years ago. "I have to think about this some more, Rhoda. I shouldn't have come here yet. Maybe I should get to know Louis a little better."

"Better than what?"

"Better than I know him now. Other than the fact that he's the best caterer I've ever dealt with, I really don't know everything that I'd like to know about the man."

"What do you think sex is for, girl? What better way is there to get to know a man? Look, you know him well enough to do business with him. He wants you. You want him. What else do you need to know? How big his dick is? How long he can keep it hard? Well, there's only one way for you to find that out."

CHAPTER 2

Rhoda's words amused me. I shook my head and let out a gentle laugh. "I know you are not going to stop until I do what you want me to do. But I shouldn't have let you talk me into doing this. I shouldn't have even told you about this man. I should not have let him get close enough to me for him to think that I'd . . . What's wrong with me? I'm a happily married woman." I put a lot of emphasis on my words. I was now at a point where I couldn't tell if I was trying to convince myself that I shouldn't be having an affair, or Rhoda.

"Happily married, my ass." She guffawed. "You show me a happily married woman, and I will show you a woman who has at least one spare. And I don't mean a spare tire."

"I'm glad most people don't think that," I shot back. "That's one of the most ridiculous things I've ever heard you say. You ought to be ashamed of yourself."

"If you are so happily married, why are we sittin' in this motel parkin' lot, havin' this conversation? Why did you ask me to lie to your husband about where you were goin' tonight? Is that what you call bein' happily married?"

"You know what I mean. Having an affair could ruin my life."

"I'm married, too! I've been havin' an affair with my husband's best friend for almost twenty years. Do I look ruined? And for the record, I am about as happily married as a woman can be."

"I should go back home before it's too late."

"Look, Annette, if you've come this far, it's already too late. Now stop actin' like this is your first day of kindergarten. Get a grip. You've got four hours to play with. And from the looks of that young stud, you're goin' to need every last minute of those four hours to satisfy him. Shit!" Rhoda laughed as she looked in the rearview mirror to check her makeup and hair, something she'd do even on her way to her execution. "I hope you douched with some vanilla extract, like I told you. I noticed his tongue, and it's long enough to make a woman very happy. He sure seems like the type who likes to do a little *grazin' in the grass*. And he should. As a matter of fact, I haven't seen a tongue that length since I saw *Godzilla*." Rhoda laughed some more.

I didn't like the fact that she was getting such a kick out of this. Now I really was sorry that I had ever told her about Louis and the fact that he'd been trying to get into my panties for weeks, tongue and all.

"You're making me nervous, Rhoda."

"You're not nervous. We're both way too old to be gettin' nervous about fuckin'. You're just confused." Not looking away from the mirror, she fished a Kleenex tissue from the beaded purse in her lap and blotted her plum-colored lipstick. "This is just, uh, jitters. But you'll get used to that. I did." She paused and gave me a thoughtful look, then a quick but weak smile. "I am so happy for you. You're finally goin' to get what you need after sufferin' for so long."

"I am not suffering," I protested.

"Whatever you say," she said with a sigh, balling the tissue and tossing it into a litter bag hanging from the dashboard. "I don't know how you've managed to last this long without mountin' the pizza delivery guy and humpin' the hell out of him. Almost a whole damn year without some dick is not normal!"

"It is for some people," I insisted. "And what's so bad about going without sex for a year, anyway? Some women go their whole lives without it."

Rhoda nodded. "They are called nuns, invalids, and freaks. None of which you are. Or we wouldn't be sittin' here." Rhoda glanced at her watch, then gave me an exasperated look. "I'm too through. Are you goin' into that motel room or what?" She started her motor and adjusted her rearview mirror.

"I'm going," I said quickly, opening the door on my side.

"I'll pick you up around eleven fifteen. I want to be home in time to watch at least part of *Jay Leno*!"

The woman who had been my best friend for most of my life gave me a hearty push with her hand. I practically slid out of the front passenger seat of her SUV and onto the ground, landing on my feet like a panther. She sped off before I could even catch my breath.

Despite all the shit that Rhoda had said, I couldn't determine what she *really* thought. And I couldn't understand how she could pressure me into having an affair and still grin in my husband's face. This was one of the few times that I wished they were not friends. But no matter what she thought or said, this was my call. I wanted to have an affair with Louis Baines. It was nothing for me to be proud of, but I had to pat myself on the back for attracting such a young, handsome brother in the first place. And he was the one who had come on like gangbusters, not me. That was something that had rarely happened to me, even when I was young.

My marriage had become a stale joke. My husband had already put me out to pasture, like I was a Guernsey cow that he had milked bone dry. Louis had come to my rescue just in time. His actions had done wonders for my ego. At least that was what I kept telling myself. But before Louis entered my life, I had almost convinced myself that my sex life was over at the age of forty-six.

I looked around the parking lot some more. Summer was just around the corner, so the weather was nice. But the wind was howling in a way that made me even more nervous. This was a rough neighborhood, so nosy acquaintances were not the only people I had to be concerned about. A couple of months ago somebody had attacked a man from behind and robbed him in the same parking lot that I was in now. A few weeks before that, somebody had dragged a woman between two cars parked behind the motel, sexually assaulted her, and taken off with her purse and jewelry.

I coughed and tightened my grip on my purse. One thing I had learned from growing up around rough people was that it was stupid to look too prosperous. The woman who had been raped and robbed had had the nerve to come to this neighborhood in a fur jacket, wearing diamonds on everything but her toes. She had to be either stone crazy or suicidal, because that was like waving a piece of raw meat in front of a wolf. I was sorry about what had happened to that woman. But like everybody else, I felt that she should have known better. I had some very expensive clothes and jewelry, which I never wore to this part of town. I rarely carried much money or more than two or three credit cards in my purse in this neighborhood, or anywhere else. I had a large can of Mace in my purse, which I prayed I would never have to use. The air was foul. It reeked of gasoline and oil, dust, and despair. I sucked in some of that air, anyway. Then I looked around and checked my surroundings one more time.

At night when the Do Drop Inn sign was turned on, some of its letters blinked on and off; some didn't light up at all. And if that wasn't tacky enough, the molelike Pakistani man who owned this motel had had it painted pink last year and had propped up some plastic flamingos in front of the entrance. There was a truck stop a block away. Tired hookers brought their tired truck driver tricks to this motel.

A huge buckeye tree loomed over the building like a gigantic umbrella. In the fall, the buckeye nuts fell off the tree and covered the motel roof like brown rocks. I knew about the buckeyes because my mother used to clean the rooms in this dump thirty years ago, and I used to help her.

Louis had told me that he'd be in room 108 and had warned me that he'd already be naked. "I just hope you can handle this dragon in my pants, baby," he'd also said. "I've got something that has made some women weep from joy and others weep from pain." You would have thought that he had a footlong brick between his legs, the way he was talking. But I knew better.

"I hope I can handle it, too," I'd replied, rolling my eyes. I didn't know why Louis, or any other man for that matter, felt the need to brag about the size of his dick. As a former prostitute, I was pretty sure that I'd seen it all when it came to sex. For one thing, there was probably nothing left that could surprise or scare me. I didn't think that there was anything that could top the trick that had a two-headed dick, which I'd encountered one rainy night. But Louis didn't need to know all that, though. As a matter of fact, he already knew more about me than I wanted him to know.

The way I was dragging my feet, you would have thought that I was on my way to a job I despised. I was glad that the room was on the other side of the motel, so I'd have a few more minutes to compose myself. However, before I could do that, a pay phone on the corner in front of the motel caught my attention. Before I knew it, I was rooting through my purse for some loose change so I could make a call.

"Hello," my husband answered on the tenth ring. Even though one of the four telephones in our house was never more than a few feet out of his reach, he always took his time answering one when it rang. This was just one of the things he did that had irritated me for years.

"Hi, baby," I began.

"Who is this?"

I gasped so hard, I almost dropped my purse. I couldn't respond right away.

"Hello? Who is this callin'?" Pee Wee asked, sounding truly annoyed.

"I want you to tell me how many women call you up and address you as baby, fool," I demanded, anger rumbling inside me like gas. I didn't know what the hell I was going to do with that husband of mine! No wonder I was about to have an affair.

Turn the page for a sneak peek at
THE COMPANY WE KEEP!

On sale now!

CHAPTER 1

Teri Stewart had no idea that two of the secretaries she worked with were secretly trying to set up a date for her with a popular male escort. It was going to be expensive, but worth every penny. That didn't matter, though. The money was going to come from the company's petty cash fund that the two secretaries controlled.

"John, if that woman doesn't get some dick soon, we are all going to be in therapy," complained one of the secretaries with a weary look on her face.

"And if this escort thing doesn't work, I'll screw her myself! I've been gay to the bone for my entire thirty-seven years and have never even *seen* a woman's pussy, so you know this is serious," moaned the terrified male secretary. "Either that or you'll have to strap on one of those dildo dicks and do it. We can't take too much more of her foolishness."

Unfortunately, the scheme didn't work. The only agency that the two desperate secretaries could afford had only one black escort. And he had dates lined up for the next two months. When the agency suggested another one of their studs, a very dark-skinned Iraqi, the two secretaries considered him until they saw what he looked like. That poor man looked enough like bin Laden to be his twin. Teri was very patriotic. She'd never sleep with a man who looked like the enemy.

"All we can do now is hope that the upcoming New Year will be better for Teri," the female secretary said hopefully. "And better for us . . ."

Teri had not been involved in an intimate relationship with a man in six months, and it was beginning to get on her last nerve. She had gradually become a tense, frustrated, abrupt Donna Karan–wearing bitch. She knew she was beginning to get on the last nerves of *everybody* she came in contact with. Just yesterday she actually saw the guy from the mailroom duck into the stairwell as soon as he spotted her thundering down the hall trying to track down a fax she'd misplaced. And the two nicest secretaries in the company had started looking at her in some of the strangest ways. She had no idea what was going through their heads, and she didn't want to know.

It wasn't that no man was interested in her. That had never been the case and probably never would be. If for no other reason, men came on to her because of her looks. Most didn't care about anything else she had to offer. Few could resist her big, shiny brown eyes; smooth mahogany complexion; and full lips. Not to mention her hourglass-shaped body on legs that would put Tina Turner's to shame and a mane of dark brown hair that didn't need a prop like a weave to cascade around her shoulders like a silk scarf.

It seemed like the older she got, the more men she attracted. She predicted that forty years from now she'd be beating off dirty old men with her walking stick. Just last week somebody had stopped her on the street and asked if she was Kerry Washington, one of the most attractive black actresses in Hollywood. So why did her pussy feel like a condemned piece of property on no-man's-land? Beauty was not the cure-all for loneliness that some people thought it was. She was probably one of the best-looking lonely women on the planet. But in her case, it was by choice. And it was all because the *right* man had not approached her in six months.

"At least you still got your health and a good job," somebody—she couldn't even remember who—had told her a few days ago. That same person had advised her to contact an online dating service. An *online dating service!* If that wasn't the last refuge for the truly desperate and a paradise for predators of all kinds, she didn't know what was. She'd made it emphatically clear that she was not that desperate . . . yet.

"I'm doing just fine, thank you very much." That was how she always responded when some busybody's nose sniffed in her direction and asked about her love life.

No, she wasn't getting any and didn't know when she ever would again. What the hell. She could live with it. She still had more things to be thankful for than a lot of other people. Yes, she did still have her health and her job and had been thinking about getting a cat.

Right now her job was the main focus in her life. She enjoyed being the Executive Publicity Director for Eclectic Records. The prestige and all the perks that went along with her high-profile position meant as much to her as the fat paychecks she collected twice a month. This was one sister who didn't have to worry much about where she was going in the hectic business world and how she was going to get there; she had already arrived.

Unfortunately, a lot of Teri's peers hated their jobs, so they didn't share her vision or enthusiasm. She didn't know of a single person in L.A. who *wanted* to be at work on New Year's Eve. It was hard enough for most people to come to work on the rest of the days in the year. But work was where Teri Stewart was tonight (she'd also worked well into the night on Christmas Eve, too). Not because she wanted to be, but because she had to be.

Teri didn't give a damn what everybody else in L.A. was doing. If nothing else, she was disciplined and considerate. To her, every commitment she made was important. Last year on a much-needed vacation to Puerto Vallarta, she had offered to take her friendly hotel maid and her kids to dinner. She didn't think to ask the woman how many kids she had, but she expected at least two. When the maid showed up with all *nine* of her kids in tow, including the eldest boy's wife and their two kids, Teri didn't back out. Now here she was on New Year's Eve trying to finish a monthly media report that was late because one of her sources had dropped the ball.

The building that was home to Eclectic Records was almost empty. But that didn't bother Teri. There was a pit bull of a security guard at the front desk on the first floor at all times. The sixteen-story building was located on a busy street near downtown L.A. Even though there had been a few muggings in the area recently, it was still fairly safe compared to other parts of the city.

Holiday lights were still in place, inside and out. The soulful R. Kelly jam emanating from a CD player in the center of Teri's cluttered desk in a corner office on the sixth floor didn't do a whole lot to make her feel more at ease. Her mood was dark, and she was more frustrated than usual. The impatient frown on her face and her pouting bottom lip, which would have made a less fortunate woman look like a hag, made her look even younger than her twenty-nine years. She mumbled profanities as she searched for a document that contained information she needed to complete her report. "Shit!" she hissed as she thumped the button on the speakerphone next to the CD player, speed-dialing her secretary at home.

"Nicole, you didn't put a copy of Reverend Bullard's report on my desk," she insisted, glaring at the telephone as if it were the source of her frustration. There was no answer. "Nicole, are you there?"

"Uh-huh, I'm here," Nicole finally replied with a mighty

hiccup. Somebody had popped open a bottle of champagne in the company break room to jump-start the New Year's Eve festivities. Like a fish with a long swallow, Nicole had guzzled two glasses before she left the office two hours ago.

By the time Teri had concluded a tense conference call with two long-winded clients on the East Coast and made it to the break room, all the champagne was gone. If she ever needed a liquid crutch, it was now. She appeased herself with the reminder that she would make up for it in a couple of hours.

"I thought I told you to put a copy of the Bullard report on my desk. You know we can't afford to not get our artists mentioned in the tabloids and the music rags whenever they do something good." Teri was convinced that a story about an ex-con preacher making gospel CDs for troubled teenagers would be good press for the preacher and for Eclectic Records. "I thought I told you twice."

"Well, I *thought* I did," Nicole said with a burp. "I meant to . . ."

"You thought you did and you meant to, but you didn't," Teri snapped.

"Will you please calm down? You're making me nervous."

"Calm down, my ass. I've got a job to do and I can't do mine if you don't do yours." Teri paused and let out a loud breath. "I'm sorry. You know I don't like to take out my frustrations on you. I just want to finish what I started and get the hell up out of this place." Teri let out another loud breath, inspected her silk-wrapped nails, and glanced around the spacious office that she spent as much time in as she did her condo near Hollywood.

"That's better," Nicole mouthed.

Nicole Mason sat on the edge of her bed in the apartment she shared with her son. With a heavy sigh, she rose and wiggled her plump but firm ass into a pair of black lace panties. "Try the file cabinet behind my desk. The report should be in the top drawer in a green folder," she said. The panties felt a little too tight, just like almost everything else she owned. Especially the black slip she had on now. She made a mental note to curtail her ongoing relationships with Roscoe's House of Chicken 'n Waffles, Popeye's, Marie Callender, and Sara Lee or else she'd have to introduce herself to Jenny Craig and Richard Simmons. "Teri, you know you are my girl, so I know you won't take this the wrong way . . ."

Teri responded with an exasperated snort.

"Girlfriend, you need to get a life," Nicole told her. "You know it and I know it. Everybody else knows it, too."

"I have a life, thank you. I am on my grind," Teri reported, as she continued her search. She entered Nicole's work area, which was right outside her office. She fought her way through an assortment of large, live green plants on the floor that decorated the area like a rain forest. She found the green folder right where Nicole said it would be. With another frown, she returned to her office with the folder and leaned over her desk, glaring at the phone. She sucked in her breath so hard her chest ached, but before she could speak again Nicole's voice cut into her muddled thoughts.

"Miss Girl, I thought we were supposed to be hanging out tonight. Come on, this is New Year's Eve and we happen to be in one of the most exciting cities on this planet. And, in case you forgot, Lincoln freed the slaves."

"I have a job to do, Nicole," Teri reminded her.

"We all do. But we all have lives outside of our jobs, too," Nicole said firmly.

"I know, I know. I just need to tweak a few more sentences on this damn report. It won't take that long. And why are you rushing me? You are not even dressed yet."

"How would you know that?" Nicole quipped, tugging on the waistband of her panties.

"Because I know you," Teri remarked. Flipping through

the green folder, her eyes got big and a smile formed on her lips. "I found it!" she exclaimed, clutching the missing document to her bosom as if it contained the secrets of the universe. She breathed a sigh of relief and flopped down into her chair, which was so comfortable with its soft black leather and adjustable seat that she didn't want to move again. "Let the games begin!"

Nicole rose and stood by the side of her bed, which was just as cluttered as the rest of the bedroom. She ignored the clothing and music magazines that she had tossed to the foot of her bed. "Uh-huh. So, now you can—" She was cut off by the annoying buzz of a dial tone. "Hang up on me then, bitch." She laughed, shaking her head. "I'm too scared of you."

CHAPTER 1

I saw my best friend kill her vicious stepfather on the night of our senior prom. While our classmates were dancing the night away and plotting to do everything we had been told not to do after the prom, I was helping Valerie Proctor hide a dead body in her backyard beneath a lopsided fig tree.

Ezekiel "Zeke" Proctor's violent death had come as no surprise to me. It happened sixteen years ago but it's still fresh on my mind, and I know it will be until the day I die, too.

Mr. Zeke had been a fairly good neighbor as far back as I could remember. When he wasn't too drunk or in a bad mood, he would haul old people and single mothers who didn't have transportation around in his car. He would lend money, dole it out to people who needed it, and he never asked to be repaid. He would do yard work and other maintenance favors for little or no money. And when he was in a good mood, which was rare, he would host a backyard cookout and invite everybody on our block. However, those events usually ended when he got too drunk and paranoid and decided that everybody was "out to get him."

When that happened, barbequed ribs, links, and chicken

wings ended up on the ground, or stuck to somebody's hair where he'd thrown them. People had to hop away from the backyard to avoid stepping on glasses that he had broken on purpose. There had not been any cookouts since the time he got mad and shot off his gun in the air because he thought one of the handsome young male guests was plotting to steal his wife. In addition to those lovely social events, he'd also been the stepfather and husband from hell.

Valerie's mother, Miss Naomi, bruised and bleeding like a stuck pig herself after the last beating that she'd survived a few minutes before the killing, had also witnessed Mr. Zeke's demise. Like a zombie, she had stood and watched her daughter commit the granddaddy of crimes. Had things turned out differently, Miss Naomi would have been the dead body on the floor that night, because this time her husband had gone too far. He had attempted to strangle her to death. She had his handprints on her neck and broken blood vessels in the whites of her eyes to prove it.

To this day I don't like to think of what I witnessed as a murder, per se. If that wasn't a slam dunk case of self-defense, I don't know what was. But Valerie and her mother didn't see things that way. They didn't call the cops like they'd done so many times in the past. That had done no good. If anything, it had only made matters worse. Each time after the cops left, Miss Naomi got another beating. They also didn't call the good preacher, Reverend Carter, who had told them time and time again, year after year, that "Brother Zeke can't help hisself; he's confused" and to be "patient and wait because things like this will work out somehow if y'all turn this over to God." Well, they'd tried that, too, and God had not intervened.

"None of those motherfuckers helped us when we needed it, now we don't need their help," Valerie's mother said, grinding her teeth as she gave her husband's corpse one final kick in his side. She attempted to calm her nerves by drinking vodka straight out of the same bottle that he had been nursing from like a hungry baby all day.

Miss Naomi and Valerie buried Mr. Zeke's vile body in the backyard of the house that Miss Naomi owned on Baylor Street. It was the most attractive residence on the block, not the kind of place that you would expect to host such a gruesome crime. People we all knew got killed in the crack houses in South Central and other rough parts of L.A., not in our quiet little neighborhood in houses like Miss Naomi's. Directly across the street was the Baylor Street Mt. Zion Baptist Church, which almost everybody on the block attended at some time. Even the late Mr. Zeke. . . .

The scene of the crime was a two-story white stucco with a two-car garage and a wraparound front porch that was often cluttered with toys and neighborhood kids like me. The front lawn was spacious and well cared for. A bright white picket fence surrounded the entire front lawn like a houndstooth necklace. Behind the house, as with all the other houses on the block, was a high, dark fence that hid the backyard, as well as Valerie's crime.

Miss Naomi's house looked like one of those family friendly homes on those unrealistic television sitcoms. But because of Valerie's stepfather's frequent violence, the house was anything but family friendly. He had turned it into a war zone over the years. Valerie's baby brother, Binkie, referred to it as Beirut because Mr. Zeke attacked every member of the family on a regular basis, including Valerie's decrepit grandfather, Paw Paw, and even one-eyed Pete, the family dog.

Even though there was blood in every room in that house, that didn't stop me from making it my second home. Over the years I had learned how to get out of the "line of fire" in time to avoid injury whenever Mr. Zeke broke loose.

That night, I had innocently walked into the house and witnessed Valerie's crime. As soon as I realized what was happening, I threw up all over the pale pink dress that had cost me a month's worth of my earnings. I continued to vomit as I watched Valerie and her long-suffering mother drag the body across the kitchen floor to the backyard so casually you'd have thought it was a mop.

Before they reached the gaping hole in the ground that had several mounds of dirt piled up around it like little pyramids, they stumbled and dropped the corpse. There was a thud and then a weak, hissing sound from the body that made me think of a dying serpent. Somebody let out a long, loud, rhythmic fart. I could smell it from where I stood in the door like a prison guard. And it was fiercely potent. I couldn't tell if it had come from Valerie, her mother, or if it was the last gas to ooze from the asshole of the dead man. It could have even been from me, but I was such a wreck, I couldn't tell. I squeezed my nostrils and then I froze from my face to the soles of my feet.

I held my breath as Valerie stumbled and fell on top of one of the mounds of dirt. Miss Naomi, breathing hard and loud, fell on top of Mr. Zeke's corpse. One of us screamed. I didn't realize it was me until Valerie scolded me. "Dolores, shut the fuck up and help us." Why, I didn't know. With the tall dark fence protecting the backyard like a fort, none of our neighbors could see her. "We need to get him in this hole *now*," she said, huffing and puffing. I couldn't believe that this was the same girl that Reverend Carter had baptized less than a week ago, in the church across the street from the scene of her crime.

CHAPTER 2

The Los Angeles experience was like something out of a movie. Literally. Things just didn't happen in L.A. Being that this was where Hollywood was located, even night didn't just happen in L.A. It made an *entrance* the same way Gloria Swanson did in that old movie *Sunset Boulevard*. Just like the demented character that she had so brilliantly portrayed, this particular night was *ready for its close-up*. And I was right smack-dab in the middle of it. I was not the star, but in a way I had a strong supporting role. It was not where I wanted to be.

I grabbed a flashlight from the kitchen drawer and stepped into the backyard. Even in the dim light, I could see that the hairdo Valerie had spent a hundred dollars on was ruined. Her usually glorious mane, matted with dirt and saturated with sweat, looked like a sheep's ass. With every move she made, the long curls that she was so proud of flopped about her face like limp vines. She leaped up from the ground, pulling her mother up by the hand. They then continued to slide Mr. Zeke into his final resting place. Well, it was final as long as some busybody didn't dig him up.

"Lo, you need to hold that goddamned flashlight straight,"

Valerie informed me, speaking in a voice I hardly recognized. There was a desperate look in her eyes that I had never seen before.

I was temporarily unable to speak. I moved my mouth, my tongue, and my lips, but nothing came out. All I could do was try to hold that fucking flashlight in place. Even with the porch light on, and the beam from the flashlight in my hands, everything seemed so dark, including my beautiful light pink dress. And nothing seemed real.

"Aren't y'all supposed to wrap him up in something?" I asked in a trembling voice. It seemed almost disrespectful not to include a shroud. I even snatched a towel off the kitchen counter and held it up, waving it, hoping they would at least wrap up his head and cover his eyes. But Valerie and her mother ignored me. Mr. Zeke went into the ground with just the clothes on his back. Almost every single inch of the white shirt he'd died in had turned red with his blood.

Valerie and Miss Naomi put together didn't weigh as much as that loathsome body that they had dropped into a hole that had already been dug. I don't know how I managed to stand there holding the flashlight in my hands, both of them shaking hard. I had to use both to hold the flashlight in place so Valerie and her mother could see what they were doing.

Mr. Zeke had dug the grave himself the day before and told Valerie's mother that she'd be in it by the weekend. No, he had promised her. Ironically, he'd dug it long and deep enough to accommodate his six foot four, 270-pound frame.

The murder weapon, a butcher knife that could have passed for a sword if it had been any longer, was on the kitchen table with half of the blade missing. I'd find out later that the missing part of the blade had been buried with Mr. Zeke, still planted in his chest like a spike. This was a horrible way for a horrible man to die, and for some reason I felt unbearably sad. Despite everything he was and had done, he was still somebody's son. Having never known my blood relatives, family had a special meaning to me.

In the kitchen, the blood on the floor was so thick it looked like you could dip it up with a spoon. There was a large puddle in front of the sink that covered the floor like an area rug, and a wide trail that looked like a thick red snake that led to the door. The spot in front of the stove was where Mr. Zeke had issued his last threat, and breathed his last breath. Pete, the dingy black mutt that Valerie and I had rescued from the street, had already started slipping and sliding across the floor, lapping up blood like he was at a hog trough. Pete stared up at me with his remaining eye. Mr. Zeke's blood was dripping from his tongue, whiskers and nose.

Besides Valerie and her mother, who died from natural causes herself about a year later, and Valerie's one-eyed dog, I was the only other individual who knew what had happened to Mr. Zeke. That night, I promised Valerie that I would carry her secret with me to my grave. And one thing I knew how to do was to keep a promise.

I had kept that promise for sixteen years. And it had not been that hard for me to do. I knew that my knowledge of the crime, and not reporting it, put me somewhere in the vicinity of the guilt. Since Valerie never talked about Mr. Zeke's murder after that night, I didn't know if she had shared her secret with anybody else. And I didn't want to know.

Even though I knew that Valerie's mouth was one of the biggest things on her body, I shared secrets with her, too. A lot of people did. When I shared something with Valerie it was usually something petty—something that a lot of our friends already knew anyway, or would hear from me eventually. But not this time.

Not only was Valerie Proctor my best friend and former

roommate, she was one of the most popular bartenders I knew, because her ears were even bigger than her mouth. She was the one person I knew who'd be more than a little interested in my confession, and the only person who would have any sympathy for me. But even before I spilled the beans, I had to ask myself, "Should I be telling this woman my business?" I didn't even have to think about my answer. I had to tell somebody. This was a load I could no longer carry by myself. Besides, what were best friends for?

"Now what's so important you had to drag me away from the comfort of my own place of business, and a possible date with one of the hottest men on the planet this side of Denzel? And it better be good," Valerie warned, her voice half serious, her eyes wide with curiosity. "Girl, I've been itching to hear some juicy news all week. I want to hear some news that is going to make my ears ring."

"Well, I've got some . . ." I said, speaking with hesitation. "And, it's real juicy . . . I think." We occupied a patio table at The Ivy in Beverly Hills.

"Who about? Paris Hilton? Nicole Richie? Lindsay Lohan? Beyoncé? Will Smith? Star Jones? Big-mouthed Rosie O'Donnell?"

Valerie served drinks to a lot of celebrities who visited Paw Paw's, the bar she owned in West Hollywood. And it was profitable for her in more ways than one. A lot of the things she heard from the famous and not-so-famous patrons had ended up on the pages of the tabloids. She was well paid by her media contacts, even for something as petty as one of the Lakers leaving a five dollar tip on a hundred dollar tab. "Who? Who?" she said, sounding like an owl. And the way her eyes were stretched open, she looked like one, too.

"Uh . . . me."

Valerie reared back in her seat so far her neck looked like it belonged on a goose. "*You?*" From the expression on her face, there was nothing I could have said that would have disappointed her more. She let out a disgusted sigh and rolled her eyes. "Shit," she mouthed.

"Uh-huh," I muttered. "Me."

"Oh. Whatever, whatever," Valerie said with an exasperated shrug. "Well, what did *you* do, mow somebody down with your Honda and flee the scene?"

I shook my head. "Valerie, I need to talk to you about something I've done. But you have to promise me that you won't ever tell anybody. I . . . I can't keep this to myself any longer," I said, speaking in a low voice. "This is serious. Real serious."

I was glad to see that Valerie seemed more interested now. She held her breath and stared at me for a moment. "Please don't tell me you've got some fatal disease," she squeaked, her eyes full of tears and her lips quivering. "I don't know what I'd do without you!"

I shook my head again. "I'm not going to die," I assured her.

"All right then. I'm listening," she replied, letting out a loud sigh of relief.